VENOM SPEAR

BLADES OF GRASS BOOK 1

AUSTIN CHAMBERS

MARC, KEEP FIGHTING FOR THE AMERICAN SPIRIT!

– Austin

CREDITS

EDITOR – Emily Rollen

FINAL PROOFER – Loren Foster

COVER BY – Ivan@bookcoversart.com

ISBN – 978-1-7360479-1-0

Published by Crossed Cannons Publishing, LLC
P.O. Box 334
Seabeck, WA 98380-0334
www.authoraustinchambers.com

In Memory of "Dave Wolf" and all of those other friends we never actually get to meet.

And dedicated to my best friend, Dorothy. She loves me despite my demons.

Venom Spear

Blades of Grass Book 1

PROLOGUE

Over the Hindu Kush Mountains, Afghanistan

"Danger close!" 1st Lt. Freeman Louis "Super Bert" Caldwell heard in his helmet headset. "T-Man is on the ridges to our north, west, and southwest. One hundred meters and closing!"

Caldwell knew that was what the Joes called the Taliban. It sounded like the mother of all firefights raging in the background. Americans were about to die.

"Bert, I just went Bingo," he heard his wingman say. Captain Scott "Snooze N" Nethers was his closest squadron buddy and mentor. He was letting Bert know that he was now at the point in his fuel level that he had to make the twenty-five-minute flight back to base and land. The pair of Fairchild Republic A10 Thunderbolts—known affectionately by the ground troops as the "Warthog"—had been providing close air support for almost three hours. They had already performed an aerial refueling before receiving the call for support, meaning they were now bound to return to base. Not that it mattered—both planes had already run themselves low on ammo.

"I'm good," Super Bert Caldwell replied. "I can make at least two more passes!"

"You're full of it! Let's go. Ratchet and Clank will be on site in thirty minutes." Snooze ordered.

"Listen to those guys, Snooze!" the young pilot countered. He was three months into his first combat tour after college and training. "They're surrounded and cut-off from their QRF! They don't have thirty minutes!"

"Bert! Stop!" the more seasoned pilot warned the rookie. "See that fog that's rolling in?!"

It was too late. Freeman Caldwell—Lou to his friends back home—lined up on the southwest-to northeast approach into the valley once more, disappearing from Snooze's view as he did. The greenish-brown electronic map in the upper-left corner of his cockpit dashboard moved the mountains slowly as he once again progressed along the canyon walls. He reached down to his left. He felt for the correct switch to move from the HF frequency he had been talking to his wingman back to FM.

"Echo 3, this is Whisky Flight 2! Keep your heads down!"

Super Bert reached down to near his left hip and flipped the little red safety cover over the power cutout to his GAU-8 30mm cannon. He was hot, once again, to spew his depleted uranium projectiles into the enemies of brethren unmet. He had achieved his nickname as a token of supposed embarrassment from his squadron mates. The seven-barrel rotary cannon in the Warthog's nose makes a very loud "brrrt" belch-type sound when firing at its fixed 3,900 rounds-per-minute rate. Pilots would normally fire in one to less-than-two second bursts. Super Bert had demonstrated the ability to make precise micro adjustments in flight, engaging as many as fifteen percent more targets on each pass when compared to his peers.

Left hand on his throttle, he trimmed his ailerons and reduced throttle just a bit, nudging his right hand on the joystick a hair left as he did. He was trying to get right in line with the top of a canyon wall he could no longer see due to incoming fog. The reduction in throttle caused a slight loss of lift. He couldn't mess with this technique too much—the cannon was calibrated to shoot 4000 feet ahead when the craft was at a down-attitude of thirty degrees. Sweat built on his brow under the already hot helmet. Super Bert shot his eyes back and forth from the left side display, his heads-up display, and the window, nervously trying to find the top of the canyon. A quick altimeter check...one last look at the HUD...

BRRRRRRTTTTT....BRRRRRTTTTTT....BR-RRRRRRRRRRTTTTTTTTTT! Lou Caldwell hit the throttle and re-engaged the cannon's safety switch, pulling slightly back on the yoke. If he had the fuel to make one more pass, he didn't want to waste it climbing to altitude and rolling over to look when visibility was garbage anyhow.

"Whiskey Flight 2, Echo 3!" he heard the ground troops' TACP, or Tactical Air Control Party, call him once more. "Nice shooting, flyboy!" The operator on the ground had the training and expertise to manage all aircraft involved in the mission. "Stand by! Standby. EVAC units are inbound! Visibility is nil. Copy?"

"Copy, Echo 3. I'm past Bingo. You'll have Whiskey 3 on scene in ten mikes," he said in the military radio jargon that meant ten minutes. "I'm RTB."

"Echo 3 copies." As Super Bert began to head back to Bagram Air Base, he switched his radio back to pre-programmed HF frequency and began the procession home.

BACK IN FOB CAMARO NEAR JALALABAD, A SENIOR COLONEL had been listening to the entire operation from the Tactical Operations Center. The Brigadier General-select had already been given his flag announcement, due to take over as Inter-Agency Operations Director at Joint Special Operations command as a new general in two months.

His Rangers had been stuck on this Charlie Foxtrot mission for almost two days, and he wasn't going to sleep until they were home. It wasn't until two hours later that one of the TOC's radio technicians informed him that they heard Whiskey Flight 2 had crashed four miles short of making it back to his home runway. Apparently, the Air Force Pararescue had already scooped him up—alive but banged up...and probably done flying for good.

Not if I can help it, Judah Montgomery thought in response to knowing exactly how the military worked. "Find out where they took him, Specialist," Colonel Montgomery ordered. *That man had the balls to stay in the fight,* Montgomery thought. *And we don't leave anyone behind.*

CHAPTER 1

THE PENTAGON

BUZZ. THE OLDER GOVERNMENT-ISSUED IPHONE SILENTLY vibrated with two short bursts in Lou's right pants pocket next to his thin wallet. He was finishing washing his hands after draining the afternoon coffee. *A work email,* he knew by the two short bursts, which distinguished it from a text. He would just wait the two minutes until he got back to his desk. The forty-one-year-old 'light colonel' checked the button line—or 'gig line'—on his light blue shirt, ensuring it was perfectly in line with his dark blue trouser zipper. He left the bathroom in the Pentagon's C-ring, the closest facility to his office, nearly getting run over as he did.

"What the—?" he exclaimed, quickly cutting himself off. The hall was alive with commotion, and active duty and civilians alike were scurrying about—some back to their offices, others to somewhere they'd just been summoned. *Something's happened,* Lou thought, concerned. *This feels big. Like 9-11 big.* In thirty-five seconds he'd dodged two more near collisions, darting down the highly polished, off-white tile floor of the long hall and making the left turn back into his office. The non-descript wood door led to a not-so exciting office staffed by mid-level officers of every branch.

United States Air Force Lt. Col. Freeman Louis Caldwell, Lou to his friends, was but one of twenty men and women who comprised the Inter-Service Task Force for Consideration of Consolidation. The ITFCC was deep into a several year study and evaluation of every pro-and-con and nook-and-cranny of what it would mean for all branches of the U.S. Military to merge under one banner. Their collective roles were pretty far down the pecking order of units that would be scrambled for... *Whatever the hell this is,* Lou thought.

He swiped his badge in the card reader and entered the large monotonous room. He was fortunate enough to share one of the individual offices on the far wall with another Air Force officer. There were three other combined offices. The remaining ten officers with two civilian project managers shared the common space in the center with stereotypical cubicle walls. At the far left was a conference room which was visible behind a glass wall. He could see most of the staff cramming in there as one of the Army majors was trying to log in to the room's computer and pull a feed up on the seventy-two-inch monitor.

Lou pulled the phone out and scanned it as he started walking that direction. He hadn't even managed to get through his password entry by the time he reached the room. He dropped the phone back into his uniform trouser pocket.

"What's going on?" he mumbled to Air Force Major Pete Soffet, his office mate. The DOD logo that had been playing 'Pong' on the large monitor at the end of the room suddenly evaporated into an aerial feed.

"Mt. Rainier erupted," Pete whispered, eyes glued to the screen. The Army major had logged onto a secure Pentagon feed. "But before that they had an earthquake."

"Yeah, earlier," Lou concurred. "A few hours ago, like a 7.0, or somethin'."

"No." Pete corrected, looking at Lou. "Just now. Didn't you see the email? They're saying this thing was huge—in the ballpark of nine. Or bigger," he added.

Lou let out a low whistle. "That's gonna leave a mark," he said to nobody in particular.

"Who's flying the drone?" he heard one of the team members ask on the far side of the conference table. People had started seating themselves, mesmerized by the giant dark-gray fist shaped column of rock and earth growing out of the south end of Puget Sound on their screen.

Good question, Lou agreed internally. *What feed are we looking at here?* He thought about what would've already been in the air somewhere within a couple of hundred miles. *Probably an MQ-4 out of Whidbey Island,* he thought. *On an autonomous mission. The thing will fly in a high-altitude loop for hours.*

He listened to one of the other officers explain to his peers that if it lost signal, there were fail-safes that would allow it to be piloted from any of several other locations around the country. "We learned the hard way a couple of times. Always have a redundant station ready to send new instructions via satellite."

"Holy crap!" a Navy Lieutenant Commander said as the drone's camera broke through the rain clouds over Seattle. The room grew deathly still as that totality of destruction presented itself. They could see fires everywhere. Highway overpasses were pancaked in many areas. About a third of the Seattle skyscrapers were now piles of rubble and debris being swamped by tsunami water. None of those still standing had much in the way of glass left on their window frames. *Like steel skeletons,* Lou thought, just as shocked as everyone else. Cargo and cruise ships had sunk and caught fire right at their piers. Destroyed vessels of all sizes littered Puget Sound as far as they could see. The waters were brown and frothy. The shorelines in many areas showed massive landslides right into the Sound, taking entire neighborhoods with them.

"Where's the Space Needle?" another asked with a crack in his voice. Though the famed landmark was conspicuously absent, the altitude was too high for seeing fine detail. As if on cue, the drone began a rapid and steep descent.

"Someone's obviously taken control of this thing," one of the team members announced.

Buzz. Lou heard and felt his phone again. *Buzz-buzz*. Everyone had their phones on vibrate and they were all sounding at the same time. He retrieved the device as he left the conference room and headed for his own office. *Can't stand trying to read emails on these little screens.* He pulled his ID card from its badge holder on his chest. When he sat at his desk, he slid it into the slot on the keyboard and punched in his PIN. As he waited for the screen to finish the log-in loop, he scanned the screen of his phone. It was a text from his wife.

[Julia] You seeing this thing in Seattle? Can you skip racquetball? We need to talk.

Lou sighed audibly. *I don't need this right now,* he grumbled to himself as he queued up his computer to see if CNN or Fox News had anything to expound about the big disaster. But that wasn't unusual—he and Julia had not had an easy go the last fourteen plus months, their marriage barely hanging on by a thread. And as happened multiple times each day, Lou felt himself begin to drift down the long, sad tunnel in his mind. Each time he thought of his wife, he also thought of their own personal apocalypse that had been the beginning of the end—their son Terrance's suicide.

The sixteen-year-old had it all seemingly so well. He was a varsity starter on the football team and had recently obtained his driver's license. Lou had felt the double-crush of both regret and guilt ever since that horrendous day. Still officially a pilot, he had up to that point been the primary co-pilot for the C-17 that flew The Beast—the Presidential limo—ahead whenever he or she travelled. When he reported his family tragedy to his Commanding Officer, the Air Force had rightfully and understandably removed Lou's status as a flight-qualified officer. It was a protocol to allow flight crew time to grieve—and prove they were still mentally sound. It was the second and final time Lou had lost flight status in his career.

He had travelled a lot before that day, as most crew in the 89th Airlift Wing did—often and consistently. And in the course of his career after that fateful plane crash in Afghanistan, he'd worked hard to re-establish himself as a trustworthy pilot and officer, somehow managing to keep flight status in the cargo delivery portions of the branch. It was due to this life of long and unpredictable absences that Julia had since blamed Lou for being the ghost-father that had ultimately led to their son's decision. And try as he might to hold the marriage together, it just didn't seem in the cards—a person could only stand the sight of someone they came to hate for so long. *Is this the day?* Lou asked himself as he re-read the text.

To add gas to the fire, in the months after Terrance's funeral, Lou had taken to alcohol for comfort—a lot. *I'm allowed,* he told himself nightly as he felt the cold buzz start to dampen the deeply embedded depression. *To hell with anyone who doesn't get that.* Still, the Air Force noticed. His attendance had started to suffer, as did his punctuality on the days he did make it to work. Eight months earlier he'd been transferred to the current task force he was on, a clear message that both he and the Air Force were merely buying time until his commission expired. At 5'10", Lou wasn't an overly big man to begin with. But the sedentary job and nightly love affair with Pendleton whiskey had grown the pooch over his belt-buckle. He hated sunny days because his shadow was a mirror that didn't play tricks on his mind about it.

Lou had started to play racquetball three days a week as a coping mechanism. In his forethought, he figured it was about trying to stay fit. Deeper in his psyche, it was just one more way to avoid going home. Ironically, it was Julia that wanted to sell the house. After the suicide of their only child, she left her career in real estate to mourn and never went back. She couldn't stand the thought of living in the same house her sole baby had hung himself in. Many fights in recent months had revolved around the collision of that fact and Lou's desire to stay—it was the last and only place he still felt connected to his son's memory. His counselor had told him that despite popular misconception, the divorce rate for parents in his circumstance was not significantly different than for other groups. In Lou's mind, despite loving and wanting to reconcile with Julia, divorce was a matter of time—though he refused to be the one to pull the trigger.

Lou ignored his booted computer and yanked his access card out of the slot on the keyboard. He scanned his wristwatch and stood. *1610,* he saw. *Must be early afternoon in Seattle.* Those folks are in for a whole different world. He grabbed his brown A-2 bomber jacket off the coat stand near the door on his way back into the larger office space. Still technically a pilot, he was allowed to wear it with his service blue uniform, and it was much more comfortable on a bright and chilly October D.C. day. *Drinks are half off 'til 6 on Tuesdays at The Stowaway,* he remembered. *I guess I can skip stopping in just this once,* he lied to himself.

SOUTHWEST OF TUCSON, ARIZONA

THE FALL DESERT SUN WOULD SOON MOVE FROM ITS ZENITH TO start skewing west over Mt. Ruby in the Pajarita Wilderness. Luckily, the autumn days were better for patrols than those super-hot days of mid-July, but the trade-off was longer shadows in the evenings and much chillier nights. The preserve was a safe refuge for migratory birds, part of the Coronado National Forest.

Forty-nine-year-old Granger Madison was stumped, sure that this old route for smugglers would've reopened by now. He and his all-volunteer force of veterans had but one mission every time they braved the hot days and cold nights in the Arizona desert—find and report human traffickers.

This wasn't your average band of mostly well-meaning and sometimes-chubby American patriots fighting the surge of people trying to cross the southern border. Some of those groups had gained notoriety in the recent decade, sometimes due to unfair treatment by the press, sometimes due to their own poor decisions. Granger's Road Runners were a tight-knit group of combat veterans who went to great lengths to stay quiet about what they did. Their mission wasn't about coyotes smuggling poor people, most of whom just wanted to better their chances in life. As egregious as that tragic tale was for those refuge-seekers...as much as Granger wished he could just start sniping the coyotes...he knew it would be like fighting the tide. His team's mission had been solely about finding the cartels—those who had evolved beyond the role of coyote into experts at smuggling narcotics, weapons, and children sex-slaves. In the nearly eight years since his team had formed—just he and one other at the very beginning—they had reported twelve routes to the United States Custom and Border Protection branch of the Department of Homeland Security.

There were six Road Runners in all. Three other seasoned operators joined Granger to make a patrol that would plant themselves for several days—each of them a veteran in long range reconnaissance patrols in the Army, Navy or Marines. The other two were both capable as a support crew, a pair of older and less-agile vets. These men would drop off and pick up the Road Runners with the intent of leaving no evidence that the team was even out there—they were the insertion and extraction team. Those men were all-in, too—even from the comfort of home, they had to be ready to respond at any moment the entire time the Runners were in the field.

As a civilian group, Granger's men tried to play by the rules—mostly. Regarding communications, they all used HAM capable radios, though their primary form of communication was simply a group text. They found cell signal to be spotty in the valleys and slopes and somewhat reliable near the crests of the sage covered mountains. Each of them had a mesh network antenna they would set up with a small foldable solar panel, and their phones could text each other quite reliably in a private chat, even when they would spread themselves out. At that moment, Granger had an earbud inserted from the HAM radio, listening to an AM channel blare a classic rock song, a small measure to keep the mind awake when staring at nothing active in the desert. He didn't do that but for a few minutes every hour or two, not wanting to lose focus on why he was out there.

"So as Boston winds down...if you've been living under a rock today," he heard the afternoon DJ commence, "we have an update on that nasty event near Seattle. A massive earthquake that the USGS estimates as being nine-point-oh on the Richter scale struck the coast of Washington State. Mt. Rainier has erupted. California and several other states are reporting blackouts, and several corporations are now reporting issues with accessing their cloud-based storage. Relief efforts here in the Tucson area have already started. Please go to the Red Cross website..." <Click> Granger shut down the radio and picked up his phone. *Nothing from Claude or Bob...* he thought. His support team was part of the group text.

[Granger] How bad is this Seattle thing, Bob?

[Bob] Bad. Too big to describe here.

[Granger] Roger. Pick us up at Extract 1 in 3 hours. Thx.

[Granger] Unless anyone has anything new, let's pack it and meet at RP6 in 30. Will explain then.

After the usual replies, Granger began to square away his position. After putting away the binoculars, radio, and small remnants of MRE trash, he rolled up the sniper's mat he always used to lay on the desert floor. He then used a piece of scrub brush to wipe away the tracks in the sand his body and mat had made laying there. They always worked in pairs, so he'd be meeting up with Dave Wolf in just a few minutes as they hiked to the far end of their valley, down into the basin to meet Tracy and Mick at Rally Point Six. *This route is dry anyhow,* he mused a bit disappointedly. He stood and stretched, confident nobody had been counter-surveilling the valley after having been in control of it for forty hours.

The medically retired Tucson firefighter double-checked the hole he'd been using as a waste-privy, covering it with one more mound of dirt and a few stones. As a young man in the Marines' Force Recon—

once again called Raiders—he used to enjoy the alone time in the brush as a form of proving his mental toughness. Now at forty-nine, it was solace—a respite from a society he was feeling less a part of, particularly since the fire that ended his career and covered the left side of his face and shoulder and the back of his legs in scar tissue.

The plastic appearance that ran from his left eyebrow down across his now-malformed ear and all the way to his left shoulder usually drew strange looks in grocery stores. The burns had been only second degree on the shoulder, thanks to the Kevlar and Nomex in his bunker gear. The side effect of that, though, was that not all the nerves had been killed. It was somewhat painful to wear a backpack. In the years he'd been running the Road Runners, he'd morphed his system into a right-shoulder-only sling-pack. The graying 5'11" Granger slung his pack and wrapped the waist belt around, ready to start moving toward Wolf. *I think we need to look farther west.*

JOINT BASE ANDREWS

THE VH-60N CARRYING PRESIDENT JEREMIAH ALLEN AND First Lady Francis Allen approached and settled on the tarmac at Joint Base Andrews a little after 9 PM. POTUS, call sign "Snake Charmer" to the United States Secret Service, had finished a series of meetings in the West Wing as quickly as he could. He wholeheartedly agreed with his Chief of Staff that they should get to the west coast as quickly as reasonable to survey the damage from the mega-disaster. It was the *presidential* thing to do.

After the last "presidential shuffle," Marine One wound up in the left-rear number-four-spot of the constantly shifting diamond formation. The five helicopters—Marine One and four decoys—constantly shuffled whenever Snake Charmer flew, an active security precaution to ensure an engaged enemy would have his hands full trying to shoot down the correct rotor wing aircraft. This was one of several craft the Marines used to shuttle the President, and usually the model sent for a rapid pickup and drop off that hadn't been planned.

Snake Charmer's primary protection agent stepped out of the craft first and assumed a position just past the Marines who had opened the hatch. The Marines, in dress blue uniform, saluted sharply as President Allen passed by after stepping out of the forest green craft. He held his hand back toward the craft to assist his wife down the one folding step and onto the tarmac. He returned the salute, always uncomfortable that he was breaking some sort of protocol doing it. They began their procession toward the Boeing 747, known to the Air Force as VC-25A and the rest of the world as Air Force One.

Chief of Staff Shannon Sahr and Julia Jacobs, Jeremiah's personal assistant, were waiting at the drivable tarmac stairs that abutted the aircraft, along with a few other Secret Service agents. Most of the staff and invited press corps were already on board. About one hundred yards to the right of the president's approach was a facility that ushered people through the "cleared to board" procedures.

"Would you get Secretaries Smith and Williamson on a video call as soon as we're past takeoff?" Jeremiah asked Shannon before she could say a thing.

"First thing, sir."

Shannon had already been dealing with the Secretaries' staffs all afternoon, as it were. The Secretaries of Energy and Interior would be the most directly in the public eye aside from President Allen. It was mere bad timing that they couldn't be on the flight. Secretary Craig Smith had been at an energy conference among his European peers that week in Switzerland. Secretary Lashay Williamson was on personal leave in Indiana. She was already arranging her own tour to start the next day.

The entire entourage hurried into the plane so they could get airborne and maybe catch a little shut eye before they got to the

Rainier Impact Zone. The craft was buzzing with the normal beehive of activity that always accompanied the president. Some military personnel were double and triple-checking their pre-flight tasks. Others were already fully on-line at their communications stations in the big craft's "hump" aft of the cockpit. Various Secret Service and members of the president's staff were getting themselves situated for the flight.

President Allen turned right to head back toward the conference room, completely ignoring his office. All chairs on Air Force One were capable of being secured for take-off and landing. *No need to wait,* he thought. Francis made the left to take her spot in the Presidential bedroom in the plane's nose. Jeremiah waved off the usual chorus of "G'evening, Mr. President" echoing from everyone he passed on the way.

"Good evening, all. Look—sorry to drag you all away from your loved ones on such short notice." He genuinely was sorry.

The former Pennsylvania steel-mill manager turned politician had always connected with people. It was his strength. Born in Ohio, the son of the mill's superintendent went to work in the family business right out of college. Early on, he was able to bridge a fiercely growing divide between labor and management, something that did not go unnoticed by the local Democratic party members. The course of his life had been a slow progression through state and federal positions. The bulk of his career had been as a congressman, though four years before he ran for president, he switched from the Democrat party to the Libertarian party.

Jeremiah Ethan Allen had become disenfranchised with his party in recent years, feeling that the growing love for political dissention in America made the time ripe for a strong third party to grow. Unlike the Green and Constitution parties, he felt the Libertarian party was less divisive, able to appeal to reasonable minded folks from both sides of the aisle. He was the first Libertarian to be elected to Congress, and the following cycle two-years later, eight more Libertarians had been elected to the House and one to the Senate. When he ran for and won the Presidential nomination that election cycle, the media had done their very best to paint any votes for him as a waste, no matter which party he was stealing them from. It was truly a sign of the strength and foresight behind the Constitution, as he won the requisite electoral votes by a thin margin over both of the major party candidates.

Grabbing a seat along the side of the long table, he got right to it as Shannon and the rest of the key staff filed in. "Before we discuss the horrifying death toll predictions again, let's start with the things we can look at outside the destruction area. Transportation." His assistant Julia brought him an iced lemonade without asking.

Shannon was seated to his immediate left and nodded toward one of her staffers crammed into the room. "Go ahead, Terrell."

"Mr. President." The staffers almost always began with a direct address to Jeremiah. It was a protocol he hated and had tried more than once to order stopped, to no avail. "Secretary Vu's staff reports all major shippers, both domestic and international, are aware of the issue and are taking steps to conduct redirects on land and sea to every port from Oakland-San Francisco and south. The port at Eureka in northern California was wiped out by the tsunami. Long Beach is expected to take the brunt of the overflow. The initial reports of trucks and containers lost today is based on tracking devices that went off-grid—currently over 2,500 trucks. Counting containers of goods lost in the Seattle-Tacoma area and ships that were capsized in the tsunami, the estimate is over one-hundred and twenty thousand. Both numbers are expected to rise."

After two more minutes of the shipping and transportation report, Jeremiah's mind wandered to the infrastructure issues already being felt. "Thanks, Terrell. Who has energy? I want to know how California will be handling all of this extra shipping."

"Mr. President," stated Sam Gilson, Shannon's operations director. "Bunky is still in the communications center arranging the video chat with Secretary Smith. Despite coal plants only comprising point-four percent of California's energy plants, thirty-three percent of what they use is coal powered, purchased from the surrounding states. They've made big strides toward solar, but the output will fall as it gets closer to winter. The loss of hydroelectric from Washington and Oregon will hurt them, but it won't cripple them." He went silent for one second before adding, "Yet."

"Yet," the president caught. "Meaning what?"

"The secretary's staff was emphasizing the domino effect from today's events. As the demand for coal and natural gas increases in all western states from the loss of hydroelectric, those states will be selling less to California. But as California demands more for an exponential amount of port traffic, the trucks needed to haul the coal won't be available — compounded by the loss of trucks and qualified drivers today. Then there's the human factor..."

"People getting tired and such," Shannon added.

"Partially," Sam said. "But I guess I was referring to a more primal pessimism."

"You've opened the door, Sam," Jeremiah said patiently. "Just walk through it."

"I guess I'm looking down the road, sir. What happens when people who make their money online, not just corporations, but the thirty-three percent of people at the bottom of middle-class—can't work from home because the electricity isn't there. Or the internet."

This made everyone in the room get quiet for an unusual eight seconds, only to be broken by an announcement from the co-pilot that they were preparing to takeoff. Very little information was available this early into the catastrophe. The plan was to avoid the ash plume from Mt. Rainier while en route. The crew would attempt to find out the status of SeaTac Airport on the way. Initial reports from scout planes were bleak at best.

"If nothing else," Shannon had told the president two hours before they departed, "we can always land in Portland and drive up."

CHAPTER 2

MORNINGSIDE, MARYLAND

"WELL, THIS SUCKS!" JULIA CALDWELL SAID. "I WAS THINKING about going to a real estate conference in Seattle next year."

"Hmmph," Lou half grunted, sipping on a sweaty lowball glass of whiskey. "Pretty sure they ain't having that. Besides—" he stated, looking at her with drunken disdain, "you gave up bein' a realtor."

The pair had been both mesmerized and traumatized by the images being played over and over on the news, as had most of the country. One couple who had been visiting the Washington state coast for their anniversary had posted a goodbye video to their adult children and grandkids on their Facebook profile as the giant coastal tsunami rolled in and marched itself a few dozen miles up the highway.

"As long as we're playing 'Captain Obvious'," Julia yelled back from her easy chair, "you said you wouldn't stop and drink on the way home tonight!"

Lou stood up, rocking a little to steady himself. "I didn't wanna hear it, Julia. You said you wanted to talk. But it always turns into a giant guilt trip you dump on me!"

"I can't help it if you take it that way!" she screeched. "If you feel guilty about Terrance, that isn't on me!"

"I miss him, too!" Lou yelled back. He started to head to the kitchen, noticing that he had some sort of grease stains on his light blue uniform shirt. "Damn bar food..." he muttered under his breath.

"You are such a jerk," she yelled with fire and anger in her voice. She was long past tears for Lou. "We can't keep up with this!" She stood to follow him out of the living room. "And you have got to clean yourself up! Before..."

"Before what?" He turned to challenge, assuming she was going to use the d-word.

"Before they kick you out, Lou! Before you kill someone drunk driving! How many 'befores' do I need?"

Lou clammed up and set the glass on the small breakfast table, trying slowly and with impaired motor function to keep upright and move while unbuttoning his shirt. He stumbled toward the sink.

"You'll never get to fly again if you don't—"

"Fly!" he exclaimed at the incredulous idea. "They're never going to let me fly again! I'm on that dead-end task force until I retire!" he yelled through the fog of the whiskey.

"Then what are you going to do, Lou?" Julia asked, not quite yelling anymore, but emphatic all the same. "Drink? Is that your life's mission now?"

Lou turned back around to find a clean washcloth. "Been thinkin' about that," he said lowly. "Prob'ly start flippin' houses or something. You could market them, and we—"

"You don't know the first thing about it!" she exclaimed.

"I know I wouldn't have to work with anyone!" he yelled, staring. "Where's the clean dish cloths?"

She reached into his space, yanking the uniform shirt from him and heading toward the laundry room. "Don't even bother," she said loudly and coldly. "Just take your drunk butt to the spare room already."

Lou rocked a bit back and forth, eyes watching her disappear down the first-floor corridor toward the back. Inside Lou's head there was a completely sober man, talking to him. *You're going to regret this tomorrow. You should've stopped four drinks ago.*

USS JAMES L. HUNNICUTT, SSGN-93, NORTHERN YELLOW SEA

MASTER CHIEF DARREN JORGENSON ROLLED OUT OF HIS RACK in the "goat locker"—the private space for all Chief level NCOs on a US Navy ship. *0513,* he said to himself, glancing at his Casio G-Shock wristwatch as he started his usual mild stretch routine. The space's red lights were still on, casting their eerie hue on everything. *Getting too old for this,* he told himself, as he did every morning. Unlike the top Chief on a surface ship, the COB, or Chief-Of-the Boat, was part of the normal watch rotation. His normal watch started at 0600, though he always tried to be there fifteen minutes early. His morning routine consisted of a quick shower, one piece of toast, and a glass of "bug juice."

After completing his morning facility stop, he donned his blue "poopie suit" coveralls common to all submarine sailors. He grabbed his water bottle and left the chiefs' berthing compartment and headed up and forward to the enlisted mess—another difference between sub and surface chiefs. On a surface ship, the chiefs had their own small eating space—on a "boat", they did not. There just wasn't enough room, even on this specialized, one-of-a-kind spy-submarine. This one had been built from the ground up to be its own class, while still using many of the same parts and components as the other subs in the fleet. Even its predecessor that had ushered in the new millennium had been a modified version of its own class. Building this one as a unique submarine had actually been a lesson from the ballistic fleet, though.

When the Navy converted the four oldest Ohio Class submarines into a new class for a new type of mission, they immediately began improving the coming Virginia attack boat class. Like most classes of ships that take twenty to thirty years to build, the Virginias had a series of mid-class feature changes that would forever distinguish them from the earlier models. But the Navy went one step further, knowing that these new "SSGNs" wouldn't last forever. Over half of their hull-life had been used up before the conversions even began. But their missions had proven so valuable—delivering multiple SEAL teams and well over 100 cruise missiles—that naval architects began to build a new class from scratch.

This had coupled with the fact that they really only had one fully capable spy-submarine, which tended to need an extraordinary amount of TLC. The only way they had been able to procure the funding had been through the concept of taking the strike-capable SEAL delivery submarine concept and blending it with the best features and capabilities of the predecessor spy submarines. What had been born was the USS James L. Hunnicutt, with one other in sea trials and four others in various stages of construction. The sub was just over 500-feet long and thirty-eight feet wide in the main "breadth" of the hull. It was not quite as maneuverable at speed as a true attack submarine, but it wasn't meant to be. The beast had specialized LOCs, or "lock-out chambers", that could push up to four 8-man SEAL teams in and out at the same time. It contained two rows of eight missile tubes which each contained six Tomahawk cruise missiles. It was fully capable of carrying any Swimmer Delivery Vehicle the Navy used, and it had six torpedo tubes. It was also outfitted with several auxiliary propellers that could lower out of the ballast tanks. This allowed the sub to hover in one spot and even travel sideways into unique bodies of water. She had specialized compartments in the bottom that allowed the deployment of unique sensors, recording devices and UUVs, or unmanned underwater vehicles.

"Mornin', COB," a few of the enlisted sailors muttered to Darren as he strode into the tight confines of the mess and went straight to one of three toasters bolted to the counter and plopped in a piece of whole wheat. Darren filled his cup of juice and guzzled, looking to fill his water bottle. It was a small morning game each day to see if he could get through this process before being bombarded with the day's issues. As a senior enlisted person, his primary job, other than acting as the Diving Officer during battle stations, was to be the liaison between the Commanding Officer and the crew. If morale was tanking, he needed to be on top of it.

"Morning," Darren would counter to each young man or woman as he passed them, usually offering up a small piece of "How ya, doin' today, Petty Officer Thomas?" or "Seaman Smith" as he passed them. Each person in there was getting themselves fed and ready for their shift. In recent years, the US Navy had switched back to a 24-hour day after decades of running sub crews on watch for six-hours and other duties or rest for twelve. "Other duties" usually comprised at least half of that twelve hours. The Navy had a noticeable reduction in the number of minor and major mishaps involving submarines ever since.

On the James L. Hunnicutt, the Executive Officer had aligned with Darren in successfully lobbying the captain to allow the eight-hour watch to be split into two four-hour watches. This allowed the various chiefs and leading petty officers to schedule maintenance and other duties for junior sailors in just one of the two remaining eight-hour windows. *It might be my imagination,* Darren thought, *but it feels like this crew's morale is the best I've ever seen.*

Darren plopped himself in the bolted swiveling dining chair next to Senior Chief Carlos Alford, his "bull-nuke". Carlos was his senior enlisted counterpart for all things at and aft of the ship's reactor.

"What's happenin', Senior?"

The two men were on different watch rotations, and this was their usual chance to have a direct face-to-face for the day. In the informal hierarchy, it was still Darren's job to present any major issues to the CO on Carlos' behalf.

"One of the electricians got caught snoozing on watch last night. EM3 Christianson. Chief Clark will be forwarding the write-up to Lt. Smythe this morning. And..." Carl paused, searching his tired memory, "...Aux 2 seawater pump is being tagged out so we can investigate an increase in the dynamic pressure during cycling. Pretty routine stuff," he smirked.

Darren made a note. The Chief Engineer would route the info on the pump as needed. His job was to make sure the CO was aware of personnel issues. In the case of the sleeping sailor, there was a chain-of-command to respect that would relay that, too. If the sailor had been caught leering at a female sailor or some other highly sensitive issue, Darren would have already been on the way to brief the XO and CO. There was a balancing act when it came to being a COB—knowing when and what one needs to expedite versus letting the team fix for themselves.

As the two men made their morning small talk, a petty officer approached. "Sorry to interrupt, COB. CO sent for you." The messenger immediately turned to return to the bridge.

Darren stood up. "Thanks, Senior."

First names would've been used in the goat locker—out here, it was always about maintaining unit discipline. He grabbed his water bottle and headed up and forward once more. *Never would have allowed water bottles in a sub at the start of my career,* he pondered. When the 'Hunny' class was designed, water bottle holders were installed at every watch station. Every sailor was issued a special stainless water bottle coated in a sound dampening rubber lest they drop it. He made his way past the missile firing control center and turned right—starboard—and headed up the steep inclined ladder that led to the aft port side of the bridge.

"Ma'am," Darren greeted his XO upon seeing her. Though they both reported directly to the CO, Darren and the ship's Executive Officer Lieutenant Commander Carla Gingery treated handling crew issues as a two-person team. She had confided in Darren about the occasional issue with junior officers, choosing to lean on the forty-eight-year-old's full career of experience. In the two years since James L. Hunnicutt had been fleet-ready, they had developed a good working rapport.

"Skipper's in his stateroom, COB," Carla said before turning back to her conversation with the Officer-of-the-Deck.

Darren nodded and scanned the status of the submarine's 'brain' before heading back down the ladder and forward a few feet. The COs stateroom—about two-thirds the size of a tiny bedroom—had an open doorway that Darren swiveled his body into. The brownish laminate in the hall had a fake wood-grain pattern that was traditional to US submarines. Darren always wondered why they didn't go with something brighter to assist in the sunlight deprived environment.

"Sir?" he said to announce his presence.

"Mornin', COB," Commander Brody Woodward said. "Close the door," he instructed in a voice that said something was wrong.

Darren complied and turned back to see the CO handing him a clipboard with radio message traffic on it.

"Picked this up on VLF just a while ago," Brody said. He paused to let Darren absorb what was being read.

Leaning against the now closed door, Darren started reading the message from COMSUBPAC—Commander Naval Submarine Forces, Pacific—silently at first. As he read and re-read he started to mumble and eventually read out loud to ensure he was actually comprehending what he read. "...massive damage to all piers and facilities in Washington State. Death toll expected to be several hundred thousand or higher. Task Force being organized. All units remain on station." Darren looked up at the CO. "Captain, our families...our homeport is just...wiped out?" His face was twisted with worry.

"I know, COB. I don't have magic words for something like this. I need you to help me figure out how we're going to break this to the crew. Two people in the radio room are the only ones to know. We need to get ahead of this before the scuttlebutt starts."

Both seasoned operators had a half-century of experience between them—experience that allowed them to be sailing undetected in the front yard of their nation's most formidable opponent. Yet neither knew how they were going to break this to 168 other sailors and expect them to perform their dangerous tasks flawlessly.

MORNINGSIDE, MARYLAND

LOU WALKED PAST THE BLOOD RED GMC ACADIA MINI-SUV IN the driveway. Tempted as he was to take it in the mid-October cold, the little sober man in his head knew he was too trashed. He would drive home buzzed, knowing full well that might be his undoing someday. But there was no denial that evening—he was drunk and on a mission. And while The Stowaway was too far to walk—he wasn't *that* drunk—Snuffy's Tavern was but three blocks away, part of the closest strip mall.

It was past dark, and his bomber jacket was zipped up fully, the padded collar engulfing his chin, neck, and ears. He started to pass a cold looking man, obviously homeless by the attire and demeanor. One could just tell when someone else was carrying everything they owned in the world, and the baby stroller stuffed with trash bags and an old suitcase was a dead giveaway.

"Got any spare change?" the man muttered slightly to Lou. Like most homeless, he'd long lost the mechanism—shame—that kept him from making eye contact. His gaze pierced Lou.

Lou felt in his trouser pocket for the paper he'd gotten back from the two twenties he'd plunked down earlier in the evening. He pulled them out, staring at a wad that he started to pull apart. *Three ones and a five,* he counted in his head. "Take it," he said, stuffing the whole wad at the man. Lou figured they were probably about the same age, though the man was obviously weather-beaten and street tested. He reached out and took the bills.

"God bless you, friend," the man said as he stuffed the bills into a pocket on the inside of his holey coat.

"God don't exist," Lou muttered under his breath as he turned to walk away.

"Come again?"

This made Lou stop. He was too drunk to walk straight, but he was certainly not too drunk to spew an opinion. He turned back. "You're welcome. Get a meal. Hell—get a drink. I really don't care. But don't ask God to bless me, whatever you do." He turned back and continued his journey.

The homeless man started to do the same, but after a few seconds he turned back around, speaking to Lou's shrinking figure. "Whatever happened, man, I'll say a prayer for you..."

The Hell? Lou put on the brakes and started stumbling back the twenty feet toward the man. "You do that, you'll never get another red cent outta me." *There.* He started to turn back but was just too inebriated to let it go. "Just who the hell do you think you are, telling me you'll pray for me!" He started to raise his voice. "Look at you! How on Earth can you believe in God when you live on the damn street?"

"It's just a figure o' speech, mister," the man replied. "But I seen enough times in my life I shoulda been dead to know He's up there." The man pointed up with a gloved finger but kept his eyes on Lou. "He didn't put me on the street—I did."

Figures I'd find the one homeless guy who doesn't babble with psychosis, the internal sober Lou thought. "Yeah...well...good for you then," Lou replied. "But no loving God would've taken my precious son from me! No loving God would've killed like a million people in Seattle this morning! You wanna believe in the tooth fairy, go ahead. But don't dump your security blanket on me. I know better!"

"Sorry to hear 'bout your boy, mister," the man said with a grizzled voice. "If there is a Heaven, I'm sure he made it." Lou turned and started stumbling toward the bar again. "But you need to figure out who you're really mad at 'fore it's too late," he heard.

MORNINGSIDE, MARYLAND

THE LYFT DRIVER DRAGGED HIM OUT OF HIS CAR AND DROPPED Lou right on the cold sidewalk, cussing him out and thanking nobody in particular that Lou hadn't puked in his car. Lou rolled over onto one shoulder, pushing with one hand on the front lawn. The only saving grace was that at 11:30 at night, no neighbors were still awake to see him. He slowly clambered up onto both hands and both knees. He felt a wave of nausea spin the earth as a cold sweat broke out in the chilly air at the same moment his stomach rejected the abuse it'd received all night. After two minutes of spewing and hacking, Lou slowly stood and made his way to the garage door in a stupor.

He found the little keypad on the side of the door frame. *All threes,* the little sober guy said in his head. *Remember? You changed the code to one button for nights like this?* Lou punched the three button four times and the door started to rise. The opener's light grew in intensity in the dark driveway as the chain-drive pushed the solo door up. Lou stumbled past Julia's car, over to the workbench. He pushed the spare garage door remote he had hanging on the pegboard over his workbench. He yanked on the chain that controlled the one bulb over the bench and plopped himself in the chair as the door descended. He looked left and found the trusty trash can. *It's been a couple of months since you got this jacked up,* the little voice reminded him. *Your nightly buzz has been holding you together for a while.*

He found his backup pint of Jameson hiding in the bottom drawer of his benchtop toolbox right behind his head. As he took a pull on the small bottle, he stared at the hole in the large load-bearing beam that ran across the garage. He could still see a fiber from the rope that Terrance had run through it. In his nightly ritual, Freeman Louis Caldwell started crying in the memories of the beloved son he would never see again. The garage opener's light went out, leaving the weeping man in the small glow of his workbench light.

CHAPTER 3

MANHATTAN, KANSAS

MORRIS DOOGHAN SAW THE PROFESSOR'S TEACHING ASSISTANT stroll in and fire up the 80-inch smartboard. The Kansas State senior had wondered if they were going to even try to hold class, what with how the power had been flickering that morning. *Still don't get why we're having power and internet issues just because Washington had an earthquake a week ago,* he had texted his buddy a few minutes earlier. The economics major was knocking out the last class for his aerospace minor, an Introduction to Mechanical Engineering class. He watched the last of the students trickling in to take their normal seats when the power flickered and cut-off once again.

Morris heard a small percentage of groans and sighs as he once again checked his phone's charge. *Twenty-three percent. Going to have to find that backup battery at the bottom of my junk drawer.* He opened his MacBook Pro to check it. *Still at eighty-nine percent. Good.* The night before, he'd found that a lot of his cloud storage was inaccessible. The internet was spotty, and that morning he received a slew of emails. In addition to the normal junk, there were a few from his credit union, explaining how they were trying their best to get the system back up and running normally.

He got a text just as he looked up to pay attention to the TA, who had called out to the class. "Just got word that morning classes are canceled," she said somewhat nonchalantly. Everyone began to pack up by the daylight trickling in through the third-floor window. Morris checked his text:

[ThatNub] Lemme know if ur class gets axed

"ThatNub" was William Easton, Morris' roommate at a near-campus apartment and part of his core group of friends. The junior was the number two to Morris' leadership role on their airsoft 'mil-sim' team, 'Cat Scratch Fever', so named in honor of their university mascot. The team didn't get to play together in summer, so they tried to practice two to three times per week. There just wasn't enough interest in the sport for it to have any kind of intramural league at the college. Instead, the group played in a monthly Saturday league a few towns over and tried to travel to Kansas City, Kansas, known to the group as KCK, at least once in each half of the school year.

Not really in the mood to text, he thought. He didn't want to waste his battery on a fairly trivial conversation when he'd be walking back to the apartment in a few minutes. *He probably just wants to set up a practice, anyhow.* He pondered that for a moment. *As if there's anything else to do with no class and no internet.*

THE PENTAGON

THE STAFF SERGEANT KNOCKED BEFORE ENTERING. "COLONEL Caldwell?" he asked.

"Morning, Staff Sergeant." Lou said politely.

Could this be it? he asked himself with butterflies in his stomach. In the ten days since the massive devastation in the Seattle area had started sending a slew of trickle-down effects across the American west —*and the world it seems,* Lou thought— he had made the decision to apply for retirement. Despite knowing it was the best choice for his life, and that it would undoubtedly be approved, he still felt a bit of melancholy. The entire half of his life since college had been all about the United States Air Force. Drawing that closed was an emotional decision even though he'd felt disconnected from the military ever since Terrance's death. *This calls for a drink.*

Lou took a large yellow envelope from the clerk's hand. "This feels a bit thin, sergeant," he mused as he began to untie the string enclosure that held the flap closed.

"Congratulations, sir!" the enlisted member announced as Lou pulled a single sheet of paper out of the envelope. Having handled the Lt. Colonels' retirement package personally, he was looking forward to this presumably pleasant surprise.

Lou scanned the paper in confusion. He looked up at the E-6 clerk, and then re-read it, finally settling on the names at the top and bottom. "T-there seems to be some sort of mix up, Sarge...." He trailed off, waiting for an explanation.

"This one," the sergeant said, pointing at the paper with some abnormal emphasis, "is not for me to spill the beans on, sir. You can tell it's coming from the top." He pointed at a certain slip in the folder. "You can see you have an appointment with Colonel Jackson on Tuesday, sir."

"Colonel Jackson..." Lou trailed off, looking into his memory. *Old Seely Jackson?* he asked himself. *Nawww... he retired last year. At least I have the weekend to mull this over.*

"General Montgomery's assistant... Sir...?" The staff sergeant had a tone that sent out his confusion. Other than the Secretary of Defense, this was General Montgomery's building. How could this lieutenant colonel not know who the Joint Chief's assistant was?

"Really?" Lou asked in disbelief. "*That* Colonel Jackson? What would he want with me?" he wondered aloud. *They don't reward drunks with promotions,* he knew. *What's happening?* The pit of despair started to fester in his gut. *Can't they just leave me alone?* he complained in his thoughts. *I just want to retire already.*

"No idea, sir. But congratulations!" the staff sergeant said with entirely too much enthusiasm as he turned and left.

Had Pete Soffet been in the office, Lou might've bounced his frustration off him. As it were, he had to wander out and find someone to vent at, and the army seemed like a good place to start. He got up and headed out into the primary room, turning left and entering the office of two majors without even knocking.

"What's up with your boss?" he said with a hint of snarkiness as he laid the paper on the desk of Drew Wenk.

The Army Major turned his head to greet Lou, then scanned down at the paper lying next to a framed family photo. He picked it up and immediately recognized the seal on the top as belonging to the Joint Chief, Army four-star General Judah Montgomery.

"You mean 'our' boss..." Drew said as he scanned the letter.

Lindy Walton perked up at the possibility of new gossip. Drew just chuckled and slid the paper over the back of his desk to land on hers across from him.

"Guess you're not as desk-bound as you thought," he muttered as he turned back to his computer screen.

Lindy already had her reading glasses on, scanning the paper. "You're getting promoted?" she asked in disbelief. "I mean, no offense, but..." She didn't have to finish. They all knew Lou was at the end of his career. She started her re-read of the document.

"None taken," Lou returned. The office grew silent again as Lindy read, and Drew had already tuned out the conversation. "Seriously," Lou said. "You guys are Army. Why would he do this?"

Drew looked back up. "Probably denying all retirement requests because of all the military buildup between China and Russia. I hear we're starting to make major troop shifts to the west. They're spinning it as helping out the National Guard in all the rioting cities, but my colleagues in Operations allude that it is something...bigger."

"Allude?" Lou asked with a smirk.

"You know—" Drew said. "Saying it without saying it," he grinned.

Lindy chimed in. "Didn't you say you once met him? Back when you flew Warthogs?" She was hesitant to dig too deeply into Lou's past.

"Kind of," Lou concurred. "My near-career-ender saved a bunch of his men, and he sent me a case of scotch and a very nice letter. We met briefly several months later. I doubt he even remembers my name."

"I wouldn't be so sure," Drew kicked in, realizing Lindy's point. "Monty is notorious for keeping tabs on his favorites."

This opened a can of teasing from Lindy. "Ooooooo, you're one of Daddy's fav-o-o-o-rites!" she teased emphatically, causing Drew to laugh and Lou to grin sheepishly.

"Hardly," Lou said, finally chuckling at his own expense. "But it would explain this, I guess." He looked up from the paper Lindy was just handing back. He shifted his eye contact back to Drew. "The buildup makes sense. Ever since Tuesday last week, the whole world seems to be on fire and shifting dramatically." Then back to Lindy, who had stood from her desk and was filling up a couple of Army coffee mugs, handing one to Lou. "But what can I offer?" Now he was at the source of his confusion. "They won't let me fly anymore."

Drew stood up and brushed past Lou after smelling the java, on the way to get his own cup. "That's a good question. I'm sure that meeting tomorrow morning will clear a lot of this up."

Freeman Louis Caldwell didn't normally get sentimental. But these weren't normal times. As he turned to leave, he began, "Look if I get transferred...I just want to say that with this last year and all..." He had, after all, been ushered into their office as a 'loaner' who needed a spot to work for just a bit.

"Shush," Lindy warned. "We got you, Air Force. The pleasure was all ours. I can't imagine what you and Julia have been through—just know you'll always have a desk in this office, as far as I'm concerned."

As Lou tried to turn out into the hall and head back to his own desk, Drew grabbed his hand to shake it. "Congratulations on the full-bird, Colonel. That crash all those years ago may not be quite the career-ender you thought it was."

That's not the crash I've been worried about, Lou thought.

El Paso, Texas

"You done gooood tonight, baby!" Eddie Gonzalez yelled from the musty-smelling bedroom.

Sweat dripped-off him as he basked in the resurged ego that normally needed recharging nightly. The thirty-eight-year-old Texan sat up to start pulling his clothing off the floor. He paid for this crap-hole apartment, but it didn't mean he wanted to stay there. Eddie's girlfriend lived there, but he lived at his home. He had a serious trust issue—and two other girlfriends. Though an American, he was an established Captain in the El Aguila cartel, the Mexican cartel that controlled the drug trade across from El Paso and all the way to the Gulf. Like most large cartels in recent years, El Aguila had adopted a horizontal command structure rather than a vertical one. Take downs of central cartel leaders like "El Chapo" Guzman had driven cartels to operate in a more cellular structure. They had councils now, not "bosses."

Eddie was one of but a couple of key members in the El Paso branch that was running the majority of their purchased influence. Him being an American only helped the matter—he could visit a crooked cop or judge who needed some reminding of the terms of their lifelong commitment without the complications of being a foreign national.

Eddie wandered into the bano to check on his side chica, 'Carmela Fuentes', the cover name he believed to be Rosie's real one.

Rosie was brushing her teeth and smiled softly at him through the coal black hair she had not yet tied back out of her face. She bent down to rinse and some of it spilled into the sink as she did so. "Getting ready to go, tiger?" she asked playfully.

"Uh-huh," Eddie confirmed as she stood back up, reaching around and grabbing her around the waist as he nuzzled his nose and mouth onto the right side of her neck from behind.

Rosie pretended to like the firm after-play, as she always did, passively nudging him back out to the dusty bedroom of her meager apartment. "Stop, tiger! You should get going before she gets nosey."

"I know, I know," Eddie said, once again grabbing her waist, this time from the front. He pulled her in for one last kiss. "I'll call you tomorrow. Gonna take you out to eat. Somewhere nice," he promised as he let go and found his other sock and boots.

Rosie continued the rest of the normal process, promising to "stay beautiful" like she always did when he complimented her. After she was sure he was gone, she went and put the laundry that had finished washing itself while she performed her unpaid services on Eddie into the dryer. Double checking he was indeed gone, she went back to the bedroom and found the screwdriver she kept staged under her mattress as a last-ditch defensive weapon. She went to the strike plate on the door jamb to her bedroom and removed it like she did on those lonely nights she needed an extra reminder. She removed the folded picture with her damaged right hand, the one missing two fingers from a childhood accident. The tears started to fill up the bowls around her eyes.

She opened the picture to view two young women—a much younger her and her mentally challenged sister, Angel. It was this person for whom Rosie endured everything she did. She suffered heavily from depression—she needed this boost occasionally, but lately it felt like it was every night. *I don't know how much longer I can keep this up!* she thought, and she started to bawl hot salty tears. *He disgusts me! They never said I would have to do these things! Thank God Angel can't see me like this! Oh, Angel! I miss you so much. You're why I'm living in this hell!*

Angel lived in a San Antonio home for special needs residents. If Eddie or anyone in the cartel knew she existed, Rosie would certainly suffer for days before dying a horrible death. Former San Antonio Police Corporal Rosalita Ortiz was deeply undercover, having been recruited by the Texas Rangers to produce a full list of the corrupt police, politicians, and judges in El Paso. The corruption in the El Paso Police Department was so deep they couldn't trust anyone to know of her existence. She was truly isolated, other than routine contact with her handler through a dead-drop system that rivaled any cold war spy movie.

Years earlier, the Rangers had worked up a profile on the rising star named Eduardo Gonzalez. He had...a fetish, known scientifically as acrotomophilia. They knew he had a...thing...for amputees. Rosie had been the first female missing digits from her hand to become a police officer in San Antonio PD history. Once she agreed to go undercover, the Rangers worked hard to remove that story from the internet. They planted her as a maid in a motel known to be used as a meet location by Eddie. That was almost three years earlier. Rosie took one last glance at the photo and put it back into the hiding spot. She found some tissue, blew her nose, and jumped into the shower—her nightly attempt to wash away shame and grime that never seemed to leave.

TUCSON, ARIZONA

LEAD ROAD RUNNER GRANGER MADISON HAD SPENT THE better part of the fifteen days since Mt. Rainier blew her top working on his preparedness items. He didn't consider himself a "doomsday prepper." To him, it wasn't about labels, but rather just common sense. And he found the more he drifted from his security background—like constructing raised garden beds in his suburban front yard, despite the HOAs complaints—the more he was enjoying learning new things. *Never thought I would enjoy canning tomatoes I grew myself,* he once told his mom, who still lived in his New Hampshire childhood home.

The divorcee's ex-wife and kids had moved back to her native North Carolina a few years earlier, their marriage strained by her binge drinking. Granger didn't really hold it against her, as it was her way of coping with their issues through his several post-injury surgeries —*Caring for a burn victim is nasty business,* he realized. *I don't think I could do it,* he admitted to himself on many occasions. His anger in not being able to be a regular part of his daughters' lives was justified in his mind, though. She left when they were getting into sports and hunting, things he desperately wanted to teach his girls. Their absence was one of the things that drove him to keep the Road Runners going.

His original motivation for it had been born as a result of seeing the ill-effects of human trafficking firsthand as a Tucson FF/EMT. He could not recall the number of calls he'd been on that involved assisting the police with medical needs when they initially busted-up a ring. As badly as he felt for anyone who fled their country, the kids being sold into sex-slavery angered him the most. *That, and how the American media pretends it ain't happenin',* he reminded himself. He credited this mission as the one thing that was probably keeping him from diving into the bottle, which was the reason he felt somewhat sorry for his ex.

Granger had the website Zoom.Earth opened on several tabs on his laptop, sitting back in his easy chair. He had the TV on as background noise. Occasionally they would mention some tensions between China and Russia that would cause him to perk his ears. Usually, it was just berating the president for a failed response to somehow land large planes of supplies in a region with no working runways, highways, seaports, or railroad tracks. The various tabs of the website were opened to different HD satellite photos of the same mountain range near the Mexican border. The difference was their dates—Granger could look at the same spot on as many dates as he wanted. It was a painstaking effort as he zoomed in on a specific location on multiple tabs looking for any sign of unnecessary activity. Occasionally he would think he's onto something, only to discover through web searches and phone calls that it was a university team doing field research, a rancher, or some other legitimate reason.

The Buenos Aires National Wildlife Refuge... he thought slowly. *This could be something.* He went back and forth on the same pictures covering three days a week for two months. He eventually started looking at a farm on the southern side of the border with Mexico. *Maybe... just might be time to see if the Runners can get some time off work and go scouting...*

CHAPTER 4

THE PENTAGON

"COME IN, COLONEL!" THE TALL AND FIT BLACK MARINE SAID.

Colonel Ryan Jackson brought Lou in from the main reception area of the Joint Chief's office to a short hall. They passed a pair of restrooms and a water fountain to meet an impressive steel door with no windows. There was an electronic badge scanner and keypad on the right side of the frame. Colonel Jackson entered his access card, punched in a PIN, and placed his eye in front of the retinal scanner embedded a foot higher up the wall.

Lou followed the Marine through the door into an ornate hall. The blue carpet had a two-inch-wide border of red along the walls, which were covered in polished oak paneling and large framed photos of the U.S. Military in action. The pair transited past a few offices belonging to other staff members of Joint Chief Montgomery. Just across the hall from the large conference room on the left, Ryan Jackson turned right, leading Lou into his own office.

"The birds suit you, Colonel," Colonel Jackson said as he rounded his desk for his chair. He was referring to Lou's new rank insignia.

Lou was wearing his full, dress blue uniform with coat, tie, and ribbons fixed in their spot above his left pec muscle. "I appreciated having Monday to go hit the uniform store, Colonel," he replied. "I have to admit the letter was a bit shocking." He took a seat on the near side of the desk. "And there is a small part of me that wants to plead my case for retiring instead." *Liar,* Lou called himself. *It's the only thing you want.*

"Ryan, Lou. Call me Ryan. And that's a great starting point. Do you think retirement would suit you?" Ryan leaned forward, resting his elbows on the edge of his desk and crossing his arms. He peered deeply into Lou's eyes.

"I'll just cut to the chase, then, Ryan," Lou responded. "I'm sure you know what happened in my family... my flight status. My issues getting to work the last year. Hell," he snorted, "if I were my own employee, I'd be counseling me right now."

Ryan Jackson's face curled up at the corners of his mouth in a small smirk. "Let me rephrase my question, Lou," he said. "What would happen to you if we let you retire right now? What would you do?"

"I thought about flipping houses, I suppose," Lou started. *This guy's gonna call me out, ain't he,* Lou told himself.

"Colonel Caldwell," Ryan said, leaning back in his chair. "Like you, I've seen a lotta guys and gals retire in the course of my career. And the ones who started moving on a plan before then are doing well. Sure, there are a few who moved to Mexico or the Philippines and live like kings just on their retirement. But the ones who retired in reaction to something don't fare so well."

"Begging your pardon, Colonel. But interventions don't usually come with a promotion. You'll forgive me if I play my words cautiously," Lou said for the setup. "But you all know I have depression and a drinking problem. None of this seems right. Just what are you up to?"

"The General said you were a man of action," Ryan said with a warm smile. "You're right. He has plans for you. The promotion is less about rewarding you and more about having you fit a role. In fact, that's not exactly accurate. It is only about the role. If you were any other lite colonel with a drinking problem, your retirement package would be being expedited right now."

This caught Lou off guard. "Huh? I'm out of flight status right now. Surely there are other pilots the general trusts. I—"

"Let me be frank, Lou," Ryan said, leaning forward again. "As the general's top aide, I have advised him against this course of action. I think you're a liability. But he keeps tabs on certain men and women, and that includes those who stepped up in moments he needed them to."

"So. This *is* about that day in Afghanistan," Lou said slowly. "I kind of had a hunch."

"That was the catalyst, Colonel," Ryan Jackson said. "This is about you. The general has a need. He wants you to fill it." Ryan went quiet for a moment, then added, "Consider this him rescuing you."

Lou snorted and shook his head. "I don't need charity, Colonel Jackson." He started to stand. "Please just tel—"

"Sit down, Colonel," Ryan Jackson commanded with the authority due a prestigious Marine officer. "You seem to be under the impression you have some sort of a choice." Lou plopped his butt back down and gave the Marine an irritated stare. He said nothing. "In twenty minutes, you're walking into the general's office. So, get it all out here. In case you've been too drunk to watch the news, there's a large skirmish building between Russia and China. Why do you think that is?" His tone had evolved into full annoyance.

Lou was seething in his head. *Go to hell, jarhead. I may drink, but I'm not an idiot.* He stared at Colonel Jackson for a good fifteen seconds, but it became apparent the Marine was going to press the silence. Force Lou to submit, so to speak. Finally, he spoke. "Two weeks ago, those natural disasters kicked us in the nuts. The infrastructure out west is toast. The disappearance of the tech companies based out of Seattle have had trickle down effects on the functionality of the internet. Our emergency response has been for crap because every highway, airport, and seaport is completely obliterated.

Our markets tanked. Inflation is starting to skyrocket because the Port of Long Beach can't take all of Seattle and Tacoma's traffic. Highways and trucks were lost. The tsunami wiped out cargo ships throughout the Pacific. It also hit Hawaii, Alaska, Japan, and Russia hard. If I had to guess, Colonel," Lou said with a bit of disdain, "I'd say they're getting ready to fight for the top dog spot." *Happy?* he didn't add out loud.

"Very good, Caldwell," Ryan acknowledged. "Despite dealing with your tragic hand at the bottom of a bottle, you seem to have a clue. Now, how this affects you... We're making strategic moves to the west. Some of it is to be ready to help the western governors with the coming social unrest—"

"What unrest, Colonel?" Lou interrupted.

"Come, now, Lou," Ryan said with a skeptical chuckle. "People now-a-days riot if Facebook goes down too long! You really think they're not going to get pissed when the power outages start lasting for days? Anyway, that's only part of it. If our two friends across the Pacific do, indeed, start a shooting war, there's no telling where that'll go."

"What's all that got to do with me, Colonel Jackson?" Lou asked. "All I want is to close this chapter."

Ryan pointed at the clock on the wall to his left. "General Montgomery will fill you in in fifteen minutes. My sole job here has been to make sure you understand that when he asks you for a favor, he isn't asking."

USS James L. Hunnicutt, SSGN-93, Southern Yellow Sea

In the two weeks since Cascadia had destroyed their homeport, the crew of the USS James L. Hunnicutt's morale had tanked, making Darren's job as Chief-Of-the Boat extremely difficult. They had orders—they were on a mission, and national security issues didn't stop when the volcano blew her top. If anything, they had ramped up significantly. The spy and special operations boat had seen activity increase in China's fleet an astonishing nine hundred percent. It was obvious they were preparing for a major engagement.

The Hunny's mission had shifted. *Pretty sure the brass can see all this activity from space,* Darren thought. The sub had been using super-quiet unmanned underwater drones to map the floor—or more specifically, all the sensors and equipment on it—of the bay immediately outside the People's Liberation Army-Navy, or PLAN, Northern Fleet's amphibious base. Ever since the evening after the Cascadia event, the base had been in some sort of major alert status. Captain Woodward exercised caution and moved south sixty kilometers to a secondary mission using the Hunny's hovering capabilities to retrieve recording devices they'd placed on the ocean floor near the Northern Fleet's submarine base and place new ones. These devices allowed the US Navy to get hyper-accurate recordings of every submarine's "signature" —the sound it makes. In the old days, it was just a submarine's unique "screw" noise—the noise made by the propeller—that identified it. In the 21st Century, technology accounted for every noise—seawater suction, pumps, even the hydraulics of water passing around the sub's sail, which was the cowling around the periscopes so often seen breaking the surface in movies.

The Navy's recording devices were high tech, covered in space age polymer that absorbed active sonar attempts to locate them. During the Cold War, the Navy had been embarrassed by the then Soviet Union when they discovered one of the old models that was wire-tapping their undersea military communications cables. The Soviets had dissected the device, finding a "Property of US Navy" label on a part on the inside. Ever since then, great lengths were maintained to keep all facets of these operations as "in the dark" as possible.

The Hunny had finished the recording device swap outs when they received their new orders—head to Guam as quickly as possible without risking detection for immediate off-loading of the recording devices and slew of electronic intelligence they had gathered in the obvious haste of the PLAN's northern fleet activities. From there, they would head to the South China Sea to monitor PLAN training missions that have ramped up at various naval bases. *Suits me fine,* Darren thought. *They must really be up to something to make us take the devices in mid-mission like this.* His crew had been riding in ultra-quiet mode for several days straight, and it was enough to fracture anyone's nerves. The garbage had been piling up in the special cans meant to sink it. Certain maintenance had been skipped to avoid dropping a tool and giving away the sub's position. It enhanced people's stress levels. These sailors knew something that most everyone else didn't, including the other branches of the military—*if they find us, they'll sink us.* What the USS James L. Hunnicutt and her crew were doing was akin to a foreign navy parking a submarine right in Chesapeake Bay and observing the fleet in Norfolk.

Darren called a junior sailor into a small office the chiefs used that was outboard of the diver's lock-out chambers on the third deck of the ship's missile compartment.

"I don't understand how you're almost out of time on getting your dolphins, Mr. Turner," he scolded the young Seaman, "but still have time for *Call of Duty* during your down time." The young sailor had joined the crew several months earlier and was lagging behind in the strict and rigorous training and qualification cycle—earning one's 'dolphin qualified' uniform insignia—that was notorious to submarine sailors.

"I don't have a good answer, COB," the sailor said, knowing making excuses would go over about as well as farting in church.

"Didn't your LPO assign Davis to mentor you? Is there some other factor? Different watch schedules? Can't stand each other? What? What is it?"

One of Darren's biggest duties was ensuring he and his CO had enough qualified positions to completely staff the ship at all times. Since the crew ran on three shifts, that meant having more than the requisite minimum, as there was always a need for people to be training in the next position up. If Seaman Turner was lagging, then someone else couldn't move into the next training and qualification position up.

"Nothing like that, COB. I—"

"Battle stations!" they heard being passed verbally down the passageway. Sailors were scrambling by. Had the crew been in a more stable, open-ocean environment, there would've been an alarm sounding. As it were, the Yellow Sea's average depth was a very shallow forty-four meters. They traveled slowly to ensure they had time for sensors to pick up any underwater anomalies—it would still be twelve hours before they were in the slightly deeper East China Sea. Depth was their friend.

Like everyone else, Darren and the junior sailor hastened to get to their battle stations. By the time he arrived in the Control Room, it was packed with bodies as positions began to be augmented with additional people. Unlike the control room in most of the preceding submarines, this one was one deck down from the top level, largely due to modern technology leading to smaller periscopes. Several of the watch positions that older subs used were non-applicable to this class. This, too, was due to modern electronics—the ship could now steer and control depth, ballast, and trim—all from two positions. This space savings allowed the ship's torpedo fire control systems and all sonar and other sensor systems to be controlled in this location. In older submarines, there were separate rooms for some of these functions. The cruise missiles and various special systems like the UUVs were controlled in a space farther aft.

He assumed his spot behind the ship's pilot and co-pilot, relieving an ensign as the Diving Officer for battle stations. Darren's ears were clued keenly on the dialogue between the CO and the sonar operators as his mind tried to catch up on their situation.

"Submerged contact bearing three-five-five, estimated range twenty thousand!"

"That's a third sub, Sonar?" Commander Woodward asked, calmly trying to ensure he had the facts straight. He was peering right over the operator's shoulder, looking at the computerized display. "Nav," he ordered without looking at the navigator, "find the deepest water you can between relative one-twenty and one-ninety. COB, what does our current course show for depth?"

Darren scanned the instruments next to his seated pilot. "Computer says we have three-hundred-and-thirty-feet and slowly getting deeper, Cap'n," Darren replied.

"Very well. Pilot, make your depth three-hundred and maintain course at four knots."

Darren surveyed the situation. They had three submarines all to the north, driving them toward four surface ships all to the south. *They know we're here,* he thought. *But they don't know where.* Like the CO, he knew the best course of action was to go so slow they would be impossible to be heard—and hope no loud sneezers got a tickly nose.

THE OVAL OFFICE

PRESIDENT JEREMIAH ALLEN HAD NOT BEEN HAVING THE BEST weeks of his life. Quite the opposite, in fact. He was becoming all too familiar with his cabinet—particularly the secretaries and their staffs in the defense and state departments. In administrations past, there would have been a Homeland Security secretary, too. Making good on his campaign promise to the Libertarian Party that helped him get elected, Jeremiah dissolved the department. *This country lasted two and one-quarter centuries without one,* he stated during the campaign. *Defense and Homeland Security are synonymous terms,* he liked to point out to critics.

The president's daily brief, called the PDB since the 1940s, was usually delivered by a senior CIA official who worked for the Director of National Intelligence, Thomas Berry. Though not called a secretary, his was a cabinet-level position. In the fifteen days since the Rainier events, Director Berry had joined mid-term replacement Secretary of Defense Kelly Fitzgerald and Secretary of State Dee Buttermaker in reviewing the PDB. President Allen's administration had moved the brief back to the world of paper versus electronic delivery, as China had assumed leadership in the world's cyber warfare. In two weeks, China and Russia had become the dominant topic of the discussion—over the domestic issues, over the worsening inflation, over the Rainier relief efforts. *It's all tied together anyway,* Jeremiah reminded them all at least three times per week.

The reason was due to the actions immediately taken by both Russia and China to 'help' after the disasters. While the Navy had immediately started working on Task Force Truxtun to move supplies and people to the Slaughter Peninsula area, the two superpowers across the western pond had started mobilizing forces within a day. Both had sent immediate offers of assistance via the formal channels, as well as the secret back-systems of communication.

As the first few days turned into a week, cities police forces were overwhelmed as simple protests over the lack of government response had evolved into something more organized and on-point to push an agenda. The Chinese had started mobilizing their northern fleet on a scale not seen in years. Russia had loaded two divisions of their army onto trains and were starting to amass them on the roughly 2,400-mile-long border with China. What was more telling to Joint Chief General Judah Montgomery and Defense Secretary Fitzgerald was the number of troop transports the Russian Navy had started moving.

All ten of their nuclear-powered ice breaking ships were plowing passages through the Northern Sea Route, Russia's portion of the international trade routes that navigated the entire Arctic Circle year-round. More than three dozen amphibious type naval vessels had started showing signs of deployment on satellite imagery.

"If Ivan was truly worried about sending supplies to help, Mr. President," General Montgomery had explained a week earlier, "they would be loading the ships already present in their eastern district bases."

On this day, at Shannon Sahr's urging, President Allen had invited the chair and co-chair of the National Governors Association to sit-in on the meeting. Each state's governor, as well as those of the five American provinces, were automatically members. There was always a member of each of the two parties in the top two spots. *Wonder how that will play out as more third parties get elected,* Jeremiah wondered. *Not just Libertarians—the Green or Socialist parties could pull a surprise off in a blue state one of these days...*

"Thank you for having us, Mr. President," Governor Burton of Iowa said as he entered the Oval Office. He was followed by Governor Teresa Santiago of Florida, the council's co-chair. After the round of handshakes and informal greetings was over with, they took their seats on one of the two yellow paisley couches that faced the mahogany coffee table.

"Please proceed, Director," Jeremiah said to Thomas Berry.

The director was sitting on one of the two blue and yellow high-backed chairs at the end of the office opposite the president's desk. He took a sip of water to wet his throat, setting the heavy glass back onto the end table near his left. "Mr. President and distinguished members and guests, we'll start the briefing today with the continued buildup of Chinese and Russian forces in the Pacific theater, and—"

"Sorry, Thom," Jeremiah interrupted.

"Of course, sir."

"Governors," Jeremiah said, "you're here to learn. Ask questions if you want. I need you to help educate all the governors of what's at play —within the bounds of the non-disclosure you signed this morning— regardless of party. I know we don't always agree on policy and decision making, but I want you all to see the transparency here and remind your peers, particularly the eastern governors, about the complexity of world events. Things have been moving at lightning speed."

"Of course, Mr. President," the Democrat Iowa Governor Phillip

Burton said. He nodded at Republican Governor Santiago. "I think we both are looking forward to this. Thank you for the opportunity."

"Agreed," Teresa Santiago said, nodding in return.

After a nod from Jeremiah, Director Berry continued. "As you see in the briefing packet, Russia's navy is now distributed in the Pacific to a strength of sixty-one percent of their forces, expected to be seventy-five to eighty percent within two weeks. The majority of these transfers have been with amphibious landing ships for landing troops and tanks. Their ground forces continue to creep toward their border with China and Mongolia, mostly by rail. Since yesterday's brief, eleven percent of their short-range tactical missile launchers have departed their western and mid-country bases. The only thing they've left untouched in all of this is their Black Sea presence."

The director grabbed another sip and continued. "China has had an unprecedented level of activity in their northern fleet. Our submarine USS James L. Hunnicutt has suspended operations in the Yellow Sea. I'm sure Secretary Fitzgerald will cover that in more detail. The short version, as you can see in the report, is that sixty-eight percent of China's northern and central fleet submarines are at sea, as well as fifty-three percent of their surface combatants. It sure appears they're trying to flush the Hunnicutt out of there. As well as the one known Russian sub in the East China Sea.

"Pardon me, Director," Governor Santiago interrupted. "A question...?"

"Of course, Governor."

"Why would our natural disasters trigger all of this military activity over there?"

"I'll take that one, Thom," Secretary of State Dee Buttermaker said. "At the least, Governor, it is posturing. Both countries have pledged to send support, so now they're trying to show the world who is the more capable caregiver."

"What about 'at worst', Madam Secretary," the other governor, Phillip Burton, asked. "Has our earthquake—or rather, the trickle-down effects from it—made us vulnerable?"

"Well, in the unlikely scenario that they want to try something over here, they would first be forced to contend with each other," the secretary stated. "That takes a series of events to happen on the world stage first."

"Like what?" Governor Santiago asked.

Secretary Buttermaker looked at President Allen. She served his office and wasn't sure how much he wanted to share with the governors. "Like the collapse of the dollar," Jeremiah started. "Combined with the domino effects to the world economy if the internet quit working, hackers were able to hold international corporations hostage with ransomware, and foreign trade with America came to a grinding halt."

"That's what *is* happening, isn't it?" Governor Santiago asked, confused.

"Yes, Governor, it is," the president said matter-of-factly. "This is why the supplies that came flooding into the western cities for Washington continue to sit at airports. For one, there's no way to get them there, at least not in the sheer volumes needed. For another, as you've seen on the news and heard from your fellow governors, those cities are getting downright upset and vocal about the rolling and days-long blackouts and internet issues. Our analysts tell us those same relief supplies will be needed where they're at in three to four weeks."

"Several of the western governors have been mentioning gang violence has exploded in recent days," Governor Burton admitted. "We can't put our finger on it, exactly."

You know exactly why, Jeramiah thought to himself with no more than a casual glance. *You all are so busy trying to divide everyone into left and right, you haven't noticed the giant chasm in the middle—the same people who elected me.*

"It's because nature abhors a vacuum, Governor," Jeremiah stated. "It's why you're here today—to see that what the media calls feckless lack of leadership is actually patience in the face of something much more dire and complicated going on in the background. And might I add that your peers in Idaho and Oregon activated their National

Guards to secure their borders with Washington less than five days ago. And the legislatures of those and every other state that exports hydroelectric, wind, or solar power passed bills banning the sale of electricity for two months."

Ignoring the barb, Governor Burton asked with a skeptical chuckle, "Do you actually think one or both of those countries could be jockeying for a position to attack us, Mr. President?"

"Would you suggest I wait until they decide the answer to that, Governor Burton?" Jeremiah countered.

CHAPTER 5

The Pentagon

Colonel Jackson led Lou past the general's civilian administrative assistant at the appointed time. Army General Judah Montgomery's door was already open. He gave a lite rap on the door frame and proceeded in as the general called out, "Enter." Lou followed and straightened his blue uniform jacket, holding his garrison cap in his left hand as he proceeded through the door.

"Good to see you again, Colonel Caldwell!" Monty shot Colonel Jackson a quick glance as he strolled in. He and his primary assistant had developed a code of communication based on shot looks. But in Monty's mind, Lou was the center of attention. He had a warm smile, like they'd once been softball buddies. "I hear you don't really go by Super Bert anymore. Okay to call you Lou?"

"Yes sir. Of course," he said, his nerves still frayed a bit from the prior half-hour's slap in the face. He scanned the room to get his surroundings down. Ryan Jackson had gone back behind Lou and casually shut the office door.

"Have a seat, Lou," the general said casually, motioning toward the couch, chairs, and coffee table that adorned the very center of his office.

As he moved toward the couch, Lou scanned the office a bit more observantly. The floor was covered with a beautiful and expensive rug bearing the logo of the Joint Chief. There were cabinets and shadow boxes containing memorabilia all around. Some were items in their permanent homes, left by previous Joint Chiefs until they found their way to the National Archives. Others were various awards, flags, and photos from General Montgomery's career. Lou stopped and looked at one of a much younger, one-star General Montgomery standing with a group of operators at a Forward Operating Base in Afghanistan.

Lou hadn't realized he'd started flashing back to Afghanistan in his own head until the General said from right next to him, "FOB...Rhino, I think? At least half those men owe their lives to you."

Lou snapped his head. "Sir?"

"Have a seat, Colonel," the general once again instructed with a warm nudge.

Lou sat on the opposite end of the couch that Colonel Jackson had already planted himself on, and General Montgomery sat on the opposite side of an ornate marble coffee table. A silver platter and coffee urn had been placed on it. Lou could smell the fresh brew, but he was not going to be bold enough to just grab a cup.

After sitting in the red, leather high-back chair, General Montgomery opened the chat. "Lou, while that door is closed, just call me Monty..."

Lou looked at Ryan Jackson for some back up, then back to his superior officer. "I—I don't think I can do that, sir..."

Colonel Jackson just grinned but remained quiet, knowing his place and opinion was fully at the general's beck-and-call. Monty continued. "Suit yourself, Lou. I'm guessing you have a lot of questions..."

"That'd be an understatement, sir, and I'm all ears. I'm sure you know why I was looking to retire, so I'm still a bit confused about this role I need to play."

"I need a colonel to play special assistant, Lou," Monty started. "I know Colonel Jackson went over some of our expectations with you. Before I go into 'the what', I need you to look me in the eyes right now and tell me you can dry up while you're working for me." His grandfatherly gaze pierced Lou's soul.

"I know I haven't handled my son's suicide the best way possible, sir..."

"I'm not here to judge you, Lou. But I need you back in the game, and so I guess you could say I'm here to kick you in the butt." General Montgomery was being respectfully blunt. "Your file never once indicated a drinking problem before the event. This seems to me to be more of a 'self-medicating' thing than a true medical addiction."

"That is true, sir. I've tried counselors and whatnot—none of them have ever helped me make sense of Terrance's suicide. All they do is make me angry."

"Son," Monty said. "Look at that brandy snifter over there."

Lou turned his head to a shelf full of trophies and other memorabilia. Right at chest level was a large glass container. *Just like what lounge piano players get tips in*, Lou thought. It was about a third full of beer bottle caps. "Okaayyy..."

"Those caps—they don't represent the men I've lost in combat. They represent the men I've lost here at home. The ones who couldn't leave the war behind."

Lou felt his eyes start to well, as if he was being scolded politely by his father when he was a child. He kept staring at the snifter to try to hide his emotion. "That's quite a few men, sir."

"Lou, I may not have lost my own son to suicide. But I know the devastation it causes to those left behind—deeply. I'm sorry about your boy, Super Bert. But I want you to promise me here and now—I'll never have to drink a beer and drop a cap in that snifter for you."

The salty tears started to escape their pens around Lou's eyes. "I'm sorry to have disappointed you, General," was all he could think of to say. He kept staring at the snifter.

"It starts here, Lou," Monty continued. "You need to reverse the

Charlie Foxtrot you've made your life into. And unfortunately, I need you on the road while you do it." He stood and retrieved a tissue from the bookshelf behind his desk, handing it to Lou to force him to stop staring at the snifter.

Lou took it and wiped his eyes. "Sir, I'm taking all of this to heart. It isn't all about Terrance. Julia and I are at a precipice right now. Can I have a couple of days to talk to her?"

"Sure, Lou. We can prep our backup plan. I'll give you 'til Thursday to report back to Colonel Jackson."

"Thank you, General. So—what's the job?"

"We're making a lot of moves in the field," he started. "Big moves. I need a set of eyes and ears on the ground to let me know that the things I'm being told are legit. At least, that's it on the surface. I want to know the buzz in the air, too. The vibe. Not just on post, but in the communities, as well."

"I'm confused, sir. It takes a colonel for that?"

"You'll open doors as a colonel, Lou. Ryan here has built a cover profile. We'll have you coming out of the Pentagon's public affairs office. If they know you're reporting directly to me—"

"They'll tell me what they think you want to hear," Lou finished for him.

"Precisely. There are some posts and bases we need you to hit. But your schedule will be flexible enough for you to travel at will. Visit places unannounced. Make your own schedule, so to speak. There's a few more specifics that we'll cover once you've made your decision." With that, General Judah Montgomery stood up and stuck his hand out as he came around the coffee table. "I've always been fond of you, Lou. I never forgot what you did for us in '07."

It was at that moment that it all clicked for Freeman Louis Caldwell. The teasing from his office mates a day earlier had been spot on. This man was the one reason Lou had been able to have a continued flying career, despite being re-purposed to C-17s. Lou stood and grabbed the general's hand. "It was the only choice I felt I could make in that moment, General."

"And that's why I want you for this, Colonel. I know you'll do the tough, right thing in a moment of hard choices. Think about it. You go on the assignment for me, and I'll push your retirement through at the end." Judah Montgomery started to escort Lou to the door out of the office.

Lou tried to grab one last piece from his extremely valuable mind on the way out. "Who do you think will win in their showdown, sir?"

One didn't get to be the Joint Chief without being able to dodge and answer a question at the same time. "If you're about to get into a school yard fight, Colonel... Does it matter if the other kid is Chinese or Russian?"

SANCHES FARM, NORTHEAST OF MANHATTAN KANSAS

"BEE, WATCH YOUR RIGHT FLANK," MORRIS 'THUMPER' Dooghan yelled into the headset at his teammate. "Elvis is coming around that stack of tires!"

"I know, Thumper!" the fiery Jordan Croft yelled back. Like most MilSimmers—people who participated in military simulation fight leagues—Morris' team used call-sign type nicknames. Jordan's was 'Super B', or just 'Bee' on the radio, because of her normally icy exterior and hot temper. "I'm not an idiot!"

As the words were leaving her mouth, she pivoted her position behind the old refrigerator and started laying suppressing fire in the form of small biodegradable BBs at the tire stack. To an untrained observer, this scene would look very much like two small squads in a fight to the death, minus the actual noise of a gunfight. While most MilSim teams used airsoft equipment over paintball, they also went to great lengths to buy all the CGG, as Morris jokingly called it—*cool guy gear.* Camo, padded military clothing, chest-mounted magazine carriers, radios with headsets, battle belts—and tons of magazines...though sometimes tournament rules limited how many of those could be carried.

Morris was squatting behind an old car door that was propped up. The team was practicing in the back property of an uncle of Jon 'Superfly' Sanches, who lived just a few scant miles to the northeast of the college town, near the Big Blue River. Jon's uncle Jorge was a farmer. Like most farms, it had built up a collection of old vehicles, tires, spare parts, and junk that made for a good battlefield—and it was free to use. Morris straightened his back to get a better glimpse at the 'battlefield,' convinced their game of four on three was about over.

Airsoft was an honor system game, depending on people who felt themselves get hit by the small non-hazardous BB to stand up and wave their hand to indicate they were dead. Thumper and Bee had lost their teammate, David 'Goldilocks' Faust. By Morris' math, Elvis and Superfly were all that was left—he'd seen ThatNub and Misty Meaner wave out already. Morris felt a BB rattle his face shield as he was squatting back down. *Shoot,* he thought. *What'd that take to die—half a second?* He stood up and waved out.

"We got ya, Bee!" Morris heard Elvis taunting Jordan. "Might as well give up!"

Jordan wasn't falling for it. She asked Morris over the headset, "Which way'd he get ya?"

"Nope," the team's leader replied. *Freshmen,* he thought. *Sheesh...* "You get busted talking to a dead player in KCK, you'll get us kicked out of the whole tourney," he lectured.

Bee replied with a choice cussword and began to creep backwards towards Morris' car door, trying to protect their dirty, ratty Pikachu doll. The 'flags' in the group's capture the flag training were a pair of old Pokemon plush dolls that had been handed down from prior team leaders long gone for more years than Morris knew.

Morris began to walk out of the small training arena to join the other recently deceased. He approached the awaiting beer that his roomie ThatNub was holding out for him, retrieved from Morris' small, purple K-State cooler. "Thanks," he said in his usual calm and smooth baritone demeanor. As the team leader, it was Thumper's job to ensure there were a few cold brewskis iced down. None of the college students had much money, especially after budgeting for their airsoft gear—he took the cheap, non-craft beer and popped the top.

"She is good, but man can she trash talk," Morris told Nub. "And she tried to get me to tell her where Fly was."

"I heard," Nub told him. The team used small 21-channel family radios and would often switch to the other team's frequency after getting shot to listen in. This wasn't the first time they'd warned the freshman about trying to bend the rules.

The pair listened to the rhythmic cycling of three compressed-gas powered AR-style fake rifles become two as Elvis stood up and shot wildly at Bee's hiding spot. She took the bait, trash-talking to take him out, completely missing the fact that he'd just sacrificed himself to allow SuperFly to get to a spot to kill her. A team could win by capturing the flag/Pokemon or just eliminating the rest of the team, which usually happened in the tight confines of their training area.

Thirty minutes and several small conversations about tactics later, the entire team was circled around the small firepit behind the farmhouse. On top of the normal one to two Saturdays per month they tried to play over at the paintball park in Salina, they were gearing up for a big tournament in December in Kansas City.

As 'Elvis' Floyd Presley grabbed the last of the twelve-pack, he changed the subject to current events. "Whatta y'all think of the power outage and riot stuff?" It had broken the ice on a semi-tense conversation that had become more recurring every time the team practiced.

"Not this again!" Jordan stated in an annoyed fashion.

Super B is the perfect name for you, Morris smirked to himself. "Like it or not, Bee, the world is shaken. Might as well wargame it a bit..." the pragmatic leader suggested.

"That's what I'm sayin'," ThatNub agreed. "I mean—what if people start rioting in Manhattan?"

"Ain't gonna happen, brah," David 'Goldilocks' Faust said, his wild and wavy long golden curls hanging in his face. The California native put off a certain laid-back surfer vibe just about everywhere but on the field, where he turned into an aggressive MilSim beast. "People back home are just ridin' this out on the beach..." he grinned.

Not where I'm from, Morris thought, looking at the rolling fields of Uncle Jorge's farm to the west. Morris thought of his parents back in the KCK older neighborhood of Roeland Park. His father white and his mother black, the tall slender senior was just glad his twin brother Marvin would be getting out of the army and returning home soon. The family had always worked hard and been thrifty, but they'd never saved enough to get away from the old suburb. Morris had really taken to the laid-back atmosphere in the college town, and he hoped to one day find a place farther away from Kansas City—particularly the gang-infiltrated Missouri side—to move his parents to.

"My ma says there are organized protests every day down at City Hall." He pondered for a moment. "You all should think about calling your folks, too...Find out how they're doing."

An empty, crushed beer can came flying at Morris as the group mostly groaned collectively. Several, "Yes, dad" snide comments flew his way, too.

"Whatever," Morris said, deflecting the teasing. "I might just go home this weekend to check on things. Constant power flickering and now classes getting canceled. I heard the internet is acting up because Microsoft has been vulnerable ever since that earthquake—hackers and ransomware and such."

"Now *that* I *can* confirm," said Maria 'Misty Meaner' Bannerman, so named after getting ticketed for streaking her sophomore year. The information systems junior was watching those activities as closely as the spotty internet would allow. "One of my study partners is double majoring in socioeconomics and says that financial institutions around the whole world are having big issues—and that China and Russia are both calling for their currency to be the world's reserve currency... whatever that means."

How'd I miss that? Morris scolded himself. *I'm a finance major!* "I think it means that things are only going to get shakier for a while..." Morris advised, draining the last swallow of warm and unsatisfying brew.

100 KM NORTH-NORTHWEST OF SHANGHAI, CHINA

"SIDE-LOOK SONAR SHOWS A RAPID DEPTH CHANGE!" DARREN heard one of the sonar operators inform the USS James L. Hunnicutt's Control Room. The CO was hovering over him in a second, looking at the emerging geologic issue re-created electronically on a high-resolution multi-colored screen.

"All thrusters 270-relative at 100 percent!" the captain ordered. All six secondary propulsion thrusters were deployed from the ballast tanks and aimed to try to push the sub directly sideways to the port. Because they were each off center of the ship, they lowered from a spot a little farther up the hull, which meant they only added a few inches to the ship's overall depth-profile.

I've never heard him this tense before, Master Chief Darren Jorgenson thought. The Hunny had been forced to move closer to the shore of China—dangerously close, as they continued a cat-and-mouse evasion of several surface and submarine pursuers. Each time they tried to make a dash into open water, another destroyer or frigate from the PLAN had joined the hunt. Additionally, the commercial vessels traveling between Shanghai and Korea were crowding the surface waters. The already shallow sea was now only thirty meters deep—hardly enough to conceal the sub from a high-flying aircraft if the day were bright enough. The ship's main hull was thirty-eight feet thick, but it also had the height of the sail, the rudder, and two SEAL dry-deck shelters on top, specialized rooms on top of the lockout chambers designed for SEALS to store their delivery mini-subs in.

Had they been hovering in one spot they might have felt the sideways thrusting taking place. As it were, they were maintaining six knots, trying to make headway in the East China Sea. They had managed to put over one hundred nautical miles between themselves and the nearest known submarine in the past thirty hours. That bought them some reaction time, but in the age of modern sonar equipment, it was hardly any room for error. One wrong sound, and the Chinese PLAN Shang-class nuclear powered submarine that had been hounding them would be all over it. While the Hunny could outrun it easily, they still had two known Chinese subs and two frigates ahead of them.

The diesel submarine, while older and slower, was also quieter during the hours it could run on its batteries. Daren knew they should be due to surface and recharge batteries with their diesel within another hour, based on knowing when the last time they recharged was. It was the other nuclear-powered sub that worried him. There was a thermal layer out in the deeper waters of the east sea she was hiding under. The water temperature created a sort of floor in the ocean that passive sonar couldn't penetrate. And they certainly weren't going to ping the active sonar, as that would be a dead giveaway of their own position to everyone out there. The crew of the Hunny had no idea where that other sub had wandered in the three hours since she slipped deep under that thermal layer.

The Hunny's side-look sonar used high-pitched micro sonar bursts, much too high in frequency for normal human hearing, to pulse out and paint a picture of what was to the sides of the sub. It was their last and best piece of gear to show them any undersea obstacles to their starboard side as they crept south along China's shore. At only two miles offshore, they were definitely going to get attacked if they were discovered. Suddenly the wall on the sonar's screen went nearly white.

"Obstruction!" the sonar technician yelled out.

"Sound collision!" Commander Woodward ordered the Messenger

watch station. A series of electronic beeps played mildly throughout the ship, the volume being downplayed by the ship's system automatically as they were 'rigged' to be as silent as possible. The SLS had shown what could only be described as a wall to their starboard, which had run distinctly off the screen to the left, indicating it was also ahead of them.

GRRNNNNGGCHHH! The USS James L. Hunnicutt bellowed out across the entire sea as she smashed into a piece of undersea canyon at a lucky, slow rate of six knots. People had been given less than two seconds to grab something when the alarm sounded. The crew had done admirably storing items as part of silent running, but nobody was perfect. A few items in the ship's galley had clanged around in their storage compartments, mugs had slipped off countertops...

In the control room, a series of alarms started to scream as systems detected damage to the ship's bow and front starboard ballast tanks. The Hunny started to lean to the starboard. Men and women were thrown to the decks and into the bulkheads as the ship came to a sudden stop. In a deadly world where the sound of a dropped wrench could get you killed, the crew of the USS James L. Hunnicutt had just screamed to the pursuing Chinese fleet exactly where they were.

CHAPTER 6

MORNINGSIDE, MARYLAND

"GO!" JULIA SCOLDED. "THE SOONER THE BETTER, AS FAR AS I'm concerned! Take off on your little 'work-cation'! But don't expect me to be here when you get back!"

"C'mon, Jules!" Lou yelled back as he followed her into the bedroom. "You know as well as I do that we could use a little space! This time apart will give me a chance to dry out some..."

"You can fool yourself with that BS," she retorted, "but I'm not buying it!" She dropped the laundry basket she'd been carrying onto the queen bed and spun around. "I can't believe you're going to leave me in this house all alone!"

"Let's be honest, Julia!" Lou fired back. "You're not exactly happy when I'm here. What will be so bad about—" He frowned as he cut off his own question. *The garage,* he reminded himself. *She won't go in it. No wonder she's been hinting at wanting to sell so much.*

She stormed out of the bedroom, bumping his shoulder as she did. "Get out of my bedroom," she commanded sternly.

"Julia..."

"No!" she demanded as Lou followed her down the stairs. "You go, Lou. Get the space you need! Leave me alone in the house where... where..." She burst into tears as she reached the kitchen.

"Jules. Just listen," he said as he tried to put a hand on her shoulder. She pulled away with force, turning back toward him and pointing toward the front of the house, no longer a home.

"Get out!" she screeched. "I can't look at you anymore! Disappear, just like you've done our entire marriage! Just like you did when your son needed you the most!" Her face was on fire, flush and red as she both screamed and cried emotion at a hundred miles per hour.

Gut punch. Lou felt his knees buckle a bit as the deepest fears he'd told only Jack Daniels and a therapist back at the beginning came back and slapped his face—*Did I somehow cause my son to kill himself by being absent all the time?* He turned in shock, knowing all along that's how she felt, but having never actually heard her say it before. He felt for the key fob in his pocket as he slowly wandered to the front door. His hearing went blank, unsure if she was still yelling or not, as the sudden shock and guilt started to resurface in his psyche. *I need to get out of here,* he realized. *If I take this trip, my marriage is done. If I don't, my marriage is done. And I don't want that either way.* He opened the door and headed outside. *I need a drink.*

TUCSON, ARIZONA

ALL SIX MEMBERS OF THE ROAD RUNNERS WERE STUFFED INTO Granger Madison's suburban garage. Granger had several printed pages laying on the workbench, while Mick and Tracy squared off on the pool table under the 70s era hanging Coors lamp. The night air above the driveway full of SUVs and pickup trucks was a brilliant blue-to-burnt orange combo as the sun started its final descent below the western mountains. The Wednesday evening air in the open garage was a very comfortable 65 degrees Fahrenheit.

"You guys wrap that up and check these out," Granger nudged his team.

Dave and Bob had their noses under the hood of Bob's 2015 Suburban out in the driveway. Claude rocked himself out of the folding camping chair he was plopped in, letting out an old man's groan as he did. The would-be pool-sharks set their cues on the table. Soon, everyone was looking at the color photos Granger had printed and spread around.

"So what makes the wildlife refuge seem like a hot spot to you?" the white-haired Dave started off the questioning. He was extremely fit and capable, though as a man in his early 50s, was not looking forward to yet another fruitless mission sitting in the desert for two or three days.

"Well…I found these tracks here that I can't find an alternative explanation for," Granger started.

The entire team was well-versed in the investigations Granger always performed to not waste their time. Like a paranormal investigator, he looked for other explanations that were both plausible and legal before telling the crew, *let's go catch some dirtbags.* He would call government and university offices and research labs. He would go look at recent ranching and farming sales and activities for that area on the internet. He didn't want to sit in the dusty heat any more than the next man.

The leader continued, "I also noticed this old farm on the south side"—everyone knew that referred to the border position— "is extremely active with absolutely no cattle or sheep."

"You thinking 'tunnel'?" Tracy asked. The former Navy special warfare boat operator was the team's youngest at thirty-three.

"Maybe," Granger concurred. "But let's not get ahead of ourselves. I think this is worthy of a long-range recce to check it out. We'll need at least three days—it'll be a good hump just to get in there."

Pronounced 'Recky', it was their lingo for a reconnaissance patrol that would take a long time just to get to the objective, which was to set up and quietly observe. The obvious question to an outsider might've been, *wouldn't the operators of the refuge just tell the Border Patrol something hinky was happening?* The team all had the experience to know the rules the cartels played by—those who they needed silenced were bought off, first with cash, then with threats to that person's family. The willingness to commit unthinkable evils was a very effective way for them to conduct business.

"We're swamped at work," Mick said. "Julio's always good about granting me time off, but I can't leave him hanging. With all the shipping issues and trucks being re-routed for this earthquake thing, diesel mechanics are at a premium here in the southwest right now."

"Roger that," Granger said. "You all think you could start next Wednesday?" he asked, scanning their faces.

Bob sighed. "I promised my grandson I'd come to his school thing on Thursday next week." The support crew had a little leeway, unlike the field team. "Claude and I are always good about letting each other know when we have things that could interfere with a pick-up. As long as that's okay...." he trailed off.

"No sweat," Granger said. "But keep us in the loop. We'll need to be ready to self-extract if Claude has a Murphy moment at the same time. What about everyone else?" Granger re-queried. He received the expected *shouldn't be an issue* type statements from everyone else.

Changing the subject, Dave Wolf said, "Anyone else been noticing that just about every city has some sort of protests and riots on the news lately?"

"I don't even watch the news, anymore," Claude chimed in. "Too much propaganda."

"Mmmm," Bob groaned in concurrence.

"I have," Mick agreed. "I hear that Oregon and Idaho actually sealed off their borders from Washington state. Too many people trying to cross in from that disaster. Riots, theft, spikes in crime...folks bringing their dysentery with them."

Granger added, "That, and the sudden overnight inflation and stock market dips have people freaked out, I think. And the internet has been glitchy. I couldn't even get Amazon's home page to open earlier this week."

"What about the China-Russia thing?" Wolf prodded his teammates. "Thoughts?"

"What Russia-China thing?" Claude asked, a bit confused.

"See, you can't ignore the news and then complain you don't know what's happenin'," Tracy half teased.

One of Claude's fingers extended toward Tracy. It was a normal Army-Navy greeting system that vets felt was a rite of passage. This caused Tracy to chuckle. "Seriously," Claude said, looking back at Wolf.

"They're both building up troops on the border, lots of rhetoric on the news. Not too sure exactly why, though." He looked at Granger.

"Me neither," the old Marine and firefighter admitted. "But I don't think it's a coincidence that it started after that volcano kicked our legs out from under us..."

MORNINGSIDE, MARYLAND

<TAP-TAP!> THE HARD NOISE OF THE COP'S GLOVED KNUCKLE against Lou's driver side window startled him awake. "Rll mowm duhh wnndwsir," Lou heard a muffled voice calmly commanding outside. The glass, combined with the groggy and buzzy nap, was enough for him to shake his head in startled confusion.

"Unnghgh..." He looked around and the sight of red and blue light waves dancing all round him jostled him upright. The seat had been reclined, and now he had to rely on soft ab muscles and grabbing the steering wheel to hold himself upright. He squinted out the window as his mind started to catch up. He wasn't particularly drunk, but he'd been so tired after the evening fight with Julia that he'd stopped before getting trashed and headed to the car for a nap. He started to open the door.

"I said to just roll the window down," the police officer stated. "Just stay in the seat."

Lou did as commanded. As his wits gathered, he realized he was talking to a Hispanic female officer. Her SUV was parked behind Lou's GMC, effectively keeping him parked in front of the tavern. Lou thought he could detect radio squawking and realized there was probably a partner behind his car.

"How much have you had to drink?"

"Literally just two, Officer," he said with a sheepish chuckle. "I know you always hear that, but it happens to be true."

"People usually don't need to nap after two, sir," she countered. "License."

Lou pulled his thin wallet from his right-front pants pocket, struggling for a moment to get it past the hem in the awkward position. "I get that, but I didn't want to go home, and I was just too tired to drink tonight. Gotta lot on my mind. I came out to think, and I must've just fallen asleep."

When he opened his wallet to dig out his driver's license, she noticed his military ID card. "You active duty?"

Lou just handed the card with his license to answer the question. While she was surveying the two identifications, Lou explained, "I left the key fob out on the tire. Just in case you all got called, I'd be able to show I'm not starting the car." He was pointing toward the vehicle's rear. "Can I reach for my phone?"

"Hold up," she ordered. Another officer strolled over and told the primary that the vehicle check had come back clean. "Sure thing."

Lou reached behind himself into the cup holder and grabbed his phone. *11:37? Sheesh...*

"What time did you come outside?" she asked.

"I think about 8 - 8:30. There was a basketball game on the bar's TVs when I left."

She handed Lou's ID cards back to him. "You really should find other places to get rest, Colonel. Not good to look so 'passed out' right in front of a bar."

"I got no excuses, Officer. Just some domestic issues that are best thought about *not* at home."

"Drive safely, sir. I'd advise you just get on home." She turned around and barely heard Lou thank her.

After getting out to fetch his fob, Lou reoriented himself in his mini-SUV and closed the door, tossing his wallet and cards into the small tray under the radio. *Whew,* he thought. *I wonder if being active duty is why she's cutting me a break.* He felt bad about lying to her, but in his current state of tolerance six really was like two. He felt on the seat and finally found the toggle to drive it back up into its proper position. After the police left and made it to the main road, he fired the rig up and slowly made his way out to the avenue. *I do believe a DWI would've changed Monty's mind about me,* he thought with both glum and relief. *But it also would've subjected me to both civil court and UCMJ. That could've been bad for a man trying to retire.* Lou's new promotion was temporary, so if they'd decided to bust him back, it would've been starting at his recent rank, not his gifted one.

Lou had gone to The Stowaway to avoid that homeless 'preacher' near Snuffy's. This afforded him a few minutes to contemplate on the drive home, which he made with his cruise control set on the exact speed limit. *I can't control it now. Maybe my marriage is over... maybe it isn't. But I have to do something different. Snap out of this vortex. I think Monty's right. I think maybe I do need to get outta dodge for a while. If I have something to do, I'll be able to keep to three or four drinks a night—maybe less.*

THE PENTAGON

"I MUST ADMIT, LOU," COLONEL RYAN JACKSON SAID FROM behind his desk. "I didn't expect you to say yes, and I certainly didn't expect the decision until tomorrow." The surprise registered on the detail-oriented Marine's face.

"Well, Colonel, let's just say I had a pretty clear sign last night," Lou said, leaving it vague. "I know this trip carries a lot of responsibility. I won't let the general down."

"Oh, I know," Ryan said, nodding a bit. His tone was mysterious, tipping to Lou there was something he knew that Lou didn't. He reached forward to his desk and took the phone handle off the cradle, punching in two numbers onto the device's keypad. "Captain, can you come to my office?"

Lou's confusion registered. "May I?" he motioned toward one of the two chairs in front of Colonel Jackson's walnut desk.

Ryan nodded as he set the phone back into its cradle. "Admittedly, it would've put us in a slightly larger pinch to detail another colonel for this assignment," he told Lou. "I'd already been working on that plan. My Plan B... well, like I said, I didn't figure you'd accept."

"Sorry to disappoint you," Lou said with a slightly perturbed tone. *What. A. Prick.* He didn't dare say it aloud. There was a knock at the door.

"Come on in, Captain," Ryan Jackson ordered.

Lou turned his head and saw what he thought was probably the poster boy for the Marine Corps' recruiting department. Though not a giant at probably an even six-feet tall, the man in his late twenties appeared to be chiseled out of stone. His perfectly buzzed brown hair was textbook high-and-tight. *Sheesh,* Lou thought, *his teeth and eyes are even sparkling. Looks like he could do pullups for days...* And the Marine junior officer had a smile that could sell a car salesman life insurance if it wanted to.

"Lou, meet Captain Brandon McDonald," Ryan said.

Lou stood and stepped out from the small space between the chair and desk, extending his hand. "Captain," he said nodding as they shook hands. "Freeman Caldwell." His uniform gave away his rank and branch of service.

"Sir, good to meet you!" Brandon said, his grip accidentally squishing Lou's hand into a 'dead fish.'

"Looks like you'll be heading out tomorrow instead of Friday, Captain," Ryan said. "The colonel here will pick you up at home. Zero-eight hundred. That's all."

"Great, sir!" He looked Lou squarely in the eye, his handsome face beaming. "Looking forward to it, Colonel! I can't wait to get an inside look at your career and the Air Force mission as it shifts in the 21st Century."

Oh, Gawwwddd, Lou thought. *I must be in hell.* The Marine captain broke the handshake and departed back to his cubicle. Lou looked back at Ryan Jackson as he moved back to his seat. "A babysitter? Seriously?"

"As a heart attack, Lou," Colonel Jackson said with no kidding in his voice. "I told you, Plan B. In case you actually accepted."

"Or as a way to make me change my answer," Lou countered. Ryan's face did not change one millimeter, giving away nothing about his motives. "You're out of luck, Colonel. I need to go on this assignment. It'll do me some good."

"I truly hope you mean that, Lou. But the kid is still going. The general wants you on this assignment because you stepped up once. That doesn't mean you have my unfettered trust."

"Understood," Lou said. "Just make sure he takes a few downers first. Those giant gleaming teeth might blind me while I'm driving."

Colonel Jackson was not amused and completely ignored Lou's joke. He slid a folder and a box over to him. "Here's your cover story, orders, rental car. There's a required itinerary of some commands we've set up for you officially to visit as part of the public affairs cover. There's enough flexibility in between those that the two of you can determine some other bases and commands to visit impromptu. General Montgomery will expect some sort of detailed write-up after each of those. There's also a satellite phone programmed directly to me and him. Use it for something urgent. And a laptop. Try to keep up on your email. You can get onto wi-fi on the bases and send secure reports. Stay off the hotel wi-fi. It's a hacker haven. If you must, you can use your phone as a hotspot."

Lou stood once more. *I'll need to hit the liquor store after I pick up the rental car.* "I'll try not to let him down," he said as he left the office.

EAST CHINA SEA

"WHERE IS THE KEY WEST?" THE CAPTAIN OF THE USS JAMES L. Hunnicutt asked his navigation team curtly. When the boat had suffered her damaged front-starboard quarter from running aground, the very first thing the captain had done was send an emergency distress to the fleet. In the sixteen hours since, they'd deployed one of their trailing wire antennas to receive a Very Low Frequency transmission: *SSN 722 enroute.* It had included encrypted coordinates of the USS Key West's position when they were ordered to assist.

"Best guess, assuming they haven't been detected, still an hour out, sir," the young female Lieutenant Junior Grade replied.

Commander Woodward checked the positions of the PLAN subs, frigates, and destroyers once more. Ever since their undersea collision, they'd been making a beeline for the US spy sub. In the best of times, the Hunny could've danced circles around their foes, much quieter and speedier than almost anyone on the planet realized. There were several horrible effects to their damage, however, the obvious being attracting the enemy. The not so obvious included having a list toward starboard that required keeping their port side ballast tanks partially flooded to counteract in such shallow water. They also had to trim out the aft end tanks to keep the nose from getting too heavy. The sub's speed and quietness underwater depended on keeping the proper alignment for traveling forward, something not possible with a damaged and flooding set of forward-starboard ballast tanks.

The decision for a slow evasion had been bittersweet in hindsight. Had they opted to make a speedier run for open sea, they quite possibly would've been undetected. But in the very slow speed they had been hugging the coast to slip out when the collision happened, they had received no interior damage and no personnel casualties. *Not fighting fire and flooding at this moment is just Murphy going easy on us,* Chief-Of-the-Boat Darren Jorgenson decided. *As bad as this situation is, it could be worse.*

Backing up the pilot and co-pilot in monitoring the sub's traveling condition was exactly Darren's job. On older subs, there would've been another station dedicated to just the ballast, trim, and list of the ship. The Navy's newer subs, though, operated on a literal joystick, sending electronic signals to all the controls via very expensive computers.

"COB, are we as trimmed out as we're gonna get?" the CO asked tensely.

"Aye, sir. We're stable at this depth with a four-degree down bubble."

Darren's team had diving planes at both ends of the ship to control the boat's flight much like an airplane. The starboard plane on the forward end was high up in one of the ballast tanks that had taken the hit. Though most likely undamaged, they had retracted it just in case. They were traveling at their current top-speed that would allow them to remain quiet—twelve knots. Something in the damaged area was making a thumping noise when they tried to go faster, which constantly sent a signal to their pursuers where they were. *I bet it's a piece of the sound dampening coating,* Darren thought. *Flappin' in the breeze, so to speak.*

"Conn, Contact Sierra Three has re-surfaced above the thermal, bearing one-fifteen! Range 3000 yards!" the Chief Sonar Operator yelled out.

"Is she turning toward us, Chief?" the skipper asked.

"Not yet, sir!"

"Pilot, maintain speed, make your depth six-fifty, crank us hard to port!" the CO ordered. The pilot repeated the orders back as he began the evasive maneuver.

He's trying to maintain our maximum silent speed and get us below the thermal that Shang just popped out from. Darren began to adjust settings to assist the co-pilot with the mangled depth, list, and trim issues as the pilot drove the sub down. Everyone was already walking around on a slightly sloped deck, but now it began to lean forward even more as well as list downward on the port.

"COB, I don't care if we have a list—keep some air in the port forward tanks!" the CO ordered.

"Aye, sir!"

Makes sense, Darren realized. Being able to recover depth from unknown damage to a ship designed to sink and resurface was now a very scary wildcard factor. Being fast and silent meant nothing to their lives if they could never recover from gaining depth. Darren made the adjustments. With air only in the port side tanks, the Hunny felt sluggish as she turned and dove at the same time. The normal hull-popping noises that accompanied submarine depth changes was another possible factor that could give them away, though on this descent it was mild.

"Depth six-fifty, Captain," the pilot announced.

"Make your bearing zero-five-zero," the CO replied with a little more composure.

"Zero-five-zero," the pilot repeated.

"Sir, the transient is back," one of the other sonar operators reported.

This is the first time we've been this deep since the damage, Darren realized. *Water is under greater pressure, a little more saline dense, too... Maybe twelve is too fast...*

"Contact!" the chief sonar operator yelled. "Sierra Three, bearing two-twenty, range 1800 yards!"

"Depth?" the CO demanded. While not always readily available information, the modern submarine force largely had a series of sonar arrays on each side of the boat. When they all picked up the same noise, the ship's computer could use trigonometry based on the slightly different angle to provide a probable depth.

"Five-hundred feet, Conn! She's back under the thermal."

"She's flooding tubes!" screeched the other sonar technician, who was barely able to maintain her calm in the realization they were now engaged in combat. The flooding of torpedo tubes exposed weapons to salt water, creating extra work when they weren't actually launched. There would be no other reason to do that except for its primary purpose of getting ready to shoot.

"All ahead full, right full rudder!" the skipper yelled. "Countermeasures to starboard on my command! Weapons, flood all port tubes!" Both the pilot and the weapons-and-counter-measures stations acknowledged their orders.

A common evasive tactic was to try to create a knuckle in the water by turning hard at a high rate of speed. Create turbulence in the water that would cause a torpedo to lose its track. *That hasn't worked for us against the Ruskies for nearly three decades,* Darren thought. Then he remembered that China's first nuclear subs were based on old Soviet designs. *Maybe they're still using outdated equipment.*

"Outer doors opening!" the junior sonar operator yelled.

They'll be shooting in a few seconds!

Then the dreaded words no submariner wanted to hear their sonar operators say... "Torpedoes in the water! Tracking two torpedoes, bearing two-three-zero, range 1500 yards, speed fifty-five knots!"

CHAPTER 7

ARLINGTON, VIRGINIA

"COLONEL, COULD YOU AT LEAST COME MEET MY WIFE BEFORE we head out?" Marine Captain Brandon Andrew McDonald asked as he loaded his day bags into the back seat of the cobalt blue Chevy Cruze.

"I suppose," Lou grumbled as he opened the driver's door and stepped out onto the suburban neighborhood street in the Old Dominion neighborhood. He followed the handsome young man up to the front porch, where an equally beautiful pregnant woman holding a toddler was waiting.

"Hope, this is Colonel Freeman Caldwell. He's Air Force. Sir, this is my wife Hope and our current youngest, Sarah."

"So pleased to meet you!" she said with the same semi-obnoxious enthusiasm her husband seemed to channel.

A hint of Georgia peach, do I detect? Lou asked himself about her country twang. *These people must binge watch the Hallmark Channel.* While there was no sign of the seasonal pumpkins and faux fall leaves that adorned most homes, Lou could detect a very warm cinnamon smell wafting from the house. He thought he could see a cross and Bible scripture hanging on the wall. "Likewise, Mrs. McDonald. Thanks for letting your husband come be my bodyguard."

This caused both of them to laugh. "I still don't get what your two are doing," she admitted, "but I have faith that the Pentagon knows what it's doing."

That makes one of us, Lou thought with ingrained cynicism. "It's kind of a spot check on the military," Lou advised. "We're making a lot of movements in response to that big disaster in Seattle and other world events. So Brandon and I are tasked with checking out the troops' morale."

"Well, I'll be praying for your safety and fast return!" Suddenly the largest dog Lou had ever seen squirmed through the gap between Hope and the doorframe and let out a loud but non-threatening woof. Lou took a nervous half-step back.

"Samson, calm down," Brandon commanded as he squatted and gave the giant dog a big pat on the head. He switched to scratching behind the tan Boerboel's dark brown ears. "He's a friend."

"Holy crap!" Lou exclaimed. "Why in the world do you have a horse in your house?"

Two-year-old Sarah cracked up with delight. "He not a horse!" she squealed.

Brandon stood back up, laughing. "He does eat the most in the family! But I feel a lot better going on deployments with him at home."

"I can understand why," Lou said. He pointed to his wrist, which like most pilots, still held an actual watch. "We should get going. Pleased to meet you," he said to Hope as he turned.

Fifteen minutes later, the pair of officers were turning onto Interstate Highway 95, making their way south. "Oh, shoot!" Brandon called out.

"What?" Lou asked, still trying to fiddle with the radio while driving. "Forget something?"

"Forgot to say a prayer. D'ya mind if I lead us in a prayer, Colonel?"

Oh, brother, Lou thought. *This just keeps getting better.* "What—like out loud?"

Brandon laughed. The Marine was used to his military brethren not being particularly religious. "Don't sweat it, sir." He bowed his head.

Lou looked over and thought he could just make out muscle movement on his partner's lips. *He's being serious,* Lou realized. *Jackson picked the perfect person to make sure I don't drink. Well, I still outrank this kid.* He kept an eye on him and waited two full minutes before he saw the young man's head pick back up.

"Look, kid, while we're in the car and hotel and stuff, just call me Lou. 'Kay?"

"It'd feel weird to do that, sir, but I'll give it a try."

"Seriously. We're going to be travel partners for a couple of weeks. This 'colonel' garbage is going to get real old, real fast," Lou warned.

"Roger that, Lou. So—where're we headed?"

"North Carolina. We have a tour at Bragg on Monday. Figured we could meet an old buddy of mine at Pope Air Force Base tomorr—" Hoooonnnkk!!! Lou laid on the rental's weak horn as he got cut off in the morning traffic. A middle finger was extended out at Lou from the driver ahead. "Effin' jackwad!" Lou yelled at the windshield. "People have no patience or manners anymore."

"Everywhere," Brandon concurred. "Civility is a lost art, a reflection of a real spiritual decline."

"Alright, McDonald, I'd better just let you know right now. I don't wanna hear a bunch of Jesus talk on this trip. I don't care what you believe, but if there's a God—and that's a mighty big if—he doesn't give one iota about us. Sorry if this comes off as rude. Just trying to get it square early so we can have a less stressful trip."

"Understood, Colonel," Brandon said.

"Really?" Lou countered with a slight sneer. "We're back to that?"

"Sorry, Lou," Brandon said. "It just felt kind of like an order, that's all."

Lou fell silent as the crawl south started to loosen on the road to Richmond. After five minutes of listening to commercials on all the channels Lou tried, he finally opened back up. "Sorry, young man. I don't want to set a tone of being a jerk right off the bat. I'd rather you figure that out slowly. I suppose you got a brief on my recent past?"

"I did."

"And? I suppose it makes sense why they need you to tag along... Keep me out of trouble?"

"That's only one perspective, Lou," Brandon said. "I may work for the military, but they aren't the ultimate authority in my life. You don't want me to talk about my faith or God? I can live with that. Most Marines don't want me to, either. I'm used to it. But I'm not just here following orders. I'm here because it's where God wants me."

"Alright, kid. Heh...Kid. How the hell old are ya, anyhow?"

"Twenty-nine."

"Well, Brandon. When we get to Richmond, God's gonna want you in the driver's seat."

EAST CHINA SEA

"SHE'S STAYING BEHIND US, CONN," THE CHIEF SONAR Operator answered his captain. The skipper had launched two countermeasures, which were basically bubble-generating devices similar to giant Alka-seltzers, to try to give the enemy torpedoes something else to hit.

"Pilot, come around to starboard! Make your bearing zero-nine-zero, depth three hundred. We're going to go for distance and try to close the gap to the Key West!"

The pilot relayed and followed the orders as Darren and the co-pilot fought to maintain the best list and trim attitude they could manage with the damage as the ship fought for shallower water.

"Time to impact?" the CO yelled to the sonar station.

"Thirty-five seconds, sir," the sonar chief said. "Range 900 yards. Computer has added a few seconds back as we gain speed."

"Both torpedoes bypassed the counter-measures," one of the alternate sonar operators reported. "Too much transient noise from our damage, sir. Coming straight at us!"

"Three hundred feet, sir," the pilot interjected their new depth to the captain.

"Very well, maintain heading!"

"Four more torpedoes!" the sonar station reported. "Bearing three-three-zero relative! Range 400 yards...Wait!" There was a tense moment in which time stood still. Nobody dared breathe. The smell of sweat was dense and unnoticed as all three sonar operators were pressing their headsets to their ears as tightly as they'd ever worn them. "They're Mark-48s!" she practically yelled with relieved excitement. The new torpedoes were American.

The USS Key West had taken advantage of the extra noise the Hunny was emitting to sneak up on the unsuspecting PLAN submarine. The US Mk-48 torpedoes were highly sensitive and programmable. The first two had been shot out of the older Los Angeles attack sub's two portside tubes, aimed directly at the oncoming PLAN torpedoes. The starboard tubes had a different mission—send a message to the PLAN—*don't bite off more than you can chew.* The older guardian passed her wounded sister at full speed, headed directly for the attacker.

"Two of the 48s are headed directly for the inbound fish!" The room was still, every sailor resisting the temptation to ignore their own panels to watch the sonar and weapons station operators. "Impact in five seconds at four-hundred-eighty yards!" All three headsets were yanked off heads by their wearers.

The explosion and concussion of the torpedoes were felt by the crews of all three submarines, first one, and then two seconds later the other, as four warheads exploded with what would have boat-sinking force. After ten seconds of shaking, the operators put their headsets back on.

"Sierra Three is flooding tubes!" the chief yelled once more.

"She's cranking up speed and attempting evasive actions!" another yelled.

"Status of the other two 48s?" the skipper asked, a bit more calmly than he'd been in the preceding hour.

"ETA forty seconds," the chief replied.

Even if the American weapons quit hearing the enemy sub—*and they won't,* Darren knew—the torpedoes played out a thin wire as they ran. The Key West's weapons crew could steer them as easily as playing a game with a joystick.

A moment later, the operators removed their headsets once more, and the crew of USS James L. Hunnicutt let out a giant sigh of relief. Another concussive explosion... then, after another lag, they redonned their gear and described listening to the sounds of a submarine sinking. The hull screamed with crunching and resistance as its lost structural integrity gave way to the weight of the water.

They weren't out of danger yet, but the older, slower diesel subs were too far north to be an effective threat at this point. The surface fleet was too easy to detect and evade now that the hunter-killer was not there to keep hounding them. And so began a twelve-knot limp to Pearl Harbor Naval Shipyard under the protection of their older, smaller sister ship. Darren and the rest of the crew joined an extremely small club that day—*How many people survive an enemy torpedo attack?*

EL PASO, TEXAS

. . .

"GO GET US SOME MORE DRINKS, BABY," EDUARDO GONZALEZ instructed Rosie.

She knew that was his way of saying to get lost while he and the other two men chatted. Rosie had learned that he usually needed about ten minutes in these clandestine, dark restaurant meetups. She also knew that her relationship with Eddie had developed to a certain level of laziness. *Not trust,* she reminded herself. *He doesn't trust anyone.* But in the course of two years, Eddie had stopped doing thorough searches of her purse every time they went out for dinner.

She carried a very specific box of feminine supplies, a small plastic box that happened to be the same size as a small battery-powered digital recorder. After six months of seeing that tampon container over and over again, Eddie had learned what it was by feel when he felt around in her purse for anything he considered contraband. After noticing that he no longer unzipped that particular interior pocket the third time, she swapped it out for the recorder. Her pulse was pounding so loudly the first time she used it she was afraid that was all that would play back. She was wrong.

In the fifteen months since that first recording, she'd dead dropped nine of those identical devices to her handler. Each of them carried one to two hours of conversation between Eddie and local officials he was bribing or providing instructions to. *We need photos, too,* the handler would instruct via dead-drop.

In the entire time, she'd only had one in-person meet with her handler, Jared—the time he informed her that Angel had a bout of pneumonia but had recovered from it. Part of Rosie's cover had been to attend church—St. Frances Xavier Cabrini Catholic Church to be precise—as they had an outreach program that occasionally took their elderly members on field trips. Rosie volunteered to be a chaperone to Carlsbad Caverns on one such trip. Meeting with Jared had scared the living hell out of Rosie—it had given her nightmares for three weeks.

Eddie had never let Rosie take her phone with her anytime they went out together. To counter that, Rosie was instructed to get Eddie to take her to a specific mall for dinner. When they did, she would 'window-shop' at a particular jeweler. That jeweler had lost not one but two children to gang violence and was a very willing participant in the James Bond like ruse. He knew to be looking for them and guided Rosie and Eddie to a very specific broach... A deal too good to pass up. Rosie would have to play her part, of course, begging and squealing with delight. It was not lost at all on Rosie that she had Eddie purchase the high-tech recording device she would be using against him.

But how will it take pictures? Rosie asked Jared.

As long as you have wi-fi and keep it charged, you'll never have to do a thing, Jared promised. Rosie was able to lay it on the same inductance charger that her electric toothbrush used. And that broach was worn on every dinner-date since, providing the Texas Rangers pictures that Rosie could take by brushing a specific fold in the metal.

On this evening, Rosie took her cue and left the men while she went to the bano to freshen up. She'd already gotten her pictures. Her purse would record the conversation. Rosie had recognized the old one as a judge, but the younger one she'd never seen before—and he had scrutinized Rosie for so long that Eddie had finally been forced to say something.

"I'm sorry, Eduardo, please forgive me," the police lieutenant said. "She just looks...familiar."

After freshening up and having a cigarette, Rosie ordered a new round of drinks from the bartender and slowly meandered back to her table, wondering if this would be the night her cover had finally been blown.

HIGHWAY 301, NORTHEAST OF RICHMOND, VIRGINIA

. . .

"...AND SO TO PUT IT INTO TERMS YOU CAN PROBABLY RELATE to, I figure that life—like a plane—when left on autopilot unchecked will eventually fly you into a mountain."

Holy hell, does this guy ever come up for air? Lou wondered. "Look, I know we're only to Richmond, but how about we stop and top off. I need to go drain the coffee."

"Sure thing," Brandon said. He cued up his cell phone and saw on the map that there was an early lunchtime traffic jam building up, as indicated by the annoying red dashed lines. "I'll try to find a gas station near the next exit."

Up in Fredericksburg, the team had opted to slip over to a state highway to spend a little less time smelling semi-truck exhaust.

They had spent over an hour discussing the state of things in America, particularly in regards to their mission parameters in the face of what was happening out west. They had been given a milestone of getting to Fort Bragg early as they knew several elements were already being prepped for deployment west. As much as the federal government was trying to help the folks in the Rainier Impact Zone, the increased gang violence in every major western city coupled with China and Russia's obvious military buildups were demanding even more attention.

"Got one," Brandon announced. "Very next exit."

Lou started trying to signal and gap his way to the far-right lane. "I saw when I picked you up you brought both a duffle and a suitcase..."

"Yes, well, there's no telling how long we'll be out, right? I'm sure we'll be flying some, too. I figured it was a redundancy in case one bag never shows up."

"Same," said Lou. "I don't mind checking two bags since we're on orders." He started to make his way off the highway and could see backed up traffic on the local business feeder road. Lou reached up and turned the talk-radio station down. "And I brought a durable backpack, too. Seeing the news about rolling and extended blackouts, the spotty internet issues, the hacking...it's enough to give me a pessimistic feeling about us getting delayed or stuck at some point."

"What brand is your go-bag?" Brandon asked. "I like a good quality Maxpedition myself."

"Mystery Ranch," Lou answered. "Not so tacti-cool looking. Where are we..." he asked, more rhetorical than anything.

"Mechanicsville," Brandon answered.

A cacophony of horns played a song of discontent as Lou tried to squeeze into the far-right lane where his off-ramp exited onto a multi-lane one-way road. He could see the 76 station just a couple of hundred yards ahead. There was a long line of stopped cars in the right lane that he was barely able to get into, all trying to get into the gas station.

"Whoa!" Brandon whistled. "Is this an honest to goodness old-school gas line?"

"Don't look so enthused there, Poster Boy, I need to piss pretty badly."

Brandon guffawed, almost more comically than a super-jock normally would. "Wha? What? 'Poster Boy'?" he repeated.

"It's your call-sign," Lou said, looking at him quickly as he kept trying to keep an eye on the gridlock around him. He pointed to the buff young Marine's exterior. "For obvious reasons. Look, we need to do a Chinese fire drill so I can run ahead and hit the latrine."

"You got it, Super Bert!"

Lou shot him a look as both men exited the parked car, drawing an immediate honk from the Toyota behind them. "Colonel's prerogative, junior. You ain't earned it yet." He started speed walking south.

Several minutes later, Lou found himself relieved and in the gas station's store. He noticed that the shelves were about a third empty, the sole exception being the full racks of cigarettes behind the attendant. It reminded him of being in Afghanistan all those years ago. Once the users of any tobacco product ran out of their vice of choice, those non-users with a little foresight and ingenuity began to sell their own strategically purchased supply for a huge mark up. He looked back at the water bottle cooler he'd spotted near the restroom. Although he'd brought a double walled aluminum bottle, he decided it wouldn't hurt anything for them to have a few in the car. Lou bought four bottles and a few snacks, also picking up a paper map. He could see Brandon just getting to his pump as he went back outside. He strolled over and placed the items on the floor where his feet would be when they resumed their trek.

"Man, people sure are tense!" they heard an overly friendly voice call out from the other side of his pump, an older man next to a beater pickup.

"Is this area always this congested?" Brandon asked the man in reply.

"Durin' rush hour, sure," the friendly man said. "But I'm retired!" he laughed. "Ain't no skin off my back!"

"Must be nice!" Lou said, feeling a tinge of bitterness about being manipulated into postponing his own retirement. "Is the gas line always in the street like that?" More honking out in the road reinforced his question.

"Well..." the older man pondered, pushing his ballcap back on his head a bit. "I only come through here 'bout twice per week—take groceries to my mother in her assisted home, ya see—and...I guess not, in the grand scheme. But it was like this three days ago. Peculiar..." The man readjusted his hat.

"Yes," Lou said. "Peculiar for sure. Seems like people's tempers are a lot shorter now. That isn't good when the supply chains are getting so slow. Imagine how people out west must be getting, huh?"

"True 'nuff," the old man said, as he started to shut down his pump and close his tank. "Can't help but wonder if any of this is tied to the shipping issues caused by that earthquake..."

"You may be on to somethin' there," Brandon chimed in.

Lou scanned his phone, looking at the map app—even the main roads off the highway showed the distinct orange and red lines of gridlock he didn't want to see. He looked up at his junior partner as the other man drove off and the next car came screaming into place. *I wonder if I should go in and see what other paper maps they sell?*

CHAPTER 8

WHITE HOUSE SITUATION ROOM

"DAMMIT, KELLY! HOW DID THIS HAPPEN?" PRESIDENT Jeremiah Allen yelled at his Secretary of Defense.

They and a slew of other cabinet members, Joint Chief Montgomery, Vice President Heather Crenshaw, and several military officers were crowding around a conference table and staring at several feeds. The blue carpet and dim lighting only enhanced the already ominous feeling in the room as several screens put off their electronic glow. The room smelled of stale coffee and the air practically reeked with sweat, stress and cortisol.

On the biggest screen was a message from the commanding officer of the USS Key West, verifying the torpedo shootout and pending escape. As the Hunny had continued its slow escape, the Key West had taken herself to periscope depth, daring to send an eight second encrypted burst transmission. The sub had a slew of antennas at her disposal, and one of those had an aimable parabolic shape that pointed itself directly to the sky when raised out of the sail. When it broke the water's surface, and with GPS synchronized accuracy, it sent a narrow-beam transmission directly to the highly classified position of a secure satellite:

[Fr: CO, USS Key West: engaged and sank one Shang class PLAN submarine, unknown hull number, fifty-three miles southwest of location Hotel-Echo 12, approximately 0500 Zulu. SSGN-93 reports starboard bow grounding damage to ballast tanks via underwater phone. Max speed twelve knots. Estimate arrival at PHNS in eight days.]

"First we lose the El Paso in that drydock in Washington State, and now this? What about the Halsey? Will we be getting her out of her drydock before it fills up for good?" Snake Charmer was referring to the fact that the US Navy's only west coast nuclear qualified shipyard in Washington State had been all but destroyed in the catastrophic natural disasters. The submarine USS El Paso had been right in the middle of having its nuclear fuel rods replaced when it struck. Several people had died, and they were fighting an ecological disaster just to keep the contaminated water at bay while they tried to button up the ship.

At an even greater strategic threat, the aircraft carrier USS Halsey was in a drydock that couldn't seal up its leaking. This happened to be the day they were expected to run out of emergency power—not the ship, but the shipyard proper. The entire shipyard was dependent on a series of dewatering pumps. As soon as they stopped, leaky drydocks started flooding. The shipyard team that had managed to stay at work despite the grave threats to their family had performed with honor—but was it enough? *Time will tell,* President Allen realized. *Mere hours.*

The screen changed to a satellite feed of the shipyard. "What's with the grainy view?" Jeremiah asked. It was 9 PM, and he'd not been getting good sleep for weeks. It was starting to reveal itself in how he talked to people.

"Heavy rain on site, Mr. President," answered an Air Force officer who was clacking rapidly on his keyboard, trying to get it to clarify. As the screen cleared up and zoomed in, the room grew quiet.

One of the other screens contained a secure video chat between General Montgomery and USMC General Roderick Conway, the

Commander of all US Forces in the Pacific, known in DOD lingo as PACOM. On the bottom of the screen a text chat between the men could be seen, as they had opted to mute voice while the others in the room were reviewing the submarine shootout.

"General?" Montgomery heard the President say.

With no additional prodding, an Army officer near the general unmuted the video call and moved it to the alternate big screen, right next to the feed of the shipyard operation.

"General Conway, what are we looking at here?" the president semi-barked, still tired and short-fused, but not angry.

"Mr. President, the very last pieces of the Halsey's shafts have been reinstalled. The shipyard workers are trying to get the seals torqued down properly and to correct specs. Otherwise, the ship's shaft compartments won't be able to keep sea water out."

"Is that drydock supposed to be flooding that quickly?" Jeremiah wasn't holding back.

"No, sir. The shipyard commander and her team have been working feverishly on this and the El Paso issues. Everything there took massive casualties in the event, sir. Cranes toppled over. Broken caissons. Flooded drydocks. Collapsed buildings. Broken crane and train tracks. She's confident the team will finish."

"What happens when their backup power runs out?" the president asked, looking down at the various reports in front of him as he did.

"In true Navy fashion, Mr. President, they'll try good old-fashioned damage control by hammering large wooden plugs and wedges into any hole they can find. An old school answer for a millennium old problem."

After ten more minutes, the president called for the meeting to wrap up. "Kelly, I want to know as soon as it's clear that the Halsey is floating and not sinking in a drydock." He stood up, triggering everyone else to do the same as the various officers began to shut down the monitors. "And I want a full briefing ready for Secretary Buttermaker in time for tomorrow morning's brief. We need to be ready when China accuses us—rightly—of sinking one of their submarines. Figure out how we can leverage this thing."

With that, Jeremiah Allen headed off to his White House residence for yet another night of fitful non-sleep.

FAYETTEVILLE, NORTH CAROLINA

LOU LOOKED AT THE GASOLINE GAUGE ON THE RENTAL, NOT really needing gas, but deciding to shut the engine off anyhow. There were one or two angry looking local residents who were out of their cars, complaining. Most of the gawkers, though, were just passively watching the long slow procession of rail cars as they crossed Country Club Drive headed east by southeast. It was one of those railway crossings in which drivers grew accustomed to never having to stop at. This was a dead-end line running out of Fort Bragg, which eventually connected to the CSZ "A" Line, a north south arterial line that was almost exclusively for freight. Lou and Brandon had decided to make their first unannounced run, opting for a spot check at the Special Forces group.

Lou and Brandon got out of their vehicle, which was twenty-three cars back in line. Lou could hear the rhythmic clickity-thump-thump of flat-car wheels as they crossed over the road at an annoyingly slow twelve miles-per-hour. *We're gonna be here a while,* he realized. He could hear the four engines barely a half-mile east, blaring their horns as they continued to cross lanes of traffic in the busy morning commute, heading toward Fayetteville proper to turn south.

"Where d'ya think they're goin'?" Lou and Brandon heard the southern drawl of an older middle-aged black woman say, another driver standing on the now parking lot avenue. The three were but a small part of a growing on-looker crowd staring at the equipment of the 18th Field Artillery Brigade and the 82nd Airborne Division slowly cruise by.

"Beats me," Lou said, not really considering that he'd just lied. *No need to alarm people when even the generals aren't really sure what's happening yet,* he rationalized with himself. "Probably some sort of training out west?" *There... a smack of truth.* He smiled at the lady, who gave a polite grin back.

"Hardly ever see this crossing being used," she said, happy to educate this obvious Yankee in a rental car with Maryland plates.

"Oh yeah?" Brandon said. "You live here long?"

"Most of my life, youngin'" the woman said in her country charm. "My husband was career Army...retired here back in the 90s. Seems like they use these lines once or twice per year—but not *nearly* this long of a train," she mentioned, the realization showing itself in the faded smile.

Looking up and around, Lou changed the subject. "Beautiful morning, though. I don't mind being stuck here for a bit. Lovely area," he said truthfully.

"I'll be mindin' if this thing make me late fo' work!" the woman said, her good nature betraying the mild annoyance she was feeling with a grin. She had started to turn and move back to her car, two behind the cobalt Cruze.

"Let's scoot on up there for a bit. Oh—sorry," he said to Brandon. "You're from Georgia, you said?" Brandon nodded suspiciously. "Let's mosey on up thar for a spell," Lou teased. Though not yet willing to admit it, the young Marine wasn't totally horrible to have along. If nothing else, he would serve as a willing target to Lou's bored wit.

They passed several cars, about half of them turned off, their drivers opting to stay put. The pair approached a group of three women standing and chatting five cars back from the crossing arms. The clanking was much louder. He was in his Air Force blues, not completely uncommon in the community that also hosted Pope Field. Brandon's unique Marine Corp camo uniform stood out even more so.

"...daughter is married to a soldier," the apparent know-it-all of the group was saying. "A gal in her family support group was saying that my son-in-law's unit may get deployed to the west coast for extended drills."

"Really?" one of the women said. None of them gave Lou a second thought.

The third one asked, "Which unit is he with?"

"The 16th Military Police," she answered, her drawl getting thicker the more excited she got. "Now why on Earth would MPs need to deploy west for an extended amount of time? It's those stupid people rioting. I just know it!"

"Ya think?" one of the other two asked.

Both of them look like they could be married to soldiers themselves, Lou reasoned. "Pardon me for interrupting," he said, trying to more actively become part of the small circle. All three turned their heads to eye him and his junior cohort. Once the sight of his uniform registered, the older lady's look turned from annoyance to that of one peddling snake-oil. "Do you all know where all this gear is headed?" Lou asked.

"We were just talking about that!" the commander of this sudden social clique perked up. "Maybe you can shed some light on it. Though probably not," she frowned. "You're only in the Air Force." Disappointment filled the air.

"Wanda!" one of the younger ones scolded. She looked at Lou in shock.

"It's alright," Lou laughed. "I say that all the time!"

"I'm sorry," Wanda said. "I didn't mean it to sound that way. Thank youuu..." drawn out with pure fake hospitality, "...for yer service."

"You're most welcome," Lou said, having long ago conditioned himself to be polite to that comment that most every veteran and active-duty member didn't like. *It's not that we don't appreciate people's appreciation,* Lou once told Julia. *It's that we don't like being singled out as having done something special when we're just doing the job we signed up to do to begin with.* "Anyhow, to your point—we're actually with the

DOD public affairs office. We're trying to find out what your thoughts as Americans are on the various military activities in this community."

It was the first time Wanda had taken a full look at Brandon. Her demeanor perked up. "I think that young firecracker needs to be on some sort of calendar!" He smirked in embarrassment and looked away.

Her friend gave her a disapproving look and took over. "This—" she said, pointing at the train clacking as it continued to drive artillery, Humvees, trucks, and Conex boxes off the base, "worries me."

"Why's that?" Lou said with a serious tone on his face.

"Because they never send this much out at once." She went quiet.

The quietest of the threesome added, "Unless they're going to war."

ROELAND PARK, KANSAS

"WHADDYA MEAN MARVIN ISN'T COMING HOME?" MORRIS Dooghan asked his parents.

Morris hadn't waited for the weekend, opting to come home on Friday night. Classes had been canceled almost the entire week. Even as the power had been somewhat reliable, the computers at the school had been hacked—most of the professors had canceled classes with the full confidence that the I.T. department would fix the issue and everything would go back to normal. Morris knew better. He wanted to see just how tense things were getting in his old neighborhood.

"It's called a 'stop-loss', son. Instead of drafting, they just tell the current members they're not allowed to leave."

"That's such BS!" Morris yelled, though he didn't mean to. The normally reserved young man apologized to his mother. *Dad knows I wasn't yelling at him.* "Sorry, mom..."

"It's okay," she said. "You've always been protective of your brother. I know that."

"It's my fault he's even in the Army," Morris said, putting down his fork and mashed potatoes dejectedly. "If I'd pushed him harder in school instead of giving in to this airsoft thing he wanted so badly..."

"Your twin brother has always been an adventurous spirit, Mo," his father said. The medically retired construction worker had broken his back seven years earlier. But Morris considered him the smartest man he would ever know—especially after being at university all those years. Those professors may have had more education than his blue-collar father, but most of them were much too arrogant in their biases to be as well-rounded in intelligence as his dad. "He alone is responsible for his failing grades. Not you."

Morris looked at his father. "I know what you're saying makes sense, but you just don't get it. As his twin, I know him better than anyone."

"Excuse me?" Morris' mother said with just a tinge of fake offense. "I carried you boys for thirty-eight weeks!"

"Maaaa...." Morris groaned, dreading to hear for the umpteenth time that she had brought them into the world, and she could damn well take them out.

The family banter continued, turning to slightly more serious tones of conversation. The house Morris had grown up in felt smaller. It was his castle—his foundation. Yet the WW2 era home had started to wither and fade, Morris' father starting to have more troubles with it as his broken back continued to decline. As conversations turned to protests, gang violence, power outages, and world affairs, in the back of Morris' mind he couldn't help but wonder if his family should abandon their cherished abode for somewhere safer. *They'd put up a fight,* he realized as he pondered trying to convince them to leave for his Aunt Janet's over in Chanute. Conversations evolved into reminiscing and eventually everyone settled in for the night.

Morris staged the old camping lantern near his childhood bed to start flipping through a textbook. Out in the garage, he'd found that the old gallon of white gas had almost completely evaporated right out of its metal can. They hadn't camped in years due to his dad's injury. *These small paper-thin things might not even light up,* he realized, not remembering they were called mantles. His family had but two flashlights, both of them old plastic ones with nearly dead batteries. His parents had one on each of their bedroom nightstands.

The power flickered and popped out for the second time that evening. *Uggghhhh,* Morris thought. *Glad I charged my phone.* He scanned the portable computer and saw that the cell-signal showed the XG had disappeared and was replaced with LTE. *Huh,* he wondered. He spent a few minutes scrolling Tik Tok for mildly entertaining videos and then decided to crash.

CRASH! Morris woke with a start. He looked at his phone. *2:30!* He threw the covers off and headed for his door, not even thinking about putting on shoes. He slept in long-sleeve shirt and sweatpants in the old drafty house, so he was able to get to the upstairs hallway quickly. At 896-square-feet, the old track home was reflective of a bygone era in American living. He made it to the top of the stairs.

"Shhh," he heard down in the kitchen. "...food...listen—stop!"

The voices disappeared like a ghost. *Oh, Hell, no!* Morris yelled in his head. He flew down the old creaky stairs, grabbing the baseball bat from its familiar spot in the corner that turned ninety degrees three steps up from the bottom. He put the bat up to a high-ready position and turned right onto the main floor.

"Morris?" he heard his father's voice trickle down the stairwell walls.

Bang! Crash! "Ow! Mothuh F—" he heard a voice yell as it was rapidly flying out of the kitchen and disappearing into the cold night in the back yard.

Ignoring his father, Morris scrambled into the kitchen, hoping... "Get back here, you piece of—"

"Morris!" his mother yelled as the lights flicked on and both parents came scrambling into the tiny kitchen. There was a pile of glass on the floor near the back door, having been scooted around after the would-be burglars gained entry. The door was agape to the cold night air.

Morris spun around, bat still high at the ready. His eyes were wide and nostrils were flaring. "What! Oh!" he said as he lowered the bat, trying to de-escalate his emotions. He looked at his father. "Tell me again you don't believe in owning guns!" he said as he brushed past his dad to go to the closet and find the dustpan and a pair of slippers for his bare feet.

"Not now, son! This is a one-off event. Just some people down on their luck, probably. No need to take it out on me!"

"Dad!" Morris said with emphasis, trying to control his emotions. "This is only going to get worse! Look around town! Mom! Just tonight you were saying you couldn't believe how expensive groceries had risen in the last few weeks! People are pissed off! It's not helping that there seems to be an organized effort to go out and burn businesses and set cop cars on fire over in KC every night!"

Morris grabbed the dustpan and started sweeping with the little brush as he crouched. His mother started scanning the fridge and cupboards for anything missing. As his father went out to the small detached one car garage to fetch something to cover the window, Morris realized he was suddenly glad he didn't own a car to get broken into. *Is this the new normal*? he wondered.

Pope Field, Cumberland County, NC

"Super Bert!" Major Wallace Matthews hollered at his old buddy. "Get in here for some Hair Force love!"

Lou felt himself get wrapped in the big man's bear hug and get squeezed. "I'd forgotten about this part," Lou grunted in mild agony as he felt his shoulders do their best to connect in front of his chest.

It was Monday, and knowing they'd be swapping some old war stories, Brandon had dropped Lou off and headed over to Fort Bragg for another spot check. Lou wasn't sure, but he had a sneaking suspicion the kid was trying to make a report on the fact that he'd been hungover on Sunday morning.

The giant officer gave his much shorter comrade a final squeeze before letting his feet fall the four inches back to the floor and letting go. Several of the officers and NCOs we're chuckling completely at Lou's expense, having been victim of the major's lovefest at least once themselves. Wally was former enlisted Army before going to college and getting a 'zoomie' commission. He had brought with him the love for both hi-jinx and making people slightly uncomfortable that had been ingrained in him as a grunt in the Army.

"What on Earth brings you to the 43rd, old buddy?" the big man said loudly as he led Lou back into his office.

Lou followed his old friend from Afghanistan into the glorified cubicle in the corner of the common room. "Wally, I believe you might get a solid sixty percent from the V.A. for that hearing when you retire. Or lack of it. You sure the folks on the flight line didn't hear ya?"

That made the big man chuckle as he sat down at his desk. He pointed at the Keurig coffee maker on the small table next to the worn padded chair Lou plopped himself down at across from his desk. "Life blood?" he motioned to Lou.

He glanced at it. "Ahh, no... No thanks. I'm going to be on the road quite a bit. Decided I'd cut back so I don't go pee so often," he said as nonchalantly as if he'd been talking to his best friend. "How's Helen and the kids?"

"Good. Yep, she stays busy with her job. Sharon's in all prep-classes. She's a senior this year!"

"No kidding..." Lou said more than asked, knowing his old friend may not have heard about Terrance...bracing himself emotionally for the return question. It was something he'd prepped himself for when given this assignment, knowing he would run into people he hadn't seen in many years. "And your son?" Lou drifted, his eyes searching off as he looked for a name he no longer remembered.

"Marcus? Oh, he's a real scallywag, that one. I mean I love him and all, but...between you, me, and the wall, I'm pretty sure that boy'll have a job with his name sewn on his shirt! Y'know what I mean?" The offensive lineman-sized man started laughing heartily, made funnier in Lou's eyes by his sparkling clean-shaven dome.

Lou busted up laughing, something he hadn't expected.

"What about you all?" his friend said. "I heard the tragedy, old friend. Nobody ever knows what to say, but just know my heart went out to you. How is Julia?"

Lou felt himself get emotional, though he was not too prone to tearing up about it anymore, at least not in public. "We're coping," Lou said. "I'll try not to spin it. We're both trying to feel it out a day at a time." He drifted off on that thought.

Wally decided to get off the topic. "So why are you here at Pope, Lou?"

"Well, as you may know, once Terrance killed himself, I was no longer able to fly for the 89th," Lou reminded his buddy, referring to the 89th Airlift Wing responsible for anything related to flying the president. "And I get that. It sucks, but I get it from their perspective. They've been letting me ride out my term and career working for the public affairs office. The brass has sent me out to check on the morale of the troops."

"Well, as you can see, we're getting busy," Wallace said, stating the obvious by all the activity. "We're prepping to start moving the 82nd Airborne to Arizona and California. Probably some of 1st Special Forces, too."

"Interesting," Lou commented. "How's the team? You guys getting all the support you need? Have enough birds to support the mission?"

"Yeah, yeah, I think so," the normally jovial man said, putting his 'major hat' on for a bit. "We'll be coming home once the move is done. I mean—you're a 17 driver, right? You get it! It's just across the country...no need to keep the planes and crews deployed once the ground-pounders are at their training locations."

Lou thought about what he'd heard. "I'm assuming airborne will be getting some jump practice in southern Arizona..." His mind was thinking about the facilities for an entire division being moved out there.

"I see the gears spinning!" Wally said, chuckling. "Like I said, Cali, too. They'll be rotating units down to Arizona from Hunter-Liggett." He was referring to a large Army training base in Central California.

As he and his friend continued to chat for another half-hour, his mind was already thinking. *Arizona? I wouldn't mind getting out to Davis-Monthan again. But there's so much to do! Bliss... Hood... Norfolk... Pendleton...* It started to dawn on Freeman Louis Caldwell that he and Brandon might be at this for more than a week or two.

CHAPTER 9

Kansas City International Airport

"What are you saying exactly?" Lou grilled the Avis rental car attendant. He glanced out the window to his right, then to his wristwatch. *7:30 I wonder what we can find for supper around here.* "I can see like thirty cars right there." He pointed out the window to drive home the emphasis as he tried to maintain his cool. *As if they don't know that,* he reminded himself.

"Sir, I'm very sorry," the short thin man said, his pencil-like mustache showing a bead of sweat. "Our system has been down for two days straight. Maybe you heard most of the rental agencies were hacked? On the news? Several hundred million dollars of collision claims have been filed with our underwriters overnight. Until our people can sort through what's real, we've been ordered to ground the fleet. All of the rental services are experiencing the same issues."

"What do you suggest?" Brandon asked, keeping a higher level of composure than Lou. They'd caught a flight straight after their meeting at Fort Bragg.

"You said you two are heading to Fort Leavenworth?"

"Fort Riley," Lou corrected. It was the third time he'd mentioned the name.

"Honestly, you guys should just take an Uber to the bus depot downtown. Oh—" the youngster caught himself.

"What?" Lou asked, unamused.

"It's just that...well, there's been a lot of volatility down there every day..."

Tired and a bit hangry, Lou picked his things back up off the countertop. "Thanks." *For nothing...*

"Thank you, sir," Brandon told the counter attendant, who was obviously in his early twenties. He caught up to Lou as he made his way through a set of sliding doors. "I'm thinking chow next," he suggested. "Then maybe a hotel?"

"Food, yes. Hotel... maybe." He'd contemplated getting to the bus depot and crashing in the terminal. "Now," Lou paused as he tried to figure out how to use his Uber or Lyft app, "we need to—"

"Here it is!" Brandon said with his usual 'Leave It to Beaver' boyish charm. A newer silver Honda came streaming up to the curb near the car rental section of the airport. Lou gave him a confused look. "I ordered it like two minutes ago!" Brandon explained with humorous enthusiasm.

BUENOS AIRES NATIONAL WILDLIFE REFUGE, ARIZONA—NEAR the Mexico Border

GRANGER HIT THE TRUCK WITH A QUICK ONE-SECOND BURST with his laser range finder. 456 meters. He laid the device back onto his sniper's mat, picking up his mechanical pencil and made a few notes in his 'rite-in-the-rain' notebook. He pulled his ghillie suit completely over his face and head, burying it down in the hole in his mat. He reached both of his hands around each edge of the mat into the troughs he'd dug below that were just the right size for the lower half of his arms. Down in the dark hole he found the cell phone below his face. *Dang! Forgot to check for scorpions! Got lucky...*

With his entire head blocking the only path for light to escape into the cold desert air, Granger began to text the rest of the team. They were using their GoTenna mesh network transmitters coupled with an app on their android phones called ATAK—the civilian version of a secure private texting network used by various special operations forces.

[Granger] I count seven, range 456m

It usually took everyone a few minutes to get secure and check their messages.

[Mick] Concur 7 339m

Two minutes went by. Each of the men's spotters were less than 50 meters away, so they weren't going to bother responding.

[Granger] Anyone eyes on the source? *Only two showed up in the old truck... Where'd those other five pop up?*

He received three 'negative' responses and the chat went silent again.

Granger knew his men knew their stuff—like he was doing just then, they were all re-checking their perimeters, looking for counter-surveillance. After ensuring nobody was coming up to slit his throat, Granger began to use the magnifying night vision scope on his AR-10 to scout the far wall of the canyon. He was looking for any cartel spotters or scouts that might sneak up on Mick and Tracy.

This had been a productive trip for day one. They'd seen evidence of recent transient border crossings, though probably not for at least a week. This just validated the cartel activity to the Road Runners. The cartel would let the local coyotes find a good route, then shut them down to use it themselves. After a half hour, Granger grabbed a stick and stuck it down into his phone hole a few times, remembering to try and shoo out any scorpions this time. He repeated his light-securing procedure and texted the team.

[Granger] Let's get some winks. 2-hour shifts. Spotters first

He went back to scanning the active valley below himself, thinking about what they would do the next day to try and move quietly and find the suspected tunnel exit.

The next morning the Road Runners performed their usual near flawless pack-up. Rather than backtrack, Granger had consulted his highly detailed paper map he had bought and printed off mytopo.com. The maps came to the specific grid patterns and scale he wanted, deeply showing every contour line, stream, and manmade obstruction. He instructed Mick and Tracy to hike one valley farther west to progress south while he and Dave did the same to the east. They would each reconvene in a good roost about one kilometer south, which would put them within a mile of the border.

There was an old dry pool out there, part of an old cattle cistern system. It would be one valley farther south of Mick and Tracy across their current southwest to northeast running valley. Granger could see the saddle in the hilltop down the way that the other team would need to squirt through, should they need to check that valley and old cistern out.

Another important piece of data was that they weren't positive what they saw the night before. *It was probably drugs or weapons—not enough humans for a trafficking ring.* But that didn't mean that the trafficking wouldn't eventually come this way. And the activity was quite heavier than they'd ever seen. It was some time in the early afternoon, and he'd finally settled into his new position. Wolf was farther south this time, taking the role of scout sniper for day two. It was a mild 72 degrees Fahrenheit, and Granger had managed to score shade off an old mesquite tree. He didn't ever get within ten feet of them because of wasp nests.

Buzzz! Granger's phone wanted his attention. He carefully checked it and saw that Tracy had filled his screen with enough bad words to make Samuel L. Jackson blush.

[Granger] ???

[Tracy] Just had the biggest #@$%!* tarantula I've ever seen park on my shoulder for last #@$%^ 20 mikes!!

It took the entire team every ounce of discipline they had to not blow cover with laughter. Bob and Claude were both plugged into the texting through the mesh network public antenna registration. Each of them had the liberty to conduct full and hearty belly-laughter, which they did.

[Granger] No Medevac then? :-D

[Tracy] Bob, Need clean skivvies delivery. Most ricky-tick.

[Bob] Negative, Ghost Rider. The pattern is full.

This usually happened somewhere about mid-patrol. The men would blow off some steam when it wasn't too big a threat to do so. Granger always allowed it—after all, they were all volunteers, some of them cashing in vacation days to be here. And he just hoped it wasn't all for naught. In the last several months, the local Agent in Charge of the CBP had been slowly building a stone wall around his government agents. *And here it should be the other way,* Granger thought. *If anything, they need more of us.* This thought, like the hundred times he'd had it before, festered itself as a sliver in his mind. *As much as I don't want to, we may need to start training and growing some of those 'other' groups of unofficial border guards. If the amount of stuff we saw last night is any indicator...*

Greyhound Bus Terminal, Kansas City, Kansas

The mismatched team took their second Uber in eleven hours, from the small airport Motel 6 Brandon had convinced Lou they needed to the bus terminal on the Missouri side of downtown. There was a daily Greyhound that went to Fort Riley every morning. The cup of cheap motel tea hadn't been enough. Assuming he'd find a restroom on the bus, he opted for an even cheaper cup of coffee from the cadre of terminal vending machines. *I still think the kid might be a commie,* Lou thought. *I mean—I've been trying to cut back on coffee some. But he doesn't like it? What kind of Marine doesn't like coffee?* Out plopped a 14-ounce red paper cup with red playing cards printed on the side. Under the cards, the cup instructed the patron to look at the bottom of the card for their 'bonus' card. Lou scanned his playing hand and realized that much like his life in the last year, there wasn't much to look at. He ignored looking at the bottom.

He wandered back over to his two rolling duffle cases and the hard plastic chairs and parked himself one seat over from a snoozing coffee-hater named Brandon. Lou thought about a time in his service that he could sleep anywhere. Now he could hardly sleep at all. The nightcaps served to dampen the guilt, but it also messed up his brain chemistry. Scanning the crowd, he could see...tension. The overwhelming majority of people there didn't want to make eye contact with anyone. They just wanted to move along in a fashion that said, *Leave me alone and I'll do the same.* There were a few monitors with no noise playing throughout the terminal, mounted high up on the walls. Lou could see mild graffiti on some of the walls, and at least one spot a monitor used to exist. *Did it break? Or get stolen,* he wondered.

Most of the screens were dedicated to scrolling through travel schedules. A couple were playing local morning news. Despite the volume being turned off, he could see the predictable cycle of news reset itself every few minutes—weather, traffic, sports, and puff pieces. *Nothing about that mob the driver said he was avoiding,* Lou noted. He started scanning the crowd again. It was a typical urban American collection—white, black, a few Hispanic or Asian. The young looked bored. The old looked weathered. Most people were looking at their phones. A few had hoodies pulled up to catch a catnap. It was November. Lou couldn't figure out why some people would use a cheap cotton hoodie instead of a good winter coat. One thing stood out above all, though. Tension was in the air.

"Attention in the terminal," the PA system blared. Brandon stirred, his blue eyes wrinkled from the mini-nap. "Now boarding for Lawrence, Topeka, Manhattan, Fort Riley, and Salina. Terminal D."

The message repeated itself as the herd started to get up out of seats and wander out through the glass doors that led to the proper side of the terminal to find slot D. Lou handed his two rollers to a grumpy middle-aged attendant who was tossing bags into the bus's underbelly as if he was getting a bonus for style. He kept his blue backpack with himself, pulling it from two shoulders to just one as he migrated through the slow line. Brandon repeated the process behind him. Most of his fellow travelers were using their phones to show an electronic barcode as their boarding pass. Lou was feeling much older than he was when he handed the other bus-barn attendant a paper pass, trying to keep the cold unfinished coffee from spilling. The man paid no attention to anyone as he boarded people.

Feeling the coffee do its magic, Lou decided he needed an aisle seat. *No need climbing over someone. Gonna be several stops until Fort Riley, may as well be ready to go.* He moved back through the filling bus, remembering they always had a unique metallic, diesel, and polyester smell to them. There were no more rows with side-by-side seats still open.

"Looks like we're splitting, partner," Lou said in a hushed tone back toward Brandon.

"Good!" the young man quipped. "I can go back to my walk with the Lord!"

"Is that what you're calling sleep now?" Lou posited. He decided to take an aisle seat on the right side, next to a tall slender man who was already leaning against the window, hoodie over his head as he napped. Within ten minutes, the bus was crawling the four blocks out to Highway 670, the temporary name for Interstate Highway 70 for the downtown core of KC.

After a few more minutes, the bus was rolling smoothly, most of the traffic being on the east-bound side during the morning commute. Lou had just stowed his flight cap, called a garrison cap by non-pilots, and zipped up his brown leather A-2 flight jacket to try to catch a few winks himself, when he heard, "'Scuse me." He looked up to the young man seated next to the window. "Sorry, sir, I need to go to the lav..." The young, lighter black man with blue-green eyes was striking in appearance.

"Of course!" Lou said, hopping up and forward. He turned around to be ready to reseat himself. "Will be needin' to head that way myself in a minute!" he joked.

The young man gave a quick courteous grin that quickly dissolved back into a look that said he just wanted to be left alone and headed toward the rear toward the lavatory.

I-70, KANSAS

AFTER WASHING HIS HANDS, MORRIS SPLASHED A LITTLE water on his face. *Might as well wake up a bit.* He was still worried about his folks. He'd gotten a text from ThatNub that classes were continuing, sending him back on a Friday to try to make his afternoon class and at least go talk to professors and TAs about other makeup work. He left the lavatory, and his seatmate was right there, stepping aside to replace Morris in the tiny water closet.

A few minutes later, both men were back in their seats. "Mornin'," Morris heard.

"Good morning," Morris replied, using the polite speech for strangers his mama had drilled into him and Marvin from day one. *What's this dude's deal? Air Force?* "I see the flat cap," Morris said pointing to the 'pisscutter' cap he'd spotted hanging on Lou's left hip earlier.

"Yeah," Lou acknowledged. "Colonel Freeman Caldwell at your service," he said politely, sticking his right hand out. "Everyone calls me Lou."

"Morris," he replied. "Dooghan. Everyone calls me Thumper."

"Thumper? Like the rabbit?" Lou inquired, intrigued.

"I guess," Morris said, smirking and rolling his eyes as he turned to scan out the window at the highway. *Where are we...*

"Well, don't leave me hangin', Thumper!" Lou prodded. "We got a lot of minutes to kill. I'm heading to Fort Riley. You?"

"I go to K-State," he replied. The look on Lou's face was semi-blank. "In Manhattan, right before Riley," Morris explained.

"Ahhh," his seatmate said as the bulb came on. "So why Thumper? You kill a lot of rabbits or something?"

Morris grinned a bit more. "Heh—no! It's...it's a call-sign." Then he realized he was staring at a bomber jacket. "Oh, wow! I bet you got one o' those, too. Are you a pilot?" Suddenly this conversation was worth having.

"I used to be," Lou explained. "Now I push pencils," he smiled softly. "Going to go push some pencils at the army base for a few days.

"What'd you used to fly?" Morris asked, hoping the man would regale him with a few cool fighter-jet stories to pass time.

"Mostly C-17s," Lou gave his canned answer. He'd learned long ago not to mention the A-10, as people always wanted to know why he'd stopped. "They call it the Globemaster." He could see the blank look on the young man's face. "For hauling large volumes of goods. Everything from pallets of food to vehicles."

"That's cool, man," Morris said, slipping out of stranger manners subconsciously. "What's the coolest thing you ever hauled?"

Lou expected that question next. "On my last flight assignment, I was the primary co-pilot for hauling the president's limo or the Marine One helicopters around the world."

"No kidding!" Morris said, more excitedly than he'd felt in weeks. "That's cool, dude! Which president?"

"Mostly the last knucklehead," Lou said. "But I flew one trip for good ol' J.A. back when he made his first post-inaugural trip."

"President Allen? Really? Did you get to meet him? Was he cool?"

"Uh—no. I mean no, I haven't met him. I hear he's cool, though," Lou said, smiling at the young man's enthusiasm. "Do you like him?"

Morris thought for a moment. "I don't think I like any of them..." He thought for another two seconds. "But I like that he left his party and shook things up. My folks have always been democrats. They're both in big unions. But even they're getting a bit put-off by things. If someone held a gun to my head and said pick a party, I guess I'd pick Libertarian...now that they're actually winning races."

"So that's part of the cycle, isn't it," Lou suggested. "People always vote for the lesser of two evils because they think they have to."

"Right!" Morris said. "They aren't even voting for that guy or lady anymore. They vote against the other one! That seems so jacked up to me."

"That's 'cause it is, Thumper," Lou agreed.

"So did you get a good hand?" Morris asked.

"Uhhhh...." Lou said, confused.

"The coffee..."

"Oh...nope. Garbage hand." He raised the paper cup to look at the bottom. "But an ace in the hole!" he said with forced enthusiasm. "I wonder what that means....?" He looked back at Morris. "You still haven't explained that call-sign to me."

"Oh—right!" Morris said to his new friend. "It's from MilSim," he explained. *This Air Force dude is lost, isn't he? Oh, the irony...* "Military simulation? Airsoft?" he quizzed Lou to gauge if he knew about any of it.

"Riiiight...gotcha, now," Lou said finally. "Like paintball."

"Sort of. Different guns. We use biodegradable BBs. We can use realistic rifles and magazines. Most leagues revolve around teams playing some version of capture-the-flag," he explained.

"So you must lay a lot of suppressing fire, if your call-sign is Thumper," Lou guessed.

"Back when I started, yes. That was in high school. My twin brother was the one who was really into it. I just did it to make sure he wasn't getting recruited into a gang or somethin'."

"You still play?"

"Captain of my team!" Morris smiled. "We're a man down, if you want to come to practice tonight!"

"I have a couple of meetings today and tomorrow," Lou grinned. "And I'd probably pull a hammy or something! Don't want you college punks showing me up!" Both men got a good laugh at that. Lou got serious again after a moment. "So the gang thing. Was that an issue where you grew up?" he wondered.

"Still is," Morris told him. "I'm from an older neighborhood in KC. It's getting real bad. Thing is, people are actually starting to support them. The gangs are getting bolder as people riot."

"Where do you stand on the protest stuff?" Lou earnestly wanted to know.

"Well, I get it. There are bad cops out there, and it seems like white folks are having the hardest time accepting that. But I also know they ain't all bad. We had a school resource officer that was cool as sh—" Morris caught himself. "Well, he was chill. But when the whole defund movement started, he was the first to lose his job." Morris turned his head toward the window again, remembering. "Ironic."

"Where's your brother now?" Lou asked. "He at K-State, too?"

"Uhhh, no...He wasn't good about keeping his grades up in school. Was always too eager to play around. He went into the Army, but..." The new-found anger resurfaced on Morris' face.

"What?" Lou prodded.

"He was supposed to get out next month. But my folks just told me they extended him for a year."

This surprised Lou. "Stop-loss? Hell, I didn't even realize they were doing that," he said, embarrassed.

Morris looked at Lou again. "I guess that doesn't affect officers, does it?"

"No, actually, they can do it to officers, too." The pair grew quiet for a minute. "Did your brother say why?"

Morris searched his memory. "My folks said something about trying to avoid a draft." He turned back to scan the highway, missing the new concerned look on Lou's face.

Lou stood up and retrieved his backpack from the shelf above the pair of seats. He unzipped the top pouch and dug around for his business card holder. After fishing out a card he had made to fit his mission, "Here, Thumper," Lou said, shoving the card in front of the college student. "Send me an email or text sometime. It's fun talking with you anyhow, and I can't help your brother. But knowing how it affects you and your family is somewhat related to the pencils I push."

Morris took the card. "You know, most folks just use QR codes on their phone now..." he educated the Air Force officer.

"Well... as an old pilot, I guess I still believe in paper checklists, so to speak. I mean, what happens if you need a number in a desperate moment and your phone gets broken... or stolen... or there's not power..."

"Alright, alright...you got me!" the young man concurred. He scanned both sides of the old-school tech. "You know, you never told me what your call-sign is, either..."

Lou finally relented. "We don't really use them in the delivery fleet. But when I was a young pilot, I flew A-10s. It was Super Bert."

Morris cracked up. "Like that Muppet from Sesame Street?" He kept grinning as he looked back out the bus window. *This cat's pretty cool for an old dude...*

CHAPTER 10

Bachelor Officer Quarters, Fort Riley, Kansas

Sir,

Thank you for allowing me to skip the evening reports for the first several days of this mission. Henceforth, I will submit one every night, pending a proper Wi-Fi connection that allows me to access the secure server. Per your instruction, I'll leave specifics out of the written report and call you directly via the secure SAT phone for serious matters. Other than some domestic travel issues related to hacking and internet disruptions, both Captain McDonald and myself have had an uneventful trip thus far.

I started this assignment with a certain expectation of what I would find. Regarding the deployments of the units I was briefed prior to leaving for Fort Bragg, there are no anomalies to mention. I spoke with contacts at Pope Field, who were somewhat surprised about the domestic nature of their mission, but otherwise in high spirits. We also had a chance to meet the Sergeant Major for one of the airborne companies. He admitted that the troops are a bit confused as to why they're deploying in such large numbers for training so soon after getting back from their last deployment, but he also advised that morale was not an issue.

We've had a chance to discuss the sudden movements with some of the civilian populace. The vibe they're picking up on, sir, is that something is 'amiss'. One group of ladies surmised that simply from the volume of cars on a train carrying equipment. We've struck up multiple conversations with civilians—restaurants, hotels, buses, gas stations—there is a general feeling that they're being 'hoodwinked', in the words of a Vietnam veteran in the hotel dining room this evening. There seems to be a declining faith in the current administration, particularly by anyone who is concerned about the Rainier event and the uprising of violent riots in most cities.

I've spent two days touring and talking to elements of Big Red 1 in Kansas. The troops are aware of the movements at Bragg and the rumors of deployments run rampant. This is being validated, in their minds, by the announcements last Friday re: unit deployments from Forts Hood and Bliss. One savvy corporal even mentioned the ship transfers from Norfolk to the west coast. As expected, he did not have kind things to say about the mothers of his brother and sister sailors, but he saw the movements as an obvious indicator that they're not being told everything.

One Captain from the Seattle area admitted in my confidence that she is considering going AWOL. She is extremely concerned about family, as I imagine most from the northwest states are. It isn't just the willingness to abandon post, sir. She's angry. I can't sugarcoat it, and I know you wouldn't want me to. She feels that the troop movements to the west are misplaced political theater. She demanded I let my superiors know that she feels betrayed by the president. Her words, sir.

We've traveled now by car, plane, and bus. The latter was due to the computer ransomware attack on the rental car companies that made the news. That and the other cyber events, coupled with the rapid inflation and spotty power and internet issues, is starting to eat at people's moods, both military and civilian. But despite all this negativity, when I have time to really discuss life with folks, such as on the bus ride yesterday, I get a sense of hope. I'm not sure at this point if it is naivety or wishful thinking. But that could just be my own pessimism, too.

Tomorrow we'll attempt to try a car rental agency once more. We're moving towards Killeen. And I hope to let you know, General, without sounding too forward, just how much I appreciate this detail. I met a young man yesterday... Later in the evening as I reflected on our ninety-minute conversation on the bus, it made me realize just how much I miss Terrance. I was moved to tears, something that young Kansas college senior will never know. I miss my son, sir, something I'm sure you can relate to, given the number of bottle caps in your snifter. I guess this trip is helping me clear my head a bit.

V/R, Col. Caldwell

SANCHES FARM, NORTHEAST OF MANHATTAN, KANSAS

"WE REALLY NEED TO FIND US AN EIGHTH PERSON FOR THE team," William 'ThatNub' Easton told his roommate.

"Agreed," Morris said. "But it needs to be someone with experience." The thought of dealing with another hothead freshman with no actual experience–like Super B—made them both shudder. "I'd rather have seven than another freshman." Practice had been over when it became dark forty minutes earlier. Most of the team had slipped out already.

"You're probably right," Nub said. "I figure if there were any not already on a team, we'd have heard by now." The pair, along with Jon SuperFly Sanches and his uncle Jorge, were sipping lukewarm beers around the firepit. Morris hadn't had the time to get ice. The power outage that afternoon had lasted four hours. Jorge was conserving his ice for cooling freshly hunted deer for his planned coming hunting trip.

"You boys be sure to clean up your cans tonight!" Jorge instructed as he stood to go inside. "Mama been getting' on me. No Bueno!"

"Sorry, Tio," all three college students chimed.

Morris immediately stood to start picking up the cans and cardboard boxes. "Let's go," he nudged Nub with a tap to his foot, which was resting on a piece of stood-up firewood.

Nub stood up, as did Jon. "How's the bike running, Fly?" Nub asked, eyeballing the street legal enduro bike. It was a six-year-old KTM 350 Jon had picked up used in the summer. It had the requisite horn and lights for riding on the road. Much like a motocross dirt bike, it was meant for rugged off-road riding, with a beefy and high-riding suspension. Enduro bikes normally came with engines that were more durable and larger gas tanks, as they were meant for races across broad forests and deserts, not loop tracks.

"Running good! I just got new skins for it!" he said excitedly, showing off his new knobby tires.

"You just might be able to ride that thing when the snow finally gets here," Morris said as he tossed the paper bag of burnables into the fire pit. He had a plastic bag of beer cans destined for the nearby recycle tub.

"That's the plan—say!" Jon said, suddenly eyeballing Morris wildly. "The dude at Dirty Dick's Motorsports said they have a Husqvarna on consignment! You should think about getting one so that poor Nub doesn't always have to haul you around town!"

"Damn, SuperFly...that's the best idea you've had in months, amigo!" ThatNub agreed.

Morris smirked, suddenly feeling ganged up on. "I'd probably kill myself on one of those..." *Still...it would be kinda cool,* he thought.

"Come sit on it!" Jon encouraged.

Morris was hesitant, but he started to walk that way, caught in the beastly bike's tractor beam. Then he stopped and shook his head. "Nope! Nope. I want to get some new gear before the tourney, including a set of nods. The print-on-demand store hasn't been doing too well now that summer's over," he admitted.

Like many youths, Morris had learned early on the best way to make money as a college student was in some form of online business that he could run at his own convenience between his variable college schedules. His ex-girlfriend had been his designer, making several dozen cool graphics for a print-on-demand/direct ship tee-shirt shop he had online. His best-selling line was a collection of shirts about an airsoft-playing cat called 'Combat Kitty'. In the spring quarter, he really ramped up production on new designs before summer break that would earn enough to pad his income over the trickle-in sales the rest of the year.

"What's wrong, old-man?" his roomie joked. "Chicken?"

"Yeah, they got a couple of quads, too, if you're scared," Jon agreed in fake seriousness. "You can get a rack for taking your walker with you when you go places."

Morris started heading for Nub's car, trying to evade the onslaught before it devolved into jokes about adult diapers and discount meals at Denny's. "You knuckleheads actually watch the news lately? There're massive shipping delays due to the trucks and ports being jammed up after that earthquake. You boys might want to think about saving your money for stuff like food."

"Or airsoft gear?" Nub countered.

"Hey! I said part of it was night vision," Morris objected. "That would be extremely valuable in a world with no food!"

"Easy, bro," Jon said, smiling. "We're just jokin' here. You startin' to sound like one of those survivalist dudes!"

You might be on to something, Morris agreed in his head. "Catch you manana," he said in his normal calm and collected nature, turning toward the passenger seat of Nub's old Ford Bronco.

Nub and SuperFly made their goodbyes, and Nub hopped into the driver's seat. He let the older rig warm up while they watched Jon fire up the bike, don his coat and helmet, and scooter back toward Manhattan and campus.

Still looking down the dirt farm road at the departing bike to his left, Nub asked, "Are you serious about getting more gear? Nods, even?"

"Thinking about it," Morris said. "I have some money saved. Part of me wants to keep holding onto it... part of me thinks my money might be worth more now than later." The finance major had been conditioned in college to look at safe, long-term investments. He believed in those, but the thing they never talked about was that those also relied on a stable social situation. *Sometimes spending your money on things you'll need later is a form of inflation protection,* he had figured out on his own.

Nub slipped it into reverse and cranked the wheel left, just nosing out and around the Sanches' farm truck. They started down the trail of Kansas dust just stirred up by SuperFly. "Like what?" he asked.

"New mag pouch," Morris started, closing his eyes for a moment to see his shopping cart in his head. "Not just a belt pouch, but a chest carrier...Let's see... new quick-disconnects for my weapon mounted gear..." He paused for a moment, finally cautiously adding, "Was even thinking about getting a ten-pack of AR mags." *Wait for it...*

"What! Like—real AR mags? You don't even have an AR!"

"Uh-huh...well...after what happened at my folks last week... that's gonna change, too..."

"What!" Nub exclaimed. "I'm your best friend! Why is this the first I'm hearing about it?"

"Geez, Nub! Calm down!" Morris laughed. The entire team had often pondered the day they would all be able to afford pistols and rifles and go take some real tactical classes. Morris knew his friend was being excited, not opposed to the idea.

ThatNub's voice suddenly changed to the deep rasp one might hear from an old Kentucky Colonel. "I say son—I say, I say son!"

Morris cut his buddy off. "Stop! Not the stupid Foghorn Leghorn thing, bro. Not again!" Nub was famous for doing horrible impressions at moments his friends were trapped with no choice but to listen.

"I say son!" Nub continued imitating the southern gentleman

chicken. "You and I ah' gonna head on down to the lo-cull gun-stoah, seeee...."

Both young men busted a gut, laughing about it as Nub continued the thirteen-minute trek back to their apartment. He'd pointed out that their teammate Floyd Presley—call sign Elvis—had a sister and brother-in-law who owned a gun store over in Rossville, near Topeka.

"We haven't had classes in over a week. I guess we're grabbing Floyd and heading to Rossville tomorrow," Morris said. In all the uncertainty he'd been feeling for a few weeks, he suddenly had a moment of anticipatory excitement.

THE WHITE HOUSE

"THANK YOU FOR HOSTING ME FOR THIS INTERVIEW, MR. President."

"Well, Angelica, as a few of my predecessors have found out the hard way, a *60 Minutes* interview is like car insurance."

This caused the renowned and expert journalist Angelica Brash to laugh and smile a bit. "Like a policy you don't really want but know you have to have?" she laughed.

"Something like that," Jeremiah Allen confessed with a small chuckle. He knew that soon enough, he'd be feeling the heat in both his collar and the chair he was sitting on. "Necessary evil," he said, keeping the politician's grin charade up for as long as he needed to.

"Tell me, Mr. President...Why did you choose the China Room for tonight's discussion? In recent administrations, the Map Room has taken on a role for these types of interviews..."

Softball questions to get started, huh, Angelica? Jeremiah thought. "Something different," he said. "I wanted the American people to see the wonderful collections of China that date all the way back to President Washington."

The seasoned journalist and former Washington D.C. CBS affiliate lead anchor listened and stared for an awkward second. This interview was perhaps the one thing she still needed to land the coveted lead national anchor spot. "I see," she said with a mild tone. "Such a beautiful gallery," she agreed, looking around.

Seems fitting considering where tonight's conversation is headed, Jeremiah added inside his own head.

"We'll start with the Air Force hacking incident, sir," Angelica said, getting the show truly started. "Does the FBI have any leads on whether or not it was hactivists versus foreign cyber warfare?" She was referring to the incident that happened several days prior. Out of the blue, several units across the Air Force received orders to man crews, load planes, and drop supplies over the Seattle-Tacoma metro area. Those supplies were almost immediately confiscated by various gangs. "I mean, here we are at just past three weeks since the largest natural disasters in recorded history..."

Here it comes, Jeremiah thought. His staff had been prepping him for the following questions for two days straight.

"...and it took a hacker to trick the Air Force into loading C-17s and C-130s and airdropping supplies to the people in Washington State." She left it dangling there, having already asked one question in the mix. She was saving rapid-fire questions for when he started to squirm.

"This was obviously a serious breach of cyber security. There's a large collaboration of agencies investigating. The FBI is in charge of the overall investigation, but CISA, the DIA, the CIA, the Air Force, Space Force... there are a lot of elements involved. It just goes to show how fast these types of technologies evolve." *Just answer the question asked,* Jeremiah reminded himself. *Don't dig the hole for her...*

"So, you're saying your administration had no intention of shipping those supplies?"

"That isn't what you asked, Angelica..." He'd been advised by his staff not to play vernacular chess with her, but he just couldn't help himself.

"Meaning..." she prodded with the grin a snake might have if it could smile.

"Meaning please don't phrase a statement about an answer you've asked that wasn't part of what I said," he smiled back.

"That seems a bit defensive to the American people, Mr. President," she stated.

Now you speak for all Americans? With almost any president in his first term, this would have worked. Jeremiah Allen, while not wanting to damage re-election chances like any president, knew things were at play in the coming months that would make people long-forget about this interview. Might as well stand my ground a little, he realized. "I feel it is honest, Angelica. Not defensive. You ask a question. I'll answer it. You ask another question." He left it at that.

"Very well, did you have any intention of sending the supplies from Texas, Oklahoma, and Delaware?"

"We have been—"

"How do you respond to the allegations that you're failing the people of the pacific Northwest? Are you the least bit concerned?

Need to remind her I'm not afraid. Jeremiah sat there with a poker face, not saying a word.

Finally, after five seconds of prime-time Sunday evening silence, Angelica Brash prodded," Mr. President..."

"Just making sure you're done cutting me off, Angelica," he said coolly. "Of course, we care. The jet-capable airports of every runway within four hundred miles of SeaTac airport have taken damage that makes them impossible to use. The vast majority of piers in Puget Sound are broken, many with vessels that were broken and sank right where they were tied up. The highways are clogged with broken overpasses and areas where the earth split wide open—"

"You're telling us what we already know, Mr. President. What I—"

"Stop demanding a simple answer to a complicated question, Angelica," Jeremiah countered, cutting her off in return. "Because the infrastructure is broken, we've been forced to send in supplies by airdrop, which we have done. We—"

"So now you're claiming that airdrops had already happened?"

Jeremiah stayed calm, knowing this was coming. He could feel himself getting a bit warm from the studio lights nestled in two spots on the China Room's beige carpet. "We did that within two days, but we made some discoveries."

"Like what, sir?"

"For one, the Emergency Operations Center, which was destroyed and had to be re-established in Vancouver, Washington, reported that the bulk of the airdrop supplies never made it into the hands of the local agencies."

"Oh?"

"And—" Jeremiah continued, "our specialists in FEMA evaluated the amount of supplies we could send. If we ran ten planes constantly, around the clock, just today, we would be hitting three percent of anticipated needs."

"Mr. President, that seems like an awfully low—"

"And," Jeremiah was on a roll, "there is an energy issue in the west that both complicates, and is complicated by, the disaster's impact to the internet and the economy. We've had to order the remaining relief supplies to remain staged in their current locations as the unrest continues to unfold in most western cities."

"Yes, sir, about that—as the nation's first Libertarian president, where do you stand on the curfews and National Guard deployments in Denver, Phoenix, and Sacramento? And do you think that will continue to be an ongoing action by the governors?"

"First and foremost, I do support the governors making the decisions that best suit their states, more so than me telling them what to do." Angelica started to open her mouth and Jeremiah just put a hand up to stop her. "Yes, I know that both of the other parties will jump all over that statement. I don't care. I tread cautiously with things like curfews, but I do understand them. In part, it is a by-product of the system we've allowed to trickle into place since the beginning of the twentieth century. We have a court and criminal justice system that gets bogged down with trials and appeals for far longer than they should be. Our horribly high prisoner ratio as compared to other countries reflects that while some people get locked up for far too long, some never do. As a result, there is a criminal element in most cities that is taking advantage of the issues at play. The curfews may be the mayors and governors only option to give their police and Guard forces a chance to regain some control."

"You've always claimed to be a pro-rights candidate, Mr. President," Angelica shifted the conversation, "and that includes guns. Do you feel that was a mistake as we see the levels of gang violence escalating by three...four-hundred percent in some of these cities?" She nudged her large reading glasses back up her nose.

"Two parts to that, Angelica. One, I am proudly pro-rights, and yes, that includes responsible gun ownership. Two, you need to call this creature by its real name—cartel violence."

"Cartels?" the journalist asked, with just short of a mocking tone.

"I'm sure you're hearing the rumors about a cartel organization in the northwest," Jeremiah continued. "Our intelligence suggests this may be part of a larger organized effort. Call it a 'bloc' of several cartels, if you will. But as you are well aware, there are extended blackouts happening in California, Arizona, Nevada, Colorado... The Cascadia disaster was just the first domino. Now that it has fallen, the subversive players are helping things along with everything from hacking to organized crime."

"If that's true, why would you be telling us tonight, sir? Isn't that the sort of thing you don't want them to know that you know?"

Gotcha! "There's enough leaks, Angelica. Of course they know we know. But shouldn't our public know? Shouldn't your viewers have a full realization of what's happening in their communities? Shouldn't me admitting it tonight happen if there's even a chance that they'll rethink whatever they're up to?" *Don't your viewers' lives matter?* he stopped himself from saying as he went quiet.

"Can you share more, Mr. President?" Angelica said, knowing the point was carrying in his favor for the moment.

"I don't want to be too specific, obviously, in a way that could endanger on-going investigations, but I will say this—this administration will assist the governors to the best extent possible. On a federal level, I've been asking all the federal agencies to augment the Customs and Border Protection folks with ten percent of their active agents. This does bring with it a risk that those agencies are letting other critical investigations go idle, but—"

"Do you regret shutting down DHS?" she said suddenly, trying to put him on the defensive once again.

"Absolutely not. Remember, in the age of air travel, every state is literally a border state. We're actively helping the states beef up their Guard units and city-ran port security details. As it should be."

Angelica Brash was quiet while she consulted her tablet notes, hoping the president would get nervous and talk on his own. Jeremiah had been reminded in his prep work not to fall for that trap. After nine slow and awkward seconds, she looked back up. "Mr. President, what is your take on the growing war drums between China and Russia, and have you and Secretary Buttermaker been engaged with them at all?"

"I think that for thirty years, there's been a growing shift as those two countries took certain strides to become superpowers—once again for Russia, and for the first time, China. Perhaps all that strength in one hemisphere is looking for an outlet. And yes, we're engaged to the extent that they want us to be. Both countries have offered to assist us in this trying time in our nation's history."

"But..." she led Jeremiah, sensing he was holding back.

"But they seem to be more intent on focusing on each other. They've both been moving their navies closer to each other. They've both been sending troops to their mutual border. I think the world has enough problems right now."

"Would you support one country over the other, if they did go to war?"

"Our position, as long as I'm president, will always be to stay out of other countries' conflicts and support our allies if seriously threatened."

"Then why is your administration shifting troops and even part of the east coast fleet west? What is it you're not telling us, Mr. President?"

That China tried to sink one of our submarines, I suppose, he thought to himself. Jeremiah gave an ever-so-slight upturned grin, one of warmth. "There's a lot of turmoil in the west, Angelica. Government's only purpose, in my eyes, is to protect the citizens and their rights. That is the motive behind any and everything you see this administration doing."

CHAPTER 11

Motel 6 East, El Paso, Texas

"Morning, Carmela!" the hotel's assistant manager, Lupita Suarez, said in her usual cheerful tone.

"Good morning, Lupe," Rosie replied in her usual forced fake enthusiasm. *Not exactly what I thought I'd be doing undercover,* 'Carmela' thought daily. She'd worked at this hotel for over two years. It was but one of many stops in El Aguila cartels revolving list of places to conduct drug trafficking business. Knowing it was on the rotation, Rosie had landed herself the job using her disfigured hand as a selling point. *Now you can claim you employ the disabled!* she had told them as she aced the job interview. It had not taken the cute Latina's missing fingers very long to attract Eduardo's twisted attention.

Rosie was a part-time hotel maid, which required being at work in time to stock her cart and get started cleaning the rooms after the early departures. The hotel sat just north of Interstate Highway 10. There was no removing the ingrained smell of burnt diesel and desert dirt, but that was true of the entire city anyhow. She went to the supply closet on the outside of the B building in the corridor that led between it and the primary A building. After stocking her cart, she checked her list of rooms ready to clean and moved the cart down toward the courtyard. Taking a right at the pool, Rosie pushed the cart to the far end of the B building rooms.

She took her RFID card and opened room 147, starting a process that she could have easily performed, even if the room hadn't been on the day's cleaning list. She walked directly to the window and opened the curtains and blinds. After turning off the air conditioner —*Why do they always leave it running*? — she stripped the bedding and dragged it out the door to rest near her cart. Casually looking around to ensure another maid or maintenance worker wasn't in the vicinity, she went back into Room 147 and closed the door. She moved to the queen bed's nightstand, the one furthest from the bathroom, and got down on her knees next to it. Reaching past the lamp and phone cables she felt around as far back as her arm could reach, finding the familiar one-gallon Ziploc bag.

Standing up, she pulled the cheap burner cell out of the bag and plugged its cable into the small USB charging port built directly into the base of the modern hotel lamp. Rosie spent fifteen minutes prepping the room, just as she did fifteen to twenty times per day. Before she left, she picked up the cell phone, checking its memory to ensure no guests had found and played with it. Seeing everything was clear, she opened the text feature and typed in the memorized number, texted the digit "1". She gave it three seconds, erased the sent message and phone history, reversed the process to power down the phone, and put it back in its hiding spot.

Rosie had just performed half of the modern dead-drop procedure —the half most people thought of as *leaving the mark*. In the Cold War, spies would literally leave a chalk or sharpie mark on the side of a mailbox or other such permanent feature to let their handlers know they had planted something to be retrieved. In the modern era, hiding a burner phone was so much simpler. Phone booths were removed. Mailboxes were routinely tagged by artists, particularly in El Paso. There was just too much risk an outside and unplanned factor would make the mark disappear. Only once had Rosie ever turned the phone on and seen a "1" waiting for her, followed by instructions—the time Jared met with her to let her know her sister had been ill but recovered.

After finishing Room 147, Rosie finished walking off the open-air corridor to her right, directly into the motel's back lot, taking the room's trash with her. She headed to the dumpster and tossed in the trash. Looking around once more and seeing nobody, she went behind the dumpster and retrieved the small plastic bag and recording device from the pocket in her maid's smock, sticking it behind and slightly underneath the dumpster's right rear corner. Within an hour, a seemingly homeless Texas Ranger would push his old beat-up shopping cart —complete with holey tarp and trash bags full of clothes— up the alley behind the hotel and search the dumpster for something to eat. And a half hour after that, The Texas Rangers would be listening to the most recent of several meetings between El Aguila cartel's El Paso division, corrupt Judge Jefferson Moyer, and El Paso Police Department Lt. Troy English.

INTERSTATE HIGHWAY 35, SOUTH OF OKLAHOMA CITY

"I STILL DON'T GET WHAT YOU'RE DOING," JULIA'S SLIGHTLY irritated voice played over the rented Ford Explorer's speakers.

Lou was trying his best not to raise his voice. *She knows Brandon is listening,* he thought. *I'm going to be pissed if she starts up in front of him.* He glanced over at the Marine, who was donning his earbuds to listen to an audiobook on his phone. The soft rolling plains of grass, occasionally dotted with small groves of elm, oak, or pecan trees slid by the Explorer's windows at 70 MPH, a blur under the light gray sky.

"We're just out making sure that what the brass is being told is legit," he said, downplaying why. *Just be happy with the promotion and don't ask too many questions,* he said in his head.

"But you had no problem getting the rental car today?"

"Was easy-peasy today. Not sure why. Heh—" he snorted as he thought out loud. "Maybe they actually paid the ransom to the cyber hackers." *That's a scary thought. It'll never stop once they do.*

After a long silence, Julia finally broke the ice on something. "I talked to a realtor yesterday."

Lou felt his temples flare as he instantly got hot with anger. "You aren't doing a damn thing with that house while I'm on the road. Especially list it for sale."

"We could have enough from a sale to put a nice down payment on something smaller. Something a little closer to your hometown. Probably have a really tiny mortgage." Her voice was cold and methodical, like she'd rehearsed the speech.

"I still need time, Julia," Lou said firmly. "I just don't know if I can close this chapter just yet."

"What about what I need?" she pled. "You're not the only one suffering, Louis!"

"There's bigger things to worry about, right now," he retorted. "We just saw a massive protest in Oklahoma City. Luckily, they stayed on the city blocks and didn't block the freeway, like what happened in Denver and San Francisco the other day. There's something afoot in this country, Jules. Or...multiple somethings. Please! Please just wait on this house selling garbage for a while."

"And there lies the real problem, Lou! What I want is 'garbage' to you!"

"I get that, I really do," Lou replied. "And I'm sorry I chose that word. We've been listening to a lot of AM radio on the road, where they talk about these events in more depth. The farther west we get, the spottier the utilities are, sometimes for days now. Inflation is starting to take off. There are foreign hackers toying with our country constantly. People are getting pulled out of their cars by coordinated mobs. Some states have stopped exporting power and started blocking travel from certain directions. Every city is now activating National Guard units. The internet and cloud are spotty at best. It makes it difficult for me to send secure emails to my bosses. There just seems to be a dog-eat-dog vibe that I can't quite expla—"

Honk-Hooonnnkkkkkk! Screeeeecchhhh!!

A semi-truck that Lou had started to pass cut off his Explorer, blaring on the air horn and hitting his brakes. Lou swerved onto the left shoulder of the highway, crossing the small, grooved strips meant to wake people up. *Dammmmnnnn!* He hit his own brakes, the anti-lock feature pulsing his car down without skidding as he rapidly approached a large chunk of old, blown-out truck tire. Brandon stripped his earbuds off and grabbed the handle built into the column by the window.

"Lou? Lou!" he could hear Julia screaming in the speakers.

"Wait one!" the old pilot yelled.

It was only his years as an Air Force pilot that had trained him to be able to speak while operating in his fight-or-flight reaction. He cut back to the right, now safely behind the semi who was fully in his lane. *What the hell!* Lou looked to the right and couldn't believe his eyes. A long procession of Harley Davidson motorcycles was entering the highway with no regard, jamming up the on-ramp and right-side lanes. Hundreds of them. *This ain't no joy-riding club!* Lou thought with anger and amped-up adrenaline.

"Lou!" Julia continued to yell.

Ignoring her, he checked his mirrors, realizing that everyone had slowed. *No danger of getting rear-ended, I think...* There was a growing group of vehicles behind him, though, that very well could start piling up. The semi ahead of Lou was holding steady at 25 MPH. Lou eased up a bit to create a safety gap. He also wanted to check out the procession. Even though he was now close to two hundred yards past the on-ramp, bikes were still entering the highway.

"Whew! Nice flyin', Super Bert!" Brandon exclaimed with great relief.

"Some sort of motorcycle gang just came onto the highway," Lou explained to his wife. "A semi nearly ran me over trying to get out of their way. Dozens of them—maybe hundreds!"

He was slowly calming down, feeling his pulse slow a bit as the sudden threat dissolved. The rumble of the choppers, created by their big twin-cylinder engines with zero-baffle exhaust pipes, roared past him on the right. It was deafening. He looked at the bikes and their riders.

"Red and gold patches. Identical on every one of them. Most of them have whips hanging from the handlebars, too. These guys look like they just rode out of a Mad Max movie!" Lou wasn't much of a sport shooter and had only ever owned one shotgun. He suddenly wished he were armed.

"Maybe you should find a place to pull off and take a break," he heard Julia suggest.

"Nice to know you still care," he said. She said nothing in reply. Finally, "Look, I'll call you tonight." The pair hung up without even saying goodbye.

"What's going on with that gang?" Brandon asked, still shocked, still mesmerized as the horde of bikes continued to file past in a loud roar.

"Until today, I'd have argued over calling a motorcycle club a gang," Lou said. He silently continued to analyze what they'd just experienced. *That truck could've just wiped them all out. Shoot—even I could've in this rental. So what happened?* He thought more deeply. *It's about respect... territory... animal instinct. The truck driver was worried about their lives. The bikers knew that and took his right-of-way. They knew at the risk of their own lives that they were above the rest of us in the pecking order... the food chain. It's almost as if the packs are starting to form...*

Tucson, AZ

Granger turned right out of his Catalina Foothills neighborhood onto River Road, headed west. In a scant five minutes he would reach his destination. He punched the touchscreen on the F-250's radio, turning off the podcast app on his smartphone that had automatically cued itself as he started the quick trek. He switched to a classic rock station, but as expected, it was at a commercial break. *11:45*, Granger thought as he glanced at the screen's clock. *Running on time.*

He was on the way to a noon appointment at the Customs and Border protection office on nearby Oracle Road. *If you're not ten minutes early, you're runnin' late,* the former Marine and firefighter had often told his daughters when they still lived in Arizona. He scanned his fuel gauge. *One-third. Crap.* In recent years, Granger had made a habit of never letting his fuel level get below one-half. And that week had been the exact reason why. Tucson was entering day three without power to several portions of the city. It had been out at Granger's house for nineteen hours.

Over the years, he'd accumulated several gas and diesel cans, mostly of the plastic variety. He was kicking himself for never prioritizing moving out of the suburb, let alone getting some sort of farm-style fuel tank. Because he would always drive a larger truck for hauling his 'toy-hauler' travel trailer, he had purchased a portable diesel generator. But he kept a supply of gasoline for his quad and lawn equipment, too.

The traffic was moving slowly, as the major intersection up where he needed to turn two hundred yards to the west was being controlled by a pair of motorcycle cops. The right lane was at a near stand-still, as several cars trying to enter the defunct gas station were holding everyone else up. Honking abounded. Granger could see people shaking their fists, and as he passed the gas station from the left lane, something caught his eye. He muted the commercial for a car-wash chain and rolled his window down.

Watching a man defend himself from the shoving of another man and the slaps of a woman, he could barely make out the yelling. "... yours, man! I was here fir..." And like that, Granger had pulled out of earshot. *People are turning into real pricks,* he thought, feeling his hip with a subconscious check to make sure the Sig P365 was there. He owned several guns. The Road Runners had all standardized themselves on Glocks and ARs as their two platforms so they could share mags if need be. But in town, Granger preferred the feel of the less clunky Sig Sauer platform for his inside-the-waistband holster.

He made his left turn through the intersection, scanning the police officers as he did. *They look exhausted.* He traveled the three-tenths mile and turned left into the office complex. *Someone tagged their sign,* he thought. A month earlier that would have amused him. The large brick structure near the driveway entrance which bore the CPB name and crest had graffiti on it. He'd seen enough of it during the fire department days to know it wasn't just a random tagger—*that looks like a gang warning,* he thought. *That's just a bit concerning.* Granger parked, grabbed his manila folder of intel, and headed into the main building in search of the office he'd visited many times over the preceding years. He could hear the low buzz of several generators emitting from behind the fenced area that separated the public parking from the back area and agency vehicles.

"Gonna need to see some valid I.D.," he was ordered as he stepped into the lobby, the glass door not even closed behind him yet.

The reception style desk with uniformed CBP officer that Granger had normally encountered had been replaced with an airport style body-scanner. There were now four officers staffing the checkpoint. All were in full duty belt and ballistic plate carrier, wearing blue uniforms instead of the green that the unit down at the Sasabe border crossing normally wore. While a little surprising, Lou wasn't overly concerned —*Damn! My pistol!*

He dug out his wallet, playing it off. Handing his enhanced driver's license over to the nearby officer, he said, "Meeting with Lieutenant Martin. But I forgot some papers, be right back." He was not going to explain to these folks why he was trying to carry a firearm into a federal building. He'd done it every time he'd come, not too worried about what he felt was a bad law. But he wanted to keep as low a profile as he could. He jogged back to the truck and slipped in. He pulled the entire holster system out and stuffed it under the driver's seat. Three minutes later and wearing a visitor's badge, Granger found his usual point-of-contact's office.

"Knock-knock," he said without actually knocking.

"C'mon in," Lieutenant Jim Martin said, still looking at his computer screen. "What can I—" He cut himself off as he looked up and recognized Granger. "Wow, is it noon already?" he said, looking at his wristwatch. "Sorry, Mr. Madison. I've been busy and totally spaced what time it is."

"That's ok, L-T," Granger said, using the moniker he had taken to use for the man in the several months since the prior point-of-contact had retired. "You guys look a little spun up," he poked. "Something going on?"

"Nothing specifically to tell you, except that business is booming," the seasoned border officer quipped. "Look, Granger, it isn't that we don't appreciate what your team is doing—"

"We don't need to rehash all this, Jim," Granger cut him off. "Either you guys want this intel or you don't. But I gotta tell you—this is hot. We found something active this time." He handed the folder over.

Lt. Martin picked it up and began to scan through the pages. "This is what, sixty? Seventy miles southwest?"

"By vehicle," Granger admitted. "Probably less as the crow flies. We still haven't found it, but we're sure there's a tunnel there. As you can see in the photos, there's plenty of vehicle traffic on both sides. But we don't dare walk down through the valley to find the entrance with as much traffic as we've seen. A Ben Franklin says they have the area under physical surveillance."

"At least," Jim mumbled.

"Beg yer pardon?" Granger mumbled back.

Jim looked up from the file. "Probably drones, too, if this is as hot as you say." He paused for a moment, keeping Granger's eye contact. "Look—you guys could very easily find yourselves in a pickle out there."

"We can handle it," Granger said, a small sliver in his mind reminding him that four was an awfully small number... Reminding him there were other less capable but well-meaning citizens who just needed the proper training and conditioning. "We have I.R. and thermal blocking gear we can don if we need to."

"I'm sure you guys could put up a helluva fight," Jim started. "But you have no quick reaction plan. I need you guys to stand down. We'll look into this when we get a chance."

When you get a— Granger's face, despite the plastic appearance of grafts and scar tissue, did not bode well with being put off so easily—almost insultingly. "Look! This is actionable," he began to plead, voice growing in agitation. "We're not those knuckleheads posing on Instagram. You guys have a real leak, here. And based on what's going on downstairs, there's a lot more happening than you're saying!"

Lt. Martin flipped the manila folder closed and leaned back in his office chair. "I mean it, Granger. I'll pass this to the right folks, but you guys need to back off before you get into a firefight...or worse..."

CHAPTER 12

ROSALES MANSION, MISION DE LOS LAGOS—JUAREZ, MEXICO

"HEY, BABY!" ROSIE SAID EXCITEDLY TO EDDIE WHEN SHE opened her door.

Oh no! she thought. *A guayabera shirt...* She knew that the only time Eddie had ever worn the shirt common with affluent men in Mexico was when he'd been called to his bosses' mansion over in Juarez.

"I love the pleats on this," she said with fake enthusiasm. She really did like the look, but any moment with Eddie had become a big mental challenge for her. Each occasion seemed more and more like an Oscar winning performance in her own mind. She ran her hands up and down his tattooed chest over the pleats and large pockets, slowly lowering them under the bottom hem of the un-tucked shirt and onto his skin.

Eddie pulled her in for a passionate kiss. "Dame un beso," he commanded.

She complied by opening her mouth onto his waiting lips. After two excruciating seconds, she was relieved when he ended it abruptly.

"Grab your stuff," he ordered. "I have a special day planned for you."

Sure, she thought. *You planned being ordered to Mexico?* "Where are we going?" she shrieked.

Over the course of their relationship, he'd usually gone to Mexico with other cartel soldiers. The last time, though, he'd brought her along in his black 1968 Pontiac Firebird. It had been for his Jefe's daughter's quinceañera. She had learned nothing of value on that day-date four months earlier.

"It's a surprise," he said with a smirk of pride, holding her hands in his down by their waists. "Grab your stuff! Let's go!" he ordered again. It was his expectation that she had learned her place, to comply when he demanded. It was a role Rosie had adopted well and would not miss one bit if she lived through this ordeal.

Forty-five minutes later, they were pulling up in the posh Ciudad Juarez neighborhood of Mision de los Lagos—Mission at the Lakes. It was a country club resort that rivaled the best in Miami, Florida—quite the contrast from the dusty cement, tin, and adobe structures they'd passed after crossing the Bridge of the Americas. Texans were second first-generation Americans, raised by immigrants in their native tongue. Eddie's English had been so bad in elementary school that he was fourteen and shaving by the time he'd made it through sixth grade. Failing grades and ridicule by neighborhood thugs had taught him that school and being laughed at were things that would never fit into his life.

Eddie slowly drove through the neighborhood. On the surface, all appeared normal. Rosie could see well-dressed cartel guards stationed in vehicles throughout the roads surrounding the mansions. Though not all residents were part of the El Aguila cartel, they all benefited from the protection. Nary a resident dared to cooperate with the policia or the federales. Not that it had been a real threat—most of them were on the payroll as it were. Passing a beautiful row of tall palm trees, Eddie turned the Firebird that he saved for special occasions onto the perfectly level cobblestone driveway. At fifty feet wide and nearly three hundred feet back to the mansion, there was plenty of room for the vehicles and well over thirty cartel guards. All were dressed casually, and some were spilling onto the manicured, fenced lawn to patrol for threats.

Oooooooh, Rosie thought. *This is big...* She began to mess with her wind-blown hair. Switching to Spanish, as she would for the rest of the time in Mexico, Rosie asked, "Baby, can we put the rag-top up for the trip home?" *I will be going home, right?* She wondered.

"Sure thing, Carmelita," Eddie said lovingly. "You look beautiful!" He bypassed her at the front of the car and began to greet other men he knew and recognized, most of them with a jovial hug and embrace.

Maybe it's just another party, Rosie thought. *Still, this is a lot of guards.* Slowly they made their way into the mansion as Eddie continued the parade. Over the course of the next hour, Rosie and Eddie enjoyed the company of over forty El Aguila leaders and their wives or girlfriends. There were even several kids present. The bulk of the party happened by the two pools, a beautiful dark turquoise in color. The bigger, deeper one had a kidney shape, while the smaller children's pool was rectangular. The golf course looking lawn was spacious and surrounded by an eight-foot stucco wall. Security cameras covered the entire area.

"Hello again, Carmela!" Inocencio Delgado greeted Rosie, leaning in and giving her a fatherly kiss on her left cheek.

Rosie lowered her cocktail glass and returned the greeting, smiling widely. "Senior Delgado!" she exclaimed in perfect Tejano-Spanish. "So wonderful to see you!"

"Do you remember my Lupita?" he said excitedly, pulling in his fifteen-year-old daughter for the warm party-style greeting.

"Si!" Rosie gave the beautiful young cartel princess a hug, instantly filling her heart with missing her own sister, Angel.

Lupe Delgado hugged her back, remembering the friendly Texan woman who was missing the third and fourth fingers on her right hand. The two women giggled and made small talk, eventually finding seats near each other at a poolside table.

As she dined, drank, and enjoyed conversation, Rosie snapped a few photos with the high-tech broach. She hadn't dared bring a recorder to this meeting—that was virtually guaranteed to end in death that followed days of torture. The jewelry looked nothing like a camera, and while away from being charged, it emitted no signals of any kind. All the women and children were eventually politely excused as the men began their conversation.

Rosie, Lupe, and the other women moved back into the mansion. After fifteen minutes of casual drinking with the other women, most of whom were Mexican, not American, Rosie excused herself and made her way to the sound of video games and teenage laughter emanating from a home theater. She wandered in and saw several kids and teens sitting around and watching two others battling in soccer on the biggest television Rosie had ever seen. Insults were being hurled, of course. Lupe saw Rosie and headed her way.

"Want to play next?"

Rosie literally laughed. "I never play those things! I wouldn't even know where to begin."

"You're welcome to join in, if you want," Lupe said warmly. She stayed with Rosie near the entrance to the room, behind the couch, recliners, and commotion.

"Thanks," Rosie said. "I don't really fit in anywhere...I'm not a wife...I'm not Mexican...I'm not a teenager," she said, motioning toward the group ahead.

"You Chicanas are just as Mexican as you are American," Lupe said eagerly, trying to comfort her new friend. "And if Tio Eduardo is bringing you around—twice now! —you're closer to being a wife than a girlfriend."

"You think?" Rosie asked in genuine surprise.

"Of course!" the young lady said.

"How long have you known Eddie?" Rosie said, wondering if she could glean any usable intel.

"My whole life! He's always been kind to me!"

Of course, Rosie didn't say. *He doesn't want your father to kill him one day...* "Do you think they'll be long out there?" Rosie asked.

"There's no telling," Lupe said, turning to watch the faux soccer match again. "I haven't seen one this big since I was about seven or eight."

Rosie searched her memory for the El Aguila history she'd been forced to learn. *That aligns with when they violently killed El Toro and his entire familia and established the council in his place,* she remembered. *Something big is happening.*

AIR FORCE ONE, OVER THE PACIFIC OCEAN

"I'M STARTING TO NOT GIVE TWO DAMNS ABOUT POSSE Comitatus!" Jeremiah Allen said emphatically. After a deep breath and exhalation, he continued. "Of course, I don't mean that. But what we've seen down there is nothing short of an invasion! I don't care if it is drug dealers! Invasion is invasion!" *Where's that damned Tylenol I asked for!* he yelled in his head. He turned his attention from the video chat with Attorney General Roslyn O'Donnell to Vice President Heather Crenshaw. "And Heather—I need you and Senator Gregory to come to terms on this emergency resolution. If he knows you'll break the tie, he and the Whip should be able to get those fence riders to make it 50-50!"

"It's been our top priority, sir. SecDef made his presentation to the Senate Armed Services and Security committee this morning. I think they've seen the big picture—all three parties. There's still a lot of partisanship going on." She was referring to the Democrat controlled Senate and the Republican controlled House of Representatives not working together on the legislation sponsored by the Libertarians that had been elected to both chambers. The president was trying to get emergency funding and some leeway in the National Defense Authorization Act so he could declare the cartel problem a legal foe.

"And we're working around the clock on the legal definition of a foreign invasion," AG O'Donnell chimed in. "Not only have we had some pushback in the Senate, but my counterparts from several Central and South American nations have sent messages of concern."

"Which ones?" Jeremiah wanted to know. "Mexico?"

She nodded. "As well as El Salvador, Venezuela, Columbia...even Argentina."

"I don't give two f—"

"Mr. President, your Tylenol," Julia Jacobs, his primary assistant, interrupted. She knew when she could get away with it.

He snapped his head at her, and within a half-second remembered his recurring order to her—*Anytime I'm flying off the handle, feel free to save me from myself.* "Thanks, Julia," he said, taking the glass and two pills from her. He looked around the conference table in the plane's meeting room. "Thoughts. If I'm wrong on this, tell me. And remember—I'm looking beyond the obvious Seattle thing. If they can overrun and align an entire prison into their organization there, they can do it anywhere. Just how the hell did we ever let them have such advanced weaponry..." he pondered, not really expecting an answer.

"It's just a fifty-year precedent set by the other governments we mentioned, sir," AG O'Donnell said. "They're so corrupt with the reach and influence that there's no changing it. It wouldn't surprise me, sir, that if we truly went after the cartel on our soil, they'd start filing complaints with the U.N. over the mistreatment of their expats in the U.S. They even have a deep reach into the pockets of some of our own cities, Mr. President."

"That BS needs to stop," he said coldly. He looked around once more. "Alright. Thanks for the call. We have a meeting here on the plane with Secretary Buttermaker in just a moment." The video conference ended, and Jeremiah stood up, triggering the rest of those seated in the room to, also. "Take a few folks," he instructed, heading forward to go relieve himself in his stateroom's lavatory. He could hear Shannon and her staff discussing the coming agenda as they cued up notes on the big monitor.

Jeremiah stepped out of the conference room into the fore-to-aft passage on the plane's port side and started forward. He stepped into the seating area, causing his primary Secret Service agent to stand up. "It's okay, Mike," he said, having gotten used to the agent popping up on alert when he entered a space. "Just gotta piss."

"Yes sir," he heard, followed by Mike mumbling into his microphone, "Snake Charmer moving forward."

Jeremiah and Mike repeated the process three minutes later as he made his way back. He grabbed a cherry danish from the tray next to the door as he reentered the conference room. Julia handed him a piece of paper. "Your schedule as soon as we land, sir."

"Mphhank-you," he said through delicious, warm cherry and flaky dough stuffed into his mouth.

He scanned as he returned to his seat. *Greeted by Prime Minister Ito and honored guests... arrive at U.S. Consulate at 12:30 local... state dinner at 7 PM...* The president was on his way to Japan to assure them that the United States was fully committed to the existing defense agreement. When Jeremiah Allen had won the election, one of his big promises was that in his tenure, the United States was finished meddling in the affairs of other nations. This had caused a small ripple of concern amongst many countries, both in Asia and throughout Europe. He'd had to go on a small world tour within a month of his inauguration to assure those leaders that we would still fully honor existing treaties.

As the only nation to homeport a United States Navy aircraft carrier, Japan's defense was critical. *Don't worry, Kazu,* the president thought when the prime minister reached out six days earlier. *We need you just as badly as you need us.* PM Kazuhiro Ito had sought an audience with the president to assure his own people that the increasing tension between China and Russia would not affect them. Tensions had become strained in recent weeks in the Pacific, particularly after

China had started a near embargo on any traffic passing through the South or East China Seas a week earlier. All this unfolding three weeks after the Cascadia events wasn't a coincidence, the president knew.

"Good morning, Dee," Jeremiah said to Secretary of State Buttermaker as he sat down again. She and her key aides had arrived from their own small pre-meeting in the president's office in his small intermission.

"Morning, Mr. President," she replied. "Ready when you are." He gave a nod, setting down the paper Julia gave him and reaching for a napkin. She continued. "After this morning's chat with Minister of State Watanabe, it's clear that Prime Minister Ito will be enacting the emergency defense clause of their constitution. Calling up their version of reserve forces. They don't want us to be surprised, and they are going to want our full backing when China and the Koreas protest."

"Maybe we should add a quick hop to Seoul while we're over here," Jeremiah mused. *Don't have time for all this nerve soothing,* he thought to himself. *Got enough problems.*

"I'm not sure there's time, sir," Dee echoed his thoughts. "Not if you want to stop in Guam and Saipan and get back by Tuesday."

"Well, shoot," he said aloud. "And I do. We need to let our territories out here know they aren't alone. There's probably a few senior citizens on those islands who were alive when they were pillaged in World War II."

"Yes, sir," Dee said. "I'll reach out to South Korea personally and remind them we're committed to them, too." She shifted topics. "Are there any new developments in the Russia-China arms buildup that I should know about?" As she was speaking, Shannon Sahr's phone started vibrating, as did several others in the room.

"Sir," his Chief of Staff interrupted. When she did, people listened. She looked at her assistant Terrell. "Get Bloomberg on the screen," she politely ordered. "And CNN."

"What is it?" Jeremiah asked. *Not another crisis. Please.*

"The CME" she said with a concerned look.

The Chicago Mercantile Exchange, often just referred to as 'the

Merc', was the largest futures and options exchange in the world. Originally formed to stabilize the price of commodities like wheat and pork bellies, it had grown to an inflated proportion. Whereas there was no way to ever truly know how much physical money existed in the world, it was widely accepted that the CME traded more than that—a lot more. Estimates on the US currency supply usually landed around seventy trillion dollars. The world supply totaled roughly tripled that number. The CME exchanged well over one and one-quarter quadrillion dollars every year. It was called 'betting on futures.' It wasn't the exchange of physical goods so much as the anticipated performance of investments yet to come. It had been widely anticipated that this 'bubble bursting' could cause a massive and aggressive worldwide economic depression.

"What?" Jeremiah poked, not liking the delay.

"It crashed..." she said, shocked. "Someone hacked it and cleared all the databases!"

FORT HOOD, TEXAS

LOU WATCHED THE LARGE TANK-LOOKING DEVICE DRIVE forward to a sharp ravine approximately eight feet deep on both edges and over twenty feet wide. Above the tracks, it looked like nothing he'd seen on the battlefields of Afghanistan from the blur of his old A-10 cockpit. Engineers employing tracked or floating deployable bridges to keep combat units rolling forward wasn't new. But it wasn't widely needed by the allies, and the Taliban and Al Qaeda certainly hadn't possessed this type of equipment.

What made the M1074 Joint Assault Bridge unique was how it had converted the existing M1 Abrams tank body into the delivery vehicle.

The use of an existing system meant gains in efficiency, not just in training people, but in having parts readily available. On top of the body was where things looked differently. A large hydraulic rack carried a folding bridge, in this case eighteen meters long. It could plant a pivot leg on the ground in front of the vehicle, and within three minutes, a bridge capable of carrying tanks and howitzers could span a wet or dry chasm up to eleven meters wide.

Lou was on his second day checking out units at Fort Hood. This piece of gear was owned and operated by the engineers of Engineer Battalion, 3rd Brigade Combat Team. Tanks and mobile howitzers from other battalions were lining up near the practice trench, taking turns crossing over the bridges. In all, five delivery vehicles had landed five bridges to speed up the process.

"Once we land a bridge, we can get out of the way within a few seconds," explained Staff Sergeant Elise Tardy.

"What happens to the launch vehicle once the combat units have moved across and forward?" Lou asked, yelling slightly above the heavy noise of diesel engines and rumbling tracked vehicles. The central Texas dust was kicking up, coating everything in a fine powder. Lou coughed a bit.

"The transportation unit may be able to bring additional bridges up on flatbed trucks," she explained. "If that's not planned or if speed is of the essence, the JAB can cross the bridge and pick it back up from the other side."

"Oh, I see," Lou said. "Just move it forward until needed again?"

"Precisely, Colonel," Staff Sergeant Tardy concurred.

"Do the Gray Wolves have enough of these?" Brandon chimed in, asking the major, who was also present.

"We have eighty percent, Captain," Dewey Cook answered. The Gray Wolves was the fighting moniker of the 3rd BCT, and Major Cook was the engineer battalion's Executive Officer. "Which is actually doing well. These are a fairly new system, still being delivered."

"Gotcha," Brandon said. "I was headed for tanks myself after ROTC, except a little birdy told me the Marines would be phasing them out entirely. Sure enough, that started happening by the time I was a first looie."

"What'd you wind up in?" Major Cook asked. "Infantry?"

"All Marines are infantry, Major," Brandon said, beaming from ear to ear. Major Cook laughed, though with the noise of the equipment pounding the Texas plains, it was hard for any of them to hear. "Yes, sir. Specifically in light armor recon."

Lou watched the bridge building, fascinated. As a former destroyer of heavy mechanized equipment, he was enjoying the chance to get an up-and-close experience that few in his profession ever did. He scanned his watch. *1030. Should probably get moving.* "We have an appointment with Colonel Corey in a half-hour. Do you all think we should get going?" he asked politely.

"Roger that, Colonel," the major said. "Sergeant, here, will get you back." He turned to face Lou and snapped to attention, saluting crisply.

Lou returned the courtesy and then stuck his left hand out, already loaded with a business card. As the major started to take it Lou said over the noise, "If you ever find yourself near the Pentagon, Major, give me a call!" With a quick handshake, he and Brandon followed the staff sergeant back to the parked Humvee two hundred meters away near the edge of Elijah Road.

"Where you from, Sergeant?" Lou asked her as she turned the rig around for the trip.

"Mayport, Florida, sir," she replied. The Humvee's top was installed, as the mild Texas fall had started to cause lots of dew buildup in the wee hours of the morning.

"You didn't join the Navy?" Lou asked with a grin and a wink. She turned right.

"No, sir," she said with a sheepish grin.

"It's, okay, Sergeant," Lou said, looking out his window at rows and rows of the army's newest M1 tanks. Some were desert tan, some were green, and a few of the newest looked as if they had pixelated paint schemes combining both colors. *That's kinda cool,* he thought to himself. He looked back at her. “Nobody likes the Navy. I don’t blame you!”

She grinned and laughed at the small talk. “Thank you for understanding, sir!”

Lou wanted to keep pressing. “What’s your thoughts on everything that’s going on? Seems like most units here at Hood have been left alone in this wonky deployment thing...”

“Not sure having thoughts on the matter is within my paygrade, sir,” she replied, already briefed by everyone from her company sergeant major to Major Cook not to say anything that could reflect poorly on the Gray Wolves.

“I’m not asking you to rat, Sergeant,” Lou said. He’d learned at Fort Bragg that he needed to establish some trust with the enlisted first. “I mean, how do you feel? Apprehensive? Confused? Demoralized? None of those?” Lou pressed. He could see her wheels spinning as she chose her words. Brandon sat silently in the back, seeing an open side to Lou he hadn’t expected.

“I guess a little of all that, sir.” They both went silent. Lou waited patiently, knowing the pump was almost primed. “I’m dating a guy in a different unit—a radio operator assigned to a headquarters company. He tells me things that concern him. Bad things he hears are happening in Seattle. Things not being talked about in the media.”

“Oh?” Lou said, genuinely surprised. “Such as?”

“I’m sure you’ve heard all of this already, sir,” she said as she clammed up.

“I really haven’t, Sergeant Tardy,” Lou replied honestly. “We’ve been on the road for days, and I’m a desk pilot for public affairs. I’ve been at the same mercy of civilian media reports as everyone else.”

She looked at him earnestly, before turning left in the parking lot of the Brigade Headquarters Building. After she pulled near the front, she opted to park instead of to drop Lou off directly in front of the building’s entry. After parking, she turned her head once more. Lou could see the tension in her brow.

"Just tell me, soldier," Lou said in an informal tone, not wanting it to come off as an order. "What has you this concerned?"

"Sir—"

Man is this kid frightened, Lou thought.

"—have you heard anything about a large gang taking over Seattle?"

CHAPTER 13

East Tucson, AZ

Granger stared at the pool in Dave Wolf's backyard, subconsciously wondering just how warm it was. He was very leery of exposing his burns to Tucson's summer sun… *But November?* he questioned himself. *Maybe…* Most people thought it might be anxiety about exposing his horrible burns to the general public. Granger—and by default the Road Runners—weren't prone to be anxious people. He pulled the lowball glass to his lips, taking another small sip of the Crown Royal whiskey, letting the aroma drift to his nostrils.

"We may need to think about expansion," he advised the team.

The Road Runners and their families were enjoying BBQ at Dave's 'House of Shenanigans', watching the kids and grandkids in the heated pool play with super soakers and screaming with delight. It was late afternoon, and the sun was already getting low to the west. Dave and his wife owned a chain of seven In-N-Out Burgers in the greater Tucson area, a job that had grown to the point that they allowed a general manager to deal with the worst headaches. They usually had the team over to their Houghton neighborhood pool five or six times per year. They had become...*family.* As the veterans had all grown to trust each other with their lives, their families had bonded, too.

"I thought we were opposed to that," Tracy Rogers said. The team's youngest member was only thirty-five. As the newest member, the former Navy combatant craft crewman used to deliver SEALs into 'brown water' territories in South America. While not a SEAL, Tracy himself had gone through his own version of Hell-week. Men with his training were widely regarded with the same stigma and respect afforded to other special forces. "I even tried to suggest a couple of guys and you all shut that down."

"He's right," Dave Wolf agreed, setting his bottle of Fat Tire down for the conversation. "We've always been about quality over quantity."

In the preceding minutes, those wives and girlfriends in attendance around the two covered poolside deck tables had started grabbing items to take inside. The BBQs always wound up in some boring special operations story hour that bored them. Dave's wife Donna had slowly evolved the group of women to split off and play pinochle in the house.

Granger had just briefed his team on the response by the CBP —*thanks but no thanks for the intel. You guys need to stop.*

"Maybe it's time to hang it up," Mick Oakley suggested.

"Or a more direct approach," Claude added. The others looked at him, half with surprise and half with disbelief. "Seriously. I mean—I know I'm not out there with you guys. But I would be if I could, same as Bob," he said as he nodded.

"Damn skippy," Bob said. He was rotating his cane with his fingers, its rubber boot on the ground between his feet. "And I don't mean peanut butter."

"Define more direct," Dave said. He was calm, but the tone in his voice was skeptical.

"You know..." Claude continued. "Make it so those a-holes just disappear..."

"You're talking about actually engaging them," Dave said in annoyance, sitting upright. "You do realize that's still a crime, right?!"

"I, for one, am ready for it," Mick said. "Tired of seeing nothing happen to them. Who knows how many people they've smuggled in..." It was a statement, not a question. "Drugs...guns...terrorists...not to mention why we started this originally—the kids!"

"Hear hear!" Bob exclaimed. "I may not be a trigger puller, but I'd gladly go to prison if we got caught waxing those pedo-suppliers!"

"Everyone just take a deep breath," Granger finally chimed in. He'd heard enough bickering. "If we do ever go that route, four of us damn sure ain't enough." He let that sit while he took another sip. "And brothers, direct action combat is coming this way whether we like it or not." He looked at Dave. "How long did you need to run your generator today, just to heat that pool for the kids?"

"You're right," Dave agreed. "Maybe we wasted a little precious gas today. I felt it was important for the families." He was very level-headed, but the former special forces officer didn't like being made to look foolish.

"Easy, brother, I'm not mocking you," Granger replied. "All I'm sayin' is that sooner or later, all this crap that's happening is going to catch up. You guys've been watching the news, right?" He looked around. "They're burning cars in Phoenix right now. How much longer until that angry mentality comes to Tucson? Or Houghton?" he added as he looked back at Dave. "I think this level of activity we've seen at the new spot is just the tip of the iceberg." He leaned back in his chair.

"So. What did you mean by expansion?" Dave asked. "Certainly not those chubby militia knuckle-heads!"

"Yeah," Mick concurred. "Last thing we want is to be labeled. I get it—most of those guys aren't racists...aren't anti-government... It doesn't matter. That's the label they get because they can't keep the idiots from joining."

"And they always wind up with some sort of fed mole, too," Tracy added. This got Dave's head nodding in agreement. "Trying to pull some red-flag BS to make them look even worse."

"Guys... who do you think we've been talking to all these years?" Granger said with a slight pitch to his voice. "Border Patrol has certainly built a dossier on us, right?" Silence. "I'm not saying let's start taking open enrollment on Facebook, for Pete's sake! But like you said, Tracy—" Granger looked directly at him. "You know a couple of guys you trust." He continued his scan. "I bet we all do."

"The guys I know have started their own groups," Tracy said.

"That's what we're saying, Grange!" Dave chimed in, using his buddy's shortened nickname. "There's an exponential factor where the circle grows larger than we can vet for legitimacy."

"I get that, Dave, but there's a lot of well-meaning citizens out there. Patriotic men, rear-echelon vets or even those that never joined... Men and women who still believe in supporting this Republic and the Constitution that we all swore to defend! Those are the folks I'm talking about. They just don't know how to get started." The group was silent, some staring off at the coming sunset, others sipping on their beers. "We are not ready for direct action," he reminded everyone coldly. "They have superior numbers, drones, heavy weapons, probably even some backup from the Mexican Federales."

"They can't cross the border like that!" Claude said incredulously about Mexico's police or soldiers. "That'd be declaring war!" He guffawed at the idea.

"Where is the exact border, Bob," Granger replied smoothly, "when it's just us defending it?"

El Paso, Texas

"There sure were a lot of people at the party, baby!" Rosie said, trying to make small talk now that they were back on the American side of the border.

While she didn't think he'd been putting on a show when he dragged her out of her apartment, the thought was never far off. He wasn't easily prone to losing his temper, not like some of the enforcer types she'd seen him interact with occasionally. She knew that if he were truly falling for her, though, the perceived betrayal might be enough to set him over the edge. She hoped that the state and maybe even federal prosecutors would finally have enough fish to fry and end this investigation soon.

"Lots to think about," he replied. He'd been quiet most of the way back.

"Well, I know not to ask," she said. Usually psychology didn't work with Eddie—at least, not right away. She knew she might get him talking if she pulled out all the stops. Before resorting to sex, she decided to add a degree of complexity to the mind game. "But you seem stressed. I just wish there was something I could do..." She left the ripe fruit hanging there.

"There's always something you can do," he said, looking like a wolf as he gave her a quick grin. They turned eastbound onto Alameda Drive.

Almost home, Rosie thought. *Home. What a crock.* But it was her home, more or less—the one place where she didn't have to worry about saying the wrong thing or being seen by someone who knew her in some freak incident. "You know what I mean!" she smiled as she played it off.

Eddie took a right into her apartment complex, and they immediately saw a group of Hispanic people gathered around a few cars at the far end. Eddie pulled into the spot he normally took when making his booty call, and the pair got out.

They glanced over at the group, and a few young men started making comments about the Firebird. "Niiiiice car, homes!"

Eddie stopped. *Uh-oh,* Rosie thought.

Three of the men started toward Eddie. "Wassup, Guay?" The young man was using a word for dude that implied a sense of no respect as he walked up.

"You cholos know who you're talking to?" Rosie yelled at the obvious gangsters.

Eddie started to laugh. "It's okay, beautiful," he said, trying to calm her down, holding her arm as she tried to get between Eddie and the approaching group.

"Yo—you'd better shut your whore up, cabrone!"

This insult got Eddie's attention. He yanked Rosie back behind him. Due to the border crossing, it was the one time he wasn't armed.

"Alto!" he heard an older man behind the group yell. "Stop!" the man yelled again, running to catch up. The clean-shaven man had a baggy white shirt and tan long-shorts on over his pristine white Reeboks. He slapped one of the men—hard—on the back of the head. "Get back over there!" he yelled at the mouthy one.

All four of the bangers wore shocked expressions. "But—"

"Now!" the older arrival yelled again, pointing. "All of you idiots! Go! And I'll kill anyone who touches this car!" As they started to retreat and lick their wounds, he turned and faced Eddie. "Please forgive the disrespect. I know who you are... and who you represent. I'll educate those punks in a way they won't forget."

Eddie took a deep breath, face still twisted in anger, upset with himself for not going straight home from the border. He just glared at the man for a long moment. Finally, "Don't go too rough on them. Your crew part of our network?"

"As a matter of fact, yes," came the reply.

Eddie turned and grabbed Rosie's hand, leading her toward her building. He looked back at the tat-covered gangster as he walked and said, "Keep a low profile. Big, big things happenin' soon..."

SANCHES FARM,

Northeast of Manhattan, Kansas

. . .

"C'MON, WANKER!" MORRIS DOOGHAN HEARD WILLIAM Easton, AKA 'ThatNub', yell at him as he sprinted for the blaring cell phone near the firepit.

Morris ignored the slam, knowing the whole team would give him a hard time when the call was over. He'd just violated the one rule he harped on the others the most about—*no cells during practice.* Morris had recognized the Beethoven's 5th ringtone as his mother calling. He was just happy to know that phone calls were still somewhat reliable in the face of all the utility issues the country had been having. *Will take the load of crap to see how Mom is...*

"Mom," he said into the mobile device as he pulled it to his ear. He turned to scan the team, who had resumed killing each other with biodegradable BBs.

"I'm sorry it took so long to call you back, Honey Bear," his mother said.

"Honey Bear?" Morris said, more amused than he was letting on. "Mom, I'm not nine anymore."

"I know, Morris, but let a mother have her moment!" she commanded. "We have some things to tell you..." She went silent.

"Just spit it out, Ma," he said, calling her Ma subconsciously when she was being annoying.

"It's the city, Bear. It's getting downright scary! These gangs are getting braver about claiming territory! It's—"

"I've been telling you and Dad to get out to Aunt Janet's."

"We are, Bear! Just hol' on a second, child! I brought you into this world..."

Morris wasn't in the mood. "I know, I know, you can take me out. When are you leaving?"

"Tonight. But I wanted to see if there's anything you have to have. Just in case..." the words escaped his mother.

"Something happens to the house?" Morris finished. "Was there another break-in?" *Imma kill someone.*

"No, Bear, but there have been two daytime home invasions this week. One down the street, the other over on Chestnut."

Damn... "Don't fool around, Ma! You two grab your stuff and go," Morris said sternly.

"It's not so easy, Morris Allen!" his mother exclaimed.

Uh-oh. Middle name. "I'm sorry, Mom. I'm just worried..."

She continued the lecture. "It's not so easy to just pack and go. We have to get all the food, some clothes, what little of your father's back pain medication we have... It takes a lot of work to flee your home!"

"Alright! Alright... Just some clothes, I guess. Oh! And Marvin's airsoft stuff—all of it. He'd be upset if that went missing." He thought a second longer. "I-I guess I got everything else I need here at my and Nub's apartment."

"You don't want any of your old toys? Skateboard?"

"Ma!" Morris said in disbelief. "None of that is worth your lives! Just get going, already..." *Sheesh,* he didn't dare add on vocally.

"And Bear—I don't want you coming to the city," she instructed.

"We have a tourney next month in KCK," he countered. *Surely the Kansas side is still safe...*

"No, Morris! People here on both sides of the line are starting to fold! The riots have moved out of downtown. The gangs are setting up food distribution stations near the worst of it. People are actually supporting them! It's insane!"

Morris took it in as she went on. *No tournament? Then what are we even practicing for? This is too hard to believe...* They continued for two more minutes.

Morris had been tuning out the growing dissention amongst his teammates, but they were not giving in. Nub and Super B had jogged over to start chastising him properly, up close and personal. "Tell your boo bye-bye and let's get back to practice!" the feisty freshman ordered.

"Okay, Mom. Bye. Love you, too." Morris pulled the phone away from his ear. He looked to ensure the call had ended and then looked at the two. His expression had been enough for even the mouthy Super B to shut up.

"What is it?" best friend Nub asked. "Something wrong with your parents?"

"I dunno," Morris said in a slight amount of shock, still not knowing the phrase for it, but realizing that his parents had just committed to bugout. "My mom made me swear—Swear! —to stay here in Manhattan... What's that mean?" Concern.

The trio began to walk back to the practice portion of the Sanches farm property when another phone sitting on the cold concrete fire ring started to buzz. They all looked at it, but Nub called out, "Goldi!" trying to get David 'Goldilocks' Faust's attention. By this time the other four had started to slowly drift over. The blonde curly Californian started to jog to his phone.

As he answered his phone, the other six had all coalesced into a group. "What's goin' on?" Maria, known as Misty Meaner, asked.

"My Mom..." Morris said. "She and my dad are heading to my aunt's out in the country. They say KC is getting too dangerous to stay in..." His voice trailed off as he shifted his gaze from Maria to the others.

Floyd Presley and Nub exchanged glances, and then looked at Morris. "You gonna tell them what we did this week? Or should I?" Elvis said bluntly.

"Tell us what?" Super B demanded.

Damn! Does she ever take a day off? Morris asked himself. "Go ahead, Elvis," Morris said calmly. "It's your family."

As all eyes shifted to Elvis, Goldi got off his phone. "My sister says my parents are leaving Encinitas for her house..." He wore a stunned expression.

"Where's she?" Jon 'SuperFly' Sanches asked.

"Outside Twentynine Palms," he answered. "She said that a group of people protesting for wealth redistribution stormed my hometown and started a bunch of fires in the richer neighborhoods." The longer he spoke, the more his face shifted from stun to outrage. As did his voice. "Protest, my butt! These people are downright anarchists!

Spoiled, entitled, and greedy little babies! Just trying to steal so they don't have to work!"

"Sorry to hear that, Goldi," Morris chimed in. "My parents just said the same thing about KC." Morris was still shocked but had managed to keep his reserved tone intact.

"What's going on in America suddenly?" exclaimed Misty, confused.

"You were about to tell us some big secret," Bee reminded Elvis insistently.

"Nub, Thumper, and I went to my sister and her husband's gun store over in Rossville several days ago."

"What!" exclaimed Bee and Misty Meaner at the same moment.

"Duuuuueede," Goldi drawled out smoothly. "Straight fire!" he exclaimed in the youthful vernacular.

Superfly was a little hurt. "Why didn't you guys tell the rest of us?" Jealousy was written on his face.

"What'd ya get?" Super B asked, the usual rash 'tude dissolving into excitement.

"Funny story, that..." Elvis smirked. He glanced at the other two, looking for some support.

Morris took over. "So, after the break-in at my home back in Roeland Park, I'd told these two after practice back on Tuesday that I wanted to upgrade my gear, but I was also thinking about finally getting a rifle. And maybe a pistol," he added. "Nub remembered that Elvis mentioned his sister's gun store."

"Dat's right!" Nub added, breaking into his all too familiar and unwelcome Robert DeNiro impression. He was even trying to protrude his jaw and squint. "I was da key to rememberin' da most important fact!" A rapid and verbose chorus of insults flew Nub's way, as well as an empty magazine from an airsoft rifle.

"We grabbed Elvis and went on Thursday," Morris explained. "Clint and Beth were good to us."

"What. Did you. Get!" Super B repeated herself with emphasis. "Did you guys bring them?" That realization made her and Jon both set their airsoft gear on the ground next to the fire ring chairs. They started making a beeline for Nub's Bronco.

"Whoa! Whoa, whoaaa!" Nub said, chasing the pair down as the rest of the group trailed. They all wound up at the rear gate to the old utility rig, with both Nub and Morris inserting themselves to guard it from opening. "Chill, you guys!"

"Jon. Before we bust out any toys, I want you to go clear it with Tio Jorge first," Morris advised. As the group's leader, he was always invested in making sure they didn't overstay their welcome. "And if he says okay, maybe we can run some dry drills around the obstacle course."

"Whoa, wait. Why would we do that?" Misty wanted to know. "This is still practice, right?"

"Practice for what?" the usual placid Goldi said suddenly, catching everyone off guard. He was visibly upset. "Weren't you listening?" He pointed at Misty.

"That's not fair—" she started to protest as he cut her off.

"Don't you all realize that my family—Thumper's family? They just told us they had to bugout from home!" His face turned crimson as he started to realize how angry he was getting. He turned and stormed off to the firepit. The others mostly remained silent as both Misty and Super B guffawed at Goldi's reaction.

"Jon," Morris said. "Why don't you go grab Jorge and meet us at the firepit..." Jon took off. "I'll just grab one case," Morris suggested to Nub.

"If you say so," his roommate said, his tone still hesitant.

Morris grabbed a rifle case and headed back to the large circle of chairs, the rest following him. "Everyone grab a seat," he suggested with his usual relaxed authority. After everyone but Jon was seated, he decided to get realistic with the team. "My mom begged me to stay here in Manhattan. Begged!" he emphasized, showing a bit of emotion. *Don't cry!* he yelled in his head. *Baby!* But his friends could see his eyes moisten a bit.

Goldi got up from his chair and walked over to where Morris was seated. He stuck his hand out for the bro-shake grip and Morris stood up. The pair clasped hands and pulled into each other for a one-armed hug. “Mine, too, bro,” the Californian whispered. The seriousness of what the two young men were feeling had finally dawned on their friends.

“I wonder if I should call my dad?” Jordan ‘Super B’ Croft admitted. Her mom had passed away from cervical cancer eight years earlier.

“Yes,” Morris said as he and Goldi returned to their chairs. “You all should.”

“This sucks,” moped Misty Meaner. “You and Nub have an apartment. The rest of you have family in rural parts of the state. Goldi and I are both from out-of-state. What if they shut down the college and kick us out of the dorms?” she asked worriedly.

“We’ll all support each other,” Nub said seriously. “Jon’s folks live in town, but I’m guessing they’d come here to Jorge’s if they needed to.” He had a suggestive look. “They might let any of us camp here.”

“In winter?” Misty complained.

“Look,” Morris said as he saw Jon and Jorge coming toward the pit from the farmhouse porch. “Let’s take a deep breath and talk this through.” He unzipped the rifle case laying at his feet. “Jorge, if I’m careful can I pick this up and show everyone it is clear?”

“Sure thing, Mr. Thumper,” Jorge said as he approached the group. “Thanks for asking first.” He was just as curious as everyone else to see the cool looking rifle.

Morris picked up an AR-15, outfitted with a delta-shaped grip of some sort on the bottom of the rails near the muzzle. On top was a small black optic. The overall rifle had a green theme of modern pieces for the stock and grip. Ensuring the muzzle never pointed at anyone, he pointed the rifle into the sky and set the stock on his right leg. He used his right hand to pull down on the charging handle and used his left to lock the bolt back. He handed it to Elvis seated to his right, who immediately passed it off.

“All three of us bought one,” Elvis explained to Goldi, who took the gun.

"Cool! It's lighter than I expected!" he said, the rifle temporarily suspending his sadness.

"You said you all bought one?" Jon the SuperFly asked, looking at the three.

"My sister sold them to us at cost," Elvis explained. "They're having trouble getting their inventory replaced. But she said she'd hold a few basic models back in case any of you could afford them. We're all thinking about pistols, too."

The others looked at Nub and Morris for confirmation. "Yeah," Nub agreed. He was suddenly inspired to switch into his Christopher Walken. "And it ain't cheap!" he said in his worst Long Island accent. He winked and twitched his head. "And this here fire could use more cowbell! Yous guys want, we oughtta get some mo' guns 'fore they're all gone!"

After the expected and usual batch of hard times was thrown Nub's way, Super B stated confidently, "I bet we'd be pretty sick as a tactical team!" She started to get stars in her eyes.

As the others all started to chirp about how cool that would be, Morris had to jump in. "Yo, yo, just hold up a sec." Always the pragmatist, he needed to rein in the overconfidence. "While Mil-Sim has taught us a lot, there are some key things we need to think about."

"Whatever, Dad!" Super B said, intent on not letting the old man in the group ruin their moment.

"Seriously," Morris said. Everyone started to quiet down as the rifle continued to pass around. "After we talked to Clint and Beth when they sold us these, it became clear that we need some training to make sure we know how to use them." He chuckled a bit and pointed at the rifle. "These ain't airsoft!"

Elvis jumped in, by far having the most shooting experience out of the group. "He's right," he said with authority. "And not just about recoil. You sight these differently. You have to have them pulled into your shoulder a lot harder. And you sure as hell don't keep blasting through dozens or hundreds of rounds at one person pinned down behind a barricade."

Morris looked around. As the cool tool almost made its full loop back to him, he scanned the faces of his friends. With the exception of his brother and parents, there was nobody else he could think of that meant this much to him. *I don't even recall half the people in high school's name. But these weirdos?* he mused to himself. *They're my people. And I need to figure out how to protect 'em.*

CHAPTER 14

KILLEEN, TEXAS

<THUMP-THUMP-THUMP>

Unnnnnrrgnghhgh, Lou groaned, head pounding as the hotel room spun. *What the hell is that noise!* screamed the little sober guy in his head. *I told you you'd regret buying that rum!* An electronic tingling began to permeate the air.

<Thump-Thump-Thump-Thump-Thump> "Open up, Lou!" he could hear Brandon calling through his motel door.

<Riiiinnngggg!>

As the fog lifted, Lou started to comprehend that his phone was ringing. A still-drunk hand finally found it near the lamp on the night-stand just as it went silent. "Alright!" he called out. "Hold yoourr hors-es!" He slowly tossed his legs over the side of the bed and stepped in a cold, slimy pile of vomit sitting next to a very clean waste basket. *Awww! What the actual f—*

<Riiiinnngggg!>

"What!" Lou yelled at the phone as he wiped his nasty foot on a clean piece of hotel room carpet, staggering to the door. He yanked it open, not even bothering to look at Brandon out on the entrance balcony. He spun around, still in underwear, sweaty tee shirt, and one sock—on the foot that missed the vomit pile. He punched at the small screen on the 'hip-top computer.' It didn't register in his hungover mind that it was a cell number common to his part of Maryland.

"What!" he screamed at whoever was disrupting his one good drunk sleep-in since starting the assignment.

"Ohhh, come on, Colonel!" he heard Brandon call out as he entered the smelly room. "There's better ways to spend a Sunday morning."

"L-Lou?" he heard as he plopped on the end of the bed and laid back down, feet still hitting the floor. He was feeling around for a corner of the sheet to wipe his sweaty head with. "I-I'm looking for Lou Caldwell. It's his neighbor, Ron Fredrickson."

Huh? the little sober man asked in Lou's head. "Ron? Uh, yeah, it's Lou. Sorry. Uhhh, what's up?"

"I-I don't know how to say this, Lou. I guess I just thought you should hear it from me instead of the police." The room suddenly quit spinning. "Your house…"

"Spit it out, Ron." Lou sat back up, ignoring the wave of nausea.

"Your house burnt down, man. Like almost all the way! And don't freak out—there's no sign of Julia! No sign that she was inside…"

The world shifted on Lou. *He must be… I must still be passed out, drunk…* "Wh-what?" was all he could mutter.

Brandon could feel the shift in Lou. Despite having to come pound on the door to get the wasted colonel to wake up and answer his cell phone, ringing incessantly for almost ten minutes, he could tell that Lou was now as alert as the artificial chemicals in his body would allow.

"Your house, Lou. It's gone."

Lou sat in stunned silence for a moment. "I-I'm out of town. For work. I-I don't know…"

"I'm going to give your phone number to the fire marshal. Okay?"

"Y-yeah…" Lou hung up without even thinking to acknowledge his neighbor, still not believing what he was hearing was anything but a fuzzy nightmare.

"What is it, Lou?" Brandon asked with concern. He side-stepped the vomit to get around to the end of the bed and face his senior partner. The clean-living man, a Marine and Georgia Tech graduate, had certainly been around enough drunks that it wasn't shocking to him.

"M-my house... Julia..." Lou told him with thorough confusion. "They're gone..." He tried to stand.

Brandon shot his arm out, giving the wobbly colonel something to grab as he got back off the bed. "Meaning what, sir?"

"My neighbor just called. Said my house is gone... a fire... said the fire marshal will call. No sign of Jul—oh, hell, she actually did it!" Lou's already pale face drained of any remaining color, leaving just two dark circles around his eyes. His thinning light brown hair was glistening with sweat despite the motel room's air conditioner being set at 62 F. "She—she—" Lou started to cry as he made it to the bathroom counter. *Terrance! How will I be able to connect with you? The garage!* "Can you please leave?" Lou managed to get out through sobs.

"In a minute, sir. I don't think you should be alone right now."

Lou dove to his knees next to the toilet, managing to get his latest wave of rum and bile into the proper receptacle. Brandon started to drench one of the motel washcloths in the sink, wringing it out. Once Lou's hand shot up, he gave it to him.

Lou slowly stood, wiping his mouth off as he did. "I need to get home. I-I think I need your help getting me onto a plane today," he admitted.

"Of course. I'm going to need to let Colonel Jackson know, sir. Or would you rather..."

"You can if you want, son. I'll be calling Montgomery directly. Jackson doesn't... well, let's just say I'll have a better audience with the big dog." Lou moved over to the shower-tub and started running the water to get it hot. He had to place a hand on the wall to steady himself.

"I'll be back in a few," Brandon said.

Lou set the small motel coffee pot up to brew, hoping the shower and caffeine would be enough to tie him over a bit until he could find some food. *I can't believe... This must be a nightmare! Where did she go! She said she'd be gone if I left. She said she couldn't stand being—Oh, God! Did I cause this? She wanted to list the house... I said no!* Lou continued to beat himself up as he tried to make himself presentable to the world once more.

About fifteen minutes later, Brandon was at the door once again. Lou let him in. "Something's come up. Jackson says you should still call Montgomery. He wants me to get to Pearl Harbor."

This surprised Lou, who was trying to find his clothes to pack. "Pearl? Really?"

"He made me call from a sat phone to tell me why. We've got a couple of submarines returning to port tomorrow. They were in some sort of shootout with China. Jackson's arranging for a helo from Hood to get you down to Austin for a flight home."

MOTEL 6 EAST, EL PASO, TEXAS

ROSIE NERVOUSLY LOOKED OUT OF THE CURTAINS OF ROOM 235 at the Motel 6 once again. For what she was about to do, she didn't even want to use the room she kept her phone hidden in. *Just in case they know!* All she could see was the side of the small strip mall next door. If the window could have opened, she might've smelled the MSG in the air from the Chinese take-out place closest to the hotel. *Cars... highway traffic... feeder road.*

She hadn't been able to get much sleep since she'd pried what she knew out of Eduardo Gonzalez. It had taken rum, tequila, and performing that special thing with her mouth that almost always made her want to throw up. Eddie had gotten so drunk that he didn't even try to satisfy his sick and unique urges with her missing hand digits. But his buzz made his lips loose, and loose lips sink ships.

Rosie had blistering-hot news and she was nervous as hell about what to do with it. She'd gone to work the next morning, having cleaned eight of her ten rooms for the day building up the courage. She was so worried about being set-up to be caught, she went to a different room. With two rooms left, she decided that she needed to pull the trigger, hoping that this may finally help her escape the nightmare-ish operation. She toggled the correct button on the new recorder that the 'homeless Jared' had left for her on her last drop.

"I...I d-don't know what to say, exactly. I was taken without warning to Amarillo again." She was using the Spanish word for yellow as code for Inocencio Delgado's mansion. "There must 've been thirty...forty of them there. Plus guards."

"You should've gotten the pix! I didn't dare try to bring this recorder! I'm sure they would've found it—they made everyone put their phones in a box. Some of the guards were continuously sweeping the place for EMF. They even had several big drones pulling security." She paused, looking once more at the closed and locked hotel room door. "It wasn't until I got Eddie drunk that I was able to get him to talk. It was just a matter of setting him up to brag, as usual. This is some heavy crap goin' down." Another pause. Another scan out the window. *Need to hurry, before Juanita or Melanie comes along to help me with my rooms.* "E-Eddie says that the entire cartel network—Mendoza, Pena, Castellano, any and all of them—are collaborating in some sort of expansion move. Everyone is expected to triple the amount of traffic, especially guns and cartel members. Along the whole border!"

She set the recorder down while it was still recording and walked over to the door, peering out the peephole. Satisfied she wasn't being ambushed, she went back over to the dresser and picked it back up. "Says this is all something that's been prompted by something Mendoza pulled off in Seattle—some sort of 'gang take-over.' I don't get much news of what's going on up there, but it sounds big. They freed an entire prison or somethin'. Now L.A... Denver... Phoenix... us... even as far up as Kansas City! Everyone's being told to start mobilizing for all-out assault on the cops. And the clincher is that they're goin' for some real psy-ops stuff, here. Provide food and medicine to people as the food shortages get worse. Help agitate the protestors, ramp up the violence in all of the down-town areas."

"Look! I haven't asked for anything from you jerk-offs in two years! Now I am! Get me outta here! I don't know what they're goin' to do here in E.P., but it sounds like it involves several coordinated IEDs. On Thanksgiving! Lots of people are gonna die! Cops and otherwise! Get this info to someone big—FBI... whoever... but Get! Me! Out!"

JOINT BASE PEARL HARBOR-HICKAM, HAWAII

UNDER A TYPICAL PEARL HARBOR NOVEMBER MORNING, TWO US Naval vessels slowly proceeded into port. The sun was still low, behind Diamond Head on Oahu's southeastern shore. The temperature was a 'chilly' 68 degrees Fahrenheit, and the salty breeze was carrying south to north, directly into the harbor. Nothing else about this particular pair of vessels was normal that warm Hawaiian morning.

The USS James L. Hunnicutt was listing to starboard, showing signs of damage. Most of the island's tourists hadn't hit the Navy Base and the duck boats yet, but there were still plenty of on-lookers gawking from shore and hotel balconies. Within minutes, the pair of vessels had hit Facebook and Instagram feeds. The Associated Press office in downtown Honolulu had been slammed with phone calls from Washington—*What is up with those submarines?*

One-half mile south of the Hunny, the USS Key West cruised into port, appearing normal to anyone who wasn't brushed up on naval lore. Flying high on the sub's collapsible flagpole—just below the US flag, was a Jolly Rogers flag. Handmade by the crew, the black cloth flapped in the breeze next to and below old glory. In the breeze, the crudely sewn craft revealed a large white skull with two crossed torpedoes under it. And while the lore and urban legend bound no specific rule as to the flag's meaning, every submariner knew what it meant—*Enemy engaged and killed in combat.*

Unbeknownst to most of the American public, this had happened in 'peace' a handful of times. It never made the news, and when it did, the lore was downplayed by the Navy. *No. Of course we didn't sink another submarine. That would be an act of war, wouldn't it?* But there were those that knew. A submarine—not just any sub, but America's most precious sub—had just arrived with damage under the watchful protection of a much older and still lethal sister sub.

Due to the emergent nature of the James L. Hunnicutt's condition, the ship's captain Commander Brody Woodward had received orders to immediately park at the Pearl Harbor Naval Shipyard. She would tie up to Pier Three, the long pier next to the harbor's East Loch, where she would be poised to enter drydock in two days' time. The USS Key West would continue slightly farther into Pearl Harbor, rendering honors to the USS Arizona before turning right to tie-up at the base for a quick debrief by the Fleet Commanders.

Darren was atop the sub, as were all crew who were part of the ship's 'deck division.' Unlike surface ships that had an entire group of men and women for topside seamanship duties, it was a collateral duty for many of the junior non-nuclear trained sailors and a couple of senior NCOs. A chief was in charge of the operation, but with the unique nature of their list and trim, Darren wasn't going to be anywhere else but right in the mix. The ships' CO, CDR Woodward, was in the sail, known more officially as the conning tower. Darren watched as a shipyard tugboat pulled alongside. The harbor pilot had boarded a half hour earlier, and now the tug was making up her lines.

Over the course of the next thirty minutes, the tug turned the sub around, pointing her bow south directly at the drydock, but tying up her undamaged port side to the pier. The Hunny's list to starboard caused a few hiccups in the normal procedures for landing the gangway and shore power cables, but after another hour, the USS James L. Hunnicutt was secure. Thirty minutes later, in dress blues uniforms, Darren, CDR Woodward, and Lt CDR Gingery walked off the ship and toward a waiting base sedan. The first-class petty officer who would drive was standing next to the car and offered a crisp salute, which CDR Woodward returned for the trio. *It's going to be a loooong day,* Darren thought. The car would whisk them directly to the Fleet HQ, where they would have to explain how they almost grounded and lost their three-billion-dollar spy and special operations sub.

Darren had his work cut out for him. As the senior enlisted NCO, he now had to figure out how to keep a crew that was deathly worried about their families back in the Rainier Impact Zone from going UA —*Unauthorized Absence,* the Navy's version of AWOL. He also had to keep them quiet about what exactly had happened, keep them motivated to get the ship fixed in drydock, and find a way to quit worrying about Pam and Maya. *Impossible,* he thought. *How can they possibly expect us to keep working while we're wondering what happened to our families?* He knew at that moment it would take all his energy to patiently wait for his officers to make that point for him and the crew. He knew they would, but the twenty-four-year career sailor also knew it would fall on deaf ears at the Fleet HQ. *God help us all right now...*

As the USS James L. Hunnicutt's leaders moved off the brow and directly to the waiting car, none of them noticed a Marine Corps officer standing along the edge of the pier, quietly observing the crew as they shifted the ship into a portside condition.

MORNINGSIDE, MARYLAND

. . .

LOU'S BROTHER FOSTER HAD COME DOWN THE EVENING PRIOR to pick him up at BWI in Baltimore. The pair grabbed a hotel nearby, his brother purposefully keeping Lou away from the house until they could see it on Monday morning. The Elkton, Maryland, businessman owned a small septic pump out business that would continue to run while he took a few days off to tend to his youngest sibling. They had stopped for a couple of quick breakfast sandwiches at one of the chain junk food restaurants and were now standing in front of Lou's home, talking with the fire marshal.

"Exactly how do you know where it started?" Foster Caldwell asked the expert. The graying man had two inches height and sixty pounds on his younger brother. His wrinkled skin made him look years older than he was.

"In layman's terms, whatever disappears the most in a house fire is where it burnt longest. And we can detect the accelerant with instruments. But as you can see, there's not much left of the second floor. And we can't let you go in yet—there's just too much risk that this remaining framing will fall-in on you—but if you can see the spots I'm pointing to, it becomes obvious that the first floor got burnt out in several spots first. See how the corners are just gone?"

Lou wasn't fully listening, his mind still focused on losing his connection with Terrance. *Why, Julia...? Do you really hate me that much? Will you forever blame me for his death?* He snapped out of it when he heard his brother calling his name.

"Lou! Earth to Freeman. You still with us, buddy?"

"Yep." Lou had been staring at the remnants of the garage, the beam now a memory. The sloppy, wet black char-soup that still covered the concrete floor had a strong burn odor to it—an odor that permeated the entire neighborhood. Though Lou could see a few gawkers standing on their porches or in their yards, he didn't care. *The beam is gone, nothing but charcoal and ash,* he thought. *Eventually returned to the earth in decay, maybe washing down the storm drain the next time it rains... Is this life? Is this our purpose? To eat. Sleep. Procreate. And then die? Return to the earth in a vicious cycle of birth and death?* Lou felt himself getting angry, wondering if there really was a God, though he knew there was no point in it. No value. He turned to face the other two men. "What happens next?" he asked the fire marshal.

"Once we've finished our investigation, your insurance will send their own investigators. They'll help you hire a few different industry experts—engineers, disaster cleanup, that sort of thing. I'm sure you don't need me to say it, but the home's a complete loss. The cleanup people will knock down some of the hazardous structure so you can get in and try to reclaim any possessions. As you can see, our firefighters tried to gather any furniture and items they could and stuff them under a tarp in the centers of the intact rooms."

After another forty-five minutes, the Caldwell brothers had wrapped up with the marshal and a few neighbors who had decided to come offer their sympathies. Foster could detect his brother was getting angry with them, wondering if they were just there to gather gossip. "C'mon, squirt. Let's go get lunch."

"It's only 10:30," Lou complained as they climbed into his brother's Ram.

"You got a better idea?"

"There's a bowling alley bar a mile from here."

Ten minutes later the men were sitting at the far end of a small bar, nursing a pitcher of beer. They were the only two patrons in the dark space, filled with the noise of video games and pins being knocked over out in the main alley.

"I need a favor," Lou said with a slightly demanding tone.

"Sure, little brother..."

Lou looked at him with all seriousness. "I need to get back to work."

"Seriously?" Foster couldn't believe his ears. "No, Lou! You need to take some time to process this. Your wife just burnt down your—"

"I'm fully aware of that, Foster. And I got no idea where she is. Her folks don't know. They've been texting me for the last half hour, wanting to meet up. The thought of talking to them pisses me off. They've enabled this mindset of hers that I was somehow responsible for Terrance."

"What? Oh, come onnnn, Lou! That's a bit paranoid, don't you think?"

"It's true," Lou said as he refilled his beer. "I don't want to see them. I need to get back out on the temp assignment I was on."

"Why? What's so important? If you ask me, you're just trying to escape. This is just fleeing from dealing with your crap, little brother."

"I get why you think that, Foss. I really do. But not being at home for ten days was starting to do me some good. Getting out, seeing America, talking to folks. There's something therapeutic about it. I can't explain it." His brother was eyeing him skeptically, searching his mind for his next counterpoint. "Please. I'm not asking for much. Just come down and meet the insurance folks. Just hire anyone they say. Put anything that doesn't have to be thrown away into storage."

"I doubt your bosses will let you go back out, Louis," Foster argued.

"Normally I'd agree with you," Lou returned. "But the guy I currently work for knows what I'm going through. And he has the power to keep me on the job if I want it." Lou paused for a few seconds. "And I think I do. Foster, you don't understand. If I can get through this assignment, I get to retire as a full-bird colonel. It's what I want."

"Alright, twerp," Foster said in a way that big brothers liked to annoy little brothers. "I'll handle this mess. You go find whatever it is you're looking for."

CHAPTER 15

EXECUTIVE OFFICE BUILDING, WHITE HOUSE COMPLEX

"I'M GLAD TO SEE THE LAST REMNANTS OF THAT MOVIE PROP are gone," President Jeremiah Allen snickered to his Chief of Staff, Shannon Sahr.

"Yes, sir. It took a while longer for the pieces to sell than we anticipated."

They were in the South Court Auditorium, discussing the fake Oval Office that had been constructed by the handlers of one of Jeremiah's predecessors. And while he didn't buy into the right-wing conspiracies as to the motive of its construction, he also never bought the excuse that the actual Oval Office was too small for any POTUS to conduct publicized business with the people. *We want transparency,* he told his staff. *And that monstrosity is anything but.* One of the junior aides had suggested parceling the old set on an auction site and donating the money to a worthy charity. Jeremiah had loved the idea, and a raffle was held for the public on the White House website. The winner had chosen the Make-a-Wish foundation.

"Apparently a large YouTube channel bought the fake desk and blew it up with Tannerite and firearms."

This caused Jeremiah to laugh. "Really?" he said, not really wanting an answer.

He walked down the studio floor to the front row of gray, bolted in chairs, placing himself directly in front of the big screen on the stage. His personal staff, his entire cabinet, and their staffs had all converged at the facility. It was almost 8:30 PM, and they were all preparing to watch a live broadcast by the Chinese Prime Minister, technically the Premiere of the National People's Congress. Unlike the Chinese President, he was no figurehead. Among the few true powers of the president was the right to pick the incoming premiere. The fifty-six-year-old Chu Chin was a retired Admiral with the People's Liberation Army-Navy. He had received his Master's in Advanced Chemical Engineering from the University of Cambridge. His time in the West had made him one of the people's more trusted internal experts on their culture and diplomacy. The bulk of his naval career had been dedicated to helping stand up their nuclear submarine force. The first planned nuclear powered aircraft carrier was under construction, thanks to his leadership.

Jeremiah heard the din of several whispered conversations slowly die as everyone took their seats after he did. He scanned the room. Counting the Secret Service agents scattered throughout the room, there were close to two hundred people present. *Do we really have this much overhead?* the former steel mill manager wondered. The Wall—the 292-inch 8K digital Samsung television on the stage—shifted from a flowing red-dune sand pattern screen saver to the official state seal of the Chinese Communist Party. The room hushed almost immediately. For two more minutes, Jeremiah scanned his pre-read summary—*just an 'educated' guess,* he thought—as to what his staff of foreign policy 'experts' said to expect. He listened to one murmured conversation three rows back, but he couldn't make it out.

The official seal dissolved to reveal the inside of the Great Hall of the People on the west side of Tiananmen Square. *Almost like watching the Oscars,* Jeremiah thought glibly. The view was from a camera on the giant auditorium's gallery. The bulk of the nearly three-thousand members of the National People's Congress were on the main floor. On the stage behind the podium was an elevated grandstand, filled with the one-hundred-seventy members of the actual full-time politicians that controlled China, the NPC's Standing Committee. The darkened auditorium had a slight semi-circular design to allow all people to pay attention to the stage. Behind the committee members hung ornate gold curtains almost fifty-feet high. Jeremiah looked around at the comfortable but modest auditorium he was seated in, almost embarrassed by the thought of the fake office he'd ordered de-constructed. *Almost.*

The camera panned left to pick up Premier Chu strolling in from stage right to a standing ovation. He smiled and waved as he made a slow procession toward the stairs leading up to the stage. Those in uniform were saluting him as he walked by, and the retired Admiral returned each and every one with a grin. After five minutes, he was finally at the podium.

"He's doing this just to screw with us," Jeremiah whispered to Shannon seated to his left.

Premier Chu began to speak. The dual channel surround sound in the South Court Auditorium began to play the speech in real time at a low volume, with Chu's clear and resolute baritone voice coming in clearly. The translation of an official US Government state department employee spoke over the Premiere's words almost simultaneously. "Tongzhi... Comrades, it is with a grave heart that I address you tonight."

"Comrade," Jeremiah said to Shannon. "I thought they stopped using that. Same syllables as their LGBT movement, or something..."

She whispered back, "Chu is bringing it back, forcing everyone to use it. Shop keepers, farmers, bankers—everyone—not just party members."

"Ahh," Jeremiah whispered as he continued to watch.

"As you all know, we have extended every courtesy we can to the

United States in the face of their recent natural disasters. Our hearts and spirits reach out to the millions of starving and shivering souls in their country. We know that our allies to the north have also—"

"Allies?" Jeremiah scoffed a little louder than he wanted to.

"—extended the olive branch of peace to Washington DC. Unfortunately, they aren't quite so compassionate to those of us who call them neighbor. Even as we load our ships with supplies for the west—"

Liar, Jeremiah said passively in his head.

"—Russia loads troop carrying ships on their west coast and has been steadily bringing them through the Arctic Circle to the Eastern Fleets. Additionally, they have been sending entire divisions of troops to our border as well as to that of our friends to the west, Mongolia. I say to the people of Mongolia, China will not allow this threat to your sovereignty go unheard." The Great Hall broke out in applause.

"Uh-oh," Jeremiah whispered.

Chu continued. "And to the President of the United States..." he paused for melodrama. "Despite our peaceful intentions, your country's military has only increased its cyber campaign against China with exponential ferocity."

The auditorium was pin-drop quiet, save for the two voices on the speakers, and the clearing of Jeremiah Allen's throat. "Furthermore!" Chu continued with fervor, "One of your submarines attacked our fleet unprovoked. China has done nothing to deserve this animosity!"

We attacked him? Jeremiah felt his face getting hot. *Mother—*

"—And! Your military continues to meddle with our on-going peaceful relationship building with our rebellious south-easterly province!"

Taiwan! He literally is trying to sell the world that Taiwan belongs to them right now!

"President Allen. It is with a sad but respectful heart that the People's Republic of China must recall all one point four trillion dollars of debt owed to us by the United States."

Jeremiah Allen felt the room start to spin just a bit. He loosened his tie.

"We will accept monthly installments, to be completed by July of next year!"

"They're calling in the debt," Jeremiah heard someone from the Treasury Department staff say aloud, the disbelief thick in her voice.

The Great Hall had erupted in a standing ovation once more. After thirty seconds it died down. "And to President Nikolaev... China does not accept these threats. You are ordered to stand-down your fleets and quit amassing such a threatening force at the border that we've shared so peacefully for close to eight decades."

The speech lasted for another four minutes, and when it was over a technician shut down the speakers. President Jeremiah Allen stood up. He straightened his tie and turned around to face his multitude of staffers. Some had started to stand up, and he motioned for them to stay seated.

"If it isn't clear by now," he said, pointing at the screen that had returned to the red sandy image, "then you're in the wrong career," he finished matter-of-factly. "Both China and Russia have been leveraging this moment for the almost four weeks since America got kicked in the gonads." He started to wander slowly across the front row, gaze locked on his people. *Selling America on the inevitability of the coming war starts here,* he knew. "As if the issue in the other Washington wasn't bad enough... As if we didn't have the cartel making a power play throughout every Western city... As if we didn't have the typical republican and democrat gridlock... As if we didn't have a coordinated effort by socialist-Marxists to convert the very fabric of America—to destroy the Republic!" He let it sit for a minute to regain his calm voice. "Dark days are ahead, team." He stabbed at the screen once more. "They've all but promised it."

MOTEL 6 EAST, EL PASO, TEXAS

. . .

In the two days since Rosie had dropped off the recorder, she'd slumped into a severe depression. She was mentally fighting hope and despair at the same time. Despair was the natural mood she felt, but hope was a dangerous weed that would take over her mind and cause a deadly mistake. Either she would slip up, or they would not pull her out as she wanted. Either way—hope had to go. As usual, when she made another trash run after sending the 'bat signal' to come get the recorder, a blank one had been left in its place.

Eddie had been off grid since then, barely texting or calling and not coming over for any playtime at all. This didn't concern her so much from a safety perspective. But it did drive home just how big whatever was happening could become. Since they had no dates, she did the next best thing—she read every text and she paraphrased the one phone call he'd made in her own words. Finally, she felt there was enough to turn in. She made her way to Room 147. It was occupied, but she'd kept a close eye on it and watched the elderly couple get in their Honda CRV and leave. *It's now or never.*

She moved her cart along calmly, scanning the noisy kids by the pool as she went. She and her cart drifted from eyesight of the kids and their parents as she got near the stairs that led down from the second and third floors. With one last glance around, she used her keycard and entered the room. The cold chill of the full-blast AC hit her in the face. *One light!* she instructed herself. *Touch nothing else!* The last thing she wanted was for 'Karen' to go bark at the manager, accusing the maid staff of stealing her cheap earrings.

She flipped on the switch immediately as she entered and went through the process of fetching her phone. *No time to charge it!* She powered it up and began to type in the memorized phone number.

BUZZ! *What the—!* The little envelope icon appeared. She opened the text. "1."

She felt her knees get weak. *Could they have...agreed?* The hope began to root itself in her mind. She powered the phone back off and decided she would have to take it with her. She had the nerves to remember that she may need to text back. After ensuring she hadn't mussed up any personal items, she turned off the light, opened the door and scanned. *Nothing unusual.* She turned right and made her way out to the dumpster. *Damn*! She went back to her cart and got some trash to carry with her.

She tossed the refuse, looked around, and reached under the familiar back corner. The small plastic bag was there, but instead of a clean recorder, it had a single piece of paper. *I think I have a lighter to burn this back on the cart...* The small, folded note had one small set of instructions. "Reply with location and time for this weekend. Out of town. I'll have guests."

USS Lyndon B. Johnson, DDG-1002—Norfolk, Virginia

"Permission to come aboard," Lou heard the sailors ahead of him ask the sailors staffing the Quarterdeck of the specialized destroyer. *More of a statement than a question,* he noted to himself. He spotted that they were holding up the military CAC, or Common Access Card, as they did so. One of the four sailors staffing the Quarterdeck was checking the cards physically with a handheld scanner and then waving her peers aboard. It was one morning after talking his brother into handling his home disaster, but to Lou it felt like a sense of normalcy—his visceral decision to flee leading once again to a structured life.

He got to the end of the brow, or gangway, and showed his card with his left hand. "Permission to come aboard?" he asked with a smile, not quite comfortable assuming they would say yes. The Air Force colonel was decked out in his usual relaxed pilot's dress of blue slacks, brown bomber jacket, and blue 'pisscutter' cap. It was the first naval vessel he'd ever stepped foot on, and the smile was hard to hide.

The young Seaman Apprentice saluted the bird on Lou's cap with a nervous expression. She'd never seen an Air Force officer, but she knew that whoever this geezer was, he shared rank with her captain. Lou returned the formal gesture as she took his card from his other hand. To the surprise of both, the reader gave the familiar beep and green light of approval. "Permission granted, sir," she said politely.

By this time the ranking member of the Quarterdeck watch, a grizzly Hispanic Senior Chief, wandered from the podium and emergency control panel he'd been hovering near. He saluted Lou. "Good evening, Colonel," he said. "Captain Goldberg is expecting you." He turned to one of the two petty officers who were part of the Quarterdeck detail. "Norwood, escort the colonel to the CO's cabin." He turned back to Lou. "By your leave, sir. Just follow the petty officer," he explained with an open palm reaching toward the assignee.

"Thank you, Senior Chief," Lou said politely. *Glad I brushed up on the Navy's rank insignia!* Ironically, Lou's last job at the Pentagon was in the middle of researching the pros and cons of aligning the entire military into one structure. While strictly about cost and battle efficiency, the impact to each branch's traditions, customs, and specific roles had to be scrutinized carefully.

As the sailor began to lead Lou into the hangar bay and forward, Lou asked, "So what's the insignia on your patch mean, Petty Officer?"

"Yeoman, sir," the young black sailor said matter-of-factly. Lou detected a bit of southern twang and hospitality. "It means I push a lot of paper! And if I may be so forward, sir, what do you do?"

"Same!" Lou joked, laughing. "And it's perfectly fine. What's your name?"

"Norwood, sir," the sailor said as they made their way through the hatch at the forward end of the hangar bay. As he stepped through, Lou could sense a unique smell, not foul, but unlike anything he'd ever sensed. Like submarines, surface naval ships carried an olfactory aroma that could not be described, nor mistaken for anything else—truly unique to the Navy.

"No, I mean your first name," Lou said, still in a surprisingly good mood.

"Ooohh, Reggie, sir. Thanks for asking!"

"No sweat, Reggie. I take it you sailors use last names a lot?" Lou inquired as Reggie began to lead him up a set of stairs.

Reggie turned to face Lou, changing the topic for a quick moment. "Watch your step, sir. These inclined ladders are steeper than they look."

"Man, you aren't kidding!" Lou said.

He caught his toes twice as he ascended twelve steep steps that were barely six inches deep. He found himself grabbing onto the step ahead of his chest as he walked up, only switching to the handrails for the last four. He followed Reggie out a non-watertight hatch to the left of the ladder's top. They turned right, continuing forward in a dark, crowded hallway. It had blue speckled tile, and the off-white walls were full of electrical boxes, firefighting stations, and various signs and placards. Some of them were even painted with luminescent paint.

Lou turned his body as sailors passed him going the other direction. It was the only way to pass each other without collision. Each time, his uniform received a polite but extremely curious stare.

"Almost there, sir," Reggie said.

"Before you go, Reggie—" Lou halted him, digging out a business card and giving it to him as he did with every military member he talked to. "Part of what I'm doing is an assessment of morale, impact to families, that sort of thing. Feel free to shoot me an email if you ever want to bring anything up that you feel the chain-of-command isn't helping with."

"Right on, Air Fo'ce!" Reggie said, sounding completely like an Alabama civilian for a moment. Reggie knocked on the door that had a brass nameplate on it.

"Enter," they heard a commanding female voice say.

"I'm good, Petty Officer. Thanks," Lou said and smiled as they parted ways. He entered what he would later learn was the only carpeted space on the destroyer—the Commanding Officer's stateroom. "Captain Goldberg?"

A slender officer with a cedar shade of red hair was already walking toward him. "You must be Colonel Caldwell," she said with a warm greeting. "Please come in! Get you anything? Water?"

"No, thanks Captain," Lou replied.

"Please... call me Millie," she stated. "And is it okay to call you Freeman?"

"Of course!" Lou said. "But I might turn around and look who you're talking to. I typically go by Lou."

"Some sort of fly-boy call sign?" she joked with a grin.

"Nothing that cool," he smirked back. The pair made the usual get-to-know-you small talk of personal career and 'what's your branch like' for a couple of minutes.

"Alright, Lou," Millie said as she started to get to business. "Here's the plan. I'll address whatever questions or concerns you have regarding your public affairs tour, then I'll give you a little tour of LBJ, Good?"

"That'd be excellent, Millie. Thanks. To start with, as one of the many ships being re-homeported on such short notice, how has that impacted your crew and ship's readiness?"

"Well, that question has both sides of the coin, really," she stated. "On the morale side, we've had the expected gripes and pushback from the married sailors, particularly the younger ones. I think the sailors that are on their second enlistment or beyond are kind of used to this type of thing. But since the only other two ships in the Zumwalt class are both already ported in San Diego, I expect that operationally, we'll be better off."

"I'm guessing that has to do with parts and training and such," Lou guessed as he wrote in his notebook.

"Exactly," Millie said. "I can tell by the bomber jacket you fly, or used to, so I'm guessing you can relate with planes."

"Pretty much," Lou concurred. "I was doing some pre-reading in my hotel last night," he continued. "This is a very unique ship design anyhow, but I guess you all have a newer weapon system?" Lou was referring to the ship's extremely long, slender, and smooth design coupled with a brand-new hypersonic weapon.

"One of them, yes. Our vertical launch tubes are the same as the other Zooms," she informed, using the class nickname. "But by the time LBJ was operational, the Navy was years past the decision to never purchase and use the one-of-a-kind ammo for our surface guns. They're currently outfitting the other two ships to use the C-HGBs with their existing gun mounts. But that limits the speed of the projectiles. They designed our unique launchers while we were being built—our hypersonic rounds shoot faster than the other two ships'."

"Are those the rail guns I've been hearing about?" Lou asked. He knew more about the topic than he let on as a result of his last job, but he wanted to get the full education.

"Ahh, no," Millie said. "Like our ammo, the rail gun system was scrapped before it became fully operational. There are a few ships with it installed. But the hypersonic rounds we can shoot don't require the million amps of power the rail guns need. So...similar projectile, but much farther range and greater speed with less engineering needed to fire."

"Fascinating," Lou said truthfully as he scrambled to write, hearing a knock on the door as he finished.

"Enter," Captain Goldberg stated loudly.

The non-watertight door, technically not a hatch, opened and a lieutenant walked in. "Pardon the interruption, Captain."

The young man was the ship's Command Duty Officer. It was his job to 'be in charge' for a full day, a common assignment for qualified mid-level officers while in port. It relieved the Commanding Officer of dealing with mundane tasks. He eyeballed Lou quietly. As the CDO, he was aware of Lou's visit. He just wasn't sure if he should speak in front of him.

"Go ahead, Jimmy. The colonel works for the Pentagon," Millie explained.

"Ma'am, we've had a message from squadron that there's been some sort of terror attack in Denver. It's already hitting the news."

"Oh boy," she said with great concern. "How bad, Lieutenant?"

"Smaller in scale. Sounds like an organized attack on their city hall and-or police station. Multiple armed assailants. RPGs. A real bad situation there, ma'am."

"Well, that sucks!" Lou exclaimed. "I'm supposed to fly there tonight." *What on Earth is happening to our country?* he asked himself.

CHAPTER 16

PEARL HARBOR NAVAL SHIPYARD, HAWAII

CHIEF-OF-THE-BOAT DARREN JORGENSON LOOKED DOWN INTO the still flooded dry-dock, impressed with the efficiency of the shipyard team. In the sixty-eight hours since they'd arrived at the pier, there had been a virtual broken beehive of activity. As soon as PHNS had received word about the damaged vessel, they started building the dock setting. They had finished it the evening before as the trades-personnel from the other services —electrical, pressurized water, ventilation, pneumatic air, and a host of others— were rapidly setting up the drydock for the US Navy's most important vessel that wasn't an aircraft carrier.

The USS James L. Hunnicutt had settled onto the blocks almost two hours earlier, timed with high tide to give the vessel maximum clearance over the concrete and wood cradle as she entered the drydock. There were still a few feet of water slowly being pumped out of the dock. A team of shipyard workers was already motoring around in a small boat, taking readings for radioactive contamination along the hull. As the dock emptied completely, they would finish that process while a few others set up the lights and required firefighting stations. After that, it would once again resemble the kicked hornet's nest as trades hyper-staffed themselves to get scaffolds and environmental containments set up.

Darren, Commanding Officer Brody Woodward, Executive Officer Carla Gingery, and a slew of the shipyard's officers and engineers were staring at and discussing the ship's grounding damage. The bulbous fiberglass 'sonar' dome that covered the entire front end of the sub had escaped mostly unscathed. *Thank goodness,* Darren thought. For a brand-new class of subs, they didn't have any spare domes at all, let alone in Hawaii. The determination had already been made that the ballast tank immediately aft of the sonar dome had taken the least damage and could be repaired as-is. The ship had obviously taken the brunt of the collision on the skin of the two tanks aft of that one, as well as on the ship's actual pressure hull. *These repairs are going to take some time,* Darren realized. *More time for this crew to get antsy about taking leave and trying to get home to Washington State.*

News had been surprisingly informative. The ship's homeport base had taken an accounting of all residents on the base. As a newer base that tailored its services to America's ballistic missile submarines, it had been built to a decent standard throughout the 70s and 80s. There had been a minor percentage of building collapses on the base proper, and the bulk of injuries and deaths had been to civilian staff, not families. Many of the married younger crew had already received good news. All the married men and women who were beyond their very first stint had reached a point in life in which they lived off base in homes they rented or purchased. Not to be outdone, many of the single sailors that had attained an E-5 rank lived in apartments out in the town of Sylvan, as that was the rank that they could qualify for the allowance.

The American Red Cross, in coordination with FEMA and various volunteer HAM radio clubs, had done a pretty good job of collecting the names of known survivors. Collecting names of the dead would take years to work through and it would never be fully finished. Too many people had perished in mudslides, the mini tsunamis that made their way down Puget Sound, and building or freeway overpass collapses. Had it been an isolated event, perhaps those people could have been retrieved and provided their last rites. But the entire region had been totally devastated. Local roads had become labyrinths of zigging and zagging, with 'checkpoints' established for collecting a 'toll' by the less scrupulous. Highways were largely unusable except to pedestrians. The power grid had become a foggy memory, something that would take a couple of decades to replace.

Darren had been one of the lucky ones, learning that his wife and daughter had taken their three horses and sheltered with a group of friends at the local gun club. His CO and XO had not been so fortunate to learn anything yet, which concerned him greatly. *We could be back in this fight within a couple of months,* he realized. *Where will their heads be?*

As the shipyard's CO, naval architects, engineers, and other experts started to wander away from the damage surveillance, the Hunny's CO, XO, and a Marine slid over to Darren, who was still observing the dewatering of the dock.

"You've been awfully quiet, COB..."

"Starting to get a lot of leave chits, sir," Darren said, turning to salute the pack of officers since they were outside. The Navy only rendered routine salutes while wearing a cover on their heads, and that was normally only done outside. He received the salutes in return.

"Even though we stated a clear no-leave policy?" Carla the XO queried.

"Aye, Ma'am," Darren said, looking at her. "The crew is worried, rightfully. And those single sailors that live on base want to know why they can't just go back to their home states for leave."

CO Brody rolled his eyes. "I can only imagine the dissension that would cause..."

"Agreed, sir." *Nobody ever said being in charge is easy.* "And since we were at sea for the bulk of the time since the event, I don't think the crew has fully comprehended the issues affecting the rest of the country, sir. That is, not until that thing in Denver yesterday." He eyeballed Brandon, wondering why he was standing there.

"Master Chief, this is Captain McDonald. He's on a scouting trip of sorts for the Pentagon. These morale issues are exactly the kind of thing he's looking for."

Brandon stuck his hand out to shake Darren's. "Mostly," he said, his usual grin showing through everyone's gloomy moods. "I'm from PR. Anything you can share about the damage and the repairs would help me see the bigger picture. I'm not a journalist, and the Pentagon can verify my clearances if you're worried about that sort of thing."

"Very good, Captain," Darren said. The grizzled Navy Master Chief didn't waste his 'sirs and ma'ams' on junior Marines.

"COB, when we wrap up, why don't you introduce the captain to some of the chiefs and LPOs."

"Roger that, sir."

Executive Officer Carla Gingery chimed in. "We've been so swamped with the debrief and emergency docking, I don't think anybody has had a true chance to catch up on news, let alone find some stress relief."

"I'm open to suggestions," the CO said, looking back and forth at Carla and Darren. "I mean, we can't exactly throw a crew softball and picnic day. But we need to do something."

"Maybe just a stand-down, sir," Darren suggested. "We could still go to the softball field, have everyone not on watch come out to talk... Give them everything we know... A chance for those who have received bad news to memorialize their loved ones."

"Not bad, COB," Brody said. He looked at Carla. "XO?"

"I'll get ahold of MWR right away, Skipper."

"Any good news from the engineers, sir?"

"It's all guess work at this point, Master Chief."

"We'll be back in this thing by the time it's a surface war, sir," Darren added as he looked back at the evolution in the drydock. The unspoken truth was that in any other time, all three of their heads would've been sacrificed on the career altar. *But these are anything but normal times,* Darren thought.

BUCKLEY SPACE FORCE BASE, AURORA, COLORADO

THE COLORADO AIR NATIONAL GUARD C-21 LEARJET approached runway 32, gliding to a smooth descent in the brisk Colorado fall air. The quiet, high-pitched hum of the two Garrett turbofan engines turned into a whine as the craft touched town on the dry, high-mountain runway. When the 140th Wing didn't have much training and activity happening, the runway could sometimes go two days without fixed-wing traffic. The former Air Force base had been turned over to the United States Space Force when it was commissioned in recent years. Home to sub-commands of every branch in the military, the base had become the hum of Space Force's Delta 4 program, as well as portions of Delta 6 and Delta 7, too.

Incredibly, the attack on Denver had only served as a minor hiccup in Lou's travel plans. As Tuesday night had drifted into Wednesday morning, it had become apparent to the state and federal governments that the event —as atrocious as it was— had been an isolated occurrence. The national media quickly started calling it '11/9' in an obvious attempt to play on people's emotions. *It was a Tuesday not unlike that September Tuesday in 2001,* they said. But unlike the sight of skyscrapers falling, this just didn't have the emotional gut-punch. There were no innocent children on airplanes dropping out of the sky. And in recent years, a very specific agenda has successfully persuaded mainstream America that police were inherently bad and in need of defunding. In some cities, they were actually trying to replace them entirely with social workers. As horrifying as watching a trained and armed gang was to people, most of them suffered from sensory overload and apathy—a dangerous combination.

I wonder if the rumors about a gang taking over Seattle are true, Lou mused as the small jet prepared to land directly at the Space Force base. *No wonder it happened in Denver. These cartels are all the most soulless and brutal killers in the world. They've been emboldened. Hell, they're probably coordinating their moves at this point.* Like a lot of Americans who were paying attention, Lou's instincts were spot on, despite the lack of subject matter expertise. *Of course, everyone is a Monday morning quarterback after things like this,* Lou admitted to himself. In review of what the public had been told, he just couldn't be sure of anything.

Of the six terrorists killed, five were Hispanic aliens with no record showing them even in the country. The last was Chechnyan. At least two had escaped, maybe more. It appeared the goal was merely to wreak havoc in the Denver City and County Building, and no group had claimed responsibility. Fifty-seven civilians and twenty-two police had been hurt or killed. And since the group had been using rifles, the mortality was expected to hit ninety percent. They used RPGs to destroy the exits as people began to flee. It was suspected there were spotter teams, though the FBI had been extremely tight-lipped about that possibility.

Lou had originally wanted to hit other east coast bases while he and Brandon were split up as a team, but the nagging feeling that something was wonky in cyberspace kept eating at him. He decided to make a visit to at least one if not two bases in the Denver area that were specific to fighting America's cyber war. Then the terror attack happened. Lou figured his bosses would tell him when there was something he needed to know. Colonel Jackson did help expedite Lou's trip by avoiding the Denver airport. It was a day of firsts for Lou. Not only had he never managed to make it to Buckley in his career, but it was also his first time in a Learjet. *Sure beats traveling commercial,* he thought no more than thirty seconds after takeoff.

Could the loss of Microsoft and Amazon HQs in that earthquake really have had this big of an impact? Is this all something that could have happened even without the issues caused by that disaster? I'm a 'free-range chicken' right now, he thought. *Why not go talk to the cyber experts and find out?* He'd learned that most of the Space Delta Unit 6 was based out of Schriever near Colorado Springs—but their 62nd Cyber Squadron was stationed at Buckley. That was who Lou was on the way to visit.

"We'll be parked in about three minutes," he heard the reservist captain who had flown him back from Virginia Beach say in the headset. Both he and the co-pilot had been getting required flight hours in —picking up Lou had given them an objective besides burning fuel. Lou had hoped they would approach the base from the northwest. He wanted to see the giant golf-ball looking arrays that contained large radars. The sixty-foot-tall structures were part of America's early-warning network, coupled to satellites that helped detect and track launched missiles and spacecraft.

"Roger that. Thanks for the lift, gents! It was a good chat. Hats off to the 140th!"

"HUA, Colonel," he heard the young officers say in the typical Air Force battle cry.

After the craft finished taxiing and an airman secured the wheels with chocks, the pilot shut the engines down. While the pilots continued their post-flight checklist, Lou pulled on the locking lever of the twin door hatch and popped them open. The roof swung up and the bottom of the hatch mechanically triggered the steps into appearing as it swung down. Lou ducked and descended to the tarmac. He received and returned a salute from the immediate airman.

"Lieutenant Snyder from 62nd Cyber is in the officer's lounge in the hangar, sir," the young man pointed.

"Gotcha. Thanks," Lou said.

He stretched slowly and started picking up the pace as the stiffness dissipated from his aching knees and lower back. Clop...clop...clop... That's going to get annoying. Lou looked down at the wheels on one of his rolling duffels. One of them was missing a large chunk of its siliconized rubber coating. *Great*... The clop-clop sped up as Lou did, and he tried to ignore it across the remainder of the tarmac and through the hangar. Just as he was about to open the door into the officer's lounge, it pushed open and an intense looking 1st Lieutenant in green camouflage exited the room.

"Colonel Caldwell?" he asked as he pulled his rapid salute back down.

Lou saluted. "I am."

"Follow me, sir," the officer said in a hurry and started to walk toward the personnel door near the back corner of the hangar.

Lou scrambled to keep up. Clop-clop-clop... He made it out of the door and saw the lieutenant a full thirty feet ahead. *Must be my breath,* he thought sarcastically. Lou stopped and tightened the straps on his backpack, keeping his left hand on the tow handle of the good roller. He hefted the other duffle by its sewn handle and started to carry it. The lieutenant had reached the silver Ford minivan with government plates and turned around. When Lou finally caught up, he reached for the bag.

"Apologies, sir."

"Thanks, Lieutenant," Lou said, handing it to him. The man loaded both duffels into the back and headed for the driver's door. As they started across the base, Lou said, "I apologize if my late arrival is causing you some issues, Lieutenant."

The young officer looked at Lou. "No, sir. It's just me. I've been told I need to relax a bit." He kept driving.

"Have you always been in cyber defense?" Lou inquired.

"Yes, sir."

Must be having a bad day, Lou concluded.

Shortly, the van was finishing the four-minute trek to the secure looking building that housed the 62nd Cyber Defense Squadron. The lieutenant spent a few minutes hand-walking Lou through a security entry procedure that included an EMF sweep to ensure he had no devices on him whatsoever. He'd left his luggage and phone in the van upon the advisement of the lieutenant. Once he had the proper visitor's credentials, Lou and the younger officer passed through a manned, secure entry into the main hub of 62nd's activities.

"Sir, I'll be taking you to Lt. Colonel Santos' office. Is there anything else?"

"Latrine?" Lou said. *Considering you were in such a hurry? Good thing I didn't go in your van…*

"Right this way, sir."

Lou took a few minutes to freshen up and was surprised to see someone waiting for him in the hall. A 'lite' colonel about his age smiled and stuck his hand out. At 5' 5", he had an enormous amount of energy. "Lt. Colonel Anthony Santos at your service!"

That's quite the difference, Lou mused. "Colonel!" He grabbed the hand. "Lou Caldwell."

"We got it, Lieutenant," Santos said to the young man as he took custody of Lou. "Security explain to you that you have to be escorted at all times?"

"Yes, Colonel," Lou said. "Don't go too hard on the kid. I needed a couple of minutes after the flight, ya know…"

Anthony laughed. "I think we can let that go this one time!" They continued small talk until they got to the colonel's office.

Lou followed him in. "Seems busy around here for dinner time."

"We've been extremely busy lately," Anthony concurred. "Donna, can you get the colonel here some water? And have the mess set aside some late rations for us?"

"Yes, Colonel," a civilian seated at a desk in his waiting area acknowledged. Anthony led his guest into his office and closed the door. Lou could see two of the giant arrays off in the distance.

"Do you know much about the 62nd, Colonel?"

"I think 'Lou' is fine in here. Do you go by Anthony?"

"Only when my mama is scoldin' me!" he joked. "Call me Tony."

Lou laughed. "Understood! I must say, Tony, you're quite the contrast from the young L-T out there," he said, pointing back over his shoulder. The two men had both plopped themselves into the chairs in front of the colonel's desk.

"He thinks he's being punished," he explained, the smile slowly dissolving from his middle-aged brown face. "In our world, colonel, a lot can go wrong in a flash. Did you happen to notice our unit emblem?"

"A gorilla with a shield and lightning bolt?" Lou thought back. *Just walked by it five minutes ago...*

"Correct. There are several different squadrons in Space Delta 6, each with a different mission. While we are considered defensive, as are some of the others, we are tasked with immediate countermeasures."

"The shield...and the gorilla..." Lou slowly put the puzzle together.

"Exactly."

"I thought Delta 6 had to do with tracking our military satellites," Lou stated in hindsight to his pre-reading.

"We do. But you won't find the specifics about two squads, including ours, on anything you read before today." He smiled softly. "We aren't straight offensive in nature, but we are the offensive response element of a defensive strategy to protect our critical satellites. Particularly those that can detect strategic or hyper-sonic weapons launches."

"Begging your pardon, Tony," Lou said. "That sounds a whole lot like an 'if you tell me, you'll have to kill me' answer. Will this seat self-destruct in five seconds?" he joked, looking around.

Tony laughed. "We are prepared to do things people would never understand to protect our satellites," he explained. "While the greatest threat remains disabling them electronically, there are physical threats to consider. Portions of our squad are able to launch a counterattack at someone trying to access our satellite net—both digitally and physically. And that's really all I can say."

"Roger," Lou acknowledged. "Then let me ask you this—is everyone here as stressed as that young man? Are you all getting what you need? In other words," Lou chose his words carefully, "if I had the ability to relay anything you wanted to say...to anyone you wanted to say it to... what would that be?"

Tony's face had become as stoic as Lou had seen it yet. He realized he'd never be able to play poker against a man like Tony. "I guess it would be... what are we waiting for? The things we've had to defend against in the last month... From China, Russia, Iran, North Korea, hell even our allies... not to mention the hackers-for-hire... What is the plan to make that stop before something irreversible happens?"

CHAPTER 17

Holiday Inn Express, Colorado Springs, Colorado

Sir,

2300: After the bleakness of the last thirty-something hours, I thought you'd like to hear an update from here at Fort Carson. Hopefully you've had a chance to review the trips from the two ships at Norfolk, so I won't rehash any of that.

As is the case everywhere now, speculation of the events unfolding in America seems to be taking a life of its own. The internal unrest here in the west is palpable, surely enhanced by the attack but a few miles from here. Yet I feel that even if that hadn't happened, I'd still be sensing the same vibe. Directly after the rumors about cartel infestation and motive for the event is a general conversation about violence in the streets. The continuous power failures, the hyper-inflation, and the fact that shelves are half-full has most people concerned. In fact, I don't recall anyone asking about the progress on the Seattle relief efforts in days...maybe in over a week. The mayor and city council in Denver just confiscated any relief supplies that were bound for airdrops to Seattle. I can attest in my own experience that traveling by air or car comes with its own inherent risks. By air, one is bound to be stranded for days without luggage in an airport. By car... Well, I figure it's just a matter of time before I turn up the wrong street and run right into some sort of 'protest.' Regarding my discussion with 62nd Cyber, I'll shoot onto base first thing in the morning and send an encrypted email.

Tonight, I dined out at a local restaurant here in Colorado Springs, and I wound up in quite an in-depth conversation with a group of hunters. (I should note that most of the menu was 'off-limits' due to supply issues.) Most of them are veterans and seem to have a grasp on how the world turns. What had started out as a joke about the movie 'Red Dawn' almost turned into a running theme for the conversation. These men and one young lady represented three generations of a family. They'd just come off a late bow-season hunt and were stopping for dinner on the way back to Castle Pines. Our conversation drifted to well past forty-five minutes. They were quite inquisitive as to the nature of my trip. The one underlying vibe I picked up from this particular family could be summarized as 'preparedness', I suppose. I was left with the impression they might be preparing to leave their suburb for good. 'Timing.' They kept talking about timing their departure. I found it peculiar that they seemed like typical small-town folk, but they did not like me referring to their plans as a 'bugout.'

I'll try to get a rental car tomorrow. The flight cancellations are becoming the norm, as are the sustained power outages. Luckily the hotel here has a good generator system. I'm told we can't use the heater, but we will still have hot water. The evening desk clerk told me that the manager's uncle owns a fuel distributor. Apparently, he's been fudging the numbers on his deliveries to the local commercial fleets. I've had a quick phone con with Captain McDonald, and we're going to meet up in Tucson. He's a squared away leatherneck, sir, despite liking jazz and talking enough to embarrass a teenage girl.

I'm sure people much smarter than myself are working on the logistics of keeping all these posts supplied with fuel for their backup power. That would seem to be an obvious Achilles' heel for the deployment readiness of any unit. I understand that the Navy lost the largest west coast fuel depot in Slaughter County during the disaster. Perhaps that will be a thread for me to chase when I finally make it to San Diego.

0015: Apologies for the time stamps, sir. I think an event that unfolded this evening as I was writing is relevant to add. I heard a commotion out in the parking lot. I went out to the outside walkway that overlooks the pool and saw two groups of people in a very loud and physical altercation. The long story short is that people from both groups improvised themselves some weapons—lounge chairs, beer bottles, I think you get the idea. It took almost forty minutes for the police to show up, and the EMS wouldn't come in until the cops showed up. There were several injuries. It was unsettling to say the least. I went down and helped with first aid and gave the police my statement.

I'd like to finish in thanks. I know I already said it on the phone from Maryland on Monday, but I do appreciate you letting me continue on mission, sir. I can't quite put my finger on why, but I feel like I should be out here.

V/R, Colonel Caldwell

INTERSTATE HIGHWAY 25, NORTHERN NEW MEXICO

"I WONDER IF THERE ARE STILL HOBOS," LOU STATED TO Brandon over his phone speaker as he traveled south on I-25.

His partner was still in Hawaii, opting to take a military airlift command flight directly to Davis-Monthan Air Force Base in Tucson the next day. It was Veterans Day. Lou had a buddy who was an officer at a VFW branch in Tucson—he was hoping to make it there early enough in the evening to kill a few brain cells and swap some stories.

"What makes you say that?" the young man said over the phone's solo speaker. Lou hadn't bothered to take the time to connect the device to the rented Kia's radio system.

"The freight train to the east of the highway I'm on. In fact, it's carrying Army equipment. Must be heading to SoCal or Arizona. Hell," he snorted, "it might be some of the stuff we saw in North Carolina!"

"Where are you at?"

"Just passed through a town called Maxwell. Still up in the north central part of the state. Wait! Looks like the tracks are peeling away from the highway. Oh well. Kinda cool..."

"So..." Brandon led hesitantly. "Any news on where the missus is, Colonel?"

Lou could sense the kid didn't want to pry. Though he knew it deep in his mind, his experience of learning all about that with Brandon had somewhat endeared the young Marine to him. *He's earned some flexibility,* Lou realized.

"If I said it once, I've told you ten times—call me Lou. Or Super Bert if it suits the moment." He heard Brandon laugh with a bit of ease. "And no. Her parents are pissed I didn't meet them back in Maryland. They claim they don't know where she went, but I'm not so sure. Listen, Poster Boy, in a few minutes I'll be departing the highway in search of the loo. Lou's loo, so to speak."

"Gave up on the goal to trim out coffee, huh?" he heard the young man quip. "I figured a pilot'd be better at holding his piss!"

Twenty minutes passed after the banter and salutation was over when Lou exited the interstate highway. *Springer,* he read on a sign showing an arrow and the logos for a few gas stations and restaurants. He cut through the small town and found a gas station, realizing that the rail line passed right through it. The Burlington Northern Santa Fe line passed through and eventually headed west for Albuquerque and beyond. Lou had a pessimistic feeling that he was going to finish his potty break and fill up just in time to get stuck behind a two-mile-long train hauling US Army armor at about 20 MPH.

About the time he was getting ready to depart, the train did indeed start to pass through the town. Lou turned right on the appropriately named Railroad Avenue. He would be able to cruise a mile south and jump right back onto I-25. *Guess I won't be stuck.* He wasn't prepared for what came next.

The first eight cars behind the four massive diesel engines were passenger cars. He hit the brakes, as nearly every car in the quaint high-plains town came to a stop and started honking. The lifted Ford pickup immediately in front of him had two giant, almost gaudy, American flags tethered to the rear corners of the bed. People began to get out of the cars and trucks—and wave. Lou slowly and cautiously slid to the right of the small town's extra wide main avenue and continued south. After a mere two hundred yards, he finally pulled over, mesmerized by what he was seeing.

Where the road curved away from the track, across from the town's stereotypical diner, was a crowd gathering. *I guess that's why there's so many cars in this parking lot,* Lou thought. He parked the car and after checking both ways, crossed the street over to the crowd. *Looks like twelve or fifteen people, maybe?*

"Look, Mom!" a boy of about fourteen said. "Here's one now!"

A beautiful older woman holding a girl of perhaps three or four looked over at Lou and smiled. All three of them were holding small American flags stapled to foot-long wooden rods. A few others in the crowd turned and looked, clapping and smiling at Lou. He felt a man slap him on the back affectionately. *Like I've just wandered into a Norman Rockwell painting,* Lou thought. He couldn't help but smile a bit.

As the lead passenger cars of the train crossed the small crowd, the soldiers responsible for operating and maintaining the tanks, artillery, Strykers, and other equipment were stuffing themselves out the windows, waving. Some were recording the town's gracious crowd on their own phones. "Whhheeeeeewwww!" he heard the male and female soldiers cheering at the cheering civilians. All were wearing big smiles.

They still got nothing on Brandon! Lou thought, not realizing how big his own was.

"Are you a soldier?" the girl in the woman's arms asked innocently. Though he'd left the garrison cap in the car, his trousers and bomber jacket looked the part.

"Amy, leave the nice man alone," he heard the woman say in a polite hush.

"Okay, Gram!" Lou heard the girl reply.

"It's fine," Lou said. "Sort of," he told the girl. "I'm an Air Force pilot."

This caused the teen's head to whip. "Coooolll! Have you ever shot down anyone?"

"Christopher!" the woman hissed. She looked at Lou with a sheepish smile. "Sorry!" She laughed in embarrassment.

Lou laughed back. The sounds of the crowd were dying, making the clacking of the freight cars seem louder. With no more soldiers to cheer, most of the crowd started to cross the street and head back to the diner parking lot. "As a matter of fact—" he led the boy on "—no. Sorry pal, not that kind of pilot." The small family started to cross back over with Lou walking behind them a couple of strides. "Mind if I ask you a few questions?" he asked as they all neared a truck that was apparently theirs.

The woman looked at her children. "No, I guess not..."

"This whole impromptu cheering thing," Lou started, not exactly sure how to proceed. "How'd...I mean, what made you stop what you're doing and start waving flags like that? Waving at soldiers..." Lou could see a sadness in the woman's eyes appear as the smile slowly dissipated. *She's remembering someone,* he realized.

"It just felt right, I guess," she replied. "Chris's Trail Life group had a Veterans Day assembly at the American Legion here in town. We were already down here."

"And we had flags!" the youngster added with enthusiasm.

"Which reminds me!" she exclaimed. "Thank you for your service!"

"You're most welcome," Lou said politely, hiding his cringe face well. "Thank you for your time, folks." He turned and started to head toward the rental when he saw a sticker with a red frame and one gold star in the corner of the woman's windshield. He gulped and stopped, turning back to the woman. The boy was on the far side of the truck helping the girl get into her booster seat. "Thank you for your sacrifice."

The woman started to ask Lou what he meant when she saw him pointing at the sticker in the windshield. She sighed heavily as her eyes misted over in memory. "Daniel. My oldest. KIA in Afghanistan in 2009."

"Is she Daniel's?" Lou asked about the girl, completely oblivious about the age being far too young.

"Oh, no. Amy is my daughter's. I have custody. She got in with the wrong crowd."

"I'm sorry if I've pried too much," Lou said sincerely. He started to turn back to the Kia.

"Were you in Afghanistan, sir?" she asked, walking over with expectation written on her face.

Lou looked at her sad brown eyes. They perfectly complemented the tan desert-plain landscape, dotted with the occasional pine tree. "Several times." *Just leave it at that, Caldwell,* he told himself.

The woman walked over and reached around Lou's neck, pulling herself in for a hug. He felt the warmth of her breath on his ear. "I can see sadness in your eyes, sir. God bless you. Whatever you did, whatever you dealt with...whatever it cost you. Thank you."

ASSARIA, KANSAS

"STOP! ALL STOP!" FORTY-FIVE-YEAR-OLD SONNY DAVIS, AKA Sunny D, yelled at the Cat Scratch Fever Mil-Sim team through the radio. He hobbled over to where Super B was standing as fast as his bad back would allow. The owner/manager of the paintball park in Assaria had agreed in a private text with Morris to give them some free no-shoot small units tactical training. "This, boys and girls," he said pointing at Super B and Superfly, trying to be heard without seeming too 'Drill-Seargeanty.' "This is why I insisted on no ammo."

His facility had been carefully built on a wide-open piece of Kansas prairie, with a combination of natural earthen hills surrounding it. He had also used an excavator to craft himself a few strategically located berms. Though not a public shooting range, he and people in his inner circle would occasionally use it as such when the park was closed.

"Everyone gather around!" he hollered without the radio's assistance. "Not you two," he told Jordan and Jon. "I'm going to use you as an example." Jordan's expression turned to embarrassed anger. Seeing this, "Don't take it personally, Bee. Every Army grunt made these same mistakes in basic training and AIT."

The rest of the team drifted in from their various positions. They'd been learning to move as a unit in an engaged situation while keeping cover, trying to get a feel for the differences between Mil-Sim and actual combat.

"What'd you do?" Nub teased the Super twins with a big grin.

"Listen," Sunny D ordered, regaining control. "Y'all wanted my assistance, so listen up. I got better things to do on a chilly Thursday afternoon, *especially* Veterans Day! I know you're all itchin' to get to live fire with yer shiny new guns. Baby steps. The more playin' around we do now, the less time there is for real learnin'."

"Sorry," Nub said, turning serious.

Turning back to the lesson at hand, Sonny pointed at the positions of Jon and Jordan. "Everyone else, circle around behind me. Whaddya see?" The team was looking at the duo stacked up behind a large inflatable airsoft prop, simulating taking some sort of ballistic cover.

"Jon's muzzle?" Goldi asked.

"Very good. Where should it be? Anyone."

"At the ground," said Morris.

"Yes. And…"

"...and not stuck between Super B and the barricade?" Misty guessed.

"Precisely. And not to pick on you two," he said to SuperFly and Super B, "but Jon? You need to not sweep your partner with your muzzle. Do it again and I start issuing pushups. HUA?"

"Huh?" Jon Sanches said, confused.

"Do you understand?" Sonny said firmly.

"Yes. Got it."

"And same for you, Jordan. You—"

"I didn't—" she started, but the Army veteran wasn't having it.

"Your finger will not be on the trigger again. If I see it there, you get laps. Got it?"

The college freshman showed an unusual amount of humility. "Yes. Sorry."

He scanned the whole group again, taking off his electronic ear-pro. Though they weren't shooting, everyone had adapted them as part of their kits for Mil-Sim since their radios could plug into them. Seeing this, the whole group followed suit.

"Listen. This stuff wasn't even my real specialty. I ran a mortar crew in my seven years in the army. But there's a lot of bad habits to break here. I see it all the time. Granted, the more experienced Mil-Sim teams are also shooters. Mainly it's the paintballers. But you all are noobs at this. You guys got some bad habits to break before we evolve into tactical shooting." He could see the reality donning on the college kids. "Here's what I suggest. Let's go do some square range shooting from the bench... Let everyone get the feel for your rifle. Get that itch scratched. Then come back Saturday. The team that had the park booked canc—" Sonny paused, his eyes shifting around as if he were distracted.

Morris heard thunder off to the west. *A lightning storm?* he asked himself. *In November?* Sonny donned his electronic hearing protection again. He turned up the volume and walked a bit, trying to get a good bead on the west. Confused, Morris did the same. The barely audible sounds were unmistakable. *Boom. Boom.* Then a bunch of rapid session *boom-boom-boom-boom-booms.* Within moments, all of Cat Scratch Fever had mimicked Sonny and Morris.

"What is that?" Floyd 'Elvis' Presley asked.

"Perty sure that's the Smoky Hill Weapons Range," Sonny answered. "About ten miles from here."

"Who uses that?" Misty asked, confused.

"Army," Sonny said. "But not very often. Normally it's just the Kansas Air National Guard, and normally it's on weekends."

The loud booms continued. "Are those tank cannons?" Goldi asked.

"It's an aerial range," Sonny explained. "Probably helicopters from Marshall," he guessed. Marshall Field was the aerial support facility for Fort Riley.

"Listen!" Morris said. The unmistakable sound of a distant helicopter could be heard in the ear protection's speakers. Not only did the headset protect shooters from the deafening noise of gunfire, but it also amplified normal human hearing many times when the speakers were turned up. "I think I hear one."

"I got it, too!" Nub said. "Waa-Ha!" he added in a mock John Wayne voice.

"Everyone, shush!" Sonny ordered. He was closing his eyes, studying the noise. He started turning his head, trying to get a feel if the sound was stronger in one direction or another. He opened his eyes and started scanning.

"You got a FLIR scope of some sort?" Morris asked.

Sonny snapped his head with a wide grin. "Why, yes! Yes, I do!" He took off for his office with the others in tow.

A few minutes later, after scanning the sky, he finally said, "I got it! Right there!" He could see the craft's heat signature with infrared. "I wonder what it's doing way over here... Ohhhhh...." He went silent, which was too much for Super B.

"What!" she exclaimed.

Sonny was still holding the infrared monocular to his eye. "I'll lose it if I pass this around. It's small, but the shape is distinctive. I think it's a drone helicopter, the kind with the big camera under it and big bulbous radar over the rotors. Explains why it'd be over here. Probably making a big miles wide circle around the bombing practice to the west."

ThatNub had a thought. "We'll be passing right by Marshall on the highway on the way back to K-State! Maybe we'll see them landing!"

Buzz! Morris' phone vibrated. While everyone else was still scanning the sky to see the drone helicopter, he slipped back toward the parking lot a bit and powered up the phone's sleeping screen.

[Mom: You and William alright?! Call me!]

Huh? Morris stepped even farther away from the conversation amongst his peers. He doffed his ear-pro and removed the slung rifle, leaning it against the fender and front bumper of Nub's Bronco. He called his mother.

"Baby!"

"What're you talking about mom?"

"The protests! On your campus!" She was confused. "How can you…? The radio said…"

"We're doing airsoft over in Assaria this evening. What're you talking about?" Morris repeated himself.

"Oh, Morris! Be careful going home. Apparently, the students at State have organized a big rally to protest President Allen. The news was saying they'd taken over the Dean's building and set fires in the main quad! Are you two really okay?"

She's really worried, Morris thought. "We're fine, Mom. We'll be fine." *Don't think I can bring myself to tell her about the guns yet.* "And what exactly do they think Allen's done? Or not done?"

"The radio said he issued some executive orders today. Ordered companies that make MREs and ammunition to only sell to the government for the next six months."

Well, that sounds kind of jacked up, Morris agreed in his head.

"And a rumor he may be setting an evening curfew for all major cities west of the Mississippi in a few days. Someone leaked that out of DC," his mother said, "And as far as I'm concerned it's about damn time!"

"So much for Libertarianism..." Morris mumbled.

"What?" his mother said.

"Nothing, Ma. Just got mixed feelings if what you said is true. Look, we gotta wrap up and drive back. I'm gonna get off the phone. Tell Dad hi." After another minute, Morris was finally able to pry his phone off his ear. He grabbed his makeshift range bag with ammo, tools, and gun lube from the Bronco and returned to the group.

"What's up?" Nub asked.

"Not sure where to begin," Morris said. "But I think we need to get familiar with these rifles before we leave tonight."

CHAPTER 18

THE WHITE HOUSE OVAL OFFICE

"WHEN?" JEREMIAH ALLEN ASKED HIS NATIONAL SECURITY Advisor, Elliot Parks.

He had just strolled in through his staff access on the room's north side. Elliot and Chief-of-Staff Shannon Sahr stood up from their seats on the gold oval office couches. Snake Charmer walked over to glance at the small electronic clock he kept in his top left desk drawer. He'd kept the habit of wearing a watch but not at *0345? Why can't these jackwads ever wait until daytime?*

"Most of the Secretaries are en route, sir. Ambassador Hilton will be cued up as well. Chairman Montgomery and DCIA Chen are already in the situation room waiting."

President Allen was still in his royal blue bathrobe. "Then I'll head back up and get dressed. I'll see you down there in five minutes." He strode back out the door he'd come through and found the night steward standing by. "Ronald, would you phone JJ and let her know I'll need my first couple of hours cleared?"

"Right away, Mr. President."

Jeremiah went east along the corridor, finding the private stairwell up to the presidential residence, guarded by one of the graveyard shift Secret Service agents. "I'm sorry I didn't say hi when I came scrambling by, Cheryl."

"Not at all, sir," she said, continuing to scan the hall. She called in his return up the stairs as was protocol. It had taken some getting used to, having his every move recorded. Jeremiah used to feel sorry for the agents on a night like this—the kind where he was back and forth because of emergency meetings and wandering around in his bathrobe.

He returned to his bedroom, and Francis picked her head up off the memory foam pillow. "False alarm?"

"Wishful thinking," Jeremiah frowned.

He took four minutes to relieve himself and brush his teeth. He'd learned the hard way to make sure he took a whiz before he went into an unplanned emergency meeting. Switching to a pair of Eddie Bauer sweatpants and a taupe sweater, he slipped right back into his slippers and made his way back down the stairs. When he'd achieved getting two floors below ground, his brief respite of peace and quiet was over.

The pair of Marines guarding the entrance to the hall snapped to attention and saluted. Jeremiah returned it as best as he could without stopping. "So, who's leading this?" he asked Elliot.

"The DCIA, sir, along with an analyst General Montgomery brought along from DIA."

Jeremiah turned left, leading Elliot and Shannon into the situation room. He took his usual position at the end of the table, scanning. *Heather must still be on the way.* He didn't blame her, knowing the Vice President would've been notified a bit later and still needed to transit over to the White House. The US' United Nations Ambassador Alexis Hilton was standing by on one of the video screens.

"Morning, Alexis," Jeremiah said.

She had attended graduate school with Jeremiah's youngest sister. At nine years younger, he'd never been much interested in anything other than her intellect. He'd met her at a Pennsylvania fund raiser when he was a local state representative and knew immediately she was the smartest person in the room. As tempting as it was to tease his sister's college friend, he'd had to learn to turn that kind of normal American behavior off.

"Morning, sir. I have feelers out to Ambassadors Xu and Stoyevskiy, but we've not heard back from them. Nor the Security Council Chairman."

"Thank you, Alexis. Alright, folks, where do we start?" he asked the room.

"Sir, as you know," Joint Chief General Montgomery started, "DIA picked up on some chatter that we felt compelled to run through CIA. Based on both our and their analysis..."

Jeremiah immediately looked to the CIA Director, Rosamund Chen, who was nodding in agreement.

"...we think we're about to see a Chinese first strike against the Russians. If not today, certainly tomorrow."

"Define 'first strike,' please, General? And can someone find me a cup of coffee?"

As a Navy audio/video technician found himself scrambling to the corridor, the general looked at the monitor that was projecting the thumbnails of several satellite images. "Number three, please," he said to the Marine Major who was controlling the feed. "Low intensity, sir. Tactical, not strategic. Looks to send a message by sealing the border, but no apparent invasion plans—yet. If you bear with us, we'll explain why we think this is a non-nuclear strategic strike." The president looked at an infrared image of a series of land-based cruise-missile launchers set up in a valley. "These are DF-10A cruise missile batteries, sir. They have a 2000-kilometer range and a 500-kilo warhead. This is just one picture of a launch facility that has sprung up in the last two days. This one is north of Wangkui."

Jeremiah was moving his mouth as he counted. "What differentiates this from normal training, General? I see maybe a dozen launchers."

"There are eight such deployments, sir, and when we map their ranges out, it creates a bubble that perfectly overlaps their entire border with Russia."

"Okay, we've been expecting this. What's new?"

"Sir, the Chinese are notoriously fickle with their training budgets," Director Chen jumped in. "For one thing, they've never shipped the fueling trucks out that support these mobile launchers and the required station generators fully loaded before."

Jeremiah squinted. "Okay, I'll buy those are muddy tracks, but c'mon... You mean to te—"

"Laser measurement," General Montgomery explained. "Our satellites always measure how deep their ruts are and have built tables to account for rain as a factor."

"G-huyah!" Jeremiah audibly guffawed. "You mean to tell me the depth of a muddy tire track tells you they're about to attack?"

"That's just one piece, sir," Director Chen said. "It's going to take a couple of hours to review everything in detail." She grabbed a glass of water from the set that had been placed on the table in a haste before the meeting.

"Understood, Director, and I want to hear it all, but give us the cliff notes version so that the Ambassador is prepped when her UN co-members call her back."

"Very well, sir. They are heavily reliant on fishing the Amur River and its tributaries to feed their citizens. Fishing activity has decreased by ninety percent in the last two days, along the entire 2,700 miles. We have heat blooms on their military satellites that indicate increased power consumption for highly encrypted transmissions. The power generating stations at every one of their cyberwarfare centers have been sucking their cooling ponds dry. And we can't say too much to protect the asset, but the Australians have two independent sources inside the staffs of the Standing Committee members that confirm it."

"Also, sir, the recorders our sub recovered from the floor of their two North Fleet bases were able to give us direct conversational intel from their fiber-optic lines," General Montgomery began to add.

"Someday, General, you're really going to need to read me into that program. Just how on Earth can we tap undersea fiber optic cables?"

"Nano-technology is a helluva thing, Mr. President." He left it at that as both of them knew there was a reason political leaders were sheltered from knowing too much about how the intel was gathered. "Point is, sir, not only do we have snaps of them loading their ships for a major sea engagement, we have phone and email conversations validating it."

"Aye-yai-yai," President Jeremiah Allen muttered in exasperation, wondering for the latest of countless times why he ran for the office in the first place. "Anyone else want a coffee, or is it just me?"

TUCSON, ARIZONA

LOU WOKE UP IN THE NAMELESS HIGHWAY HOTEL. AFTER SO many in such a short time period, he was just starting to see them as different versions of the same bad and mundane dream. He didn't make it into Tucson until after 9 PM. A quick text with his buddy had confirmed that the VFW was closing. *We're all old-timers,* he explained. *Nobody here drinks like we're bulletproof anymore.*

Other than his encounter with wandering into a seeming Twilight Zone of Americana, his only other event of the previous day with any significance was paying twenty-five dollars for a paper map of New Mexico. The cost was reimbursable to him, as was his whole trip—a mere grain of sand on a thousand-mile-long beach of U.S. taxpayer debt. *My dad used to have these Gazeteer books with detailed maps of all fifty states. I sure wish Foss or I had kept those when we parted his estate.*

As he passed through Lordsburg, New Mexico, memories came flooding back of a ski-trip he and Julia had taken back when he was stationed with the 355th Wing at Davis-Monthan, his current destination. Terrance had still been a twilight dream at that early point in his marriage and career. Julia had sprained her ankle during snowboarding lessons, and they spent the bulk of the long weekend snuggling and working on starting a family to keep warm. The happy memory instantly turned his mood sad again, as the thought that Julia and he were done swept back over him. *Foster is probably right. Maybe I am using this job as escapism a bit. But I've lost her. I've lost my house. This retirement is the only bright thing I have going for me. I have to go out on a good note.*

The Kia made the noise of an old Sherman tank as it started to cross the rumble strips. Lou jolted out of his daze and corrected his course. He surveyed the post-dusk desert darkness. It was largely pitch-black, and Lou couldn't tell if it was darker than normal due to rolling outages.

The next morning, Lou got himself groomed for the day as best as he could in a hotel running on generators. *Gonna need to figure out a place to do laundry*, he thought as he gave his clothes a sniff-test. *Tonight. Brandon will probably need to as well.* He realized he may not own enough skivvies for traveling in the American west during the worst blackout period in modern history. He put away the bottle of vodka, still two-thirds full despite having been purchased in Norfolk. *Don't need the Poster Boy giving me any crap.*

Lou stuffed the old school key into his pocket, thankful that the hotel had been able to switch back to them. The modern key card had led to more than one customer being locked out of their rooms in recent weeks. Lou took the internal stairs down the two flights. *Definitely not riding elevators anymore.* He headed for the lobby, where he found a woman staffing the front desk.

"Is there an Air Force Federal credit union near here?" he asked the clerk, a Mexican-American woman in her mid-30s who bore the name tag 'Mary.' Lou was in the easternmost reaches of Tucson, an area he hadn't been all too familiar with at the beginning of his career.

Mary pulled out a paper brochure of Tucson and flipped it over, showing a printed breakdown of the immediate area. She circled a spot, saying, “On the right, just past the Taco del Mar,” with a friendly smile. “But I’d call first,” she advised. “With the blackouts and internet issues, a lot of them are only doing on-line transactions now.”

“Kind of makes it hard to get cash, doesn’t it?” Lou asked rhetorically.

“I suppose,” she agreed. “My husband and I recently took almost all of our savings out. It took several trips, as our bank had imposed a withdrawal limit.”

“Is that even legal?” Lou chuckled. “My instant reaction would’ve been to close the account.”

“I get it,” Mary agreed. “But both of our jobs require direct deposit. We’re kind of at the bank’s mercy that way.”

Lou thanked her and left. As he got to the car, he went to check his paper map that Mary the clerk had made for him, suddenly recalling her advice to call first. He discovered a fast-busy signal, which spurred him to drive there. Mary’s guess was correct—they were closed for the afternoon. *I really don’t want to run out of cash,* Lou thought. He returned to the Kia and texted his old pal that he was on the way.

Nine minutes later and fifteen minutes early, Lou was parked at VFW Post 549. He got out of the car and heard a generator running behind the building. He wandered into the veteran’s social club. “Looking for Mark Salem?” he half-asked the bartender, a pleasant looking black woman easily in her 60s named Phyllis.

“Sign in,” she half-ordered with a smirk as she pointed toward the logbook on the wall near the entrance.

The room had a dark wood interior and the blinds on the windows were half open, allowing just enough light through the slivers for Lou to make it out. The back door was open, and Lou could see what he presumed was a designated smoking area out back. He could see it was covered and had very Arizona-esque gabion walls around it to shield the picnic tables from desert winds rolling off the hill behind. The walls surrounding the pool table area were covered with all too familiar pictures of A-10 Thunderbolts and other USAF craft, along with a few action photos from the other branches. In the corner of the seated dining area was the MIA homage one would find in every VFW Post in the world. It was a place setting permanently established in honor of the fighting Americans who'd never made his or her way home.

He wandered over to the book. *What the hell is my member number?* he wondered, retrieving his billfold.

"Don't look now, everybody!" he heard an obnoxiously loud but familiar voice call out. "We got us a Super Bert in the house!"

"What's happening, Witch Doctor?" Lou asked in a noticeably more subdued tone.

He was immediately both impressed and appalled at his old friend's appearance. Retired Lite Colonel Mark Salem, about eight years senior to Lou, had been out for nearly a decade. The shorter man was wearing a Hawaiian shirt and tan cargo shorts. His balding head ended in a puffy ponytail that resembled something one might see on a fat, park-fed squirrel—if the squirrel had gray hair. Behind a pair of coke bottle glasses were the eyes of a man who'd become accustomed to drinking VFW beer way too early most days. His three-inch beard was what surprised Lou the most. It was jet-black, almost as if Mark had been dyeing it.

Mark strode over to Lou and gave him as big of a hug as a short man could. "Good to see ya, Lou!" he yelled. "What's it been? Nine years?"

"Twelve," Lou corrected as his buddy released him and headed for a small two-person table on the wall past the pool table. "And I see your hearing aids still need batteries." Nobody was playing pool at that moment. Other than Phyllis, Mark, and Lou, there were only two other patrons, both sitting at the bar. *Well, it is a weekday,* Lou realized.

"Twelve?" Mark questioned in disbelief. "I didn't see you at the squadron reunion here in Tucson?"

"No. I was at the one in Florida," Lou said.

"Huh," Mark said quizzically. "I guess the years start to become smudged, don't they? You still in, you said?"

"Yep. On a special detail right now, in fact."

"Yes, that's what your text said. You definitely got my curiosity piqued!"

"Hold on!" Lou said, cutting off his old friend. "Let's catch up first..."

This led to almost two hours of swapping stories and catching each other up on personal details. Whereas Mark had been extremely saddened to learn of Terrance's suicide, he could relate somewhat. His wife had been diagnosed with a rare form of brain cancer seven years earlier. It had taken her life in just four months. Lou specifically left out the recent event with Julia. He just wasn't ready to be peppered with judgment about why he was on the road instead of at home handling his life issues. He'd noticed that despite the story time, both he and Mark had both only barely finished their second beers. The place had acquired close to a dozen other patrons, most of them regulars.

"I notice that we're both a bit slow," he said as he glanced down at their mugs.

"Well, I've obviously lost the battle of the bulge!" his friend joked. "I try to sip them now. The older I get, the less it is about getting buzzed and more it is about just sipping on something."

"Same," Lou wrongly agreed. "I went through a rough patch of drinking after Terrance," he confessed. "Not that I'm a medical addict, but I think I've probably been hitting the bottle too much lately." The thought of cold puke on the bottom of his foot was still fresh.

"So, tell me more about this 'special detail'," Mark said while air quoting the words. "Sounds cryptic."

He pulled out a pipe and tobacco pouch and stood, leading Lou through the back door to the smoking area. As he stuffed and tamped his pipe with a sweet cherry-smelling leaf, Lou gave him the best version he could without saying who he worked for directly. Mark kept his pipe lit, pulling on it with an intense gaze of interest as Lou filled him in on most of the trip. He finished by letting Mark know that in less than two hours he had to go pick up Brandon and needed to switch to water and coffee.

"The duty van at the receiving hangar can give him a ride to the transpo center. Just tell him to catch a cab or a Lyft or something," Mark suggested.

Lou smirked. "I suppose I could do that. But I do need to slow down a bit. Like I said..."

"No judgment from me, brother. So as much as this trip is about unit integrity," his old friend summarized, "you're also out here trying to see how us grunts live without power and internet?"

"Something like that," Lou laughed. "But what has me more concerned is the devolving nature of people. Seems like more and more people are prone to tempers and violence. And I'm trying my best to avoid cities. The cartel thing has me worried, too. What if Denver was just the beginning? What if those reports from Washington State are true?" His friend had grown eerily quiet. When he failed to continue the chat with a new comment or question, Lou finally spoke up.

"What...?" He could practically see gears turning in his friend's head.

Mark put a finger up silently as he pulled his cell phone out. "Gimme a second." He shot someone a text. "I got someone you should meet. Text your leatherneck and tell him how to get here." A half-minute later, *Buzz!* Mark scanned the reply. "This guy'll be here in a half-hour. Member of the post. Former special forces officer from the 90s."

Lou was very curious. *What about the words Denver, cartel, or Washington triggered that response?* he wondered. "Alrighty. Guess we should get another round, then."

CHAPTER 19

PEARL HARBOR NAVAL SHIPYARD, HAWAII

USS JAMES L. HUNNICUTT CHIEF-OF-THE-BOAT DARREN Jorgenson walked through the noisy, furious drydock, impressed with what had been done so far. In the just over five days since his submarine had been sitting on the fir and oak topped concrete blocks, the shipyard workers had converted the giant concrete box. What had been devoid of anything but the submarine and her setting on that Sunday morning was now filled with scaffold, electrical panels, cables, hoses, and a collection of large machinery from one end to the other. While the goal was to assess and repair damage as quickly as possible, the opportunity to perform other maintenance couldn't be lost. Screens that protected large seawater intake valves had been removed for cleaning and valve maintenance. Locations of the submarine's special sound-dampening coating had been encapsulated in large plastic containments for heat and humidity-controlled repairs. From afar, the Hunny might resemble a piece of dropped candy with ants crawling all over it.

"Follow me, COB," the shipfitter boss yelled through the noise and earplugs both were wearing.

Darren had requested the chance to go see what was happening at the damaged ballast tanks, on the chance he could somehow support the 'yardbirds.' He followed the supervisor up two sets of tight metal stairs on the scaffold, rounding a couple of corners on the proper level. He followed the young lady through a slit in a virtual room of fiberglass and Nomex material hung for spark protection. The intensity of the grinding noise amplified as Darren stepped through. He banged his hardhat on a low hanging pipe, unable to see it due to the plastic bill on its front.

"Sorry, Master Chief," she yelled. "The custom levels of scaffold in here to get us into the various pockets through the damaged metal are all over the place! Move slowly and keep looking around!"

Thanks for the tip, Darren thought as he twisted his head back and forth, trying to see if the new crick would pop itself out. *Nope.* His safety glasses started to get a mild layer of vapor on the inside, a byproduct of his age and weight not reacting too well to the tropical temperatures.

"Looks like Godzilla took a bite out of us," Darren yelled above the noise. There were large grinders and cutting torches in several spots along about forty feet of the two ballast tanks. Much of the damaged hull had already been cut away and removed with cranes.

"One good thing about her design, COB," the shipfitter yelled. "The older subs keep the air bottles along the side."

"Yes, I recall the 'banana bottles' in between the frames," he acknowledged. He'd served on four other subs over the course of his career. "They mimicked the curve of the hull. You think these larger, more traditional cylinders saved our bacon, do you?"

"They're still doing the NDTs," she hollered.

Various engineers and testing departments were performing a variety of non-destructive tests all over the ship, but particularly to the pressure hull and over critical pieces in the damaged area. The tests involved a variety of procedures from using fine powders to X-Rays to look for cracks and damage that might cause issues under the weight of the ocean. Ironically, there were certain shapes and sizes that did not require immediate addressing. Those would actually become more water resilient under pressure. But ultimately, all facets of ensuring that the ship designed to sink could reverse the process were amongst the most highly regarded in the Navy. In the 1980s, after the loss of the Space Shuttle Challenger, NASA had come to the Navy for technical guidance in how to improve their programs.

"But from what I've been hearing, your pressure hull and bottles are good," she added.

"What's that mean for our schedule?" Darren asked. "And is there anything you can use sailors to help with? I got tons of those, and some of them could use something to take their minds off Washington State." *This noise down here goes right past the ear-plugs and just vibrates your bones, doesn't it?* Darren thought. *No wonder these people get paid so well.*

"Sure thing," she said. "I could use three or four for fire watches. That'd free up a few of my folks to do other things. Swing shift, too. Can you manage that?"

"No problem!"

"As to schedule, we still have a ton to do. See all this damaged piping? And your secondary propulsion thrusters are toast. Once it's all repaired, there'll still be a couple of weeks to test it all. The fitter shop is already lofting and building your replacement outer hull, but even when all of that's done, it takes weeks to get the outer paint and coatings installed properly. I've seen jobs like this take a year!"

Darren laughed, though she could only see it with the noise. "I guarantee you we don't have a year!" he said. "Big navy is going to throw everything they got at getting us back to sea."

The supervisor considered that. "If there's one thing the government has taught me, it's that they can suspend, change, or cancel the rules when it suits them. Maybe with some paperwork lifted, we could get this done at a World War Two pace. What'd you guys hit?" she asked curiously, knowing the tight-lipped submariner wouldn't tell her.

"Big frickin' mermaid!" Darren yelled, moving to exit the contained area. Once back out on the open scaffold, he didn't have to yell so loudly. He turned to see her following him. "You all have a young workforce," he commented.

"We've been hiring like mad for years," she explained. "And with the loss of Washington's shipyard, we're going to be doubly busy. I've heard that the Navy is looking to reopen Long Beach and Alameda."

"Long Be—those have been shut down longer than I've been in the Navy!" Darren exclaimed. Then he thought about what he knew... about what this young lady probably knew intuitively, if not openly. If a major naval engagement broke out with either Russia or China, there would be no way to build ships fast enough—not in the 21st Century. *The world just moves too fast, now.* Repairing ships, or retrofitting those that had been parked in the few 'mothball' fleets like in Pearl Harbor and Philadelphia, would be the only way to keep in the fight. With the loss of Washington State Naval Shipyard, the U.S. only had civilian drydocks on the entire west coast. *Makes sense,* Darren realized.

"In fact," the young lady continued, "I bet any and every sailor would be directly handed a DOD job when they get out, if they want it. Better pay and no going to sea. You might just see an exodus of your sailors, Master Chief."

Which is why the Navy just issued a stop-loss order, Darren didn't say aloud.

MOTEL 6 EAST, EL PASO, TEXAS

ROSIE HAD THOUGHT SO LONG AND HARD ABOUT HOW TO safely leave town for the ordered meetup that she'd waited until Friday to make a decision. *Naturally,* she thought with ingrained pessimism.

Eddie had scheduled a booty call for Sunday. She knew she'd be able to get him to eat first. *A big batch of the chili with corn tortillas he loves so much,* she decided. Only a healthy dose of magnesium-citrate would be included.

A day earlier, she'd gone to the pharmacy. She'd managed to sweet-talk the grandmotherly technician into giving her the stuff normally prescribed before a colonoscopy. She bought some Vaseline and a set of adult diapers, too, and hid those under her growing pile of dirty laundry. *No way will I chance making a separate batch of food for myself,* she thought, scared of the mere possibility Eddie would figure it out. She decided she'd partake in the same meal on the chance he took a spoonful of her bowl once he'd detected a weird taste. I'll just deal with the same issues and wear the diapers to the meeting. The thought of it grossed her out, but fear of an excruciating death at the hands of the cartel was a powerful motivator. The final thing that drove her choice was that if only he got sick, he wouldn't leave. She'd need to legitimately compete for the throne to get him to go home.

After going through her vigorous security process, she was finally ready to announce a location and time. She was surprised not to see a prodding text, wondering what had taken her so long. *Eddie will be over at lunch time. I need time for us both to get sick, for him to decide to go home... Carlsbad,* she decided. *That should be far enough away. If I give it a few hours, the frequency of the explosions should start to die down. [9 PM Sunday, Pancho's, Carlsbad].* Rosie sent the text with the time and location of an off-the-drag restaurant. She went through her clearing procedures to re-stow the device. As tempted as she was to break the thing and just walk away forever, she didn't want over two years of her life to be for nothing. *I could never live with myself if I can somehow prevent El Paso from becoming Denver.*

THE WHITE HOUSE RESIDENTIAL QUARTERS

"SORRY TO WAKE YOU SIR," TERRELL ARRINGTON SAID. Shannon Sahr had assigned the staff's overall utility man to work nights, knowing that the West Pacific War could kick off any day.

"I'm sure you have good reason, Terrell," the president said, pulling the bedroom door closed. Terrell was joined by an Air Force officer in uniform. He motioned for them to join him at the residence dining table, spying a folder he was about to be handed.

As they all sat, Major Kari Radcliffe handed the president a binder. "Mr. President, PACFLEET forwarded messages they received from no less than three submarines reporting a massive engagement between China and Russia."

"How long ago?" Jeremiah asked, rubbing the sleep out of his eyes. They all heard a knock at the door. "Come in," he yelled at the door, knowing who it was already.

A Navy enlisted culinary specialist adorned in a white double-breasted chef's coat opened the door and pushed a cart of coffee and danishes into the residence. Jeremiah had left a standing order with the kitchen to be ready to send some up any time the house staff got wind of him being woken up in the night. It seemed to be happening more often than not in recent weeks.

"Right here, Mr. President?" the young man asked.

"Perfect, Petty Officer, thank you." After the steward left, "How long?" he repeated patiently, standing to pour himself some go-juice.

Major Radcliffe scanned her watch. "First report came in fifty-one minutes ago, sir."

Jeremiah sat down and sipped the Arabica java as he opened the binder to look at the communiques. "I take it we've got radio and satellite evidence being prepped for me, too?"

"Yes, sir."

"So what started it all, Major?"

"The Illinois reports that she was monitoring three PLAN diesel subs in the southern Sea of Japan for the last two days. They encountered a Russian sub, identified by our subs as the cruise-missile-sub Kazan, and began to harass her. When one tried to flank between the Kazan and her homeport of Vladivostok, the Russian sank her."

Jeremiah nearly spit out his coffee. "What!"

"It gets better, sir. The other two PLAN subs attacked and damaged the Kazan, but she and an adjoining Akula class hunter were able to sink them, too."

"Damn." *So much for wishful thinking*, Jeremiah thought. "Alright. I'm going to grab a quick shower while everyone's on their way in." He thanked the pair and headed back into his bedroom while they departed.

His mind was racing a million miles per hour. When he was showered and redressed, he didn't even remember doing it. *What is their end game, really? Are they literally starting a fight over who gets to be top dog in the future? Just how weakened do they think we are?* And the one underlying thought about his own courses of action that made him shudder—*I'll undoubtedly be heading to the U.N. sometime in the next day or two, as will everyone else.*

Forty minutes later the president and most of his security council were meeting in the situation room. "Maybe we should start a punch ticket of some sort," he joked as he entered the room. Everyone stood and waited for him to take his seat. "Get a free pizza after five meetings or something."

"We have a development, sir," SecDef retired Admiral Kelly Fitzgerald said. He nodded toward Major Radcliffe, who'd logged into the DOD computer to cue up their prepared report and other assets on the room's screens. The main monitor's DOD logo display dissolved as a satellite feed began to tune in. "Go ahead, Judah," the Secretary told the Joint Chief.

General Montgomery stood and walked up to the smart board, grabbing the electronic stylus that acted as a virtual highlighter. He placed the tip on the screen, circling the area where the fight had occurred. "This area to the south of Vladivostok is where this first engagement happened, sir."

"Wait, the first engagement?" Jeremiah said incredulously.

"The Kazan is neither an attack boat nor a ballistic missile boat. She's a cruise missile sub, sir, not unlike our oldest four Ohio subs and the new Honeycutt class. Built for non-nuclear strike warfare and spying." He nodded at the major, who cued up a slide show on one of the secondary screens. "These slides show the progression of the fleet deployment over the last two days. Fully sixty-eight percent of Russia's Pacific fleet is now deployed, with a large percentage of the Atlantic fleet's troop-carrying ships anchored at Petropavlovsk loading their army and coastal defense forces as we speak. Based on where the Kazan was engaged, we believe she might have been trying to position herself down in the Yellow Sea for a strike."

"In all, sir, six of our submarines are tracking seventeen Russian subs and eleven Chinese subs, in the Seas of East China, Japan, and Okhotsk. It's getting very crowded down below and even more so on the surface. If either country wants to start something, taking out the other one's submarines is a crucial first step. But now that the Ruskies have spilt blood, the gloves are surely coming off today. I'll be surprised if we don't see escalation in the next few hours."

DAVIS-MONTHAN AIR FORCE BASE, TUCSON, ARIZONA

IT ALL HAD A VERY FAMILIAR FEEL TO IT. LOU AND BRANDON passed the north side of the base, heading westbound on Highway 810, known locally as Golf Links Road. He turned left to proceed to the north gate. *Awww, I'd forgot about the slight s-curve,* he remembered. Everything had a bit of nostalgia to it. He hadn't been here since the beginning of his career, before the lifesaving, plane-destroying incident had cost him his dream job. He made the slight curve around the visitor center and saw a large group of loud but peaceful protesters. Most were screaming, and many held signs of complaint about President Allen's 'increasingly dictatorial' response to the events unfolding in every city. "Eff your curfew!" other signs read. They pulled up to the main gate.

"Whoa! This looks like post 9-11 levels of security," he told Brandon. "Granted, I was just starting college and ROTC in those years..." It dawned on him that he had been flown onto his last base directly. He hadn't noticed a large increase in security during his one trip that follow-on morning.

"Yep, after Denver there was a noticeable increase at Pearl," Brandon told him. "I think there's more going on than they're telling us..."

Lou presented his and Brandon's CAC identifications to the civilian DOD police officer, decked out in dark blue tactical jumpsuit, full plate carrier, and Kevlar Mich helmet. Lou looked around. Both inbound lanes had a pair of security—one police officer running the ID check, and one enlisted MP providing an overwatch. They, too, were adorned in full battle compliment, right down to the slung M-4 rifles.

"You know where you're headed, Colonel?" the officer asked after the scanner beeped its seal of approval.

"Yep, thanks, Officer."

Lou cruised back up to fifteen MPH. Once through the first major intersection on base, he continued south and was immediately reminded of better days. *The park! We used to love coming here!* In addition to the usual playground implements, there were several defunct plane carcasses implanted permanently in concrete settings around the park. Home to the famous 'airplane graveyard,' Davis-Monthan was primarily the home for the ground attack wing of the Fifteenth Air Force, one of several major units that the service was broken into. Lou's old A-10 wing—the 355th—was part of 15th, which was primarily based out of South Carolina. Though he didn't have any direct personal contacts in the 355th at this juncture in his career, his reputation had preceded him as 'that guy who did that thing' that had served a stiff lesson to all pilots since—*return to base when you're at Bingo Fuel.* Senior-level officers knew he'd somehow managed to keep flying and had even redeemed himself to the point of flying POTUS' 'Beast' limo around the world.

Lou had arranged two meetings for the day. Their first appointment was just to scratch his itch to rub the belly of a Thunderbolt II once more. He'd spent the morning paying the toll—telling a couple of pilots and maintenance teams all about the mission in which he'd saved the bacon of a few dozen Rangers and Special Forces OD-A teams in exchange for his plane. Brandon had become mesmerized, finally fully appreciative of why General Montgomery had such devotion to Lou.

"So, you're the infamous 'Super Bert'?" one of the young pilots said, grinning.

Lou wasn't too thrilled about being recognized, but there was nothing he could do about it. "I am, Lieutenant. What's your call?" he asked back.

"Dumbo, sir," the man answered, pointing toward his large ears. "Not very original, I know. But I can relate to having a call you wish people would forget. Squadron Commander says it would take something epic for me to change it."

"I wish you luck with that, son," Lou said.

Afterward, a pair of tech sergeants had taken them to tour a couple of the planes. Lou and Brandon learned that the Wing had all been put on a 'leave curtailment' for an unknown duration. Being told they couldn't plan any trips home for Thanksgiving or Christmas had put a big damper on the airmen's moods.

In the afternoon, they managed to meet with one of the rescue squadrons of another element of the Wing, the 563rd Rescue Group. They, too, confirmed the leave moratorium and were surprised this full colonel knew nothing of it. *I've been off-line on a special task,* Lou had to explain. *I really need to start reading my email,* he realized. Though

Brandon had been responsibly aware, he played along with Lou's lack of knowledge to ensure his partner 'saved face.' They'd been given a good tour of the C-130s and HH-60G Pave Hawk helicopters the unit used. Many of the members were Pararescue men, the Air Force special forces men and women who were combat ready paramedics.

After a full day, they were just returning to his rental car when Lou's phone rang. He scanned it and saw it was a Pentagon number. "Colonel Caldwell," he announced to whoever it was.

"G'evening, Colonel. It's Ryan Jackson," he heard.

"Colonel. Everything okay?"

"For now, Lou. Sorry to bother you, but where are you two headed next?"

"I was thinking about Pendleton on Monday, but I was going to hit Luke on the way tomorrow..." Luke AFB was just west of Phoenix. Lou had been looking forward to the short drive.

"The general may have a detail for you in a day or two that would take you east. I suggest you just sit tight until I call you back."

"Roger that. Mysterious," Lou added as a passive hint.

"Sorry, Lou," Colonel Jackson said, catching it. "It's sensitive. When I know more, you'll know more."

"Gotcha, Colonel. Thanks for the heads up."

After he and Brandon jumped in and started to leave, Brandon asked, "What gives?"

"Not sure. Jackson said to sit tight for a couple of days. Sounded ominous. Which to me is not a good thing, given how much things are deteriorating."

"Let's go grab some groceries," Brandon suggested. "I really wish I'd brought a small camp stove or a JetBoil, now."

"Groceries..." Lou repeated. "That may not be a bad idea, young man. Load the trunk with stuff in case we can't find any open restaurants. And maybe some more underwear. And a few more sets of civilian clothes," he mentioned as they drove past the protesters outside the gate. "Busy afternoon. I'd like to grab a quick shower, too, before that guy we met last night picks us up."

CHAPTER 20

Assaria, Kansas

"Duuuuddddeeee!" ThatNub yelled as Morris was trotting over to the covered patio behind the paintball and airsoft's park's shop and office. "I say, son! I say—I say, soonnn!"

"Not the Foghorn thing, bro," Morris yelled backwards as he got to his phone. "Come up with something original." He plopped down on a bench at one of the two picnic tables. He recognized the ringtone as the one for his identical twin, Marvin. *What's it been?* he suddenly realized. *Like two months?* As Nub began yelling Kansas' most horrible Robert DeNiro impression the eighty feet toward him, Morris answered the phone. "Sup, brother? How's Korea?"

Marvin Alrick Dooghan was supposed to be transferred back to the United States, part of the time-cushion allowed for people to rotate from the forward bases. Like many in the military, he'd been corrected in the belief that his life was his own when they involuntarily extended him for at least one year. Marvin served in the 46th Transportation Company at Camp Carroll. The corporal was a Cargo Specialist, trained in warehousing duties that were part of keeping the army supplied. In his four years, he'd learned a lot about the shipping industry in general, let alone the finer details of loading food, ammunition, and military equipment into metal boxes for sea or air transport.

"So-Ko is always hoppin', brother. But the Army sucks weenie worse than ever right now..."

Morris could tell his twin was not having his best day. "Still good to hear from you, Marv. Mom and Dad are at Aunt Janet's. KC is gettin' pretty crazy, man..."

"Yeah, that's kinda why I'm calling. What da hell's goin' on over there?"

"Ever since that Seattle volcano, things have just been getting more and more unstable. You're pro'bly better off over there anyhow."

"Remember that gal from high school? Alisha?"

"How could I forget?" Morris teased. "Your faces were glued together our senior year!"

"That's rightttt..." Marvin said in smooth recollection. He snapped back out of the pleasant memory. "She called me today. Wonderin' if I was back in town..."

"Bro, I don't wanna hear about your sexual conquests. I—"

"No, not like that, Mo. Listen! She's freaked da hell out, man. Says that the local gangs have set up checkpoints. Work for the Mexican cartels now. ID checks. Is she straight up, Morris? How can it be that bad?"

"Like I said, brother, Mom and Dad are at Auntie's."

"But you're still at college!" It was a statement of disbelief.

"The university is allowing anyone in dorms to stay until the end of the semester. Nub and I have enough budgeted to pay our rent through May, so..." The pair went oddly silent for a moment. "What about you getting told you have to stay in?" Morris asked. "What's so hot they had to do that to you?"

"It's crazy, Mo. I pro'bly shouldn't say anything on the phone... but, uh—we're shipping a ton of stuff back to the states from Korea."

"Really? Like food? And Jeeps and stuff?"

"Yeah, ummm, quit watching *M*A*S*H* re-runs, bro." Marvin

started chuckling at his brother on the phone. "They ain't used jeeps in like forty years, man!" The brothers had a good laugh, then, "But, yeah. All of it. Including ammunition."

"Huh," Morris said, pondering what all that meant. *Could this be related to why that chill pilot was traveling around?* he asked himself.

"In fact," Marvin added, "I don't know what this means, but we were just ordered not to leave the base at all today. Rumor is that China and Russia are starting to fight."

Morris whistled low. After the pair talked a few more minutes, Marvin finally asked about all the gunfire in the background. Morris explained about how Cat Scratch Fever had been dabbling in learning how to shoot, move, and communicate with real firearms. After his army twin assured him that was 'sick', the pair finally parted ways. Morris returned his phone to his backpack and grabbed a beanie. Sitting still for too long in the November chill made him cold. He eased his way back over to the group, minus Superfly and Misty Meaner, who were both trying to run errands while the power was on for the day. *Feels like snow might be coming...*

Sonny 'Sunny D' Davis called for a cease fire, sensing something was wrong by the look on Morris' face. Everyone went through the process of clearing firearms and removing eye and ear protection and training gear. "Might as well go take a break," Sonny called out. The group slowly trickled over in ones and twos from the practice berm to the covered patio. "Everything alright?" Sonny asked Morris.

"Well, for one, my ears hurt from Nub's stupid chicken hawk impression." Everyone busted out laughing. Turning more serious, "I dunno, honestly. Just heard from my brother. He's in the army in South Korea."

"What's he up to?" Goldi asked.

"Worried," Morris said. "First, he's been hearing from folks back in KC how jacked up it's gotten. And then, he says the army is shipping most of the stuff back from South Korea."

That caught Sonny by surprise. "No wayyy! We're technically still their ally in the Korean War."

"Conflict," Super B corrected. "My history professor says—"

"Don't care," Sonny said. "I don't give a hot damn about your verbal judo or your socialist history professor."

"E-e-easy, big guy!" ThatNub said, coming to Bee's defense. "Not every college professor is a communist!" he said, laughing. "Your foil is getting a little tiiight!" he said in a loud and halfway decent Schwarzenegger.

"Point taken," Sonny said, conceding he didn't want to get into a political debate with five college kids.

"What does that mean—them shipping stuff back?" Goldi asked.

"I guess it means the army thinks they'll need their gear and ammo over here before they'll need it in Korea," Morris said bluntly.

NAVAL SUPPORT FACILITY THURMONT, FREDERICK COUNTY, Maryland

CAMP DAVID. ORIGINALLY BUILT AS A CAMPGROUND FOR federal employees in 1938, President Franklin D. Roosevelt converted it to a presidential retreat in 1942. Despite being secluded in the oaks of central-north Maryland, it had been heavily converted into a more functional, albeit relaxing, White House. Peace accords had been made there. Many foreign leaders from around the world had woken up with quite the hangover at Camp David. It was rumored that JFK had even had a tryst with Marilyn Monroe there a couple of times.

I wonder if we'll look back at this day as the start of World War III? Jeremiah Allen asked himself. *Will that be added to this retreat's infamous history?*

He stared at the fifty-chair conference table. The giant mahogany monolith was the centerpiece of a red-carpeted room. Centered on the back length of the conference building, the bulk of the back wall's one-hundred twenty feet of length was eight-foot-tall bullet proof glass that revealed the Maryland forest. Several Marines and Secret Service agents could be seen patrolling the patio area between the glass and the manicured lawn.

Several hours earlier, when it had become apparent that he and his security council would need more room, he decided to mobilize everyone and head out there. The situation room at Camp David was more than twice the size of the one in D.C., allowing for more staff and technicians. Technically a military base, most of the staff were already vetted and cleared Marine Corps and Navy personnel. After the Marine One revolving diamond helicopter formation had dropped off he and Francis, several Hueys and Blackhawks from the 89th Wing, assisted by the Maryland Air National Guard, began airlifting presidential and Pentagon staff. The National Security Advisor, Secretary of Defense, the Secretaries of each branch of the military, Secretary of State, Joint Chief Chairman, and top generals and admirals from each branch all dissolved into a multitude of offices upon arrival. They needed to ensure that updated data and analysis was being prepared for the main meeting room. A half-hour later they'd all converged in the conference room.

"Mr. President, we have important updates coming in," Chief of Staff for the Air Force, General Bryan Shadbolt said, entering the conference room and finding an open seat.

The events were just running too quickly for everyone in all the chains to report the usual way. *Exactly why I moved us out here,* Jeremiah thought. "Go ahead, Bryan."

"The People's Army has just conducted air strikes on most of the border, sir."

"Can we blind these windows and cue this up?" the president asked nobody in particular.

The corner of the room contained a door to a control booth. Multiple military and state department technicians were situated in the booth, observing the room through a two-way mirror. A Navy

Operation Specialist entered a command on her keyboard, which triggered the thin, adhesive electro chromatic film on the windows to transform magically into an opaque gray. The natural sunlight disappeared as the recessed lights in the ceiling dimmed to fifteen percent. Monitors in several locations turned on. The large screen on the long wall opposite the window wall cued up the satellite feed about twelve seconds later.

"Put Feed three, Camera four on the main screen," Secretary Shadbolt ordered, reading his tablet. "And rotate Feeds one and two through all their camera positions on the secondary screens."

The primary screen immediately cued up a zoomed in live video image of a smoldering bridge, the end closer to the north completely destroyed. Twisted metal could be seen dangling precariously into the river below. Fire and smoke poured off the cars and buildings closest to the Russian end. The other screens began to display similar shots in other locations.

"Back the main screen out eighty percent," the secretary ordered. As the feed shifted to show a much wider view of both Russian and Chinese landscapes, he continued. "This is Blagoveshchensk, Mr. President. It would seem the Chinese have just destroyed almost every bridge and train trestle on the shared border. We'll need a little time to completely analyze the entire thing, sir. Aside from the naval engagements, we have not yet seen a corresponding force-on-force attack on the land, yet."

"What the hell!" Jeremiah Allen yelled. "Options, people. You first, Kelly," he pointed at the Secretary of Defense.

"Sir, by this time, NORAD will be moving us to DefCon Three," he started. There were five defense conditions. Reaching 'One' meant nuclear war.

"Why not two?" the president asked.

"That would trigger all of our nuclear capable forces to be at an unsustainable level of readiness, sir, considering this isn't our fight."

"Gotcha," Jeremiah said, nodding. "What does moving to Three get us?"

"To start, it solidifies some of the actions we'd already started. Canceling approved leave and vacations, enacting a stop-loss of anyone due to discharge honorably. It also puts all units into a more rigid training cycle and requires a more rapid deployability readiness. Moving to Three will release some of my budget automatically. It also binds the various branches into a more frequent and thorough information sharing schedule with non-military agencies like CIA and FBI. That's the short version, Mr. President."

"Good. Dee?" Jeremiah said, moving along.

The Secretary of State looked at two of her staffers seated farther down the table, who were busy reading an instruction from her on their tablets. "We're reaching out to my counterpart on Premier Chu's staff at this moment, sir."

"Good," Jeremiah concurred. "Set me up a call with him for as soon as they'll agree. And the same with Nikolaev, obviously." He continued. "What is China's next move, General Montgomery?"

"Mr. President, the Chiefs and I all concurred that given their history, they'll be conducting an increase in their already massive cyber-attacks on Russia—and us, probably—for several days from here forth. Not just to disrupt our flow of intelligence, but to cause panic in our markets. Also—and this is not analyzed yet, I want everyone to understand that—we see them preparing to launch space-bound rockets. Not, I repeat not, ICBMs."

"What do we think are in them?" Jeremiah asked. "It has to be satellites or weapons, right?"

"Most likely, sir. Perhaps Director Chen's team has something solid?" he suggested, looking at the head of the CIA.

"Mr. President, as the general has said, we're still trying to confirm our information. But we know they've been testing microwave directional EMP weapons that will be satellite based. It is possible they're pushing those into activity."

"Directional EMP weapons!" the President asked, hardly believing it. "As in, they can be focused for tactical targeting?"

"It's... not... that far-fetched, sir," Kelly Fitzgerald said.

"Wait! Are you saying we have those and I don't even know about it?" Jeremiah asked incredulously.

"Sir. This is a discussion that should be contained to the proper audience," SecDef Fitzgerald advised.

Jeremiah Allen looked at the cold cup of coffee in front of him, stress etched on his furrowed brow. The untouched beverage contained no answers no matter how hard he stared. *If I don't find a way to show these two countries we're still strong despite our problems, millions of people will die.*

TUCSON, ARIZONA

GRANGER AND MOST OF THE ROAD RUNNERS SAT IN A RING OF chairs in his driveway, staring at the tall, metal portable firepit he'd picked up at the local Walmart several years earlier. The flames danced on the charred mixture of juniper and oak, dry and seasoned. In November as the sun dipped, the desert air was becoming a comfortable crisp. Granger could still see the remnants of pine kindling he'd used to start the fire, its waft of aromatic resin long burnt away. The flames made him think of an assortment of fires he'd fought with Tucson FD in his short career. He tried not to dwell on the one that had nearly cost him his life too much. He'd been part of the RIT on that call—the Rapid Intervention Team. He and one 'probie' just four months out of the academy had been designated to stand-by at the Incident Command Post, ready to deploy directly to a brother or sister who was in trouble. On small structure fires, like single-story homes, such an assignment tended to be somewhat boring. *On the night of that warehouse fire, though...*

"Grange," he heard Bob Salvage say as he felt Bob's cane bump him in the shin. The old Ranger, a veteran of both major ops in the 80s—Grenada and Panama—recognized the slow creep of PTSD crawling across his friend's face.

"I'm good, brother," Granger replied, clearing his throat. All five men heard the throaty diesel of Dave Wolf's nearly new Ram 3500 pull through the neighborhood.

"Who're these cats Wolf's bringin' again?" Claude asked. "Is this part of the 'training others' thing we discussed?"

"Naw," Granger said casually. All five men watched Wolf's giant truck park right across the end of the crowded driveway. The twilight reflections kept them from seeing the passengers. "Some dudes from the Pentagon he met at the VFW last night. Thinks we should hear them out. Or the other way 'round. Not sure which."

"I trust Dave's instincts," Mick chimed in, as he turned to go grab a beer from the garage fridge.

Granger saw a non-descript man descend out of the passenger seat of Wolf's lifted truck, slowly using the 'nerf bar' step to plant his feet on the ground one at a time. The man's thinning light brown hair and ever so small office-job bump over his belt buckle made him somewhat forgettable, in Granger's mind. Like most former operators, he tended to size men up on their apparent lethality subconsciously. He was still a student of the adage that men couldn't truly be peaceful unless they could first be deadly. This average looking colonel looked harmless, not peaceful. Then he saw Brandon. *Whoa. Marine. Oorah, I'll never get sick of seeing chiseled warriors with high and tights. What an odd pairing...*

Navy vet Tracy Rogers was the first to wander over to the pair as Wolf made his way around the truck to drag his guest through the cars. "Evening, bro," he said, giving Wolf a quick one-handed bro-hug. "I'm Tracy," he said, shaking hands first with Lou and then Brandon.

"Freeman Caldwell," Lou replied with a slight grin. "I go by Lou."

The trio wandered up through the two rows of vehicles to the firepit, set just about eight feet from the eave of the garage's roof. The men went through the procession of introductions. As a pilot, Lou had mastered the art of rapid memorization in his tenure, a necessity for complex cockpits. Remembering the names would be no problem.

Granger pulled two more folding chairs from the garage and inserted them into the ring of seats around the firepit. "Wolf says you used to fly here at Davis?" he asked Lou. *Still need to learn to trust you myself, first,* he thought.

"Affirmative," Lou said. "I switched platforms after my first tour in Afghanistan. I made a bad call, flew a Thunderbolt into the ground when I shouldn't have. I had curried the favor of someone important, so it didn't end my career entirely."

Now that's honesty, Granger thought, immediately impressed. "What year was that?" he asked with direct respect.

"Oh-seven," Lou answered, understanding that he'd have to play this game to get deeper into what Dave Wolf had started educating him about a full day earlier.

"And you have Corps written all over you," Granger said to Brandon. He nodded toward Mick. "Mick and I are both Marines. He was a sniper. I was Force Recon back when they called it that."

"Oorah," Brandon said. "Before D.C., I was a Platoon Commander for 1st LAR Battalion at Pendleton."

Lou asked the Road Runners, "Did any of you make it to the sandbox?"

Granger started. "I made two deployments in the early years, both OEF," he said, referring to Operation Enduring Freedom in Afghanistan. "I was burnt out after twelve years. Came here to Tucson for a job."

"I was there in '05 and '06," Mick Oakley answered. "Six years and out."

Claude laughed, "Bob and I were already farting dust by then!" the old man joked. "But we both have Army experience enough to be the Road Runner's support team."

After a few more minutes of swapping stories, Lou finally broke the ice on why they were there. "So, I know I have to give a little to get a little," he said matter-of-factly. "I'm going to give you all the skinny on who we're working for... And in exchange, I'm hoping you'll let us know in full what it is Dave here was hinting about last night. All I know is that you all spend time watching the border for traffickers. But I'd like to hear more."

Hmmm... Granger thought. "We've been burned by the CBP enough times that we have some trust issues, Colonel," he said. He added the title to remind Lou they weren't all buddies, yet. "How much we share will depend on what you share. We have a legit Op-Sec concern—we all have families that would become real targets if the cartels ever found out about us."

"I'm hearin' ya," Lou said. He took a pull on his water bottle. "Our cover is that we're collecting feel-good stories for military morale as they shuffle troops around the country. I'm sure you men understand better than most what's happening in the cities..." A couple of heads nodded. "There's more to it than that. The stage is being set for a war between China and Russia, but if you really analyze it, their motive has nothing to do with their hemisphere, and everything to do with ours." He left that hanging.

Granger was listening intently. *Go on,* he urged in his head.

"Nobody knows who Brandon and I report directly to, so we're trusting you guys—" Lou looked around to make eye contact with anyone looking at him, "—in a fashion similar to the trust you require. We report directly to the Joint Chief, Judah Montgomery."

"No way!" Tracy said.

Wolf shot a look. "Really?" He was under the impression it had been some low-level general.

Lou continued. "We travel at our own discretion. Set up most of our appointments ourselves. Keep our profiles low. Otherwise, the troops would tell us what they think we want to hear." He looked at Brandon to see if he wanted to add anything.

"That's it, guys," Brandon added. "Before this assignment I was already on the general's direct staff. That series of disasters has set into motion events that will forever change the world as we know it."

"That sounds a whole lot like World War III is coming," said Mick.

"I suppose," Brandon agreed. "And two things have stuck out in my and Colonel Caldwell's minds as we've traveled these past few weeks. One, the international news. In case anyone hasn't noticed, China and Russia are starting to duke it out. And we've been directly involved. I just saw it with my own eyes in Hawaii, though I really can't say how."

"And two?" Granger asked.

"The state of decay in the cities we're seeing. There are still good people waving flags in this country, but they're hard to find."

"Makes sense," Bob said, nodding.

"But there's more," Granger guessed.

"Very good," Lou said as he took over the talk once more. "Old Monty wants us to find out what's really going on in America. Pick up on the vibe. 'Finger on the pulse,' I believe he said."

"And?" Claude asked earnestly.

"Every day, the news gets a little bleaker, particularly since Denver. There is obviously a movement on many fronts to shift America. Any news that crosses our feeds is worse than the day before."

"What feeds?" Tracy mocked, referring to the infrastructural issues. "I've started getting all my news from a few newsletters geared specifically toward making people aware."

"Point is," Lou said looking at Tracy, "every day is just a bit more tense than the last. That set of natural disasters triggered a wave of aftershocks, if you'll pardon the pun, that people only thought they'd see in a cheap novel. Yet here it is... happening. There's a cartel army in the process of taking over every neighborhood in Seattle. And I'm betting you all have seen a massive increase of activity in whatever it is you do. Otherwise, you wouldn't be feeling so 'burnt' by the Border Patrol," Lou finished, using Granger's own words.

The crackling of the fire had slowed to an occasional pop, mostly just softly glowing orange coals at that point. Granger stood up silently and retrieved his poker and another piece of oak from the stack at the corner of the house. As the silence grew, a couple of the Road Runners wandered into the garage for another beer. "Mick, grab that folder from the workbench, would ya?" Granger called in as he closed the screen door on his pit.

The next forty minutes were spent with the Road Runners giving Lou and Brandon every detail, starting with the dry spell they'd seen in normal coyote traffic and their recent trip scouting the extremely active route. Lou hung onto every word when his phone unexpectedly rang. He let it go to voicemail. Then Brandon's rang. The men exchanged glances.

Oh, snap! Granger said in his head. *Were these dude's phone's being tapped the whole time?*

Without a word, Brandon got up and moved over to the lawn to answer his phone. "McDonald."

"Captain, are you with Colonel Caldwell?" General Montgomery asked.

"Yes, sir. We're having a chat with some civilians after dinner."

"Sorry to do this, but it is time sensitive. I have to split you two up again. Put him on the phone."

"Right away, sir." Brandon pulled it away from his ear. "Colonel!" he called out, holding the phone toward him.

Lou climbed off the folding chair and moved over to Brandon, taking the phone. "Caldwell."

"Lou, I need you to be five hundred miles east tomorrow night. You can't miss this one. Leave tonight. Give yourself time for Murphy. Call me from your SAT phone for the details when you can. And have Captain McDonald call Colonel Jackson. We need you two to split up again."

Granger and the Road Runners watched Lou's half of the exchange intently. "Understood, sir. We'll need an hour. And I think we have something critical to relay to you, as well."

CHAPTER 21

PANCHO'S BURRITO SHACK, CARLSBAD, NEW MEXICO

ALMOST EVERY RESTAURANT IN CARLSBAD LINED THE MAIN drag through town, Canal Street. *I bet she chose this one specifically because it is buried in this old neighborhood,* Lou thought. He'd tried making the usual small talk with the Texas Ranger seated across from him in the booth, but the man was too... *something.* As stressed as everyone had become, this man seemed to be far more upset. *No,* Lou thought again. *Anxious. Both, actually.* The DEA agent next to him wasn't much better.

He'd made the trip with time to spare, heeding the general's warning. The only slowdown was unexpected, but one that his military I.D. helped him with. The New Mexico National Guard had set up a checkpoint within one-half mile of the border with Arizona. Lou understood that Washington State's neighbors had started this new trend over two weeks earlier, based on the numbers of refugees from the Emerald state who were arriving with cholera, dysentery, and the other usual post-disaster illnesses. *But down here in the Southwest?* Lou questioned. *Documentos, por favor, anyone?*

Lou had received a full briefing from the general, having called via the secure satellite phone before he'd left his Tucson hotel. This contact was a Texas Ranger with a direct plug into one of the thirteen Mexican cartels that comprised MS-13. She'd relayed a flash message that had a sense of urgency regarding something they were planning for around Thanksgiving. Lou wasn't a federal cop, but he was bright enough to understand that one cartel wouldn't pull an outlandish event without at least the blessings of the others—unless of course it was aimed *at* them. But when their internal violence was at a minimum, they seemed to be a more-or-less self-policing and cooperative council of criminals.

A contact of General Montgomery's in the Justice Department used the opportunity to clear a long-owed favor. He'd relayed that the meet was happening to the general. Lou's attendance was mainly one of taking advantage of being in close proximity. General Montgomery had impressed upon him that the events the undercover contact was worried about may lead to the deaths of hundreds or thousands of people.

"I'm going to scan the parking lot again," Texas Ranger Jared Croll announced as he slid out his side of the booth. It was past the evening rush for the small restaurant.

A young waitress stepped up to the table to refill their iced teas. "Still waiting on your friend?" she asked the men.

"Just a few more minutes," Lou said. "Gracias." *I wonder if she thinks that's condescending,* he thought. *I hope not.*

"De nada," she smiled. "I'm sorry about the lack of chips and salsa," she said humbly, hoping it wouldn't affect her tip. "We've been out for a week." She left since the pair was now missing two people, not just one.

"What's your thoughts on China?" DEA Special Agent Stephen Bender asked Lou after the Latina had disappeared. He had no idea what Lou did for the DOD, but he assumed it was for the DIA.

"I work for the Joint Chiefs, but I've kind of been out-of-network,"

Lou explained. "I honestly only know what I'm getting in the unclassified emails."

"Do you think this cartel stuff plays into it?" Stephen prodded.

"Personally, I think the cartel uprising is a move of convenience—taking advantage of an opportunity. Could they be getting marching orders from China? I suppose. China would be dumb to have not at least tried to recruit them over the years. But," Lou added, "I'm not in the intel and analysis branch—at all."

"I can say definitively that China is trying to network with most of the cartels," Steve said. "To what extent is classified, but the fact that they have a symbiotic relationship is well known. What concerns me is the timing of it all. The Seattle horde is inspiring the rest of them to start acting out. I wouldn't want to be anywhere near El Paso, L.A., or San Diego in the coming weeks. Then there's Denver." The man let out an exasperated sigh. "And this intel we're all here to hear right now..."

"How's the potential terror thing a DEA concern?" Lou asked quizzically.

"I'm part of a task force with FBI and ATF," he explained. "When Allen disbanded DHS, it was under the executive order for the remaining agencies—including yours—to get better at sharing and working together. Set aside the 'cowboy mentality', so to speak."

The door at the front of the old building creaked and slammed shut as Jared returned, a semi-attractive Latina woman following him. "This is Jane," he announced to Lou and Steve. "No offense. You don't get her real name. Or her cover name for that matter." He let Rosie slide into the booth and then slid in after her, keeping his right leg out of the booth and an eye on the front door.

"I'm Fed," Steve said. "He's military," he told her as he thumbed in Lou's direction. "I did three years UC myself, once. Busted a narcotics ring for an outlaw MC in Pennsylvania. I got trust issues, tattoos, and herpes as a trade-off for that sweet deal," he added sarcastically.

I like this guy, Lou laughed to himself. *Not afraid to call it as it is.*

"Point is, I know what you're going through," Steve told Rosie. "I don't need the whole story, just tell me the part that worries you and how you got the intel." He looked at Lou as if to turn over the chance for a quick intro.

What is that smell? Lou wondered. "DOD is interested in what you're reporting because it may play into a larger and more coordinated plan we're worried about." He left it at that. *She looks nervous. She looks a bit sick. Poor lady.*

Rosie took a sip of water out of the sweaty glass that had reached room temperature waiting for her arrival. "I'm dating an American... shall we say 'Lieutenant'? Though they really don't use those TV mafia terms," she explained. "He's the handler for most of the corrupt police, judges, and city officials in El Paso. He's 'in.' The cartel trusts him as much as one of their own. As little as that is, I suppose..."

Both Lou and Steve sat patiently as she searched for the words. *Not just the words,* Lou realized. *She needs to find the courage just to say them.*

Rosie continued. "Understand, I'm reporting second-hand—I'm not in on the real conversations. There's no way I'll ever earn that level of trust. And planting a device at the compound in Mexico is just too risky. They're too smart."

"So, you've been there," Steve interrupted. "Show me." He pulled a map of Juarez out from inside his jacket pocket and unfolded it, covering the teas and waters.

Just then the waitress wandered over. They placed their orders and continued. Lou had suggested earlier that they just pay handsomely for the booth to keep down the interruptions. Steve had schooled him in the fact that something like that might actually make them more memorable to the waitress if the cartel ever came snooping.

He spread out the map, and Rosie scanned it with her finger. "Here," she acknowledged. "Nice place, fancy golf course. Security is tight. Like I said, they'll find out if I'm ever wired."

"Only here?" Steve asked, drawing a circle on the spot she'd identified. "No businesses? Warehouses?"

"Like I said, I'm connected indirectly." Rosie was a bit put-off.

"We were originally working the corruption angle," Jared

explained. "We never intended for her to infiltrate their inner circle. It just happened organically."

"How'd you learn what you know?" Steve asked. "Seems like your man would be careful."

"He is," she said. "Except when I give him a hummer while he's drunk."

Lou could tell it bothered and angered her to have to say that. His heart broke. "Jane," Lou said, his empathetic side taking over. "Thank you for what you're doing." He was being sincere. And in the emotional state he'd been in the last sixteen months, it was all he could do not to reach over and put his hand on her forearm compassionately.

Rosie's eyes teared up. "Let's just hope it's worth it," was all she could muster to say. She grabbed the paper napkin from under the water-stained silverware and blotted her eyes.

"What're they planning that has upset you this much?" Jared asked.

Rosie spent the next forty-five minutes detailing a coordinated series of IED attacks on various targets in the El Paso – Albuquerque complex. Most were aimed at the police and court system, but not all. Other than suspending the conversation for food, they peppered her for anything of value. It was still spotty information at best.

"She needs to get going, fellas," Jared said, concerned.

"One last question," Steve said. "How'd you get out of town today?"

"I spiked our food to make sure we wouldn't want to be too far from a toilet."

"That means—" Lou started.

"Adult diapers," she cut him off. "I don't recommend relying on them for a long drive." The look on her face was a mixture of disgust, shame, and straight up hate.

That's what I've been smelling, Lou thought. And for the first time since he could recall in many years, Lou did something he never thought he would. *God, if you really exist, prove it...please! Protect this brave woman,* he prayed. "I'll get the bill, everyone."

As the foursome slowly slid out of the cramped dark booth and stood, stretching their legs and backs, Rosie asked, "Where's the restroom?"

UNITED NATIONS BUILDING, NEW YORK

"THE COUNCIL CHAIRMAN RECOGNIZES THE AMBASSADOR from China."

Those eight words nearly caused a fistfight in the United Nations Security Council meeting. It didn't help that the two warring nations that would effectively trigger the third world war were both permanent members of the council—China and Russia. None of the other three permanent members—the United States, Great Britain, or France—were currently holding the title of president of the Security Council. That honor fell to one of the ten non-permanent members, each year being culled from one of the nations starting their two-year term. It happened to be Mexico. The ambassadors from China and Russia both insisted on having the floor first, each seeking the opportunity to set the stage.

"Naturally he'd pick China to speak first," Secretary of State Dee Buttermaker said to President Jeremiah Allen.

The pair was watching from chairs directly behind their direct underling, U.S. Ambassador to the UN Alexis Hilton. There were already two concentric rings of chairs built into the chamber behind the council seats situated around the three-quarter circular table. During trying times such as these, that number could easily double as leaders from around the world came to observe.

"Sure," Jeremiah whispered back. "They've allied in manufacturing and trade a ton in recent years. I'm pretty sure Mexico isn't too thrilled with me right now, so they're picking China to speak first to poke at that."

In addition to the council rings, the chamber auditorium viewing theater had been stuffed to the gills. Though there was to be a general meeting of all nations in the evening, it was the morning council meeting that was expected to produce the real theatrics of the day.

"This is outrageous!" Russian ambassador Aleksii Sotyevskiy yelled as he pounded on the table. He stood up, his face turning beet red. "The People's Republic of China has openly attacked sovereign Russian naval assets and killed our citizens in their foolish and illegal attack on our border crossings!" His speech was disrupted by the pounding gavel of the chairman, which mattered nothing to him. "The manner in which this assembly is now showing biased and preferential treatment to the aggressor nation is unacceptable! And dangerous!" he added for good measure.

"Mr. Ambassador!" council president Guadalupe Rojas was yelling as she pounded her gavel. "You will be given your chance to speak! Ambassador Chou has submitted evidence that your navy was the instigator in the initial tensions. Sit down!"

"Nyet!" he yelled, slipping into his native tongue. "The Russian people have no faith in this body or its leadership!" He turned and grabbed his chair, throwing it into the area in the middle of the giant table with theatrics that would've impressed a Manchester United midfielder. He then ripped the microphone holder out of the table and tossed it into the center carpet. He continued to spew threats and curses in his native tongue as he left the room in a tizzy, followed closely by his two staffers.

The room had erupted into chaos. The more than fifty nations that were all past members of the security council were still represented as non-voting members of the council. About half began bickering with each other, causing the mood and tone of the room to start resembling a freshly kicked beehive. The ambassadors to Iran and Saudi Arabia began to poke each other in the chest and had to be separated by their staffs.

Jeremiah Allen had seen this before, in the months of negotiations between steel-mill management and union leadership. There was a certain level of grand-standing and posturing that was expected at this level, especially by those leaders back home that had sent the chosen ambassador there to represent them. He took a good look at Ambassador Chou from China, who was patiently waiting for the din to settle so he could speak. *These smug pricks think they have the moral high ground,* he thought to himself.

"They think they're due," Jeremiah said softly as he leaned over to Dee.

"Sir? Due?" she asked, making sure she'd heard correctly.

"Yes. Due. They think the world owes them something. Just look at the arrogance on his face."

Secretary Buttermaker studied the Chinese Ambassador's fake scowl. "That's the look of a forty-five-hundred-year-old culture finally getting its turn on the world stage."

"But they're still only an eighty-year-old system of government," Jeremiah challenged. "And if I didn't know any better, I'd say that they have their eyes set past Russia already..."

"Well, we've known this day was coming for thirty years," Dee whispered back.

"Yep." *And how long until I'm the one throwing a chair into the center?* Jeremiah asked himself.

U.S. – MEXICO BORDER, ARIZONA

[MICK] DEFINITELY THE EXIT. SMALL FINGER OVER HERE IN this dell that runs to the northwest. Woulda missed if we hadn't moved right to the edge and looked down

[Granger] Plz clarify – u can see them active now

[Mick] Affirm. 8 males moving crates into back of 4wd ram. No sign of Hx

Hx was the Road Runners lingo for trafficked humans. The team had moved back out on Monday, setting themselves up before dusk. Granger had a gut feeling that the worse American society unraveled, the bolder these smugglers would become at using this route. *Still pisses me off that CBP is ignoring all this,* he fumed in his mind as he stared down into his face hole in the desert dirt.

[Granger] Roger. Stay and monitor. Moving south to monitor that farm

Forty minutes later, Granger and Dave Wolf were partnered next to each other prone in the sage and sand, staring about one mile south through their night vision binoculars, well into Mexico. They were glassing down to an abandoned sheep farm.

"...five...six trucks?" Wolf asked. "Plus two moving trucks? Whaddya think—weapons?"

"Just too dark for zoomed night vision," Granger whispered back. He'd zoomed the Aurosports in ten times, but in the dark of night and looking a full mile, they weren't putting out much detail. "Looks like crates. Whatever it is, it ain't legal..."

<SNAP!>

What the hell! Granger screamed in his thoughts. Both men went dead silent and completely motionless. Almost fifty meters east, the dead branches of a dying desert mesquite tree had turned the ground into a field of brittle bone-like noise poppers.

<Snap!> The second time it was not as loud, but it was twice as alarming. Both men knew it wasn't a fluke. And though it might've been a coyote or some small game, there had been none of the other tale-tell signs of that. Granger slowly moved his head left, trying to scan that direction. A piece of desert brush blocked his view. *Damn!* Slowly he raised his torso from lying prone on his shooter's mat to prop himself up on his right elbow. There was a light breeze coming from that direction. He thought he could make out some Spanish.

In the night, the whir was unmistakable. Whoever was over there had just launched a good sized four-bladed drone and was hovering it at about twenty feet above the ground while they checked their camera settings. The glow of an electronic screen showed the face of at least two people like a beacon at sea. *No lights on the drone,* Granger realized. *Taped over or disabled.* While each member of the Road Runners had a set of specially designed thermal blocking top and bottom they could don over their tactical clothing, they never did. Granger was suddenly filling his head with the f-bombs of twenty-twenty hindsight. *If this thing is wired for IR, we're toast!*

The little device shot skyward. Almost immediately he lost sight of it in the black of night. He lost the noise about fifteen seconds later. Granger heard his phone vibrate below him. He resealed his face to his communication hole.

[Wolf] Contact. Drone headed your way.

It was Dave warning Mick and Tracy.

[Granger] Be ready. We may be compromised.

CHAPTER 22

QUICK-E SUDS LAUNDROMAT, EL PASO, TEXAS

LOU HAD SPENT THE MONDAY FOLLOWING THE SECRETIVE meeting traveling to El Paso, intent on checking out the activities of the 1st Armored Division at Fort Hood the next day. The drive had been much shorter than anticipated. A quick phone call to Brandon had confirmed he was checking out something specific in San Diego. He didn't want to say what over the open phone, but he'd alluded to Lou that it had something to do with the high volume of fleet shifts. First, there was the loss of homeports in Washington State. Secondly there was the incoming vessels from the east coast. Lastly, the dangerous escalation in the Western Pacific was forcing ships in that part of the world to stay in the region longer than anticipated. That meant a rapid increase in training and qualification cycles for the ships slated to replace them. He would be traveling to Camp Pendleton by the end of the week, which was where the pair were to meet.

Lou took advantage of the short travel day with a long overdue nap, enhanced by finishing off the bottle of vodka. He'd set an alarm for 6 PM with the intention of finally getting around to doing his laundry.

The hotel in El Paso had seen stable power, according to the desk clerk. Laundry shouldn't be an issue. Lou had discovered a liquor barn next to his laundromat of choice. *You mean you can just drive your car through, and they'll bring what you want right to the window?* he thought excitedly. *You'd never see these in Maryland!* Still buzzing from earlier, he picked up a fifth of Johnny Walker Red Label to keep it going. Lou was two hours into his laundry, waiting for the dryers to finish. *Maybe you should call your brother,* the little sober man in his head suggested.

"You do realize it is after 10:30 here in Maryland," said a groggy and annoyed Foster Caldwell, not even bothering with 'hello'. "Some of us get up early."

"Shorry. I guesh I didn't think of that," Lou slurred.

"Where you at again?" his brother said, realizing immediately Lou was drunk.

"Texas. Where the starsh at night are big and bright!" he chuckled. He scanned the fifth of whiskey and saw that it was already half gone. *You realize you're not even feeling all of that yet, right?* the little sober man in his head asked. *Stop!* Lou grabbed the bottle and threw it into the back seat in response.

"Where are you?" Foster asked. "It sounds weird."

"I'm doin' laundry, sittin' in the car."

"Whatever you're drinking, you need to stop, little brother."

"Yesh, Mom."

"I'm serious!" barked Foster. "You're walking a tightrope, Louis. The world took a big dump on you. Accept it and move on. It is the only path that doesn't lead to a hospital, prison, or a grave."

"I jusht called to see how the inshurance thing was goin'..." Lou reasoned. "I don't need a lecshure."

"Call back tomorrow," Foster ordered and hung up.

Well, Lou thought. *How about that?* He decided to check on his laundry. After stumbling out of the car, he reached into the backseat and found the duffle bags. He staggered into the laundromat and found his dryers showed they still had four minutes. He left his duffles in front of the machines and wandered over to an aquarium on the front counter, oblivious to the stares he was getting from others. One of the men looked particularly angry. There was a disinterested employee scrolling the screen on his phone, trying to ignore Lou's presence. Lou studied the fish. "Jusht goldfish, huh?"

The employee slowly looked up, annoyed. "You need change or something?"

"Nope! Just looking at your fish while my load finishes up. One of 'em's dead," Lou said matter-of-factly.

After slowly figuring out the employee was ignoring him, he moved back over to his machines and opened them. The clothing warmed his face as he stuffed his laundry back into the two bags. The clippity-clop of the one with a wobbly wheel suddenly stopped as the wheel broke off and shot under a chair. The young attractive woman sitting in it was in heels and a pink mini skirt. She had her legs crossed over the lap of the man next to her. The same man who'd been eyeing Lou with an angry scowl.

"Awww, hell," Lou said as he stumbled in front of the people. "Shorry. I losht my wheel. It's under her—"

"Leave it!" the man in his mid-twenties ordered. His clothing and body language was a clear indicator he shouldn't be trifled with—at least to anyone sober.

"I'll jusht be a second," Lou said as he started to bend over. His equilibrium shot, he started to fall forward, and wound up catching himself right on the bare legs of the young woman.

"Heyyyy!" she screamed, pulling her legs off her boyfriend. As a flurry of Spanish cursing began to spew from her, the boyfriend shot up with lightning speed and grabbed Lou. He spun him around and ran him directly into the wall-mounted dryers face first.

<THWANG!> All other conversations stopped. Several people began to record with their phones. Lou fell back and crumpled to the floor, fresh red blood shooting from both nostrils. "Arrrnnggg!" he yelled through the drunk, trying to put his hands on his nose to assess the damage. Before he could, he felt himself being crushed under the

weight of the man, who straddled Lou, pinning his back to the floor. The man began to throw rapid, hard punches with both hands right into Lou's face. Every time Lou tried to block, the man would knock his hands out of the way and keep punching. As if that wasn't enough, the woman kicked off her high heels and started kicking Lou in the head with the top of her foot. The insults continued.

"Stop!" the employee yelled as he strode over. He reached for the man, who shrugged him off and glared at him like a wild animal. The employee backed off and headed back for the counter, grabbing his cell phone. "I gotta call the cops, man!"

The assailant shot up and ran over to the counter, causing the man to cower into the corner. "You want some o' diss, homes?" he yelled. The attendant dropped the phone and said nothing. The assailant crashed a big punch into his face to teach him a lesson, knuckles already bloody from Lou.

"That's enough!" a large man yelled as he ran into the laundromat. He'd been watching the event unfold from his car while his laundry processed. The assailant moved back around the counter. "They've had enough, dude!"

"I'll decide who's had enough, cabron!" the man said, pulling a pistol from a holster in his waistband from under his tee-shirt. He whipped it straight up into the big defender and shot three times directly in the chest. Blood began to pump out of his aorta as he fell forward to his knees, clutching his chest. He then finished falling forward, barely moving, a sick gurgling sound coming from his throat. The assailant started to move back around the center machines to find Lou, but his girlfriend screamed.

"No, baby! We got to go! We gotta go, Chico! Now!" She grabbed his other hand.

The man looked around the laundromat, finally figuring out how many witnesses there were. Some were screaming, and all of them were trying to hide behind machines. He conceded to his girlfriend after a moment. He stowed his pistol and let her drag him out of the bloody laundromat, hopping over the dying hero in the process.

HIGHWAY 24, KANSAS

"TURN RIGHT UP THERE WHERE THAT TREE IS," FLOYD 'ELVIS' Presley instructed from the back of the Bronco. "There's an old quarry I've gone shooting at a few times. Good dirt walls, no chance of losing a round."

ThatNub turned onto a dirt road when he reached it. "Are you sure?" he asked skeptically. "This seems like any of a million farm access roads."

"I know, but yes, I'm sure. Trust me," Elvis said. "I know where I'm at. There's the one farm on the left, then nothing for about three miles, then the quarry."

"What's farther down?" Morris asked.

"Not sure, never gone that far."

The three college students were returning from an ammo run at Floyd's family's gun store in Rossville. The required time for a background check had come and gone since their original visit—each of them went to pick up their pistols. Though they'd each purchased a different brand to satisfy their own style and feel of the grip in their hands, they took Clint's advice and all purchased a 9mm and a good holster that slid inside their waistbands. Once they'd trained with the pistols and rifles some, he told them they would probably have a better idea what kind of tactical holster they would want. Clint and Beth had helped the young men lubricate their new firearms and lent them the materials to set up a target stand.

Ten minutes later, the trio was parked at a heavy single pipe gate to the quarry. Meant to keep vehicles out, the young men packed up all their gear and hiked the five hundred yards down the access road. Elvis showed them how to set up the one target they would all share in a fashion to ensure the rounds were impacting a dirt wall. He reviewed the four firearm safety commandments and started running his friends through a variety of beginner drills.

A low dull humming noise began to emanate off the quarry's walls. At first none of them heard it. When Elvis had stopped his friends from shooting to review a technique, he took off his hearing protection. "You guys hear that?"

The other two followed suit. "Sounds like a plane," ThatNub decided. "Getting closer."

"Why would a plane be way out here?" Elvis asked.

"Could be anything," Morris suggested. "Just a joyride, probably."

"The sky's the limit on what it could be!" ThatNub exclaimed, instantly getting an eyes-rolling response from his buddies.

"Definitely getting louder," Morris said. "Like it's coming from over that wall," he said, pointing at the quarry wall near them. As if on cue, a small twin-engine plane broke over the wall immediately over the college students. It continued northeast, disappearing over the trees at the far side of the quarry on a downward trajectory. They lost the sound quickly.

"That thing was low!" Elvis said. "Like they were landing."

"That's the impression I got, too," the normally jokester ThatNub said seriously.

"Maybe there's a small airstrip over there," Morris said. "Or maybe it was having engine problems."

"Maybe," Elvis said. "But why come way out here to land if that's the case. I mean, pick a field!" he said, laughing.

"True," Morris conceded. "Say, fellas. What say we be getting back. This ammo ain't cheap—I don't want to blow through it all in one outing."

"I feel that," ThatNub agreed. "And we need to hit the grocery store."

Most of Cat Scratch Fever had taken to getting groceries every day, making the stop a regular part of their routines. Most nights, there was nothing new on the shelves. Morris had pointed out to all of them that the only way to get the goods when they showed up was to go frequently.

The men packed up their gear and started back to the Bronco. When they were about eighty yards away, a string of SUVs broke over the horizon on the road at the top of a small rise, throwing dust and rocks as they went. The three airsofters stopped in their tracks. The SUVs were spaced about a hundred yards apart. There were three of them, traveling at a high rate of speed. They flew right past the parked Bronco.

"They must be doing eighty!" ThatNub yelled. "That's crazy out here!"

"And a great way to destroy your paint job," Elvis agreed. "That was some real Hollywood action goin' on right there."

Morris started walking again. "You guys are letting your imaginations get the best of you."

U.S. – MEXICO BORDER, ARIZONA

BOTH PAIRS OF ROAD RUNNERS HAD FROZEN IN THEIR respective positions for close to two hours, long after the last of the cartel men and trucks had disappeared. As dawn approached, the team set themselves up on a small watch rotation to get some sleep. *We may not have found human smuggling*, Granger had said in the text loop, *but we're onto something*. After a small nap, he and Wolf moved farther north on their hilltop, then headed east and finally south until they found a good outcropping of boulders. They wanted to be in a position to find the drone operators as they crossed the desert canyon and ascended the hill that evening. They moved like snails, making every effort to stir up no more dust than a jack rabbit might.

As dusk of Tuesday evening approached, the four men each donned their Fibrotex Nightwalker thermal shielding gear. While it would be hotter, the fact that it was November made the cool desert night air tolerable in it. The gear would block their heat signature from infrared devices. After the close call the evening before, Dave Wolf and Granger once again separated by about fifty meters, trying to be each other's overwatch if one of them became compromised. Granger had reestablished his small solar panel to recharge his phone and mesh antenna. Looking down into his concealing cubby under his mat, he cued up the app *zoom.earth.* He scanned a real time display of the weather patterns, then zoomed in on the little sheep farm. The best he would be able to do to see high-res imagery of the sheep farm to the south was look at the prior day's weather feed—the live image became too grainy when zoomed down.

[Granger] Tons of tracks coming in and out

[Tracy] Frustrating. We could wax these guys before they knew what hit em'

[Wolf] Patience, young Padawan...

[Granger] We're going to find this trail tonight. Follow our normal ROE. The drone team may be a full QRF

[Mick] Propose we fwd intel to other channels tomorrow

Granger could relate to everyone's frustration. *Why are we even out here anymore? Should we just get more guys and eliminate this threat ourselves? Would we be saving lives? Would we draw more cartel or just send them to their next tunnel?* These were the thoughts that plagued Granger and the rest as dusk turned to night. When midnight had come and gone with no sign of the cartel, Granger made a tough choice.

[Granger] You two recon that exit. We r going down the trail into Mx.

The men stowed their binoculars in their packs and removed tactical 'bump' helmets, complete with traditional PVS-14 non-zoom night vision. Granger had a monocular set up to keep his load lighter on his scar tissue on his head. Dave Wolf ran a pair of them together.

Granger and Wolf formed up and moved out with a ten-meter spacing. They headed west to the mesquite tree that had been the dead give-away of their quarry the night before. About twenty meters out from it, Granger put his hand up over his shoulder, palm closed. Both men took a knee in the dirt near a small grove of cacti, looking... listening... smelling. Then he saw it. That must be the path, he thought as he spied a small divot along the rocky terrain to his left. He slowly stood and crouched as he approached it. Within ten feet he could see the dirt was worn and packed from frequent foot traffic. At three feet out he could tell that the path descended the face of the hill along a natural shelf in the rocks.

He stared down the path, following as far as one electronic 'eye' could see. After thirty seconds he looked back at Dave, who shrugged. It took most of an hour for the men to descend the roughly three hundred feet in elevation, as they traveled slowly and stopped frequently to counter-surveil for an ambush. Once the ground leveled out, both men removed their compasses and took a bearing on the small grain and water towers of the sheep ranch some sixteen hundred meters to the south.

After verifying the range with a laser range finder, Granger whispered to Wolf, "Counting the distance up to the other guys, this should be a record setter. I think that one near San Diego was less—far less."

"If that's true, we need to watch for features," Wolf said. "Ventilation screens, emergency exits, stuff like that. That one in San Dog had lights, power, a rail system for carts—pretty elaborate, if I recall..."

Granger nodded. "Why don't you take point since your nods are doubled up. It's over three kliks there and back to this point. We need to move faster than I'm comfortable with if we're gonna get this scouted before dawn."

With that, the two veterans headed out into the black night of the Mexican desert, looking to collect anything that could compel someone —anyone—to take some sort of action.

CHAPTER 23

William Beaumont Army Medical Center, El Paso, Texas

Lou tried to open his eyes, but it hurt too much. The fog was thick, but it wasn't so thick that he didn't feel pain as he re-entered the world. *What's wrong? What happened?* There was a blanket... a shadow over his memory that even that little sober voice couldn't penetrate. *Where am I?* He started to open his eyes, but his headache was too strong. *The light hurts,* he thought as he saw two fuzzy gray slits. Pinpoint pain in his eyelids shot through his nerves, causing him to immediately stop trying to open them.

"Unnnghhh," he said. He could hear a muffled voice somewhere to his right. And other noises. *Beeps. A lawyer commercial?* All were unknown to him. *Where the hell am I?*

"Nurse?" he heard a man call out, an older man, though not quite so clearly, yet. It was like he was talking through a pillow in Lou's ears. "I-I think he's coming to!"

Lou felt something touch his arm that made him jolt in his mind. In reality his arm moved a scant few millimeters. "How you feeling, Colonel?" he heard another man's voice. This one was much younger.

"Unnngghh," Lou repeated as the cobwebs continued to thin. He started to move his head at the neck a bit but found new types of pain being unmasked. "Wha... Where..."

"Relax, Colonel. Take it slow and easy. You've been hurt." He could feel the nurse's presence, almost sense the man looking over his wounds.

"What—what happened?" Lou said, searching his memory. "Was I in a wreck? I remember a dead fish..."

"That's a new one," the male nurse admitted. "Hang tight, sir. Doc'll be along in a few."

He hadn't recognized the warmth of the nurse's body until it was gone. The room felt a bit chillier. Lou started to shiver. He lay still, not wanting to move, mind awake now. *Laundry. There was a fishbowl. Am I hungover? No. Yes. But this isn't normal. Oh, no! Did I drunk drive! That other voice. I must be in a shared room.*

"Colonel Caldwell, I'm Doctor Forbes. Can you open your eyes?"

"It—it hurts," Lou said.

"Go ahead and try," he heard the man say.

Lou pushed through the pain and forced his eyelids open, squinting. "It's too bright."

"That's okay. Take your time. Who's the president of the United States?"

"Ro-Ronald Reagan?" Lou joked.

"Haven't heard that one in a while," the doctor joked back. "Do you know what day it is?"

"Ummm...it was Monday. And ummm, it feels like maybe Tuesday?"

"What else do you remember?" He felt the doctor in his face, scanning him. Suddenly there was a bright flash in one eye, then the other. "I'm just checking your pupils for reaction, Colonel," he explained.

"I think I was drunk..."

"Your BAC was .21," the doctor said. "It's probably all gone by now. It's Tuesday evening."

"I remember something happened to my... Yes, I think I got my butt kicked. It's all still blurry."

"Sit tight, Colonel. We'll—"

"Lou."

"Alright. Sit tight, Lou. We'll need to keep you here tonight. I don't think we need to do an MRI. But you've got some cracked bones in your face. A lot of swelling and bruising. You got worked over pretty hard. But still doing well, all things considered."

"Huh?" *What's that supposed to mean?* Lou asked himself.

It dawned on the doctor that Lou had no idea about the entire incident. "Just rest, Lou. EPPD will want to talk to you tomorrow."

THE WHITE HOUSE SITUATION ROOM

THE ROOM WAS TENSE, AS INDICATED BY PRESIDENT JEREMIAH Allen's chew-spit bottle. The smokeless nicotine addiction had come back in full force in the preceding five days, courtesy of a Navy cook with which the president had spotted the familiar ring in his pocket. Never a fan of smoking, Allen had taken to chew on his fishing trips. As his life became more public, it became harder to hide. *To hell with it,* he thought, as he politely asked the sailor for a chew. *I'm done caring if people care about my chew habits.* As much as he'd wanted to stay at the camp indefinitely, the polls showed he was hiding. Back to D.C. they went.

"Is this limited to the Primorsky Krai? Are they making moves on other fronts?" he asked his defense team.

They'd just briefed him that Russia's eastern coastal zone, inhabited by two million and home to their largest Pacific naval base at Vladivostok, was being placed under siege by China. Russia had spent several weeks flying troops and armor onto the peninsula. Vladivostok wasn't just militarily important. As the eastern end of the Trans-Siberian Railway, it hosted several million visitors each year, bringing in several hundred million dollars equivalent in rubles annually.

"Both sides have continually beefed up their shared border, sir," Secretary of Defense Kelly Fitzgerald stated. "But nothing indicates either side is preparing for an airborne assault in the north or west at this time. This pinch point has placed Nikolaev in a stressful position. On the one hand, their navy's homeport is under attack from a land-based force a mere hour-long plane ride away. They've saturated the west side of Golden Horn Bay with missile launchers. On the other, China's fleets are moving to choke off all routes into the Sea of Japan to contain Russia's fleet. The only elements of their fleet to the north are those still traveling through the Arctic circle, most of which are troop carriers."

"Alright, Kell... General Montgomery. I've reviewed our Pac Fleet status from last night. You think the carrier Halsey will be able to get out of the Rainier Impact Zone in a week?" He was skeptical. *But then again,* he thought, *that shipyard was able to get her shafts reinstalled and put back to pier before they lost the drydock entirely. Maybe they can pull off another miracle...* "We need her in San Diego picking up her flight squadrons asap."

"No more than eight days, Mr. President," General Montgomery answered. "We have a small task force that was independent of the resupply task force headed up to escort her through Puget Sound. There's been a lot of reports of piracy that have sprung up in the wake of the cartel thing."

Allen lightly hit the conference table in exasperation upon hearing that. "Great segue, General!" He looked at his National Security Advisor, Elliot Parks. "Your report this morning mentioned that several governors have reached out for guidance with the escalating violence. How much of this is specific to cartels, and how much is it specific to major cities?"

"My team has been allowed to sit in with Justice on their high-level intelligence briefings this week. In the wake of Denver, their multi-agency task force definitely has evidence of coordinated cartel communications and planning. I mentioned the unverified report from El Paso already. We're also hearing about two suspected new tunnels under the border in California. The border crossings in Arizona and New Mexico are at record levels. So we know they're ramping up activity, but we don't have specifics. We don't see an increase in drug arrests or overdoses, but child sex trafficking has been rearing its ugly head. There's a good chance they're using these same pipelines for moving weapons, terrorists, cartel warriors, or foreign operators."

Jeremiah picked up his spitter bottle and squirted a load of the nasty brown saliva into it. He moved his gaze back to the Secretary of Defense and General Montgomery. "Get with the AG. We need to make a clear ruling on how this is a national security issue. I've always seen a clear distinction constitutionally for local communities to police themselves, but not all foreign invasions use uniforms and capitol buildings." He scanned the room to ensure everyone was looking. "We've... scratch that thought." *You gotta own this.* "I... have been too distracted by the Pacific theater, the economy, and the failing infrastructure. Not finding a way to get troops and support into the Pacific Northwest will probably go down in the books as my biggest blunder. Now the police and National Guard in Seattle are dealing with a no-kidding criminal army of sorts. It stops here. I want to see a plan to fight these scum in every major western city by Friday. Maybe we'll send a message to those two knuckleheads in the west Pacific in the process."

EAST OF SASABE, MEXICO

. . .

"DEFINITELY THEM," DAVE WOLF AGREED. "THERE'S NO cattle, no sheep... Way too much activity for this isolated, dead ranch." He and Granger were a full two kilometers into Mexico. They were at a dangerous intersection between foolishness and tactical advantage. If they wanted to make it back across the border before dawn, the time to do it slowly and safely had passed.

"This tunnel must be two miles long," Granger said. "There must be service accesses out here somewhere. If we could just find one..."

"Yes, but we're still just two or four guys," Dave reasoned. "Your thought that we need to start recruiting and training is spot on. Patience is a virtue."

"By the time we do that," Granger argued, "this supply line will be dead and buried."

"I disagree," Wolf whispered back. "They've spent months and a fortune building this thing. They won't abandon it until some sort of big fight forces them to."

"You might be right," Granger agreed. "Let's get home and get everyone in on the conversation."

WESTBOUND INTERSTATE 10, SOUTHERN NEW MEXICO

LOU NEEDED OUT OF EL PASO. BADLY. *NO OFFENSE TO THOSE who live here,* he thought as he plunged west through the Wednesday southwestern dust. *But it'll be a cold day in hell before I step foot in that place again.*

His swollen face hurt. It was all he could do to let it distract him from driving. He was taking nothing but Motrin, not wanting to wind up in a wreck thanks to something stronger. His destination was anywhere not there. Though he hadn't yet worked out a game plan with Brandon, his goal was to go find his partner.

That morning, he'd had his interview with the El Paso Police Department. *Yes, I'd been drinking. No, I don't remember anything.* The news that a man had perished trying to save him felt unreal. Lou didn't recall anything else from the rest of the fifteen-minute interview after that. Something about 'if they catch him' and 'will be called as a witness'. To him it was all surreal, in a nightmare way. After the detectives left, he pressed the doctor for a discharge. An enlisted staffer gave Lou a ride to the private impound yard that the laundromat owners had his rental car towed to. The power had been out. The company had no intention of releasing the car to Lou without cash on the barrelhead. A trip to the rental car's trunk had convinced the slimy attendant to change his mind.

Inflation had taken a firm root since the hammer had fallen on America five weeks earlier. As had a broken supply chain. The man let Lou take the car in exchange for the entire supply. An hour later, Lou had grabbed all his items from the hotel and beat feet for the interstate. He jumped on the phone with Colonel Jackson, who had held his cards closely. *He already holds me in contempt,* Lou thought. *But if he truly detests me now, he's hiding it well.* The colonel had advised Lou to make his way east. Lou pled his case, stating that if anything, the violence he'd received had proven why Captain McDonald shouldn't be alone in his travels.

He was given a short leash, informed that they'd be ordered home soon. "Be cautious, Lou," Ryan Jackson advised. "You might think about using small highways around the major cities. There's a storm coming."

"Storm, Colonel?" Lou asked. "The weather has been fairly mild."

"I'm not referring to weather, Colonel."

In the two hours since, Lou had been alone with his thoughts, wanting a drink and hating himself for the thought. *If I'd been sober, a man would still be alive,* he remembered. As he drove, with nothing to do but talk to himself, that was the one phrase that kept repeating itself. *A man would still be alive. Why? What caused this man to step in and help? Didn't he know that people don't do that anymore? Didn't he have a family that would need him? Miss him?* Lou began to tear up. *Did I cause this man's children to forever not have their father? Why wasn't I the one to die?* He felt his face get red with anger... embarrassment... shame.

I have to make this right! But I can't! I'll never be able to right this wrong! The healing waters began to flow. Lou started sobbing as he drove, squeezing the tears out of his eyes, trying to keep them clear and on the road. His sinuses filled and then began to run. He reached into the arm rest cubby, grabbing the supply of fast-food napkins Brandon had stuffed in there to blow his nose. He saw a blue highway sign. "Rest stop 2 Miles".

And as he prepared to exit the road to nowhere, he began to understand something...new. Something of an ethereal nature. *You have to stop being so angry. Maybe God exists. Maybe he doesn't. But if he doesn't, who have you truly been mad at? If he is real, is he loving? Or is he apathetic? I'd like to think he's loving. And if he's loving, don't you think he'd help us through the trials.* Lou hadn't cracked open a Bible since junior high school. *Yes, but man has interfered with the Bible over history. Everyone knows this. But if he created the entire universe, couldn't he still speak to us? Guide us? In our minds, while also protecting the intent of the Bible from puny mankind?*

Lou exited and passed several semi-trucks and the rest area's service building, parking in the middle of several open spots. He shut the engine down and blew his nose once more, using his sleeve to wipe his eyes. The pain of his bruised and swollen face came flooding back, but it bothered him less. *I'll take ten minutes to calm down before going to the bathroom.* He sat in the driver's seat and watched a family—two parents and four children—as they packed up their evening food from a rest area picnic table and proceeded to throw away their trash and head for their minivan. An idea was born.

Lou got out and opened the rear door, feeling around for the partial bottle. Without even looking at it, he took the cap off and upended the alcohol over the grass as he walked to the picnic table trash can. *I don't know if God is real or if Heaven is real, but I do know that my beautiful baby Terrance wouldn't want me to destroy my life like this.*

CHAPTER 24

NAVAL AIR STATION NORTH ISLAND, CORONADO, CALIFORNIA

"THANKS AGAIN, LT. DELEUTH," BRANDON MCDONALD TOLD the Navy lieutenant who had just spent two hours walking him through the Osprey and its role in naval aviation.

"I told you, Marine. Call me Annette!" she smiled.

The pilot with VRM-30 was one of the Navy's Osprey tilt-rotor magicians, able to fly the half plane-half helicopters out to aircraft carriers and amphibious craft to deliver people, parts, and other supplies. The maritime versions were beefier than their land-warfare cousins, upgraded for extended range, heavier payload, and easier transportation of non-combatant personnel.

"Sorry!" Brandon said with his charismatic smile. He scanned the hangar bay as they walked through it back to the parking area. "You all sure are busy. It's not a secret that things are afoot in D.C.," he commented, taking the conversation to a more serious nature. "So I have a few questions for you. Are you getting everything you need in the form of training, repairs, etcetera? And how is morale? I mean—

the civil unrest downtown must be bothering some of your folks that live off-base, right?"

"I think we're about the same as usual for status," she said. "We tend to run about twenty percent short on our listed staffing level. From what I gather, that's the norm in the Navy anyhow. And I think with the carrier Halsey up in Washington getting ready to get to sea, we're able to focus on that to keep our minds off what's happening in town. I mean—the power outages are lasting two or three days at a shot, now. But everyone here is a lot more wary of what's happening between Russia and China than we are of getting mugged at 7-11."

"You all making runs to Halsey once she's on the ocean?"

"That's what I'm hearing, yes. But we have to wait for her to get halfway down here. She has nothing to refuel us with."

Brandon continued to chat with her for a few more minutes, then excused himself. He'd gotten a text from Lou to meet him at the Navy Lodge in San Diego. It was just past noon, so the base traffic between the two pieces of land was moderate. Brandon cruised back over the long semi-circular bay bridge in his own rental car and met up with Lou ten minutes later.

"Oooooo! Ouch!" was all he could blurt out when he saw his partner's face as Lou opened his room door. Brandon instantly regretted it when he saw Lou's face sadden. "Sorry, Lou. I didn't mean to upset you."

Lou uncharacteristically gave the younger, taller Marine a hug, sending a big look of shock across his face. "It's okay, Brandon. There's more to it than I told you on the phone. Did you get my text about finding us some vending machine goods before you left the base?"

Brandon held up his backpack as an answer. He looked around. "You want to go eat outside? It's kind of stuffy in here."

"That'll work. I need to charge my laptop anyhow. Jackson has made it clear we're probably getting called home any day now. I'd like to show you an email I'm drafting. Get your thoughts."

A short while later, having dined on vending machine trail mix and expensive flavored water in Brandon's car, Lou opened up. "I find it funny they're billing this as 'diet water'," he complained, staring at the bottle.

"It's because they flavor it," Brandon said. "Stupid, I know." He could sense Lou was stalling. He gave the older mentor a concerned look. "What is it you wanted to show me, Lou?"

Lou picked up on his friend's worry. "To start—get that girly look off your face. I'm fine."

Brandon broke into a thin smile. "You sure?"

Lou's smile dissipated a bit. "I will be." He told Brandon the entire story of his ordeal in El Paso, including weighing his friend down with how much guilt he was carrying over the would-be Good Samaritan's death. Lou could see it was bringing the usual chipper officer's mood down. "Listen. I'm okay…really. I dumped the sauce out yesterday."

"That's not what I'm worried about," Brandon admitted.

"I really don't want to have a big talk about God, Brandon," Lou said. "I'm thinking about that topic in my own mind and on my own terms."

"I get it. I can still be concerned, though."

"I'll admit it," Lou said. "My mind has gone to some dark places lately. I can't comprehend what Terrance was feeling when he took his own life. But if I could ask him, I bet he wouldn't want me to follow suit. That's the thing that gets me out of bed every day. But listen—we got time to discuss life and death on the road. I want to run this letter to Montgomery past you before I hit send."

San Diego, California

Sir,

I have an inkling of an idea about what is in motion, thanks to

Colonel Jackson. This final email is specifically about the ambiguous side mission you gave us: to find Americans and their concerns and report them to you. Our final mission reports will be filed by Captain McDonald as my erroneous judgment and actions placed me off mission, something I'm ready to own fully when I report back in person.

I'll admit it. I was more than a bit confused by this assignment, and more importantly, your choice of placing me in it. I wasn't thrilled about Colonel Jackson's decision to assign me an attendant, either (though... I fully see why he needed to.) You sent us out to put our finger on America's pulse. I think we found it, sir, but we found so much more than that, too. The tension is thick, palpable...it can be felt when you walk into the store, the gas station, or look at someone wrong. You can smell the stress as people don't know how to open up about the things bothering them. They are angry, sir, and they don't know who to be angry at. People are worried. They're worried about what happens when their kids never make it home... or they run out of gas... food... About what happens when the cartel finally sets up shop in their neighborhood.

I found angst, and I found hope. I found despair, and I found faith. I found confusion, and I found clarity. I found tension, and I found flexibility. I found average people doing beyond-average things. I found concerned people helping their communities. I found patriots fighting, sir. Fighting to literally protect their neighbors from threats, both phantom and real. The pulse of America is beating, General—hard and fast. Her citizens are clinging to the life raft. Searching. Waiting. Desperately hoping for the light to shine. For someone to say, 'hold on'... To say, 'we're coming.' 'Be strong.'

As you're fully aware, sir, the old 'blades of grass' myth from World War Two was never substantiated. The concept that Japan never invaded the mainland because of the armed citizenry was never proven. Well—I'm here to tell you, General—it is real. Our foes will find a rude awakening on that dark and fateful day. They'll find college students...they'll find mechanics...they'll find disabled veterans...they'll find brave young police officers...men and women of incredible stature. They'll find Gold Star mothers and fathers, sons and daughters. They'll find old and young, rich and poor. There's a thread that binds these people, sir—above all our differences, they'll find... unity. At least, they will once they make it past the foolish who are chasing the mirage.

It took me a while to figure it out. I couldn't quite decide what the glue that held this concept together was, as people saw the signs. They see the turmoil... the riots... the barren shelves. They see the troops taking trains and planes across America. They hear the threats from across the ocean, and they say, 'bring it.' What is that thread, sir? Love. Love for their families. Love for their communities. Love for life. Love for the right to worship God however they see fit, and to find out if He exists on their own terms. Love for sunrises, Sunday meals with their families, playing a sport, reading a fine book, spending time in the outdoors. Love for growing as a human as they age, learning to recognize and overcome their own biases. Love for their neighbors, even as they learn it's okay to believe differently than those neighbors. Learning to see the big picture as they seek their own journey into the cosmos. They don't want anything to threaten that Freedom, General. Love. There is no other word. No other word can explain why a black man I've never met laid his life down so I could keep mine. And if there is a God, I hope he is wrapping his arms around that man tonight, for he met God's own definition of the greatest love. They love America and all she stands for. After fighting each other for a couple of decades, they're finally learning to look past the sibling rivalries and fight not each other—but for each other.

Sir, the love for America runs deep in these folks, regardless of race, gender, sexuality, social class, or faith system. Our enemies don't know what they're getting themselves into. As long as these people, and millions more like them that I didn't have the privilege of meeting, have breath in their lungs...those that would invade us will never find peace.

When you sent me on this mission, I didn't know what to expect—what I'd find. I didn't expect my personal life to unravel like it did. Never did I think I'd find the courage, laughter, and hope in the face of uncertainty that I did. Thank you, General. In the face of my own personal tragedy, sir, I've found so much more. Other than death and needing air, the thing that binds us together, as humans, is tragedy. Everyone has a sad story. It took this mission for me to remember that. It took this mission for me to realize that the passion I choose for my life, whether positive or negative, will be amplified in the effects on those around me. Meeting these people, having this assignment... It has been the most rewarding thing I've ever been through—the bad and the good. I guess what I'm saying is that in finding the real America... I also found myself.

Very Respectfully,
Freeman Caldwell

P.S. If you'll still have me, sir, I'm considering deferring retirement in the face of whatever is coming.

Air Force One, Westbound over Indiana

President Allen, Chief of Staff Shannon Sahr, and National Security Advisor Elliot Parks were in the conference room. No other members of his staff had been invited to the teleconference with the senior military leaders and Secretary of Defense, Kelly Fitzgerald. The briefing, or rather the operation it was detailing, represented the Rubicon River for the Allen administration. There was no un-ringing this bell, should he decide to give the go-ahead. President Allen was making his first trip to Denver since the attack.

"It's called Operation Venom Spear, Mr. President," General Montgomery stated. He and Secretary Fitzgerald were calling from the SecDef's private and secure conference room. The other half of the screen showed each of the branches' top generals and admirals in their

Pentagon conference room. "We have three tiers, and several options for kicking it off, should you give the order."

"Venom Spear..." Jeremiah repeated, trailing off. "Let's start with the simplest version, General. The one that has the least risk to innocents." His voice was dry. *Am I really going to discuss having the military take out key cartel locations on American soil?* Had the preceding five weeks not been so unbelievably escalating, he'd almost think he was watching a bad Steven Seagal movie.

"At all levels, sir," Judah Montgomery continued, "we will invite the governors to include their State Guard units. Technically, the National Guard has been ours since several acts took effect between 1903 and 1916. I'm well aware, sir, of your desire to return complete control of those back to the states before your term ends. I'm just mentioning the current state. But many of the states have enacted additional 'State Guards' solely for their governor's discretion. Natural disasters and the like." He took a breath and a sip of water. "In the first tier, we're talking about pinpoint targeted action against known reinforced hard-targets."

"Define that, General," the president ordered. He began the process of pinching a chew out of its can to stuff into his lip.

"Primarily factories, sir. Known manufacturing and distribution sites. Obviously not every drug-house in the cities, just the well-known, high-volume ones. It also includes any site that contains evidence of terror-cell activity."

"This sure sounds like muddy water, General..." Jeremiah said with skepticisms.

"This intel is being kept up to date by multiple agencies. Justice, mostly, but CIA and DIA are integral parts, too, as we're able to follow the flow of drugs, arms, and people from foreign countries as one source of intel. In tier one, we would hit those targets exclusively with ground-launched Special Operations Forces. We're prepared to do this in all major cities, save those in the Pacific Northwest. We have intel that the civilian militia types there are about to launch a major operation against their cartel invaders. We have assets at the Bogdon submarine base that are passively assisting."

"Wait! Passively?" he asked, then immediately realized his own answer. "Oh—yes. The posse comitatus thing. I've had the assurances of the Attorney General that we are legal within certain conditions."

"Yes, sir," Secretary Fitzgerald chimed in. "The Justice Department has been engaging the state AGs and governors to press their cities to forward any and all cases of evidence asap. We're prepared to file our cases with both Congress and the Supreme Court within the deadlines, sir."

"Very good," Jeremiah said. He picked up his spitter bottle and let a dose of stress ooze into it. "I'm not worried about the political ramifications. I just want our citizens to be fully informed when the time comes. No hoodwinking, ladies and gents. Please continue, General."

"Tier two escalates by including aerial assets to land various expanded operators—Rangers and the like. It expands the target packages to include those known cartel locations that have a smaller volume of business. Mostly homes of the local cartel leaders with well-known documented and lengthy rap sheets. Or those locations that the cartel members from other nations are known to be staying. The air units will include gunships as a show of force. Some of these gangs have RPGs and possibly shoulder-launched guided missiles. This is the minimum level I recommend, sir."

Jeremiah hung his head, staring down at the stack of papers and photos that were prep work for this call. He sighed. "Keep going."

"Tier three expands both ground and air operations. We include regular infantry to help the local Guard and police with everything from arresting and corralling, to clearing buildings, to setting up large scale detainment centers. This has the largest visibility to the most populace. It is the 'slippery slope' you're wanting to avoid. We activate jets to expand the show of force. We expand the number of drones being used for keeping tabs on escaping cartel members. We activate special units intended to use electronic countermeasures against any of their drones, less-lethal force, things like that. And though we don't expect to need this, technically we have other units on standby."

"Dare I ask?" the president said, head still staring at the table.

"Cyber teams to knock out their communications, armed drones, heavy armor..."

"Armor!" Jeremiah asked, perking up. "We can't have tanks rolling down the streets of L.A., General! Surely we don't believe the gangs in Phoenix, San Diego, or Albuquerque have tanks."

"I understand it is unlikely, Mr. President, but there is one scenario that has plausibility. They have heavily infiltrated the Mexican Army through bribery, violent coercion, and just plain old enlistment. Our wargaming taught us that we have to be prepared for a scenario that includes those units acting rogue."

Snake Charmer finally looked up from the table, lips pursed in tension. "Understood, Judah. How long would it take to put into motion? I want to call President Chacon directly. I know she'll probably tip them off, but it's a necessary step when I get eviscerated by the U.N. afterwards."

"If we put the units into a heightened state of readiness, we could be moving in hours."

"Alright. Give me 'til Monday to think all of this over."

CHAPTER 25

East of Manhattan, Kansas

"Duuuuude!" David 'Goldilocks' Faust said loudly in his Southern California charm. "Those are flying in low!"

The old quarry was a solid hour closer than Sunny D's place for the former airsoft team, an ideal spot for them to begin performing basic live fire training. Though most of them still didn't own pistols, their slings and other tactical gear from airsoft had easily transitioned to make them all look like real 'mall ninjas'—without the pot bellies.

"There was only one the other day," Elvis commented. It was early Friday afternoon. The friends had taken to the training as a way of avoiding the obvious question—*how long until the university tells us to move out of the dorms and go home?* The question affected over half of them. "SuperFly, you should sneak over there and check it out."

"That's—that's not a good idea," Morris interjected.

He was bombarded by a chorus of 'Awww, C'Mon!s' as well as two quips about being geriatric.

"Seriously!" he said in uncharacteristic tension. "We have no idea what that is over there! But the fact that there's two now definitely excludes it being some sort of emergency."

"So?" Super B said. "We have every right to go and look!"

"It's okay," Jon Sanches said over the bickering friends. "I want to go. Bee—you're the tiniest. Hop on back and go with me," he said as he headed for his enduro motorcycle. "I'll go slow and you can wear my helmet." The freshman excitedly accepted and followed her teammate to his bike, which had easily made it past the gate the rest had to walk from.

Morris turned in exasperation toward the rest of them. "Seriously! They should just stay here!" He was hoping to get enough peer pressure to get the whole team involved. Nothing. He looked at ThatNub. "Not even you?"

"I kinda wanna know, bro. Sorry."

Morris looked back at the pair preparing to depart. *Maybe I should go instead of her... Nope. She'd never let that go. I'd forever be a sexist in her eyes.* He was just worried about his friend. He grabbed their rifles from laying on top of their cases. "Wait!" he yelled as he ran over.

"What!" yelled Jordan, half expecting Morris to pull a stunt.

"Take these. Keep your speed low so they won't hear you. Keep hidden in a low spot."

"We got it, Grandpa," she said, taking the two rifles from Morris and holding them tightly against her body after she dropped the slings over her neck. Jon slowly left the quarry and headed north.

TUCSON, ARIZONA

"...WHICH MEANS THE ONLY REAL QUESTION IS... WHAT DO WE do with this information?" Granger finished.

"I just want to be sure what I'm hearin'," Claude Moses said. "You guys have found basically what you've described as a superhighway of cartel smuggling?"

"Affirmative," Dave Wolf acknowledged.

"Look—" Claude said. "I know I don't got no dog in this hunt, being support crew, and all. But I think we should get whatever photos and GPS points you all collected to CBP. Give 'em another shot."

"Awwww, man, not them again!" Tracy complained. "They already tried to tell us to step back as it is!"

"I'm with Tracy," Mick said, guarding his spotter's position on the matter. "With him and Wolf sniping instead of spotting, we could wax everyone of those pedo-pushing dirtbags before they know what happened!"

"Really?" Dave Wolf challenged. "You gonna shoot their drones down, too? It would be nothing for their reinforcements to just truck right up to the vehicle bars, blow a hole through it, and QRF for those guys with about thirty criminals!" He referred to the fact that out in those few spots of isolated desert that had a border barrier, it tended to be implanted posts meant only to stop vehicles.

"Well, then what do you suggest?" Mick said with a frustrated tone.

"Men." Bob Salvage said. "Everyone take a breath and think. Goin' after each other's throats ain't the answer."

"I get that," Tracy said. "But what's the point if we can't do anything?"

"Then let's identify every option," Granger suggested. "We know one—direct action. There's a ninety plus percent chance we'd kill a dozen of them before the other unknown number killed us. What else?"

"The other obvious," Mick said. "Passing info to a bureaucracy that will do nothing with it."

"What else?" Granger pressed, looking around the fire pit in his driveway. Silence. *C'mon, Madison—think!* he commanded himself.

"Too bad it will take so long to train some more people," Dave Wolf said. “There’s some good three-gun shooters at the range. They just need the bush skills.”

“Too bad the military won’t help...” Bob said matter-of-factly.

Granger’s head popped up. “Says who?” He received looks from the rest as if a baby’s arm was growing right out of his forehead. “What...is it so far-fetched? You can read between the lines. Those officers sat right in this driveway less than a week ago, and you all know who sent them. That’s called putting out the feelers, boys...”

“You really think passing the intel on to that colonel would do something?” Tracy asked skeptically.

“As opposed to what?” Granger returned.

EAST OF MANHATTAN, KANSAS

POP-POP! POP-POP-POP-POP! SEVERAL RIFLES SCREAMED AT THE paper plates. Cat Scratch Fever had crafted several crude stands, some out of scrap wood, others out of pieces of surplus PVC piping they found on the Sanches farm. Since the other pair had left, the remaining friends started learning to move and shoot as pairs, keeping their peripheral vision on each other while actively engaging targets. Jon had run them through the drill without shooting for twenty minutes before they attempted it with live fire.

When Morris and ThatNub finished up a set, Goldi spoke up as he pulled his ear muffs off. “Listen! I think they’re coming back!” They could hear the low rumble of a dirt bike traveling at a low speed.

Morris eyeballed where the road disappeared over a small rise to the north, looking for them, but they appeared out of a small wash much closer to the quarry. The group all verified firearms were clear and started packing up. It was getting dark. Morris could tell there was a cold front moving in. After taking off his magazine chest pouch, he put his topcoat and gloves on and joined the small pack walking toward the access road to greet SuperFly and Super B.

"There's definitely something sketchy goin' on over there," Jon yelled first, killing the bike and letting it roll to a stop near the pack.

"It looked like a video game or movie," Jordan agreed. "There were black SUVs! Guards! Planes! I took pix, but my phone died because it hasn't had a full night of charging in like four days."

ThatNub said, "I'm getting flashbacks to an old movie my dad made me watch called *Lethal Weapon*." He started up his Danny Glover impression, "I'm gettin' too old for this—"

"Not now, Nub!" Morris said, cutting off his roommate.

"Sheesh, you are *such* a worrying Karen, aren't you?" Bee yelled.

Morris turned away and started walking back to his rifle case and backpack.

"C'mon, Bro," Goldi said, jogging over to him. "Don't get mad. She's a brat, we all know it. Just wait."

Morris stopped and looked at the surfer. He turned back toward the rest of the team. "You all have no idea. The gangs have taken over my old 'hood. It's getting real out there! And you're acting like a bunch of fool kids."

"Then what should we do about it?" Misty Meaner said. "We could tell the cops in Manhattan. But what'll they do? And why would a legit cartel have a strip way out here, a hundred miles from KC?"

"I think I might know why," ThatNub suggested. "My cousin is a pilot. Air controllers use two types of information from radars. The main one just shows an electronic blip, but there's way too many small planes for them to keep track of. The other one uses a code unique to the plane. That's how they know who's who in the sky."

"So?" Super B said.

"So, they can fly anywhere they want with that turned off. They could turn it off before they even take off. If they have a secret strip way out here, and they're flying low enough, they might not gather much attention from KC. They'd look like a flock of birds or something."

"That would explain all the SUVs," ThatNub said. "Did they have guns?"

"Not out in the open," Jon said. "But they all looked like dudes you don't wanna mess with."

"Anyone have any suggestions?" Misty repeated.

"I do," Morris said. "Bee. Can you go start charging your phone in Nub's Bronco? And text me those pictures? I met this military officer a couple of weeks back. On the bus from KC. I got his card."

1st LAR Battalion Admin Building, Camp Pendleton, California

"Colonel Caldwell," Brandon said, "this is my former CO, Lieutenant Colonel Leaver."

They were standing in the commanding officer's office at Brandon's last pre-D.C. assignment, the light armored recon branch of the 1st Marine Division. The battalion's Marines specialized in high-speed reconnaissance in eight-wheeled amphibious vessels. The battalion, and sometimes only certain companies of it, would be assigned to various regiments in the division based on the needs of a particular deployment. The senior Marine grinned as he came around his desk with hand extended to greet Lou. Like the Navy, Marines didn't salute indoors.

"Colonel, pleased to meet you. Please just call me Scott."

"Very well, Scott. And I go by Lou. This is just a boondoggle, nothing formal." Lou glanced around after the handshake. He was starting to see a common theme amongst Marine officers—tidy desks inside tiny offices with a sparse collection of photos and memorabilia. *It isn't until these guys get flag officer status that they start to outdo each other's toy collections,* he'd figured out. *But he does have a nice corner office.* Though a mile from the ocean, the second-floor office was high enough to have a decent view of it.

"What brings you two boondoggling here to 1st LAR, Brandon?" Scott asked. "Our leave curtailments have just been reinforced with a no-kidding Warning Order. Seems like the Pentagon has plenty enough on its plate already..." Though polite, he was immediately suspicious that one of his former officers would show up unannounced—with an Air Force pilot, no less—the same day they were put on emergency alert. "Last I knew, you'd transferred to Colonel Jackson's staff. Right?"

Upon hearing about the order, Lou pulled his government issued cell phone out of his trouser pocket and began to hunt for a secure wi-fi signal.

"Sorry, sir," Brandon said. "We really aren't at liberty. Respectfully, we—"

"Captain," Lou said looking up, "I think we can level with the colonel at this point. The general knows all he needs to by now." He went back to his phone.

"Roger that, sir," Brandon told Lou. "You're correct. We report to Colonel Jackson, and even directly to General Montgomery at times." Scott let out a low whistle as he reached for his water bottle and took a sip. "We've been on the road, mostly traveling at large, assessing unit integrity and readiness."

Lou interjected when he glanced up quickly and pointed to his face. "As you can see, the road has been a bit rough."

Scott grimaced a bit. "Yeaahhh, I didn't want to say anything, but..."

"Scott, you got anyone who can help me log on to your command net and check secure emails?"

"Oh, sure! Just ask the Marine you first checked in with when you got up here to my office." Lou excused himself and made tracks for the outer office.

He passed by a few junior officers who eyed him with great suspicion, his brown bomber jacket and blue garrison cap flat against his hip standing out like a fat kid at the all-you-can-eat buffet. He found a lance corporal sitting at the front desk. After five minutes of tedious minutiae, Lou had managed to securely log his phone into their system. He saw four chairs and a table that comprised what could be called a small waiting area, so he set himself down there to do a quick scan. He found the email he was looking for. *Wowzers*, he thought as he read. 'All combat units on emergency standdown. Suspend training cycles in progress and RTB. Suspend scheduled maintenance cycles on all ground-based equipment. Cancel all non-critical events...'

Lou read for three more minutes, noting specific units at some bases had been made exempt. He recognized a few of them as units that he and Brandon reported may be light on people or had a high number of equipment pieces in a state of repair. *I wonder if we actually gave the old man data he could use.* He kept reading, and the last few sentences almost took his breath away. 'Ensure all personnel have current Wills and Life Insurance paperwork in order. This is not a drill.'

Lou almost jumped when his phone rang as he was staring at it and thinking about that last sentence. *Dammit! That made my skin crawl!*

"Colonel Caldwell," he said sharply. He did not recognize the area code.

"H-hello? Yes." <Ahem>. "This is Morris Dooghan. I...I think we met a couple of weeks ago..."

Dooghan...Dooghan... He sounds young. "I'll need a bit more, son. I've handed out about fifty business cards in the last month."

"We were on a bus. I told you about airsoft at college..."

"Ohhh, Thumper!" Lou said. "I didn't expect you to actually call. Kind of surprised me. What can I do for you?" *That is the question, isn't it...?*

"Well, uh. Shoot, I don't know where to begin. And I don't want to waste your time. But...my team and I were out practicing and a few times, now, we've seen something suspicious."

"Well, Morris. I think you might be best off telling the local police," Lou started.

"Sorry, sir. I think this might be a bit over their heads. I'm hoping you can tell the FBI or something."

This made Lou perk up. He looked up at the office around him. There were a few small conversations going on, but they were all ignoring him. "What—what makes you say that, son?"

"I can send you some photos. It looks like a drug movie or something. Planes and cars, thugs, all meeting in the middle of nowhere. More than once."

"Did you say planes?" Lou double-checked. "Like small private planes?"

"Yeah. I mean yes. Yes, sir."

"I can take a look and forward them, Morris. After that, it is out of my hands. And I can't emphasize this enough, but you all need to not go back anymore. If it is who you think it is, they won't be afraid to hurt you. Slowly and permanently."

"So, you'll look at it, then?" Morris asked in disbelief.

"I said I would, son. Send 'em. You caught me at the perfect time for me to forward them places securely."

"Th-thank you, Colonel Caldwell!"

"Remember, Thumper—tell your friends to stay away from that area."

"I will." After they ended the call, Lou just sat and stared at the little phone. It began to buzz. *That was fast,* he thought. He opened a text from a number, not recognizing that it was completely different than the one that had called four minutes earlier.

[Sender Unknown] Sorry to bother you, Air Force. This is the Tucson driveway fire pit speaking. Please call when you get a moment. We have intel you need to send to whoever needs to see it. ASAP.

CHAPTER 26

El Paso, Texas

What are they doing here? Rosie screamed in her head. She had just yanked her eye away from the peephole on her apartment door. Two of Inocencio Delgado's scarier and more recognizable henchmen were standing on the landing outside her front door.

Thump! Thump! "We know you're in there, Carmela! Eddie's been hurt! We need you to come with us, please!" she heard the younger one saying.

Damn, Rosie! Today's the day you die! She ran across the small apartment, stopping near the bathroom. "I just sat down on the toilet!" she yelled. "Give me a minute! Sheesh!"

Rosie threw herself into the bedroom closet and ripped the carpet up from the right rear corner. She found the small cut in the plywood and yanked the temporary patch up, revealing a standard black Glock 26 with no extra magazines. It was in a lady's cummerbund style girdle with a slot for a pistol. She chose to wear it high, hoping that getting the Glock as close to her cleavage as possible might help her conceal it.

She put on an additional baggy sweatshirt and made her way to the door.

"What's with all the banging?" she feigned, followed by a string of Spanish cussing.

"Sorry, Carmela," the older one explained, the tattoos at the bottom of his jawline stretching every bit as much as his words. "Eduardo was injured. It doesn't look so good. He is begging to see you. El Jefe would consider this a great favor if you would come to Ciudad Juarez to comfort him."

"What happened?" Rosie asked, stalling.

"It was a horrible car accident. The hospital says he is too unstable to send over to El Paso. Please! We must hurry!"

Rosie knew she was being lied to, and they knew she knew. It mattered not. If she resisted, they would do horrible things to her, both before and after they knocked her out. The end result would be the same—a one way trip to Mexico. Her training had reinforced one core principle in such a situation: stick to your lies if you suspect your cover is blown. Stick to them until the very end. Admitting them will guarantee slow death.

She grabbed her phone and purse and was warned off about it. "No, miss. We must go. Now. Time is critical." The older one had an expression that was cold like a northern wind. It said not to challenge him.

Rosie found herself between the two men. Life almost felt like a dream state to her at that moment. *Maybe it's true. Maybe they haven't found out.* She was bargaining and she knew it. The older man drove the king cab pickup. Rosie got in one side, being shoved into the wall-like stature of a third man on the far side of the passenger bench. The younger one moved in behind her, trapping her in the middle.

Nobody said a word—not through El Paso, not at the border or across the bridge, and not into Juarez. She had no idea where the hospital was in this city, though she didn't expect to be going to it. Rosie tried to memorize landmarks, count seconds between turns, listen for noise both on and off the road that might help later. *Maybe they're driving in loops on purpose,* she thought. After a full forty minutes of driving through Juarez, the truck pulled into a rundown factory sector of town. They took a left into a collection of dingy gray sheet metal buildings. Rosie began to cry.

EAST OF MANHATTAN, KANSAS

THIS IS SO STUPID! MORRIS SCREAMED IN HIS HEAD. *WE GOT NO business being out here! And feels like snow is coming on top of everything else.* He'd only agreed to tag along because he couldn't stand the thought of haggling for hyper-inflated mac-and-cheese at the grocery store once again. He'd spent the morning working on any other long-term preparations he could think of. Mad he hadn't taken the modern prepper movement just a tad more seriously, he filled all the containers he'd been collecting and saving in the preceding weeks with water. He'd also discovered that the one Walmart in the area was out of almost all camping supplies. On a whim and a hunch, he found a caterer in town that was willing to sell him sterno candles normally used for keeping big pans of food warm at weddings. *At least we'll have some sort of fuel to cook with if the power goes out and just never comes back,* he thought.

That afternoon, the team had all drifted to his apartment to find out if the colonel had replied. "He hasn't," Morris told them. "I told you he probably won't."

One thing led to another and eventually Elvis busted out a paper map of the area. "See this road here? Runs north, too, but it's about four miles closer to town. If we take this ranch powerline access feeder here, we can cut across the fields relatively unhindered. Tell 'em the best part, Jon!"

"What?" Misty Meaner asked.

"I got two loaner quads and a trailer we can borrow. My friend at the powersports store. All I need is for Nub to help me tow them."

"Sweet!" ThatNub said. "Let's go now!"

He and Jon both had coats half-on when Morris raised his objection. "Seriously?" That was the beginning of a thirty-minute debate, of which he and Goldi were the only two seeing clearly. About ninety minutes later, they were parking Goldi's and Nub's vehicles in a new spot on a new road, trusting Elvis to guide them northeast with a simple cell phone compass and a gas station map. The rolling slopes of cut fields were easy enough to traverse. And with the quads and motorcycle doubled, they were able to make quick time. Goldi volunteered to stay back at the vehicles, leaving a traveling team of six.

They'd progressed at a cautious crawl of about ten miles per hour for over a half hour. Jon and Bee would ride ahead and each time they were close to cresting a small rise, they would dismount and scout the downslope and next valley.

"We've found it!" he whispered excitedly as the slow quads cruised up. Morris and ThatNub killed the engines.

"Really?" Misty Meaner said, sliding off the back of Morris' quad.

Elvis slid off the other one and stooped as he crept past the motorcycle. He got down to his palms and balls of his feet, high crawling up to SuperFly and Super B. "Nobody found binoculars for sale, yet, huh?"

"Try this," Jon the SuperFly said, handing him a cell phone with a little zoom attachment over the camera. When combined with the smart phone's electronic zoom, it magnified up to forty-eight times.

"Whoa. That is pretty slick, if you can hold it still."

He was looking at one small building and a nearly fifteen-hundred-foot stretch of grass that had been mowed down to dirt repeatedly. They were perpendicular to it, about eight hundred yards away. The crest they were laying on ran at an angle to the makeshift runway, with it passing the small building end of the runway within eighty yards. The building wasn't permanent, but a wooden shed kit from a chain home improvement store. It looked like it might be ten by fifteen feet in size. The runway at the far, north end came to a stop just shy of a grove of trees lining a stream.

"Yeah," Jon said. "I have a little tiny tripod with flexible legs I'll bring next time."

Next time! Morris thought, looking once again at the cold gray overcast. "This is super fun and all," he said sarcastically, "but my weather app shows snow coming down tonight. It feels like the temp is dropping. We came. We saw. Now let's get out of here."

"Chill, Grump-pa," Super B said. She giggled at her own pun.

ThatNub low crawled back to Morris, who was still standing lower down the slope next to the bike and quads. "Seriously, Mo. What gives? Isn't this why we started doing real tactical stuff?"

Morris almost choked on his own tongue guffawing. "Wh-What! You can't be serious! We're doing that in case... I don't know... a mob tries to burn down the grocery store or somethin'!" He pointed past his buddy at his friends. "We aren't cops or special forces, Nub! We got no business coming out here to play G.I. Joe! It feels like Goldi and I are the only two to get that."

William ThatNub Easton turned about as serious as Morris had ever heard him. "Mobs...riots...gangs back in KC—and this!" He pointed east, also. "A cartel landing strip. And nobody knows about it but us! Maybe this is exactly what we've been training for!"

"I'm going to start hoofing it back to Goldi," Morris said after several seconds of silence. "It'll give me time to think." He looked up once more. "And stay warm."

JUAREZ, MEXICO

. . .

ROSIE CAME TO IN A DOG CAGE. *UNNGHHHH...WHA...* SHE jolted with a start, the back of her head throbbing in intense pain. The room was still dark and fuzzy. She heard several men's voices. *I—I fought them at the truck!* she remembered.

"Carmelita!" she heard Eddie scream as her eyes tuned in.

A pair of dirty, leathery hands grabbed the top of the kennel and spun it hard to the right, throwing her sore head against the hard galvanized wire. Another sharp pain shot through her nervous system. "Eddie!" she screamed, seeing the bloody beaten pulp on his knees six feet in front of the cage. Inocencio Delgado was standing there, as were other men. She recognized the faces that politely abducted her. Then—"You!" she screamed. She recognized El Paso police lieutenant Troy English as one of Eddie's turned contacts. He strode over casually and squatted in front of the cage's door.

"It took me a while," he admitted. "I knew I knew you... I just couldn't place it." He stood up and stared down, spitting on her. "But it came to me a couple of nights ago. In a dream of all places. You were that cop—San Antonio, was it? The one they made a fuss over..." He looked at her mangled right hand. "The special one. It took some digging. The Rangers did a good job of burying the stories." He turned and walked casually back over to El Jefe. Inocencio was surrounded by the three abductors, as well as a few others, some close, some playing guard farther away. He refaced Rosie. "Eddie, your girlfriend's name isn't Carmelita. It's Rosie. Rosie Ortiz of the Texas Rangers."

"Arrggghhhh!" Rosie screamed as she started to kick the cage door repeatedly.

The shock of the explosion scared her into stiffness, as the back of Lieutenant Troy English's head exited the front in the violent symphony of a smoking .44 Magnum hand cannon. Brain material, skull fragments, and blood painted the front and top of the kennel, covering Rosie in a gridded pattern of crimson and gray matter ooze. Her screams evolved from anger to sheer terror until she started to black out from lack of air. She began to pant.

Eddie started to resist from his knees, hands and feet both bound behind his back. The old henchman who was driving the truck dragged an old rusty folding chair covered in dried blood over while the other two picked Eddie up by the chicken wings. They stuffed him into the chair while El Jefe Delgado strolled over to Rosie.

"I liked you," he said calmly. "Like," he corrected himself, smirking. "Funny. I still like you. My daughter...she really likes you. I'll be honest, Carm—Rosie... this one pains me a little." He could see Rosie's horrified face, not on Eddie, but on the nearly headless mess that Troy English had become on the bloody concrete factory floor. "Oh, him?" Inocencio asked. "We don't need him. We're about to change the landscape of El Paso." He laughed. "All of western America, actually," he said as he stared past Rosie in deep thought. "There are some cities in which we still need our moles, but El Paso will certainly not be one of them. But..." He squatted, much as Troy English had a few minutes earlier, completely uncaring of the bloody mess lining the cage a foot away from his face. "Now...we're hearing from our own government that your Presidente may be growing some juevos. This bought you a little time, my dear. I need to know what you know."

"Just kill me now!" she screamed. "I won't tell you anything!"

Inocencio Delgado just laughed as he walked over to his henchmen. "Make sure you take your time with him," he said as he nudged in Eddie's direction. "Make sure she watches. Then take her to the convoy forming at my estate. She's going with us to Chihuahua."

Rosie heard acknowledgments from the thugs as El Jefe left. A different man who had been passively watching from the side casually moved into the space separating Rosie from Eddie, who was still struggling to fight the bindings that had been moved directly to the legs of the chair. The scarred henchman seemed to be no stranger to pain himself. He dropped a roll-pouch on the ground and squatted down, unrolling it. He pulled out a long filet knife.

"I always like to skin the meat before I tenderize it," he said excitedly to Rosie.

He stood and moved toward Eddie. The oldest of the other henchmen started to put cheap, industrial foam earplugs in. The carver made quick work of Eddie's ears, using them to start a pile on the floor—a pile of skin, testicles, and thinly sliced muscle that would grow in front of Rosie until she passed out from shock and pleading in terror for Eddie's screaming life five minutes later.

CHAPTER 27

Tucson, Arizona

Rrrrrrrrnnnnggg! Granger Madison's phone screamed. At forty-nine, it just wasn't as easy to snap up out of bed, ready for action, as it had been in the Marines or fire department. He shook through the webs. *Rrrrrrrrnnnnggg! What the— What damn time is it? 0230! Decline.*

Rrrrrrrrnnnnggg! "Listen, jacka—"

"Be at the playground by the elementary school. The one your girls went to when they lived here. Ten minutes. Don't be late."

"Who the hell is this?"

"I set a can of chili on your counter." *Click.*

What? What the hell? Granger was grabbing for the Sig, ripping it out of the kydex appendix holster that cradled it while on his nightstand. He spun around, keeping his elbows about half-compressed. The pistol was close to his body, but level—ready to drive up to sight-picture in front of his eyes. He moved the forefinger on his support hand, ready to toggle the 500-lumen TLR1 light hanging on the bottom of the striker-fired weapon at the perfect moment. He did a quick scan of his bedroom and made his way to the open door. His room was across from the dining area. He approached the doorframe, carefully rounding it with the pistol fully extended. He was still about two feet inside his room. He continued to shift left while scanning the dining area's right. He finally approached the point where he had to go through the fatal funnel of the doorway. He did, clearing the far corner while hitting it with a quick burst of light. Nothing.

He side-stepped out of the doorway. *Probably being silhouetted by the bedroom window,* he realized. He continued to scan the dining and visible parts of the kitchen and hall. Then he saw it. Sitting right on the end of the counter that divided the kitchen from the breakfast nook was a can of Stagg chili. He knew instantly he would find nothing clearing the rest of the house. *This whole exercise was to tell me he could've killed me,* he acknowledged. It was meant purely as a trust-builder by someone who doesn't want to be seen.

Pissed as he was, Granger wasn't going to miss the appointment. He got dressed, including setting the appendix carry holster and Sig into place by his waistband. *Wait—I should bring the PCC, too.* He opted to bring the pistol caliber carbine, which used the same magazines as his Glock that he used on his Road Runner missions. He went to his Securit gun locker and opened it, swapping holsters and pistols. He grabbed the small rifle-looking carbine and two of the long, custom thirty-three round Glock mags chambered in the same 9mm. Four minutes later, Granger was pulling up to the block where his girls used to go to school, shutting down his lights before he rounded the last corner. Though he had an extremely powerful Surefire handheld flashlight, he opted to just keep it palmed in his left hand, powered off.

He got out of his truck, keeping the PCC slung close to his body and under the zip-up hoodie he'd put on. To his left were average looking suburban homes. He walked around the pickup and to its right, heading onto the school property, heading directly for the jungle gym area. As he made it through a small grove of Desert Willows planted by the sixth-grade class, he saw a figure emerge from a shadow in between him and the playground's suspended bridge.

"Well?" he said, coolly, but on fire in his mind, wondering if the cartel had finally figured him out...

"You should think about getting a dog," the shadow's voice said.

"You should buy decent chili," Granger returned. "Who the hell are you, and why shouldn't I kill you right here?"

"Easy, Granger," the discernable, black American man's voice said. "We're on the same side."

Granger took a moment. "The fact you were in my house ain't lost on me, pal. It doesn't mean I ain't pissed right now."

"Good," the voice said. The man slowly crept forward out of the shadow, trying to let Granger see him without either of them being in striking distance of the other. "You should be. And you should be scared. I know you all think you cover your tracks. But once we were told who you were, we ran a clean comparison. It took our hacker four hours to figure out who all of you were, based on a cross sectional search of cell tower usage and one satellite photo of the Suburban that infils and exfils your team."

Granger was silent. *He's obviously government. But who?* Finally, "You have my attention. Who are 'we'?"

"Good. It's good that vets like you and yours are involved. We just need you to know how vulnerable you are. If the cartel gets an inkling you're out there..."

"I know. Besides impressing me with your hacker's ability, what's your point?" Granger asked just a bit testily.

"Have you found tunnel service ports yet?"

"I ain't telling you jack squat until I know who I'm talking to!"

The man stepped a bit closer. There was a sliver of moonlight coming through the trees. *A peaceful, deadly man,* Granger assessed immediately. *Spec ops.*

"Delta," he finally said. "How'd Delta get hold of my operatio..." He cut himself off before he finished. *That colonel. Maybe there was more to him than meets the eye after all.*

"It all gettin' clear for you now?" the man asked.

It was much too dark to see many details. Even at probably 5'11", he could see the man was stout, not someone to be taken lightly. "One or two. If we had explosives it would be easy to collapse it."

"Roger that," the man acknowledged. "We need all four of you set up in that valley by dark this coming night. Find yourselves a new OP —something close to the border. I'll have one other with me. Whatever you do, don't effing shoot. You won't hear us coming. We'll say Stagg. You'll say chili. Clear?"

"Stagg. Chili. Got it. What's this all about? You've obviously read my file..."

The man sighed. "Something big." He started to walk back into the shadows, then turned. "And tell your team to get your families somewhere safe." He disappeared into the dark.

As if that exists anymore, Granger thought pessimistically.

THE WHITE HOUSE SITUATION ROOM

"WHAT DO WE KNOW?" JEREMIAH ASKED. THE ROOM WAS filled with the usual defense and security team, plus key admirals and Space Force generals.

"Satellites detected a missile launch out of China," Chief of Space Operations General George Overton scanned his watch, "forty-three minutes ago. It was a boost-glide weapon, sir, most likely an inertial guided solid tungsten projectile."

"So—not nuclear?" the President asked.

"No, sir. It's low altitude and rapid decay rate showed us it wasn't meant for strategic orbit. Cue up the feed," the general ordered the room's junior officers manning the control center. A disturbing image in infrared showed up. "It's a new night in the Northwest Pacific..."

"What the..." Jeremiah looked on in shock. "Is that a crater?"

"It's in the Kronotskiy Nature Reserve on the Kamchatka Peninsula," the general replied.

"What the hell did they hit?" Jeremiah demanded.

"Nothing of any value, sir," Secretary Fitzgerald interjected. "They shot into a remote part of the peninsula as a Russian fleet of troop carriers was sailing by less than two-hundred kilometers away."

"Is there any chance they missed?" the president tested, angry at no particular person.

"None, Mr. President," Joint Chief General Judah Montgomery said. "They've never missed one of these tests by more than ten kilometers. It's a message."

"Well, I'm hearin' it, loud and damned clear!" Jeremiah said excitedly. "Just wait 'til they try to sink one of our carriers with one of those things! Or take out our silos!" *What is the end game,* Jeremiah wondered. "We need to figure out how to stop them from taking drastic measures before this starts a world war. What are we doing to shore ourselves up right now?"

"Sir, with your permission, I'd like to keep us in DefCon Three and begin the checklist for DefCon Two," General Montgomery stated. "Just in case we need to go there. We're already at an increased state, waiting for your decision with Venom Spear. Might as well get the strategic forces aligned."

What the hell is the end game?! Jeremiah asked himself once more as he nodded his approval. "I know you all have been wargaming this, team. Tell me—what will happen when they come after us? Surely they know Russia will be sending one of their own slugs in retaliation!"

"Maybe," General Overton stated. "We can see activity at missile launch sites that indicate they may be trying to target Chinese satellites instead. But we know China has at least two satellites that can send a directional EMP pulse toward the ground. Those have heat blooms forming around them. All indications point toward both sides getting ready to go after each other's critical tech. And—Chinese intrusive cyber-attacks are ramping up on us, as well."

USAF C-130J Super Hercules, Above the U.S. - Mexico border

The turbo-prop transport craft lowered the back ramp, revealing the near-freezing night air to all who bathed in the red lights. The loadmaster was tethered to the floor of the plane with a long restraint lanyard. He stood off to the planes port side of the open ramp. The Operational Detachment Delta Special Operations soldier acting as jumpmaster bent down and got on his knees, eyeing the dark desert and scant lights of Yuma, Arizona, to the west. The majority of their forty-minute flight from Tucson had nothing to do with gaining distance. It was about getting the altitude needed for the combined HALO and HAHO jumps. From the 30,000 foot height, the jumpers would use both methods to land safely at their destinations. The first two men, destined for a spot nearly under the craft, would descend in a freefall to a height of only 2,000 feet over the desert hill they were aiming for—the 'Low Opening' of the HALO jump.

The Sergeant Major and his other three team members would open their special airfoil wings a scant few seconds after starting their freefall. This was the 'high-open' evolution, which would allow them to glide close to forty miles. They were bound for a different mission... one that required a stealthy insertion near the small city of Nogales.

Three other C-130s had been flying this pattern for three hours and would continue for two more. The craft would fly about seventeen minutes farther east than the jump point and then turn northwest to repeat the loop. Even if the Mexican military or cartels had been monitoring what was happening, they would have little chance of knowing exactly when or where any operators had deployed.

The jumpmaster stood back up with assistance from the loadmaster, part of the plane's regular crew. The parachutes, combat gear, and breathing apparatus—necessary due to the extreme height of the jump —amassed to an astounding one-hundred-fifty extra pounds of weight on the soldier. He looked back up at the small LED box just as the red one lit up—*thirty seconds to the drop zone,* the pilot was communicating.

"Standby!" the Sergeant Major yelled above the roar of the wind. He stepped up to his men and participated as they all began one last check of each other. Equipment had to be tethered tightly. There was no room for error.

The first two men, destined for a hard and fast flight to the desert floor, turned on the electric infrared lamps secured to the tops of their combat helmets. They lowered their night vision which covered their faces above the silicon half-face masks that comprised their breathing system. The duration of their freefall made the likelihood of a fatal impact very high—the IR strobes and night vision would help them avoid that. The other four wore breathing helmets that included an entire face piece, necessary to keep their skin covered. They would be hanging in the cold air, taking over an hour to glide to their destination. They would space themselves in their jumps and chute deployments and track each other only with cheap lime-green disposable glow-sticks until the final stage of their landing. The jump light turned green.

"Go!" the Sergeant Major yelled as he pointed at the pair of men.

They ran out of the plane in tight formation, leaning into tight missiles for the first few seconds and eventually flattening their bodies out with a familiar drag, using the angles of their hands and feet to stay on course with micro-adjustments.

Down in the Buenos Aires National Wildlife Refuge, four U.S. Military veterans—two Marines, one Army, one Navy—had planted themselves in a new observation post on the hilltop directly north of the border. Almost five hundred meters to the northwest of the men who called themselves the Road Runners, across a small valley, a band of cartel coyotes were loading two vans full of explosives and weapons.

Neither group was aware of the sky activity above them, as two of America's most experienced members of Delta Force descended upon the canyon under black canopies.

EAST OF SASABE, MEXICO

TWO HOURS AFTER GRANGER AND THE ROAD RUNNERS participated in the 'Stagg' and 'chili' password process, he and Dave Wolf finished leading one of the Delta operators back to one of the two service ports they'd discovered in the enormous cartel cross-border tunnel. They were all taking a knee about fifty meters from it on the off chance it opened. It was the wee hours of a Monday, but they'd been in and out of the valley so much lately, the days were starting to run together for Granger.

"The other one you found is south?" Master Sergeant Mikkel Hudson asked.

The senior operator to drop in and join the Road Runners was one of the most peacefully dangerous men Granger felt he'd ever met. Both under six-feet tall, neither of the Delta operators was a giant man, but both exuded an aura of toxic-masculinity that Granger hadn't experienced since he was in the Corps.

"Affirmative," Granger replied. *Still can't believe these guys dropped in to operate with us,* Granger thought. *Something big was happening, this guy said the other night.* "Based on bearing and pace count, it's about five hundred meters between here and the ranch. In our opinion, it has to be the entrance. It's the only place that could cover the amount of traffic we're seeing through it."

"Alright. You two keep an eye out for drones and patrols for a minute."

Granger continued to internally ponder their luck. *Wolf was on an A Team. I was in Force Recon. It's not like we're newbies.* He and Dave turned themselves east and south, watching for any signs of people or machine on or above the Mexican desert.

"Lucky Charm, Voo Doo," they heard Hudson softly say into his headset. They listened to one side of the conversation in which the junior operator reported back to Hudson what he, Mick, and Tracy were observing. "Copy all. Continue to monitor," he instructed. "Sounds like the vans took off. We don't have a drone at our immediate disposal, but my partner is getting onto our battle net to request one. Madison, stay here and cover. Wolf, follow me. We're going to rig this hatch."

CHAPTER 28

THE WHITE HOUSE SITUATION ROOM

"AND YOU'RE SURE THIS IS THEM," JEREMIAH ALLEN ASKED the two men he'd been primarily talking to in the emergency meeting. He looked back and forth at his Secretary of Defense and Leading General of the Joint Chiefs, scanning their faces.

"This is solid, Mr. President," Army General Judah Montgomery said with extreme confidence. "We had a Reaper following it from the moment it left Seattle until our AWAC from Tinker could make it on station. The ship has been under direct observation the entire time, sir."

A cartel invasion had been sent running by an organized group of citizens in Washington State. The death toll would be high... the mop-up would take years... but the people had fought back. The leadership had infiltrated in an old cruise ship painted to look like it was a Red Cross relief ship.

"The timing is key, Kell," President Allen told Defense Secretary Kelly Fitzgerald. He looked at his watch. "This isn't just political theater," he reminded them. "Doing this live will send a serious message to both China and Russia. One they can't ignore." He scanned his advisors once more. The other twenty-three people in the White House Situation Room were deathly quiet. *The evidence needs to be beyond reproach,* he said to himself. *Irrefutable.* He knew they were fully aware of that.

"Mr. President, General Montgomery has my every confidence," Kelly said, himself a retired Admiral. "If you give us the go, we can make this happen in time for your broadcast."

President Allen looked down at the cold cup of tea staring up at him from the table, feeling the weight of the world shift under and around him. He had a stern and angry resolve on his face when he looked back up. "Go. Commence Operation Venom Spear." He sighed, as if the weight on his shoulders had just compressed his lungs. "Now...who is the Skipper of the Bunker Hill?"

"Captain Patricia Cooper, Mr. President," General Montgomery answered. "May I ask why, sir?"

"Correct me if I'm wrong, General," Jeremiah said. "But she's about to command the first U.S. Navy ship to do this since the 1980s."

INTERSTATE HIGHWAY 10, ARIZONA

IT WAS EARLY AFTERNOON ON MONDAY. BRANDON WAS DRIVING their rental Toyota 4Runner while Lou was catching a nap. Both men were decked out in patchless Army uniform pieces they'd been given at the last command they toured—Fort Irwin northeast of Los Angeles—before being given the order to head for home on Sunday. Though not a fan of issuing two sets of gear and rifles to a couple of off-branch officers, the base commander knew instantly who Colonel Ryan Jackson represented when he called to order it. *Don't you two realize we're getting ready for a large domestic op?* he pled to deaf ears. They had been briefed that a massive campaign could start any day and to be prepared for potential violence in any urban area.

Brandon spent an hour at the base range running Lou through a refresher course on the M27 Infantry Automatic Rifle. As a pilot, he'd had SERE training merely for the survival and escape skills should his plane ever go down 'behind enemy lines'. But it had been a few years, and several since he gave firearms training any serious thought. They got to bed early at the hotel and then left at first light Monday. In the back of the SUV were ten five-gallon cans of gasoline and a case of MREs, also courtesy of the Army. As much as Brandon hated not being in his Marine battle uniform, the Army pieces were a relief over wearing working dress uniforms or civilian attire for this potentially harrowing trip.

Lou jostled with the startling ring of his phone. "Caldwell," he said groggily. He hit the button to put the call on speaker.

"Where you guys at?" Colonel Jackson asked.

"About fifty miles west of Tucson, sir," Brandon answered.

"You got time, then," Ryan replied. "President Allen is speaking to the world. It'll be 4 PM in your time zone. I wouldn't bank on the cell signal. You won't want to miss this. Find yourself somewhere to watch it."

V.F.W.—TUCSON, ARIZONA

LOU WAVED OFF THE BEER HIS OLD FRIEND MARK HAD brought him. Lou and Brandon both were already sipping on black coffee. "Thanks, bud. We're getting back on the road after we watch this thing. I don't need to be hitting the pisser every fifteen minutes."

In truthfulness, Lou hadn't drank a drop since the incident. He wasn't sure if he was quitting for life, but each day he didn't have alcohol things seemed just a bit less dire to him on a personal level.

"What's really going on?" Mark asked. "The activity at Davis has quadrupled in the last couple of days."

"Operationally I couldn't even begin to guess," Lou said. "But it has to do with the cartel thing. And probably with this war that seems to be catching between China and Russia."

After ten more minutes of listening to several conversations buzz throughout the VFW, the club's television over the bar changed from a muted talking head to the presidential seal. Mark got up and strode behind the bar. He grabbed the remote and cranked up the volume. The conversations started to lower a bit, but it wasn't until Jeremiah's flushed face could be seen sitting at his desk did people shut up to listen.

"My Fellow Americans..." the president began. "I come to you tonight with a grave message, vital to our nation's, and really—the world's—well-being. Thanks to the wonders of modern technology, I'll be able to show you diplomacy in action. You see, there are actors who have been trying to weaken and destroy our nation. Actors in bad faith...actors without morals...or any purpose other than one of greed, hatred, and pushing suffering onto others."

As he spoke, a feed popped up over the president's shoulder. It was gray and hard to see at first. It appeared to be the deck of a ship and waves. Suddenly the feed expanded, letting the viewers see the entire front-end of a US Navy Ticonderoga class cruiser in the foreground of the screen and some sort of merchant vessel in the background, perhaps six miles ahead of and to the port side of the Navy ship. Though nobody knew it from looking, the feed was being transmitted from the camera of a MQ-8 Fire Scout helicopter drone. The *USS Bunker Hill* was carrying one of the twenty-four-foot-long surveillance tools as part of its ship's equipment. The operators had programmed it to match the ship's speed perfectly, sending an image of both ships from an elevation of three-hundred feet.

The VFW was church-mouse quiet. Lou sat up in his chair. Like everyone else, he was staring intently at the screen.

President Allen continued. "And what I mean by actors, are snakes!" He started to get a little heated. "Snakes who have been striking fear into the hearts of Americans in almost every city west of the Mississippi! These snakes are directly responsible for the deaths of thousands, probably dozens of thousands, of Americans over the last several weeks. The ship you see is an American Navy ship tracking the snakes of the Mendoza Cartel, as they try to slither—" he screamed that word— " from Washington State back to Mexico! Don't be fooled by the red cross on the side! That's what snakes do—they pretend to help you as they bite!"

He paused briefly. "Captain? Are you there?"

Suddenly, the world heard the friendly but firm voice of Captain Patricia Cooper broadcast over their televisions as she acknowledged her presence. The president disappeared off the screen, allowing people to see both ships in high-resolution digital.

"Fire when ready," the president ordered in front of over a billion people.

"Aye-aye, sir," she said calmly.

Lou thought he heard a few gasps in the VFW as the screen showed the ship's large barrel swing and point nearly directly at the fleeing ship to its port-forward sector. There was no sound coming from the feed. The world watched the five-inch diameter shells explode out of the barrel every two and a half seconds. Ten seventy-six-pound shells sailed... ten large powder casings ejected out of the big, automated gun mount and clattered to the ship's deck. As the seventh shell was firing, the first was reaching the ship seven miles upstream.

The first two shells airburst over their prey, ripping steel apart at the seams, exposing the interior and spilling fuel out of piping. Eight more shells exploded with impact fuses, demolishing the ship in a maelstrom of fire and carnage. It began to break apart in front of the world. Eventually, the feed dissolved into a shot of Jeremiah Allen once more. He was red with rage.

"Let this be a lesson to all aggressors and agitators who are lobbying for their chance to strike at the United States while we're wounded! At this moment, throughout every major American western city aside from Seattle, the US Armed Forces are engaging in Operation Venom Spear, re-instilling law and order by actively engaging and eliminating the drug cartels. Whether it be the snakes of the Mexican cartels, the Bear of the Ural Mountains, or the Dragon by the Yellow Sea, be warned! Behind every blade of grass is an American who will kill your ass!" President Jeremiah Allen stood at his desk in the Oval Office, ripped the wireless mic off his tie, throwing the battery pack on the desk and stormed out of shot. The Presidential Seal screen popped back up showing the words *End Transmission.*

The sound of helicopters reverberated throughout the VFW. Lou and Brandon sprinted outside followed by Mark and several others. In the sky over the north end of Tucson, they could see two dozen Blackhawk helicopters flying in formation. They slowly split apart. Some would eventually deploy their infantry in Fairgrounds, others in Parkway Terrace. All were headed to locations that had been deemed inherently dangerous to the health and welfare of American citizens—houses and commercial buildings known to cater to the cartels or suspected terrorists.

Lou scanned the light blue, fall sky to the south. "What does that look like to you?" he asked Brandon.

"Planes," the young man said. "But where are they headed? Surely they wouldn't hit a target on that side of the border... would they?"

Lou looked at his young counterpart. "I suggest we hit the latrine and get back on the road. Pronto!"

BUENOS AIRES NATIONAL WILDLIFE REFUGE, ARIZONA

. . .

THE ROAD RUNNERS STARTED TO RECEIVE TEXTS FROM BOB and Claude, learning of what was happening at home. "What's happening in Tucson?" Granger asked Master Sergeant Mikkel Hudson. "This has something to do with why you all are out here."

"It's called Venom Spear. POTUS is declaring war on the cartel." He was very calm, almost nonchalant, the result of a life of combat. All six men had buried themselves in concealment at the high ridge, near the trail head they'd taken down into Mexico. They were fully alert and keeping a close eye and ear on the trail, watching for any cartel trying to send up drones.

"Because of the supposed gang war in Seattle?" Dave Wolf asked.

"Yep," 'Voo Doo' Hudson said. "Not supposed. Real."

"What about this tunnel?" Tracy asked, yawning. "You guys said you wired it, right? Can we blow this thing and go home already?"

"Not our orders yet," the Master Sergeant said calmly, trying to keep his eyes closed for some rest. "What're you guys so itching for a fight for?"

"We've been out here without any ability to act for years, pal," Granger said. *Delta or not, you're not the only operator out here,* he thought. "We're just curious as to why we rigged those hatches if we ain't gonna blow them..."

"All in due time, gents," Master Sergeant Mikkel Hudson said. "We're waiting to see what fruit that—" he pointed back toward Tucson, "produces any results here."

MANHATTAN, KANSAS

MORRIS AND THATNUB HURRIED BACK TO THEIR APARTMENT in the Bronco. They'd been at the grocery store near the highway, watching dozens of trucks and Hummers from Fort Carson scream by under the lights and sirens of the Kansas Highway Patrol. They were headed east. It wasn't until Blackhawks and Apaches flew by that the two young men spurred themselves to take action. There was four inches of snow on the ground, a bare dusting to any decent Kansan, but more was expected in the coming evening.

"Bro, whaddya think that's about?" Morris asked his friend as Nub turned onto Westwood Rd, heading north toward their apartment. There was a flurry of cars heading the other way. He snapped his head to look. "Looks like everyone's heading to the store or the gas station. Weird."

"Something big. Maybe the Chinese are attacking?" Nub guessed. He pulled up to a red light. It had been deactivated and turned into a four-way stop two weeks earlier to make life easier in the new yo-yo power system. He made his way north again. Just as he started through the intersection, he looked left and stomped on the gas pedal, throwing Morris into the seat.

"Hold on!" Nub yelled as the Bronco fishtailed. They barely cleared the way when a BMW flew through the intersection with a local cop pursuing it.

"Nice driving, Nub!" Morris yelled when it became apparent they were clear. "That moron almost killed us!"

Nub's phone beeped with a text. He tossed it at Morris as he pulled into their apartment parking lot. The friends had an unspoken code, and Morris knew his buddy wanted him to check the text. "It's from Elvis. He's asking what we thought of the president's speech?"

"What speech?" Nub asked.

"Beats me," Morris said. The men parked and grabbed their groceries. As they started up the stairs of the three-story building, a pair of men came out of one of the other apartments and started heading down. "You guys hear anything about an announcement from the president?"

"Naw, man," one of the men said. "We haven't had reliable TV in days."

"Huh," the other one muttered. "I wonder if that's why my mom has been texting like there's no tomorrow for the last fifteen minutes."

The two pairs of men passed each other. Morris followed ThatNub into their second-floor apartment. After they set the groceries on the table, Morris tossed Nub's phone back to him.

"I'll just call him back."

Morris looked at his phone, intending on calling his parents. *Dead! Crap!* He had no idea how long it had been dead. *I keep forgetting to charge it when we go out!* He grabbed Nub's keys off the counter and went back down to the old Bronco. Knowing the older, finicky vehicle might wind up with a dead battery, he opted to run the engine while he charged. *What a waste of gas,* he scolded himself. Three minutes later he tried to power up the device and managed to get it to boot up. Soon his phone was blowing up with texts. *Goldi, Misty, there we go. Mom.* He called up his phone history and scrolled to his last call with his mother, triggering a callback.

"Baby! Where in the hell have you been! Why haven't you answered! You are going to give me a —"

"Mom!" Morris said. "I'm fine! What's wrong?" Another set of police sirens went flying by in the light snow.

"It doesn't sound like you're fine, Morris Allen Dooghan! Where are you?"

"I'm at the apartment, Mom. What's happening? It's like people went crazy!"

"Oh, honey! I think you need to get down here to Aunt Janet's. That fool president is sending the military into all the cities to fight gangs! As if that's their job. For this they're keeping your brother from getting' out! I have half a mind to go to D.C. and kick that man's booty muhself!"

It all clicked for Morris. The highway... the helicopters...even the way people were acting. *No wonder we almost got creamed ten minutes ago.* "I hadn't heard," was all Morris could think to say.

"Baby, I know we're out of the way of Wichita, but do you think William would be able to drive you here to Chanute?"

I think I detect just a hint of hopeful angst, Morris thought with sarcasm.

"I know your father was going to come pick you up and bring you home for Thanksgiving on Wednesday, but we think you two should leave tonight!"

"We got friends here that don't have a way home, Mom. Their dorms are getting shut down. Truthfully..." *Oh, boy...*

"Oh, don't you even!" his mother exclaimed.

Morris saw Nub coming down the stairs, an annoyed quizzical expression on his face. Morris leaned over and turned the keys, shutting off the engine. "Mom, something's come up. When I can get a bigger charge on my phone, I'll call you back."

"Morris Alle Doo—"

Click. *Well, I'll pay for that dearly later,* he thought. He grabbed the keys and exited the Bronco. "My mom wants us to head down to my aunt's like—tonight," he told Nub.

"Funny. Elvis and everyone want to go snow camp out at the cartel airport." He turned to lead his buddy back upstairs. "I know, I know. You hate the idea."

"More than words can express," Morris agreed. "But I know I'll lose this argument. And I don't want you all going out there by yourselves."

CHAPTER 29

Delgado Estate, Juarez, Mexico

"He-hellooo?" Rosie heard a soft voice interrupt her whimpering, her sole activity while crated like a beast.

"Hey!" she tried to yell through a course, dry throat. It barely made a sound. She tried to clear her throat, but her captors hadn't brought her any water or food in what felt longer than a day. *Two days?* she wondered. The thirst was unbearable. "Hey!" she tried again. It was dark and moldy smelling. She'd been passed out when they moved her, but the one time they brought her a small amount of water, she'd been able to tell she was in the back of an old box truck. The only other items in the truck were boxes and crates.

"Is—is that you, Carmela?" she heard young Lupe call out.

"Lupe? Lupe! Yes! It's me! Please help!"

The door made a creaky groan, barely opening a foot. It was a dark blue-gray of light that silhouetted the teenager as she crawled in. Rosie burst out in emotion, barely enough hydration for tears to form. "Lupe!" she said again through raw emotion.

"Is—is it true?" the girl asked. "Are you a Federale?" Her face showed concern over disappointment.

Rosie continued to cry and grimace at the young girl, who was using her cell phone as a flashlight. “Y-Yes!”

The girl saw that Rosie had been beaten to a swollen pulp and began to cry. “What did they do to you? Whe-where’s Eddie?”

“He’s gone,” was all Rosie could tell her. “Please, Lupe! You have to let me out! They’re going to hurt me for a long time!”

The girl said nothing, though her face spoke volumes of anger and sadness. “I know who my father is…” She sobbed so loudly that Rosie worried it might draw attention.

“Shhhh,” she consoled the girl. “I-I don’t hold that against you! You’re a sweet girl! Just find me a tool to cut through this metal and slip back out here tonight!”

“It *is* night!” Lupe said. “How long have you been out here?”

“I don’t know what day it is. I got taken Saturday!”

“It’s Monday evening,” the girl said as she began to cry again. She started to get angry. “What is he going to do with you?” she asked in a low furious tone.

“I heard something about a convoy,” Rosie said. “I don’t know what they’re doing, but they have something bad planned for El Paso!”

The girl’s face turned to one of realization. “You don’t know! El Paso is like a war zone tonight!”

“What’d they do?” Rosie gasped.

“Not the cartel—your president! Your army is attacking all of your cities!”

“What! That makes no sense!” Rosie said.

Lupe held up a video of someone in El Paso that she followed on Tik Tok. It showed soldiers repelling out of helicopters and onto the roof of an apartment building while military and police vehicles surrounded it in the streets. She flipped to another video, showing a shootout near the stadium at the university. “All over the city, I’m hearing. They came from the soldier fort nearby.”

“The cartel!” Rosie realized. “They were planning something! Something big! Please! You need to let me out!”

"I—I can't!" the girl sobbed. "They'll kill my father! I know what he is, but I still love him!" She stood and started to slide back through the small gap in the large metal door.

"Please!" Rosie begged.

Lupe looked back at her. "I'm so sorry, Carmela!" She looked down at the phone in her hand and started to cry again. She let the device fall through the gap in the metal grid of the kennel and slid back out of the truck, closing Rosie into the darkness once more.

INTERSTATE HIGHWAY 10, EL PASO, TEXAS

LOU AND BRANDON HAD DELIBERATED TAKING SMALLER highways across America. As they neared eastern New Mexico, the temptation to see what was happening proved to be too great for the pair of officers. The U.S. Military was taking action against a mostly foreign threat. They wouldn't shy from seeing that. It was the end of dusk in the Texas desert. As they cruised into the city limits, they could see the blinking lights of helicopters all over the city.

"Mostly Army," Lou presumed. "But probably some news and civilian med-evac, too."

"Roll your window down!" Brandon said as his was already descending. He turned off the Toyota's radio and the pair listened. The highway was thinning of traffic, which had as much to do with people being glued to their televisions as it had to do with it being almost 8:30 at night. The men could both hear gunfire. "It's coming from the north!" Brandon said semi-excitedly.

"No, the south," Lou countered. The men exchanged a glance. "I suddenly wish those rifles weren't cased up in the back. I think we're hearing two different fights."

"Look how close we are to the border," Brandon stated as the highway went through a curve near the Rio Grande River and started heading east again. "I bet you could drive a golf ball off this highway and into Mexico!"

"Not me," Lou chuckled. "But you could. Easily."

There was no way the men could have predicted what was happening in the sky above them at that very moment. Four clusters of small drones had just flown over the river they were gawking at. These drones had never been meant for civilian use—they had no blinking lights. They were a combination of four and six-bladed copters, along with a few larger drones that resembled a traditional helicopter. Each of the clusters contained between forty and sixty of the devices. Each was headed directly for the command post at one of the major American Army and police task forces that was engaging a cartel safe house. The eight helicopter drones, each carrying eight gravity bomblets that contained a total of sixteen pounds of explosive, were headed for the City Hall building two blocks east of the interstate.

Lou saw a missile shoot skyward to the southeast. "Look!" he yelled instinctively.

"Yeah!" Brandon yelled back. "There's another in my left mirror!" Lou craned his neck, but with their gear and the vehicle's roof he couldn't see it. "What do you think they are?"

Lou immediately flashed back to a conversation he'd had with one of his peers in his combined branch task force job a few months earlier. "It might be M-SHORAD! The Army converted some Strykers into short range missile defense. For use against rocket and drone att—"

KUHHH-BOOOOMMMM! The concussion beat the sound. The shockwave hit the Toyota, flipping it onto its side as they slid three hundred feet, burning off the 65 MPH they were traveling. The angle forced them into the left jersey barrier. Lou's partially open passenger window had shattered from the blast, sending pieces of safety glass all over the right side of his face. The remaining windows all cracked in the crash, but the windshield remained whole by the thin safety film built into it. The grinding over the left side on the concrete and asphalt sent sparks shooting all over Brandon. A fireball enveloped city hall, sending concrete shrapnel in all directions. The sixty-four bomblets had delivered their one-hundred twenty-eight pounds of explosive with perfect timing.

Both men were stunned, in shock, not knowing what had happened as they came to a stop, the vehicles top crushed in a few inches against the concrete barrier that separated the east and west traffic. Pieces of concrete the size of peas, golf balls, and basketballs began to rain down on everything within a thousand feet of city hall, including the highway. Thump! THUMP!

Lou shook the cobwebs off. He touched his face, feeling bloody stinging all over the right side, including in his hair. *Eyes!* He screamed in his mind. *Yes, I can still see out of both!* "Brandon!" Thump! Lou unbuckled his seatbelt and fell down over his partner, covering the semi-conscious man. Once the concrete rain slowed, he propped himself up. "Brandon!" he screamed again.

"Unnngghhh...I...I'm okay!" he heard the young Marine call back. "Did we get hit by a semi?"

"Not sure!" Lou hollered back, feeling something way worse had happened.

He pulled his knees and feet in, eventually moving to stand on the console between the two front seats. He stuck his head and torso out of the right window frame in awe. The setting dusk seemed darker as framed against the raging fire consuming several buildings to the south. He slowly turned to where he saw the missile streak a minute earlier. There was a smoldering crater emitting fire and smoke hundreds of feet high. As he turned, he saw a similar sight in three other locations.

"We need to go! Now!" Lou screamed down. "The city is under attack!" He did a tricep extension to push his hips up past the frame. He pulled his knee up and pivoted onto the smashed Toyota's door, slowly dropping down to the ground.

Brandon followed suit about twenty seconds later. "My left shoulder is banged up!" he declared. "But it works. I can deal with it!"

He slowly climbed down, too. “Let’s get to the back,” he said as he led the way.

He pulled his pocketknife out. It had a point on the end for smashing glass, but the rear window was already shattered. He plunged the knife’s blade into the glass and sawed a hole. Pulling the camo sleeve down around his hand he grabbed the glass and began to yank it out. Like the front, there was a safety film that made its best effort to keep the glass together as a unit.

Once cleared, Brandon got onto his knees and began to pull out their gear. “Help me grab this stuff!” he hollered out to Lou. “I’ll crawl in for our backpacks afterward!”

The men spent several minutes getting geared up. They grabbed a little spare clothing from their suitcases and stuffed it and some of the MREs and bottled water into their bags.

“Pull this neck gaiter up over your nose,” Brandon advised. “It’ll help filter smoke and debris a bit.”

He did the same and pulled the winter battle coat’s hood over his scalp. Lou used a pair of skivvies from his luggage to blot the blood that had started to slow and clot all over the right side of his head. He followed Brandon’s lead in donning the gear and rifles the army had reluctantly provided.

“Where to first, Colonel?” Brandon asked with a high level of adrenaline still pumping.

“Ground zero,” Lou said. “We’re right here. We need to see if there’s anything we can do.”

Brandon stopped and took his first serious look around. The other cars and semis on the darkening highway were in a similar state. Some had people crawling out. Others did not. Lou shook him out of his daze.

“Let’s go, Brandon.”

Buenos Aires National Wildlife Refuge, Arizona

"Whatchu got?" Delta Force operator Voo Doo Hudson asked his partner, Patrick McBrogan, known as Lucky Charm to his unit team.

The radio operator had a headset on and was fidgeting with a couple of controls on the AN/PSC-5 Shadowfire enhanced battle radio. He was using a directional antenna to link to a satellite and listen to their Tactical Operation Center. "Sounds like El Paso just got waxed," the short redhead said. "Some sort of aerial attack took out several small ops simultaneously."

"Whoa!" Tracy said.

"Standby!" McBrogan ordered, holding a hand up to shoosh Tracy. His face grew with intensity in the quarter-moonlit desert. "Might've been drones. Command says we're moving to Phase Two."

"What's that mean?" Granger whispered to Voo Doo while the radio operator continued to listen.

"It means our brothers in Nogales, Tijuana, Juarez, and a handful of other locations in Mejico are about to get busy lasing targets," the seasoned operator explained. "I'll give Allen this much—the man has balls."

"What about us?" Mick asked quietly. Voo Doo held a finger up and looked at his partner. Twenty silent seconds later, Lucky Charm nodded.

"Here's the plan, gentlemen," the leader started. "We're going to give it an hour to see what happens to this tunnel. That farm has already been designated a backup target for the Reapers patrolling the border. If we see any HVTs show up, we can call in a strike. Either way, we'll blow the tunnel some time tonight."

The small band of soldiers and veterans continued to watch their perimeter, waiting for high-value targets, until a violent and explosive show of force erupted thirty-eight miles to the southeast a short time later.

DOWNTOWN EL PASO, TEXAS

BRANDON LED; LOU FOLLOWED ABOUT TEN FEET BEHIND. THE camo-drabbed men with rifles would've drawn a panic and a police response in El Paso just six hours earlier. As they passed an attorney's office complex and bank that were fully engulfed in flames, the true weight of the devastation became apparent. Where city hall had stood just a bit earlier was now a smoking, rubble-filled crater of death and destruction. The pair of men continuously scanned for the presence of any other living humans. They could hear sirens and see the dance of blue and red lights flickering to the east. The City of El Paso's forces had simply been overwhelmed.

The four drone swarms had been followed by the explosion of planted IEDs near several of the city's fire stations. What had remained had simply been overwhelmed. The city was paralyzed physically and mentally. "I haven't seen anyone since the highway," Lou hollered through the olive drab neck gaiter. "You?"

"Negative," Brandon replied. "This—I—I can't believe this..." He stood on the precipice of a concrete and steel pit. "I barely remember 9/11," he said quietly. "I was a young child. This... This..."

"C'mon, son," Lou said behind him. "Let's go north. Try to make our way to the university. If there's anything left of the Army CP, they'll probably be using the football field." He turned to leave and stopped. Brandon had become mesmerized by the overwhelming feeling of devastation. "Come on, Marine!" Lou stated with commanding authority. "Lead us out!"

Brandon snapped out of it and the men cautiously made their way back the two blocks to the highway. They used an overpass to continue north. Suddenly Lou felt his phone vibrate in his pocket.

"Hold up, Brandon," he said. "Let's find some cover."

They could see citizens starting to trickle out of homes and commercial buildings. Some were wailing. Most were in a state of confusion and despair. Lou pulled off his glove and pulled the phone out of his pocket as he instinctively followed Brandon to a corner of a building. He didn't know the number.

"Caldwell."

"Help! Please!" Lou heard a woman's voice.

Something familiar, he thought. *Not Julia...* "This is Colonel Caldwell! Who is this?"

"My name is Rosie!" cried the panicky voice, trying to whisper through hyperventilation. "I'm the UC you met in Carlsbad! Yours is the last number I memorized! Please help!"

Carlsbad! Lou realized in horror. *That girl!* "Jane Doe? Did you say Rosie? The undercover cop?!"

"Yes! I've been abducted! For over two days! I'm in a truck in Juarez!"

Lou started frantically trying to get Brandon's attention. "Pen," he silently mouthed while motioning his hand. "What else, Rosie? Any detail!" Brandon unslung his pack and started digging in the front pouch.

"I was at that location I showed on the map. But we left about ten minutes ago! A girl slipped me a phone! This is the first time it's been loud enough for me to dare make a call!"

Definitely sounds loud, Lou thought. He made a quick decision. "How much battery is left?"

Rosie looked. "Not much! It's red!" They both heard the loud squealing of brakes. "We've stopped!"

"Listen, Rosie," Lou said calmly. "Make sure that phone is on silent. See if you can turn on the GPS tracking. Then power it down. When you think it's been an hour, turn it on and text me anything you've learned! Quickly. Then shut it back down!"

"No! I need to talk with you! Can't I just keep it on? They're going to convoy me somewhere!"

"Rosie, I know you're tired and scared. So am I. Keep the phone off except when you can send a text. Okay? Your life depends on it!" As much as it pained him, Lou hung up to keep her from arguing.

"What was all of that?" Brandon asked excitedly.

Lou grabbed the pencil and paper Brandon had dug out of his pack and scribbled every detail he could remember. "We need to get hold of Jackson or Montgomery right this second."

"They're probably a tad busy right now, Colonel," Brandon argued.

"The girl," Lou said, starting to be a little panicky himself. "The—the undercover cop! The one I met before I got attacked. She's in Juarez! They've caught her. She's on a truck!"

"Dang," Brandon said.

Lou had never heard him cuss so strongly before. He pulled the SAT phone out of his pack and began to call Colonel Ryan Jackson. They updated him on their version of the explosion downtown, what ground zero looked like, and the phone call from Rosie. They relayed her phone number, too. Jackson advised them to make their way to Biggs Army Airfield, which had become the emergency fallback and rally point in the wake of the attack.

"I'll find that DEA task force guy you dealt with. And the Ranger contact. Let them know what you've reported. Double time it, men. And watch your six. Jackson out."

The blocks in this portion of El Paso weren't laid out in the cardinal directions. Brandon hit the little map icon on his phone and it worked.

"We got lucky! They didn't knock down the cell towers!" He looked at the closest street sign and business names. "Two blocks this way, and then we can go right to the northeast up a main thoroughfare. We should be able to find some sort or ride along the way," he said hopefully. "I don't want to upset you, Colonel, but I plan on praying along the way."

CHAPTER 30

BUENOS AIRES NATIONAL WILDLIFE REFUGE, ARIZONA

THE FOUR ROAD RUNNERS AND TWO DELTA OPERATORS watched two SUVs slowly cruise down the canyon dirt road to their normal stopping point. Several men walked the seventy feet up the small dell to the large collection of brush and tumbleweed that they used to conceal the lumber covering the tunnel's north access. Two of the men pulled up on the panel and hopped down. The red light emanating from the tunnel shone like a giant 'Just shoot me' beacon in the night vision devices everyone was using.

Tracy was the farthest north. "Standby," he whispered into the radio lapel mic on the front of his ballistic plate carrier. "Possible drone setting up." The men were working under reddened headlamps, and the Road Runner-Delta team was five hundred meters to the south, covering the border and observing the ranch. Tracy flipped his night vision up and pulled up his binoculars, zooming them in on the red head lamps at the back of the second SUV. "About ninety-nine percent sure they're about to get eyes in the sky."

"Contact at the ranch," Dave Wolf whispered next. "Several vehicles—wait…" He went silent for close to a minute. "Two helicopters. Too dark to tell if they're civilian or military."

The question is, Granger asked himself, *are they fleeing south, or are those others escaping north?* Though Delta wasn't monitoring the simplex channels that the Road Runners were using, each of them were still close to a pair of the civilians.

Voo Doo crawled over to Wolf and raised his own binoculars. "One of each," he whispered. "Looks like a Bell and a Huey. With a rocket pod. Fantabulous."

"It doesn't really matter which way the traffic flows, right? We give it fifteen minutes for them to be in the middle and blow it. You guys authorize it for a strike, and then—Miller time…"

Voo Doo ignored the suggestion and got on his own radio. "Alright, Lucky. What's the deal with the drone?"

"Six blades. Maybe an Aerosky… no matter. They're about to have high-rez night vision and thermal."

"Get on the net," Voo Doo ordered. "Let the TOC know this sector is about to go hot. Tell them we are clear for them to strike target package twelve kilo one."

"Wilco."

Voo Doo Hudson pulled his pack off while still in the prone position. He pulled out an explosives-firing system radio transmitter and powered it on, allowing the internal capacitors a moment to charge. He flipped the red plastic safety cover up. "Fire in the hole," he told his partner on the radio, loud enough for Lou and Wolf to hear. *Click.*

BOOM-BOOM-BOOM-BOOM! Four explosions screamed with fractional gaps in between. The C-4 charges on the first tunnel service hatch detonated the small wood frame they had been placed next to, collapsing the dirt on the tunnel eight feet down. Debris shot in the sky, barely visible in the night vision. The access cover followed suit, followed finally by the two that Voo Doo and Wolf had placed on the desert floor directly between that cover and the ranch. The noise rocked the desert for a few seconds, reverberating off the light canyon walls the men were near.

"Tell your guys not to engage yet!" Voo Doo ordered Granger.

"We just kicked a hornet's nest!" Mick said into the radio.

"They just sent the drone up!" Tracy added.

"Do not fire!" Granger said into the radio. "Your IR gear will cover your signature! Just be still and wait for our sponsors to tell us what to do!"

There was a breeze, but it wasn't too strong for the large drone. It shot up a few hundred feet from the valley floor, which still put it well above the team. It began to make large wide circles. At the ranch, even at the two plus kilometers, Wolf could see a flurry of activity.

"Looks like they may be firing up those birds!" he told Granger. After thirty more seconds, "The one with the rocket pods is taking off!"

"Everyone remain calm," Voo Doo ordered.

The helicopter had taken off in an easterly approach and as it achieved several hundred feet in altitude, it began a slow turn toward the north as if to fly over the wildlife refuge and cover the team at the north.

"The second one is getting airb—"

Woooosh-BOOMMMM! The semi-active laser from the Hellfire III missile guided the device directly into the mass of vehicles parked next to the ranch house. The ensuing explosion ripped through vehicles and caught fuel on fire. The entire area became a death torrent of shrapnel as pieces of three different vehicles ripped into the Bell helicopter about fifteen feet above ground. Every rotor in both the horizontal and vertical planes took damage, throwing the balance and aerodynamics off. The loss of stabilized flight from the tail caused the bird to spin wildly. It made most of two revolutions before impacting the desert in a heap.

"Never mind!" Wolf said. "The second bird went down!" The Huey made a rapid turn and picked up speed, doing a flyby and then a loop around the ranch.

"This drone seems to be circling our north flank!" Tracy said into the radio. "I think we—"

Ka-Krow! Ka-Ka-Ka-Ka-Ka-Krow!

"Contact!" Mick yelled.

He had been sighted-in on the one drone pilot he had an angle on at the rear of the far SUV. The dirt all around him and Tracy erupted with life as AK-47 rounds began to impact the rocks a few feet below them. The fire was coming from his slight left as eight cartel soldiers began to fire from positions of concealment from near the other SUV and the tunnel access. Mick ignored the fragmenting rocks below him, pulling his rifle stock tightly into his shoulder. He let out half a breath, verified his sight picture in his scope and squeezed until his shot cooked off. He saw one of the red head lamps fall to the ground, which verified what the night vision scope on his rifle had told him—*one down.*

"Break contact!" Lucky Charm yelled. "Move east! Move east! We got the high ground!"

As the three began to scoot away from the rim, Granger, Wolf, and Voo Doo approached. "Friendlies from the south," Voo Doo said calmly.

"Oomph!" Mick moaned as a round tore through his left ribs and chest from the valley below, missing his plates at an angle. He'd barely gotten to his hands, a mere two-foot-tall profile.

"Mick!" Tracy yelled. He tried to scramble toward his buddy, and Lucky Charm grabbed him. They could hear Mick gasping for air. The gurgling noise told the operator everything he needed to know.

"He'll be dead in twenty seconds! Stand fast, sailor!" Tracy's face was filled with outrage and disbelief. "We'll come back for him," the soldier assured. He knew the reality—this wasn't an organized mission with a QRF and med-evac. These men were just like the guerillas he'd trained in seventeen different countries over the course of his career—except for the being American part. They would have to leave this man behind for the time being.

Pop-Pop! Voo Doo dispatched the drone in two shots from his silenced HK 416 Carbine, sending it careening to the southeast at a downslope. "We're headed east and north, gents! Time to get some cardio! That Huey'll be here before you know it!"

East of Manhattan, Kansas

The seven friends had parked the two quads and motorcycle together in the dell at the bottom of the slope west of the makeshift landing strip. Jon's uncle had provided them an extra-large tarp and a few t-posts. They worked under headlamps and flashlights to set up a rudimentary shelter using the machines as an outer frame and the six-foot tall posts for some slope. They topped the posts with scraps of lumber to keep them from puncturing the tarp. After they managed to get the quiet snow to stop amassing in their new 'quarters,' it became a matter of digging out the nine inches of snow while simultaneously thumping the freshly falling powder off the tarp. Elvis had brought a foot pump and three cheap inflatable pool rafts so people could take turns using a barrier between themselves and the cold ground.

They set up a rotation, two always at the crest, keeping lookout. Around 3 AM, the snow quit falling. At 5:30, an SUV rigged with chains plowed itself up the quarry access road, snow otherwise undisturbed. Two men decked out in snow suits pulled a gas-powered snow blower out of the back and began to run back and forth along the runway. Two hours and two tanks of gas had revealed the icy Kansas prairie once more. Misty and Goldi were the current ones on watch. They observed the men yank the snow blower and a gas can into the wooden shed. They heard a generator fire up.

"I'm guessin' they have a space heater in there," Goldi said longingly from under the hood of his winter coat. He pulled his thick beanie up so he could see better. They were laying on another smaller tarp, heads barely sticking up over the crest.

"Listen!" Misty said. There was little wind. The low hum of engines could be heard. "Cars?"

A sudden thought hit Elvis. "What if it's the plane? Will they be able to see us?" He back crawled until he could push his chest up safely and turned slowly, standing as he ran down the hill. Misty Meaner figured out what he meant. She dragged their two rifles under the tarp and began to scoop snow onto it.

"Plane! Dudes, plane!" Goldi said excitedly. He started to grab the corner of the roof, pinned down near the bottom of a quad by a snow drift. As soon as he pulled and started slackening the roof, the snow that had stayed put on the tarp started to slide in.

"Hey!" Super B yelled.

Morris was the first out. "Ohhh—snap! You're right!" he yelled as soon as he figured out what Goldi was up to. "Everyone start covering everything with snow!"

"Chill!" Jon Sanches said. "We're a few hundred yards from where they'll set down."

"We're still going to stick out like a big neon sign to someone a couple of hundred feet up!" Morris argued.

At this point, he and Goldi had already collapsed the covering, forcing everyone into action. Cat Scratch Fever began to use the two snow shovels and their hands, trying to cover their gear with snow. They eventually buried themselves into the big drift at the base of the slope as best they could.

There was no denying a plane was approaching. It's engine noises died down near its touchdown point, as it had dropped below the crest of the rolling field. Morris, Elvis, and Goldi each ran up the hill until they had to get low for cover. They saw a twin engine, prop-driven plane turn around at the end of the plowed runway and slowly drive under power back near the SUV. It only took a few seconds for the engines to shut down. The shed door opened, and the two men came back out, zipping up coats and putting on their hats and hoods. The youngsters were joined by their curious friends.

"Can anyone make out what they're saying?" Jordan Super B asked quietly.

The low mumbles of the pilot directing the other two barely penetrated the cold morning air. One of the men had gone into the shed and came back out with a pair of pump sprayers.

"I bet it's de-icer," ThatNub said. They saw the pilot reach back into the plane and pull out a case. He went into the shed for a few minutes.

"None of this proves anything," Morris said. "We know that the military is assaulting the gangs in KC. We can't do anything, even if more of them show up."

"What's he up to?" Misty asked, watching the pilot messing with the ground. It soon became obvious he was going to send a drone up into the sky.

"I gotta bad feeling about this," ThatNub said in a mediocre Luke Skywalker.

"Yeah..." Morris said. "I think you're right." The little device shot skyward and began to do a counterclockwise loop around the far side of the landing strip.

"Uh-oh," Elvis said. "That things going to be over us in about thirty seconds! Look how fast it's scooting!"

In their haste to get up the slope, none of them had bothered trying to conceal themselves. The little toylike device rounded the far end of the runway and began to fly directly down the crest where they were spying. It shot right past them at about 20 MPH and then spun around in a rapid turn, hovering just past them.

"We're blown!" Elvis yelled.

The little device shot back toward the shed without finishing the loop. Morris peeked and saw the pilot frantically screaming at the men spraying the wings. They hopped down and ran to jump into the SUV. Just as the matter was about to splatter on the fan, it was compounded by the sudden fast appearance of two more vehicles coming up the road.

BIGGS ARMY AIRFIELD, EL PASO, TEXAS

THE TENANT COMMAND AT FORT BLISS WAS FIGURATIVELY ablaze with activity. Hangars had been converted into emergency hospitals for fear that the army hospital—with minimal security—would become a target. They had begun to take in civilian casualties, and infantry were playing security patrol at nearly every corner inside and out. There was no way to tell if a bloodied and burnt person was merely a victim or part of an even more cunning terror attack yet to unfold.

It had taken Lou and Brandon a mile of jogging before they were picked up by an infantry patrol in a Humvee. The unit was headed back to Bliss. Once their story checked out with people in the Pentagon, the men were given a quick escort to Biggs. Their wounds were tended to, and they were given cots to rest on while waiting for a call back from Colonel Jackson. Out on the tarmac between the hangars and the runway, helicopters were coming and going constantly.

"Lou!" Brandon said as he sat up on his cot. "Colonel!" he said a little louder, trying to roust his partner.

Lou began to stir. He lightly touched the bandages on the right side of his face and scalp. "Wha... What time is it?" he said through squinting eyes under bright fluorescent light. He pulled the camo hood back over the top of his head.

"Almost zero-five."

"Have you heard from her?" Lou asked. They'd staggered their naps—Brandon had Lou's phone charging on a small portable battery from Lou's backpack.

"Not for close to two hours. The president made a big speech last night."

"What about Jackson?" Lou asked groggily, not fully in tune with what Brandon had just said.

"He's located the DEA guy you met. The Texas Rangers' El Paso office was in the building next to the one we saw go up, which was City Hall. It took major damage and fire, too. They think he may've been working late... No sign of him."

"That means me and—" Lou searched his memory. "Uhhh...Agent Bender, I think it was. We're probably the only two faces she knows who are alive right now..."

"Jackson said Bender is flying in from Albuquerque. He may even be on the ground by now, just trying to locate us. He also reiterated we are to do nothing until we hear back from him."

Lou took a few minutes to go find the water cooler and one of the several plastic 'honey buckets' that had been set up on the front side of the hangars. He made his way back to Brandon and their two cots, one pair amongst a few hundred in this particular hangar. "So, what'd Allen have to say?"

"I'll do you one better." The young man opened his cell apps and found a segmented clip on a news site. "This is the juicy part after he mentions the attack happening." Lou took the device to watch the clip.

President Jeremiah Allen and the bags under his eyes were in front of the White House Press room wall, joined by multiple military leaders and cabinet members. Lou pressed the right-facing triangle.

"*—and furthermore, President Chacon, I call on you to help us bring these cartels to justice! For far too long, the Mexican government has been complicit in turning a blind eye to these drug kingpins. A long and established history of bribery, turning a blind eye, and even aiding these organizations has tainted your reputation amongst the just nations of the world. Now is your chance to prove me wrong. Do something. And lastly, I demand that you begin an emergency evacuation of Juarez. Since midnight, our U.S. military has been conducting surgical strikes against known cartel and terror training locations or safe havens. At 6 PM Juarez time, I'm authorizing our military to begin expanding those operations to* *include drug manufacturing and distribution locations. Make no mistake—our goal is to up-end these cartels with extreme prejudice. I advise that you start evacuating your citizens from Juarez, Elvira...”*

The clip stopped. Lou looked up at Brandon. “Well, now...” was all he could think to say. *These are the days that make not drinking a real joy,* he thought cynically.

Brandon’s sat phone rang. “Captain McDonald,” he answered. Lou listened intently. “Yes, sir. Understood.”

“What?” Lou asked as his young assistant shut down the call.

“We’re to meet DEA Agent Bender and one squad of Rangers at Hangar 12, asap.” He began to stuff his belongings into his pack. While Lou did the same, Brandon made a quick trip to the plastic latrine and then the two made their way to the assigned location.

Agent Bender was in front, decked out in his own tactical gear, talking to an Army 1st Lieutenant. They strode right up to him, rifles slung to their backs.

“Steve, was it?” Lou said as he reached out with an open hand.

“Correct,” he said somewhat somberly. “Sorry we have to meet like this again, Colonel Caldwell.” The soldier next to him scanned Lou and immediately stood at attention and snapped a salute.

Lou returned with a simultaneous, “At ease, Lieutenant.”

“Sir, Lieutenant Martel Adams, 75th Rangers,” the short but stout black officer said.

“I didn’t know there were Rangers at Bliss, Lieutenant,” Lou said, causing a slight look of confusion. “Oh—to be clear, I’m Air Force,” he explained. “Captain McDonald here is a landlocked leatherneck.”

The young officer looked at Brandon and nodded. “No sir,” he said to Lou. “We’re from Benning. My Rangers and I are part of the Regimental Special Troops Battalion, Recon Company. There are companies from 3rd Battalion here, as well.”

“The L-T’s squad is part of JSOC,” Steve interjected to Lou. “They specialize in tough recon and intelligence assignments. The plan is for Captain McDonald and half to join me and you join the L-T and the rest. We're taking two birds to go find our gal. Follow me," he said as he turned into the hangar.

He led them past a Blackhawk helicopter being prepped by several soldiers for being towed out of the hangar. There was already another outside the hangar, going through the process of having its rotor blades extended and secured for flight. They found eight soldiers standing by. One was doing burpees, another pushups, two were trying to nap sitting up on the floor against the hangar wall. The rest were occupying plastic folding chairs near a table with a map on it. As they approached the table, two pair of men—two pilots and a crew chief for each Blackhawk—came out of an office and joined them. Introductions were passed around once more.

The entire hodge-podge team fell-in around the table. "The Pentagon was able to use their persuasion with the cell companies to give us pings on cell towers in these locations." Steve pointed at small red stickers on the map.

"Most of these are on the Mexican side?" Brandon asked.

"Yes," Steve explained. "But American companies own them. I'm sure we could've hacked the foreign owned systems, but this is a rush op. Moving on, I've referenced these pings against our known intel of the El Aguila cartel's infrastructure and have come up with four locations we need to check. But..." he paused, laying a clear overlay on the map. The transparent sheet had yellow, pink, and green circles all over it that each covered several blocks, many of them overlapping. "The green is all the times she texted your cell before the president's airstrikes. The yellow is the two times since."

"And the pink?" Lou asked.

"Those are two of the four locations..." he said. "They were both factories—obliterated with 500-pound bombs five hours ago... But we've gotten the other two pings since then. You said that she said she was to be part of a convoy?"

Lou nodded. "Uh-huh...yes. She did. That was the exact word she used!"

"Nothing would make them want to boogie south most ricky-tick like their facilities blowing up," Martel Adams suggested.

"Yes," Stephen Bender agreed. "These last two pings both overlap a pair of main routes they could be on. One is Highway 2, leading west. The other is Highway 45, leading south. The question is, how do we find them if she doesn't text you anymore. We can find nothing in her texts that narrow it down. There's just too many dirt roads and old bridges."

"Maybe we hit the two locations first," Brandon suggested. "Look for something or someone there that will shed light on a convoy."

"That's kind of what we were thinking, too," Bender said, pointing to the silent flight crews. "Everyone gear up. Time is critical. We fly as soon as the birds are ready. One last thing," he said, scanning the audience of intense faces. "The Mexican government at this time is not in a cooperative mood. We'll be the only ground troops out there for the next twelve hours. Our ROE is to engage only when fired upon first. Capiche?" He got some head nods. "Good." He handed out a few photos of Rosie that the Texas Ranger's home office emailed him. "Undercover Texas Ranger Rosie Ortiz was already missing digits on her right hand. We can use that as identification. She has been a cartel captive for three days. Let's bring her home."

CHAPTER 31

BUENOS AIRES NATIONAL WILDLIFE REFUGE, ARIZONA

THE ROAD RUNNER-DELTA TASK FORCE SPRINTED ACROSS THE desert, heading into the breaking dawn. Occasionally one would stumble as the soft, sandy dirt revealed a rabbit hole or dead cactus in the last possible moment. Dave Wolf had sprained an ankle but was grimacing through the pain. He and Granger were the oldest men, doing their best not to be left behind as the group fled east-northeast. They moved off the hilltop as soon as they could, trying to slowly evade north on the next valley's western slope.

The older Mexican military UH-1 helicopter and indentured crew made a bold move by flying into the narrow canyon where the former tunnel's north entrance was. They landed south of that position, enabling the cartel soldiers there to run two-hundred level meters instead of seventy vertical meters to get to the machine. In addition to a small time-savings, they were still fresh for the coming race.

The door gunner didn't have night vision for accurate shooting of his right-side M-60 belt fed machine gun. A cartel soldier pulled a set attached to an elastic head harness out of his backpack. "Move!" he yelled when the young army conscript serving his required year tried to grab them. The young man stood his ground on manning his machine gun himself. *Pop!* The cartel soldier's silver-plated .45 presented daylight to the man's interior skull. He pulled his fix-bladed knife out of its leather sheath and cut the soldier's tether, sending the meat-sack to the desert floor. The man opened the top cover on the M-60 and verified the belt linkages were installed correctly. He pulled on the gun's charging handle.

"Get to the next valley!" one of the others ordered the pilots, who were just cresting the hill.

The mountain was relatively flat for close to a hundred meters east to west, slowly ascending to a peak to the north. The whaps of the chopper's blades bounced off the canyon walls. The nine men crammed into the helo were all trying to hold onto security belts while craning their heads and necks near the doors, looking for signs of the unknown enemy.

"I got 'em!" screamed a man on the helo's left. He was pointing frantically as the dust and motion in the morning light was slowly able to activate in the other's vision.

"Fly past them and come back where they're on my side!" commanded the one on the door gun.

Down in the canyon slope, the five men were scrambling to get down to the canyon floor into the shadows of the eastern half, which was hopefully narrow enough that the helicopter stayed much higher. Tracy and Lucky Charm were slowly outpacing Granger and Wolf, who were being shepherded by Voo Doo.

"Move it!" he was yelling. "Our only chance is to make that helo useless! Force them to land and engage on foot!"

The helicopter flew past and slowly banked itself in a turn, preparing to make a pass south down the canyon.

"They got a sixty!" Lucky Charm yelled back at his partner. "Find cover!"

The five men each stopped and tried to squeeze in behind a rock or low bush.

"There's a grove of mesquite trees down in the valley!" Tracy yelled.

They were all spread out over a thirty-meter area. The M-60 began to spit fire and noise, sending 7.62 mm bullets into the dirt, rocks, and sage brush all around the men. The helicopter kept flying south at about eighty knots. Voo Doo used his rifle's full auto function to send most of a magazine at the bird.

In the helicopter, two of the cartel were berating the pilots. "You went by too fast, cabron! Next time stay put so we can destroy them with the machine gun!"

"We have to keep moving!" one of the pilots yelled back. "These old helicopters are vulnerable to small arms fire!" They made another turn, this time regaining altitude to head north over the plateau. "This will keep them on the right side!" the pilot bargained.

"They're on the canyon floor now!" the cartel door gunner yelled. He turned on his night vision, but they were too high up in the rising sun for much effect. "Who has a FLIR?" he asked his crew. None of them answered. "What?" A flurry of cussing erupted as he ordered the pilots to find a spot north in the valley wide enough to land. "They're tired! We can land and set up a high-ground ambush!"

In the valley, the men saw the bird fly north and move out of sight in a spot where the mountains turned. Within three minutes it had returned in a southerly course and descended a few hundred meters to the south. The five soldiers were taking concealment next to a pair of small trees, all panting heavily. Dave Wolf was on his knees trying to give his swollen ankle a rest.

"I think they didn't find a good landing spot up north," Wolf panted.

"Which means they're going to give us a foot race down here," Granger said. "There's not enough cover and concealment on these slopes to hide a good ambush..."

"We could take the fight back to them," Lucky Charm suggested. "They think we're here. They think we're heading north. Let's move south a couple hundred meters and set up a hasty ambush."

Tracy nodded, still panting. "I—I'm in... Someone is going to pay for Mick!"

Voo Doo nodded. He pointed at Granger and Wolf. "You two get high on this east slope. Stay in the shadows. Provide overwatch!" He, Lucky Charm, and Tracy started jogging to another mesquite tree to the south.

As they approached it, they could see the helicopter setting down on the canyon floor less than two hundred meters south. Several men had jumped off and started to spread out.

"Hit that sucker, Charm!" Voo Doo ordered.

Patrick Lucky Charm McBrogan pulled the High-Explosive Dual Purpose 40 mm grenade out of a pouch on his battle belt. He shoved it into the breach of the M203 grenade launcher hanging on the bottom of his M4 and moved the hand guard back to close it against its trigger assembly. He took a second to get a good sight picture directly through the front iron sight, holding the rifle at a slightly upward angle. *Phoomp!*

The round used centrifugal force to arm itself about twenty meters out. It was designed to penetrate up to two inches of armor. It contacted the front right quarter of the helicopter's fuselage, detonating with a small anticlimactic flash. With a kill radius of five meters and a wound radius of one-hundred-thirty meters, the ensuing explosion of aviation fuel all but guaranteed a much more climatic finish for the ruthless mercenaries and the helicopter crew. *KAA-BOOOOM!*

"You hear that?" Granger asked Wolf back at the overwatch. "Music to my ears!"

"You can say that ag—"

Ka-Krow! A rifle shot from about fifteen meters north rang out. It passed through Dave Wolf's skull at the top of his spine and exited under the sinus cavity, leaving an unsurvivable cavern where his nose and mouth used to be.

Granger spun in horror, only able to call out a warning on pure training reflex. "Contact north!" he screamed as he slouched down behind Wolf's limp frame.

Time slowed down for the old Marine, trying to remain hidden and find the quarry, as the sudden shock of his friend's violent demise was only two seconds old. The earth around him exploded as rounds continued to pepper Wolf's body. Granger slid down the slope and made a dash for the mesquite trees. *Ka-Krow!*

"Arrnnghh!" he grunted out as a rifle round passed through his right forearm. He slid past the base of the tree as if he'd been trying to steal home plate.

He tried to raise his rifle, but his right arm refused to work. His right ulna shattered and flesh torn open, he tried to ignore the gush of blood and transition the rifle to his left. The pain was just too intense. The mesquite tree exploded with multiple rounds as he laid behind it. Granger felt another round graze the top of his left leg on the far side of the tree.

KAA-BOOOOM! The eastern slope where the shooting was coming from exploded under the concussion of another grenade. Voo Doo was at the next mesquite tree, the safety pin to the small explosive still in his left hand. Lucky Charm and Tracy plowed past Granger in a combat glide, quickly clearing the scene and then returning.

Voo Doo had already started to cut off Granger's sleeve. Using the aid-kit from Granger's plate carrier, he stuffed a z-pack dressing into the wound and secured it with a pressure bandage. "No tourniquet?" Granger grunted.

"You really wanna hump outta here with a tourniquet?" the old Delta operator grinned. "We'll add it if we need to. Sometimes pressure works. Lie down and keep it up against the tree. I'll stabilize it once the bleeding stops."

Lucky Charm came back over. Tracy went over and fell to both knees next to Dave Wolf. He removed his helmet and began to break down in emotion.

"He must've jumped out when they couldn't land. Was just one scumbag with an AK," Lucky said. "And this." He handed a silver plated .45 to Voo Doo, who looked it over.

Granger grunted through the pain. "I'm gonna want that for Wolf's family," he announced.

"Of course," Voo Doo said. He handed it back to Lucky and found the next dressing to start working on Granger's grazed thigh. "But first let's just get outta this Hell-hole little valley."

EAST OF MANHATTAN, KANSAS

THE SNOW IN FRONT OF MORRIS' FACE EXPLODED, SUSPENDING a state of disbelief he and the rest had been in. It had felt like time slowed down, or a dream in which one can't move their legs, as they watched the pilot grab an SKS rifle and start shooting at the only spot on the hill crest that had disturbed snow. They heard the engine of the midnight blue, full size Tahoe gun. The driver must not have had confidence in the beast's street tires, even with chains on. He did a quick U-turn and shot back up their small entrance, taking a short right and disappearing behind the rise in the landscape.

"Everyone—grab your rifles!" Morris yelled. "They're coming around the right side! They'll be at the quads in just a few seconds!"

He made sure the 'shake-awake' reticle on his rifle was glowing. He could barely see it. *Ka-Krow!* Whirrrrr.... *Ka-Krow!* Whirrr... The sounds of rifle rounds barely passing over his head made him bury himself tighter in the snow than he ever had. He turned up the red-dot sight as high as it would go, pulled the charging handle on the AR-15, and waited until the shooting stopped. *Train like you fight,* rang in his memory, first from the training from Sonny Davis, and more recently from the drills Elvis had been running. Morris flipped his rifle safety without looking and tried to peer at the pilot. *Ka-Krow!* Thud! That shot had been so close that it sent dirt up and onto him. He slinked back almost ten feet.

"I can't get a shot!"

In the meantime, the entire rest of the team was hunkering down behind the three off-road vehicles as tightly as they could. Elvis opened fire first. *Pop! Pop! Pop-Pop-Pop-Pop!* Soon Nub followed suit. Then Bee. The Tahoe had been charging up the little dell, throwing snow high into the air. Perhaps one person firing wouldn't have mattered. But the rapid accurate rounds of three rifles splintering the windshield had changed the driver's mind. When his passenger got hit in the neck and sprayed the cab with a fine arterial spray, he hit the brakes and rolled another U-turn, getting stuck in a snowdrift.

"Bee! Follow me!" Elvis yelled. "The rest of you cover us!"

The pair ran in the snow as fast as they could while maintaining some semblance of muzzle control on their rifles. The passenger got out on the near side and dropped to his knees as he clutched his neck. His rifle tumbled out of the door with him, but he made no move to grab it. Elvis saw the other side open, and he immediately went prone. *Pop-Pop-Pop!* His AR barked.

"Arrrgghh!" they heard from a man who'd just been hit in both ankles. The pair slowed their march toward the wounded cartel men.

At the crest, Morris had moved about a hundred feet to his right, nearly over to where the pair below had neutralized the first pair of men. He slid back up to the crest, peering cautiously, soon to be joined by Nub and the others.

"Those other SUVs are probably here!" Morris yelled. "We need to get them pinned down before they do it to us!" He pointed at Goldi and Misty. "You guys cover the plane. Everyone else—try to pin down the rest at the trucks!"

He followed his AR and sight over the crest just a bit, peering down. A dark green Excursion had positioned itself in front of the plane. It appeared that some people were hurriedly trying to get their stuff and get into it. The plane's twin propellers began to spin. A brown

Denali was closer to the shed. There were multiple cartel men running around taking positions of cover.

Morris opened fire, a course of adrenaline unlike any the airsofter had ever felt coursing through his arteries. "Spread out!" he yelled, as his friends began to follow suit, engaging the drug dealers.

A minute later, Elvis and Misty called out to Morris. "We're coming up behind you!"

"And those guys?" Morris asked.

"Dispatched," Elvis said as calmly as if he'd been a guerilla his entire life.

"Move farther right!" Morris ordered. "We need to flank their escape! Make sure they don't come up that dell again!" The pair followed their leader's orders. "Nub!"

His best friend slid off the ridgeline and yelled, "What!"

"You and Fly get on the quads and see if you can circle around north! Get to the far end of the other side of the runway! Near those trees!"

Nub's face grew into a smile similar to the Grinch's from the old Christmas cartoon. "Now that's what I call high-quality H2O!" yelled the knock-off Adam Sandler. He and Jon fired up the bike and one quad and shot north as soon as the engines were warm, turning into a tree line almost five hundred yards away.

Jordan Super B Croft, aka Bee, let out a blood-curdling scream as David Goldi Faust's head fragmented from a round, covering the snow in crimson mist. To the right Elvis and Misty had been too engaged in their firefight to hear it. Morris saw Bee start to retreat, sheer terror on the eighteen-year-old's face. Morris slid down the slope a bit and crawled over to her.

"Bee!" He grabbed his friend pulling her close as she continued to scream. "Jordan! Get back in the fight!" He looked at Goldi and nearly lost his Clif Bar breakfast. He looked back at the other two shooting, ducking, shooting...

"We need to get back in!" he yelled.

He let go of her and hoped for the best, scrambling back up to the crest to the left of Goldi's body. He cautiously scanned over and took a quick glance. The plane was in the process of heading for the entrance end of the runway. At that end, Elvis and Misty had taken so much fire from the cartel that they could no longer shoot back.

"We need to shoot that plane!" Morris yelled.

It spun into position and immediately began to throttle up. Just as Morris began to open up at it, the plane began to receive fire from the far end of the runway. He could see Jon, still sitting on his dirt bike, shooting as rapidly as he could at the plane's windows. Between a lack of practice and trying to shoot several hundred yards from sitting on a bike, he wasn't hitting much of the plane. But he'd garnered the attention of several of the remaining cartel soldiers, who began to fire at him. He dropped the rifle to the front of his chest and gunned the throttle, doing a quick tire-dragging turnaround to disappear back into the tree line.

This distraction had allowed Nub to travel into the next slight depression in the prairie. He rode the quad as fast as he could south and then backtracked west, coming over his small ridge a mere eighty yards from the back of the wooden shed and SUVs. He popped it into neutral and hit the brakes, pulling up his rifle and taking out two guards before they knew he was there. He started to draw more fire. He lowered the rifle to its sling once more and gunned it for the plane.

What's he think he's doing! Morris worried. "Nub!" he yelled instinctually, knowing it would do no good.

As the plane started to gain a decent head of speed on the snowy grass, William ThatNub Easton went airborne on a small rise, dropping onto the makeshift runway. He was pegged out in the machines' fourth gear and the plane was rapidly starting to reach its minimum take off speed. The Evangel 4500 bush plane only needed 1,100 feet of runway and they'd burnt through over half of it. The pilot made a strategic decision and cut his throttles, hitting the brakes. Nub went shooting past on the right.

As he did, the pilot made a slow arch to the right side of the runway to start a tight turnaround—he would take off to the south and not have trees to clear. One of the gangsters in the plane opened the access hatch and hopped out, doing a collapsing roll in the mild snowy grass as he did. He immediately raised his rifle and shot the quad's tires out, flipping it as it hit a rut in the carved snow. Nub was ejected off the high side of the machine and crashed into the grass, sliding... not moving.

"Nub!" Morris yelled from across his hill.

He raised his rifle, but the man had already reached ThatNub, hauling him to his feet in a daze. Morris began to run, not caring about his cover. He tripped in the snowbank near the runway, stumbling and rolling. As he got back up the plane's door was closing, ThatNub a new captive. Morris looked on in horror as the plane turned around and gunned its engines.

"Nooooooo!" he screamed as it passed him. Morris Dooghan fell to his knees, letting his rifle drop into its sling. He put his snow and grime covered hands on his head, staring at the nightmare unfolding in front of him. "Nuuuubbb!" he yelled again.

The plane gained lift and began to ascend, slowly gaining both speed and altitude. Morris was at a loss for words, a state of shock that he thought couldn't get worse... until a moment later. The lightning-fast streak and whistle of the Hellfire missile barely made an impression in anyone's senses before it blew its warhead, ripping the old bush plane—and everyone in it—into death-morsels and fire. The explosion mixed with the plane's fuel, and the remnants of burning frame began to tumble to the Kansas plains below. An Apache attack helicopter began a wide sweeping arch over the cartel runway, its M230 30mm chain gun razing the remaining cartel vehicles and shed as two Blackhawks rumbled right over Morris and set down on the runway—one to his north, the other farther south.

Morris watched as two squads of soldiers from Fort Riley spilled out and began to move out from the birds and take a defensive perimeter around them. Hands still on his head, the weight of leadership began to fall heavily on the young man's shoulders. Hot tears began to streak down his face as a tension headache set-in in the back of his skull. Morris Dooghan had just led two of his friends to their deaths in combat.

JUAREZ, MEXICO

THE TWO BLACKHAWKS WERE FLYING AT NEARLY 170 MPH. Phalanx-1, with Brandon and Steve Bender's team, was rocketing southeast. "We're headed to a large warehouse complex south of Parajes Del Sur!" Steve told Brandon and the Rangers over the headset. Even with those on, he had to speak up over the roar of the two GE-701 turboshaft engines. "We have satellite evidence that they've been manufacturing meth and packaging it for distribution from the fourth building for quite some time."

"Captain, have you ever fast-roped?" the lead Ranger asked. "Or you, sir?" he asked Steve Bender.

"Affirmative, Sergeant!" Brandon answered as Steve nodded.

"We're going to do two drops!" Staff Sergeant Duane Lopez explained. "Two of my guys are dropping onto the roof from the left side. The bird will then move laterally right and the rest of us will drop near the loading dock out the right. Easy peasy, lemon-squeezey!"

Brandon did a quick double check on his math, verifying six total in each half of the rescue mission. "Remember it isn't just about ROE, Sergeant!" Brandon reminded. "We need to interrogate!"

"Roger that, sir!"

Four minutes later, the co-pilot chimed in on the intercom. "Thirty seconds!"

The special unit felt the nose of the craft pitch up quickly as the pilot bled the speed down to a hover over the corner of the subject roof in that half-minute. Phalanx-1's left side crew member shoved the heavy black rope out the door and watched it fall a mere nine-feet to the roof top. Despite a heavy rotor-wash beating on the craft from the roof's surface, the pilot was able to keep it hovering perfectly stable. "Go!" the crewman said after verifying they had a clear route down.

One at a time the Rangers wrapped a leg around the heavy nylon rope until it made a revolution and came across the top of their ankle. With a loose grip in their gloved hands, they played slack and slid down the rope in a controlled fall. The first soldier moved out and covered the various fixtures on the surface, lest a maintenance hatch suddenly pop open. The second moved off the rope and gave a quick 'okay' wave over his head. The crew member unhooked and dropped the rope.

As he joined his buddy in providing overwatch, Phalanx-1 began to slide to the right. With Sergeant Lopez leading, the four remaining members of the special unit took a thirty-foot plunge down their rope to the industrial complex's asphalt surface.

Twenty-three miles to the west, Phalanx-2 had already landed right in the beautifully manicured front yard of Inocencio Delgado. Ten minutes earlier, five Rangers and Lou had rapidly evacuated the helicopter, which immediately took off again and began a slow loop around the mansion at two hundred feet above ground.

Lieutenant Martel Adams and his men showed complete restraint, even in the face of fire from two second story windows. They provided covering fire while moving, intending on keeping heads down while they entered the mansion and attempted a prisoner grab. Lou and the junior corporal covered the driveway and front while the four-man team cleared the house.

After a short firefight, Lou heard on the radio, "Interior clear. Phalanx-2, howzit lookin'?"

"No sign of a QRF, Lead. You're clear out here."

"Roger. Bring in our guest, corporal."

Lou and the junior soldier entered the mansion's front door. Had it not been the circumstance it was, Lou would've loved a tour of the tropically themed home. "Up here, sir," he heard another Ranger say.

They followed the man back up to the master bedroom. Lou looked down at the bloody pool around a recently deceased cartel soldier and stepped over it.

On his knees near the broken window was another cartel member, about thirty-five years old and bleeding from his right shoulder. The man was cursing in Spanish, and despite the pain, his eyes contained a rageful contempt for the Americans. He continued ranting incessantly in Spanish, causing Lou to look around.

"Anyone getting this?" He looked back at the man. "I bet my left nut you hables ingles, you terrorist waste of space!"

The man kept repeating his threats in Spanish. One of the sergeants began to translate. "He's saying mean things about your mother, sir."

"I gathered," Lou mumbled. "Look! I know you can understand me. It is in your best interest to talk to me. You see, I've screwed up—a lot—the last couple of years. I'm already set to retire. They don't care about me. And I have nothing to lose by breaking the rules anymore."

The man's cursing stopped as his eyes narrowed. In English, he expressed to Lou his desire that Lou go have relations with himself. *Krunch!* The man's nose made a sickening noise as Lou's boot sole smashed into it, the tread leaving little purple lines on the broken cartilage.

"Arrrgghhhh!" he yelled, unable to grab his nose with his hands bound behind his back. The force had sent him backwards off his knees.

"Lieutenant, if you and yours want to take a small coffee break, I'll understand," Lou said as he straddled the cartel member.

"We're good, sir."

Lou unslung the rifle and stuck the barrel in the man's mouth. "All I want to know is where and when they took the girl? Is that information worth your life?" Super Bert Caldwell had been reborn, once again flying way past bingo fuel.

The man began to squirm and choke on the muzzle suppressor. Lou took it out of his mouth.

"Ge-Geneva!" the man yelled in broken English. "No—no torture!"

"Oh, that's riiicchhh!" Lou yelled back. "The cartel asking for mercy! You're a terrorist! You don't get 'Geneva'!" He moved the rifle down to the man's privates. "Last chance!"

"J-Janos!" the man screamed. "They head to...to Janos!"

"When!" Lou yelled.

"Cinco!" the man yelled, crying. "Cinco! Big line," he stumbled over his words. "Big line trucks, big guns!"

Lou stepped out from hovering over him. One of the Rangers had already pulled a tablet out of the front slot on his plate carrier and was scrolling the electronic map. "Janos. Looks like west on Highway 2."

"What time is it?" Lou demanded.

"0710, sir."

"Damn!" Lou yelled, walking out. "Let's get the chopper down here!"

"What about him, sir?" the sergeant asked.

"Leave him!" Lou yelled, already running down the stairs.

CHAPTER 32

Highway 2, Southwest of Ascencion, Mexico

"Can you see the sun?" Rosie heard Lou scream into the phone. Wherever he was, it was loud and he couldn't hear. She couldn't stand the temptation any longer. Knowing she was dooming her gifted phone, which was running on the electron equivalent of vapors, she called the only man in the world she knew she could in the most desperate moment of her life.

"Not directly," she said as loud as she dared. "This old beat-up box truck has some cracks and holes. It's on the left!"

"Say again!" Lou yelled over the roar of the helicopter. "And how long has it been since you turned?"

"Sun is on the left!" Rosie yelled. *Screw it!* she thought. She was desperate. *This sounds like my one chance!* "We've been going straight almost the whole time, even when we slow down for a while! Are you coming?" *Please, God! Please!*

"How big is the con—" *<Click>* The phone went dead.

Rosie's heart was beating hard and fast, worried with anticipation. *Is that the last time I ever talk to someone from home?* She started crying what little moisture and salt she had. *Who will take care of my darling Angel? I'm so sorry, sister!*

FOUR MILES NORTHEAST OF CONVOY, HIGHWAY 2

"WE MAY HAVE YOUR CONVOY, COLONEL!" LOU HEARD IN HIS headset. "About four miles up the road!"

The Blackhawk had been flying at two thousand feet above ground level, trying to shave time and distance off the curves of the highway.

"And FYI. Sentry Control reports that there are two Mexican F-5s heading north from Mexico City!"

The co-pilot was referring to the American E-3 Sentry radar plane patrolling the border. Though they were over a hundred miles down the highway, the west by southwest heading meant they were still only a few dozen miles from the corner of New Mexico.

"How can you be sure it's the cartel?" Lou asked the warrant officer. "This highway has been jammed up with people evacuating Juarez."

"We have an enhanced optics package, sir! I've zoomed in. The lead and trailing vehicles are technicals. Them and several scattered throughout the middle have machine guns mounted right on the tops. Also, there's literally no traffic in front of them. It's almost like they have a free pass to travel unhindered. It's going to get real interesting!"

As the conversation was happening, the lead pilot was diving the craft down to reduce giving away their position. He started skimming the farms from a hundred feet off the ground, some still green from the mild autumn climate. "Wait one!" After a few more seconds, he got back on the intercom. "Sentry Control reports that Phalanx-1 will be delayed. They have to Medevac two wounded back to Biggs and top-off before they join us!"

Brandon! Lou worried. "That means we'll be all alone out here for quite a while, doesn't it?" he asked earnestly.

"Affirmative, Colonel!"

"What's the plan, pilot?" Lou asked. Though many Blackhawks were outfitted with pylons for attaching rockets or missiles, the two in this operation were armed only with two six-barrel 7.62 mm mini-guns —one for each door gunner.

"About the only thing we can do is zoom past and try to disable the vehicles at the front. That'll halt the column! Starting with anything that has a machine gun mounted on top. If they flee, at least they'll have to turn and head back to Ascencion!"

"What about us?" Lou asked. "How do we get in there and grab her?"

Lieutenant Martel Adams finally spoke up. "The mini guns will make short work of the technicals, Colonel. Once we've done that, we'll keep harassing them from the air. We just need to keep them pinned until 1800 so we can get more units down here to assist!"

Lou didn't like hearing that, but he knew trying to assault the cartel on foot would've been a suicide run. "Final approach!" the co-pilot yelled into the intercom. "Johnson, get ready!" he told the left side crew chief. The fuselage door wide open, the six-member team and two crew chiefs could see a convoy of cars and trucks.

There must be thirty of them! Lou thought in amazement. He thought he'd counted eight that had machine guns either on the top or in the beds. There were five box trucks and tractor trailers in the very middle of the convoy. Phalanx-2 began to slow and make an arch around the front of the convoy. Corporal Johnson opened up the electrically driven M134 at its slowest rate of 2,000 rounds per minute. These targets were relatively soft, and there were a lot of them.

The first vehicle ripped to shreds as the small projectiles began to tear apart everything in its path. It caught on fire when a ripped fuel line spilled onto the hot engine. The second vehicle tried to pass it on the left and suffered a similar fate, effectively blocking the road. Johnson then tried to take out all three of the machine guns at the front of the convoy. He destroyed the first, but the second and third were able to open up and immediately Phalanx-2 started taking hits.

"Damn!" the pilot yelled, twisting his throttle and nosing the aircraft forward as fast as it would pick up speed. "We're going to need to get farther out! Try to out range them!" The Blackhawk continued to take hits and warning lights and buzzers suddenly started blaring from the front. "Hold on! I think we just lost our tail rotor!"

The pilot made rapid adjustments to the rear fins on both sides of the damaged rotor, slowing the torque effect to the craft from the main rotor, but not eliminating it. Phalanx-2 started spinning despite both pilots' best efforts to stop it. The spinning picked up speed. Lou felt himself tightening his waist belt and grabbing onto the hand hold above him.

"We have to set it down!"

The craft was built to survive an impact rate as bad as thirty-eight feet of drop per second. The pilot pushed that envelope, trying to get the craft out of the hail of bullets, hoping that one of their mini guns would be facing the enemy when it was all over. Lou could hear the co-pilot calling in a May-Day alert to Sentry Control. The team lucked out when the craft settled into a small depression. *An irrigation canal!* Lou thought excitedly. The area was rich with farms that shared a miles-long irrigation feed. The main rotors started digging into the dirt on both sides of the man-made creek. The carbon fiber blades started to break apart and fly off. The fuselage came to a rough landing at a slight angle in the knee-high water—but only the very top of the transmission and tilt gear by the rotors was visible to the cartel.

THE PENTAGON COMMAND AND CONTROL CENTER

. . .

THE LARGE ROOM WAS SURROUNDED BY SEVERAL SMALLER rooms, which looked out on the main space through glass soundproof windows. The main control center had a series of four tiers, each containing a row of various technicians from all branches of the military. They operated encrypted communications gear and computers, allowing the Pentagon generals and admirals the ability to hover over the shoulders of their underlings. Not only could they be providing instant "buy-in" of the decisions of the actual Army and Navy flag officers making battlefield decisions, but they could, with a little time and assuming the satellites hadn't been shot down or hacked, be privy to most any electronic piece of data, including radio communications.

General Judah Montgomery knew his role, and it had little to do with managing the operation in El Paso. His would be the largest head on the chopping block if something went wrong—a school got bombed... or a civilian convoy departing due to a threat from the United States. But by and large, he and his team of branch heads served to monitor operations throughout the American west, not just one city. There had been an attempted IED on the Coronado Bay bridge in San Diego. There had been a surprising amount of cartel resistance in Salt Lake City, when two gangs had aligned forces and taken over a shopping mall. Similar stories played out most everywhere, and the greater Los Angeles metroplex had, by far, been the most volatile. But when General Montgomery's primary assistant, Colonel Ryan Jackson, had told him of a clandestine and impromptu rescue mission into Juarez ahead of the president's allowed schedule, he had given the go-ahead knowing that Murphy would surely surface.

"How long until Phalanx-1 can get down there?" Judah asked a Navy senior chief, who had been eavesdropping on the radio comms throughout the various Fort Bliss operations in El Paso.

"Approximately forty minutes, sir. Would you like me to establish a direct line with the unit commander?"

"No," he instructed. Judah would follow protocol and have his Army Chief General do that, if needed.

Colonel Jackson was trailing behind him in the C & C Center, watching him pace behind the operators on this particular tier, occasionally looking up at satellite feeds or other warzone data up on the many, supersized displays on the wall the tiers faced. He walked over to an Army major.

"We have a Blackhawk down southwest of Ascencion, Mexico," he said. "Put it on the main display, Major." He looked at Colonel Jackson, motioning him to follow as he walked back up the electronic amphitheater and waited. "The secretary and the president have tied my hands, Colonel."

"I know, sir. I just wanted you to have all the information."

Judah Montgomery let out a big sigh. "I know you haven't been a big fan of Lou Caldwell, Ryan," he began. "But I expected no less of him than to find out he's in the middle of all this." He looked at the floor, face wrinkled with the burden of responsibility.

The screen cued up and the major zoomed in to show a field of view perhaps a mile wide. Approximately one-hundred meters south of an east to west highway, Phalanx-2 sat in a man-made creek, shattered and broken. They could see a perimeter of people around it, keeping a much greater number of foes pinned down at the vehicles on the road.

"It's a matter of time before they get flanked, or the Mexican F-5s that're heading up from the south begin to strafe them," Colonel Jackson said, concerned.

"And that's not all cartel," Judah pointed out. "There's a log-jam of civilians building up east of this stoppage. It's going to become a political quagmire." He walked into one of the wing rooms, where the leading General of the Air Force was monitoring interior air operations with her staff. "General Gilbert, I need to get a few planes in the air, pronto."

CHAPTER 33

HIGHWAY 2, SOUTHWEST OF ASCENCION, MEXICO

JARRED SPINES HAD BEEN THE COMMON INJURY TO EVERYONE on Phalanx-2. The fear of dying had convinced every soul on board to push through the pain and set up a fighting perimeter. Lieutenant Adams spaced everyone, including the pilots and crew chiefs, out along the edge of the irrigation canal. A steady stream of fire was coming in, and the only thing that kept them from being overrun was the courage to stick one's head, arms, and rifle up for a second or two and return it. The helicopter's electronics were still working, something the pilots had reminded Martel. *We have to set charges and blow it up the second we think we're going to be overrun,* they said. Which in all their minds was not a question of if, but when.

Martel had pulled up a tablet that was linked to the main battle net through a satellite link up in the helicopter. He and Lou were studying a satellite image of their location. "You'd think we could link up to a satellite," Lou said.

"We could, if this had been a planned op," Martel said, the sound of hyper-sonic rounds plinking off the helicopter's roof. "Or if we had a drone! This is what we got!"

"Look here to the east," Lou said. "There's a trench!" He walked under the tail of the wounded chopper, sloshing and swimming through the cold water sourced from an aquifer ten miles away. Martel followed him. "There!" Lou pointed.

"When they figure out it's there, they'll come right down it and pop out on the flank!" Martel said. He began to reposition one of his Rangers and one of the crew chiefs.

"Wait!" Lou said. "I bet it leads to a culvert under the road! And see how the grass is overgrown?

A couple of us could crawl through and pop up over there, behind them."

"And do what?" Martel countered. "There's no way we can wage a war with them!"

"I don't mean that. I'm talking about getting into the box truck in the middle and getting the girl!"

"Begging your pardon, Colonel, but that's a suicide run! All due respect, but you don't know infantry tactics and close-quarters battle!" Martel turned and began to redirect the perimeter defense.

Lou was at a loss of what else could be done. He went into the downed helicopter and retrieved his backpack, pulling out the satellite phone. *I need to warn off Brandon,* he thought. He was sure that those coming on Phalanx-1 had already been informed of their status, but he was hoping his friend's chopper could take the technicals out from elevation and then start working the ground forces. He was about to call the other SAT phone when he heard their designation being called for on the helicopter's radio.

"Warrant officer!" he yelled, waving for the co-pilot to come over. "We're being hailed on the radio!"

The young man climbed back into the cockpit and plugged the helmet he was still wearing into the electronics. Lou replaced him on the perimeter. One minute later, the co-pilot showed back up with an elated grin.

"Glad you caught that, sir! They wanted us to verify the ends of the convoy!"

"Who did?" Lou asked, confused. He looked at the man, who was squinting and looking all over the blue Mexican sky in the westerly and north-westerly directions.

"Them!" he yelled excitedly.

Six-thousand feet above and two miles southwest of the convoy's destroyed western vehicles, an U.S. Air Force AC-130J Ghostrider was starting its counter-clockwise pattern around the intense fight happening below. Inside the four-prop plane, specifically designed for an attack mission instead of hauling cargo, a crew of two women and one man were coordinating the plane's traveling speed, altitude, and position with the onboard camera systems to lock-in on the next several vehicles behind those initially destroyed by Phalanx-2. Out of the left side of the plane's fuselage protruded two distinct barrels operated by four other crew members. The 30mm GAU 23A chain gun sent three 30 mm rounds per second toward the convoy—each filled with a high-explosive and incendiary charge originally designed to destroy enemy tanks.

The flashes of light emanating off the tip of the barrel were a thing of beauty to Lou and those around him. The plane passed south of them, raking all seven of the remaining belt-fed machine gun vehicles, each of which exploded as the rounds and their contents detonated with vengeful fury. Cartel members—or more precisely, pieces of them — raced in all directions as the flying hammer known affectionately as 'Puff the Magic Dragon' by infantry made one pass by the cartel column. It veered north and made a beeline for America with the knowledge that the Mexican F-5s were only about five minutes away from showing up.

The satellite phone Lou had stuffed into his cargo pocket began to ring and vibrate. *Brandon!* he thought as he read the screen. "Poster Boy!" he yelled into the device over the roar of the rifles around him.

"Colonel, if I'm not mistaken, you just received some relief on scene!"

"Understatement of the year, Captain!" Lou yelled over the sounds of battle. "We still need to get in and find Rosie!"

"We got about five minutes, sir!" Brandon yelled back. Lou could hear the approaching Phalanx-1's engines in the background. "There are two jets showing up to join the fun! Any idea where she's at?"

"Middle of the convoy," Lou started. "There's one box truck with two tractor-trailers on either end. I'm guessing it's that middle truck. It's the only one that looks as beat up as she described."

"Roger!" Brandon said. "The Ghostrider was ordered to only take out the belt-feds! They didn't want to risk killing her!"

Lou stuck the top of his head over the edge of the little creek's berm. Gunsmoke and the smell of burnt powder filled the field. "They've had the wind knocked out of them! They're barely firing now! Where are you?"

"We'll be there in one mike. Can you guys take advantage of our distraction?"

It hit Lou that they were at a crucial moment—an apex decision. "Yes! Keep them looking north, no matter what!" He hung up, dropping the phone in the dirt above the creek and slithered along the dirt bank over to Lieutenant Martel Adams. "Phalanx-1 is inbound! They're going to rake these guys from the north. I'm heading up the culvert to find our package!"

Lou raced past the two soldiers guarding the eastern edge of their defenses, sloshing up the cold waterway. He pulled his rifle up and pivoted on it as he got to the small culvert and stream that led directly under the road. Seeing no enemy, he laid down completely in the muddy muck and looked back, surprised to see Martel, one Ranger, and one helicopter crew member following suit.

"Keep going, Colonel! They're starting to fire at Phalanx-1!"

Completely prone, Lou began to drive his elbows and knees in coordinated fashion, keeping his butt and head below the overgrown grass. By the time he'd made it the roughly one-hundred meters to the road, his muscles were spent, filled with lactic acid. *Must keep going!* he insisted in his mind. *You must not fail her!* Driven by the thoughts of his depressed son and his missing wife, Freeman Louis Caldwell had not felt this level of purpose or importance of moment in many years. He felt Martel right on his boots.

"Now's our chance, sir! They're all trying to shoot -1, but they're staying out of range!"

Lou took two quick breaths to refill his cells, muscles tight from being worked on the crawl. He got to his knees and whipped back and forth, spotting the western most semi-truck. "Moving east!"

"Move!" Martel yelled. He instructed the two men behind him to get to the road's shoulder and hold the spot secure for them.

Lou crawled up into the grass field, keeping at a crouch. Martel joined and passed him. "Stay right on my six, Colonel!" he instructed.

There was an overwhelming noise of gunfire on the north side of the trucks as the cartel soldiers tried to pour their fire on the helicopter, which was several hundred feet up and out over the north farm. The door gunner was firing back at the east end of the convoy. Lou followed Martel along the sides of the semi-trucks. When they passed the first gap, he made eye contact with a gangster who had turned his head upon catching Martel's movement. "Look!" Lou heard him yell in Spanish. They had run past the gap and down half the length of the next semi truck's left side.

"We're about to get company!" Lou yelled ahead.

He turned around and as soon as he saw the shape of a rifle start to appear at the corner of the truck; he put three rounds right into the Kenworth's corner fender. A couple more cartel soldiers appeared out of the next gap farther west, near where Martel had planted his men. The cartel turned left and started to take aim on Lou when the overwatch blasted the pair of men in the back from fifteen feet.

"Keep going!" Lou yelled.

When the adversary in the gap closer to him peeked out to sneak in a shot, the overwatch team dropped him. Lou saw the Ranger get hit by fire from a shot from the far end of the convoy. The helicopter crew chief dragged him back into the small culvert they'd crawled up.

"One more gap, Colonel!" Martel yelled. He then blasted the box truck's windshield, recognizing the driver was just about to open fire on them. He began to receive fire from the left, coming across the gap between the trucks.

Lou looked down, realizing their legs were completely vulnerable. "Go!" he yelled as he got down onto the ground. "I'll catch up!"

He saw two pair of legs in the exact position they were in but on the truck's far side. He opened fire, continuing to shoot the men after they'd tried to run off the shoulder and into the field on the north side. He stood back up, looking at both the semi and the box truck. *God, if this is it, make it quick,* he pled. He bolted across the gap at a full sprint and caught up to Martel as he was slowly clearing the corner—'slicing the pie' one wedge at a time, as they were taught.

"Hurry!" hollered Lou. He pounded on the box truck's rear left-side door. "Rosie!" It was far too loud with gunfire for him to hear if she'd called back.

"Locked!" Martel yelled.

Lou began to let out a string of salty language but was cut off by his battle buddy. "Bottom pouch on the back of my plate carrier! There's a small master key!"

"A what?" Lou asked as he started to unzip the pocket attached to the back of the man's tactical gear. He immediately saw a ten-inch-long set of carbide bolt-cutters with extendable handles. He grabbed it and handed them to Martel. Just as the Lieutenant began to extend the handles, Lou caught a shadow on the north side of the road's shoulder. The shadow was on top of the next semi's shadow. He looked up with his rifle and caught a cartel soldier in the face just as he was peeking over. As the man screamed and slumped his head, Lou put another round right through the top of it.

Martel had made short work of the padlock and unlatched the heavy doors' locking mechanism. He swung the two doors apart a bit. He looked at Lou and his eyes went wide. "Duck!" he yelled just a second too late as a cartel soldier came around the corner. The first shot caught Lou in the back, right in the middle of the ceramic plate the Army had given him. The second got him below and to the left.

The 9 mm round passed through Lou's kidney and barely missed hitting Martel, who had whipped his pistol out of the holster low on his hip and put rounds of his own into the man's eye sockets.

"Ungghhh!" was all Lou could say as a piecing hot needle like none he'd ever experienced surged through his left abdomen. He went to his knees. "Get the girl!" he yelled. Lou could feel the warmth dribbling down the front and back side of his under shirt as he turned on his knees to keep any more surprises coming from that direction.

Martel jumped in and saw a woman in a dog cage, shaking in the corner. "Rosie Ortiz! U.S. Army Rangers!" He clipped the lock on the cage door and tossed his bolt cutters down. The dehydrated and malnourished woman was terrified. She tried to talk, but her dry voice cracked.

"Rosie!" Lou called up feebly into the open cargo box. "It's Lou from Carlsbad!"

Rosie began to crawl out of the cage, stiff... sore... eyes squinting. Martel hopped down and then held his hands out, taking hers and guiding her to the ground. Rosie had a hard time standing. She saw blood running down Lou's left butt cheek.

"Lead us out, Colonel!" Martel yelled as he fired at two more cartel trying to get around from the north side.

Lou cleared left and then right, surprised that more of them hadn't joined the fight to kill the Americans. They were too invested in the thrill of crashing a second helicopter. Lou led Rosie and Martel into the field, opting to run south and try for the canal directly. Rosie's legs and lack of nourishment made it difficult for her to run. Martel gave up prodding her and yelled, "I need to carry you!" He didn't wait for permission or a reply. In a flash he was grabbing her right arm with his left hand as he ducked, reaching his right arm down and hooking her right leg through the gap between her legs. As he stood, he dragged her onto his shoulders and began a full sprint across the dead alfalfa. "Colonel!" he yelled.

Despite the wound, Lou had already gained thirty meters on them, almost halfway to the canal. Just as he turned, two thunderous F-5

Tiger II jets rocketed from south to north, buzzing the wounded Blackhawk's attackers, which waved off their attack and began to dive and head north for the safety of the U.S. border with southwest New Mexico. The jets maintained near perfect formation as they made a tight turn to the east, beginning to loop back around.

"They're going to come around and strafe our guys in the creek!" Lou screamed.

Martel passed him and Lou maintained his position facing the trucks. He took his eyes off the jets, seeing an enormous number of gangsters begin to fill the gaps between trucks. Farther west, some of them began to sprint across the field at the wounded Phalanx-2. He switched to full auto and let the rifle eat the entire magazine at the men in the gap they'd just fled a minute earlier. He turned and began to run again, the sharp pain in his side getting worse. Lou began to feel lightheaded.

The F-5s had completed their loop and were now two miles east of the action, flying west again. One was lined up on the length of the irrigation canal, the other on the field Lou was standing in. Like a deer in headlights, Lou stopped and stared at the oncoming warbirds. *Surely, they won't actually strafe us,* he thought. His vision began to get fuzzy. *God, if you're there, please let me see Terrance again...*

The F-5s had slowed their speed for the turn and to make the best use of the potential strafing run. Lou saw a second pair of dark dots in the fuzzy vision. *Angels?* When the F-5 Tigers were only a half-mile from Lou, the one-hundred-yard gap between them filled with the screaming steel of first one, then another F-35 Lightning II American Joint Strike Fighter. *BOOOOOOMMMMM*! The two broken sound barriers screamed, as the U.S.A.F. pilots split the gap between their far-less skilled Mexican counterparts. The F-35s wagged their wings at the downed helicopter as they screamed by at a head-splitting Mach 1.4, barely five hundred feet above ground level. Some of the soldiers crossing the field had dropped at the impact of the noise slamming into them, more out of fright than physics. The two F-5s split, one left and one right, caught completely off-guard. The Lightnings had proven their name and then some, as they stayed in formation and pulled up, rocketing straight up into the sky to the west of the action. *We own your air, Mexico,* the pilots were saying. *Suck it.*

Whirrr! A crack of air snapped as a rifle round barely passed Lou. He stood again and began his run, albeit much slower. Martel and a second Ranger began to cover Lou from the canal. "Run!" they were screaming as they shot.

Lou felt his legs getting heavier as he plied them through the grass. *Pop!* He felt another burning needle, this time in his left heel. "Arrrrgghh!" he yelled as he fell into the grass. *Ka-Ka-Krow! Pop-Pop-Pop!* The noise of the firefight and rounds whipping over his head began to lull him. He began to do a pushup and get back up, intent on living. *Are they actually waving me off?* he asked himself. He could see the men in the canal trying to tell him to stay put. Suddenly the field exploded in noise and wind. It began to rain hot brass, linkages, and the smell of gunpowder, as Phalanx-1 began to hover just west of Lou, firing on the enemy convoy. Through the fog, Lou could see a muscular figure jump out of the safety of the helicopter while it was still five feet up. It was followed by others, who sprinted for the safety of the canal to reinforce their battered brothers. The figure rolled and began to sprint for Lou.

"Let's go, Colonel!" Brandon yelled. He scooped Lou up in a fireman's carry much as Martel had done to Rosie and tossed the small colonel onto his shoulders, sprinting for the helicopter. Phalanx-1 had begun to take too much small-arms fire and had to take-off, which forced Brandon to head for the canal. He slid down, with both himself and Lou tearing up the dirt as he slid all the way into the man-made creek. "We need to keep our heads down!" Brandon yelled at all of them.

"Why's that?" Martel asked, as he and the other Ranger began to help the Marine pull Lou through the water west, back to their perimeter.

The radio on Brandon's gear chirped. "Phalanx-1, Sentry Control, maintain position 1 kilo south, acknowledge," they all heard the C-3 over New Mexico say over the radio hanging on Brandon's tactical gear.

"Copy, Sentry Control," they heard their other helicopter's pilot say.

"Timber Flight, Sentry Control, you are cleared for hot in Kill Box 1. Say again, cleared for hot in Kill Box 1. Be aware, friendlies are danger close in the canal to the south. Acknowledge."

"That's why!" Brandon yelled over the noise of the firefight.

"Timber Flight copies, Sentry Control. Timber-2, happy shooting. Make sure you stop before you hit that big gap to the east," the lead pilot instructed his wingman.

"2 copies," Lou heard a familiar voice say.

The high-pitched whine of four GE TF-34 turbofan engines could be heard loudly approaching from the west. "There!" the Ranger said, pointing. They all looked up, even Lou with his fuzzy vision. Less than five hundred feet up and one mile away, in a steep turn, two A-10 Thunderbolts barely ten feet apart pulled out of their turn, lining up perfectly on the road and field between the convoy and the embattled Americans.

BRRRRRRRRRTTTTTT! BRRRRRRRTTTTTTT! BRRRRRRTTTTTT! two GAU-8 rotary cannons screamed. Timber-1 sent several hundred 30 mm shells into the field, tearing up the cartel members that were hit with severe carnage, literally destroying some of their bodies beyond recognition. Those not hit had their will to fight removed with authority. On the highway, Timber-2, piloted by a young lieutenant called Dumbo, began to shower thirty cartel vehicles with the same depleted uranium shells. The ensuing death-run would go down in the annals of U.S.A.F. history as the new generation's version of the highway of death that had happened in the first Gulf War. Only these weren't military tanks and troop-carrying vehicles, but the technical and drug-carrying vehicles of a ruthless and evil cartel, paid for with the lives and crimes of addicted Americans. Trucks were destroyed beyond recognition, some of them exploding as the high-explosive incendiary rounds ripped through fuel tanks and ammunition supplies. Fireballs propelled large truck bodies up to a hundred feet into the air.

The young pilot, soon to be called 'New Bert' by his fellow aviators, had sent many evil souls to hell in a matter of moments. Though the cartel boss had not been in the convoy, the day had been a major victory in the new war with them. As ordered, Dumbo had let off in time to avoid the civilian cars stopped to the east. The pair of 'Warthogs' screamed past the destruction and the relieved, embattled Americans. They banked left and gained altitude, leaving Old Mexico for New. The irony that somewhere in the chain of command, someone had disregarded orders to save trapped them had not been lost on Lou in the moment he passed out.

CHAPTER 34

COMSUBPAC Offices, Joint Base Pearl Harbor Hickam —Hawaii

"Good news, COB?" Commander Brody Woodward asked Master Chief Darren Jorgenson.

The pair, along with the executive officer and all department heads of the USS James L. Hunnicutt, had been at the offices of the commander for all submarine forces in the Pacific. Like the West Coast based ballistic missile submarines, the Hunny had been without home-port since the Cascadia disasters had rendered the facilities useless. As the third boat in the Navy's newest "Patriot" class of submarines, she was the only one with the many additional features that enabled her to perform critical intelligence gathering. Though a fully functional SSGN, the nation desperately needed her back in service in preparation for the active war between China and Russia.

Darren tried his best to remain emotionless when reading his 'family-grams' in front of others. Not all had received good news. *And today is Thanksgiving,* he remembered. He'd just gotten an update from his wife and daughter.

"Good as can be, sir," he replied. "This gun-range they're staying at is helping the county stand up a posse for augmenting the few remaining police and National Guard. Any news on your family, sir?" Darren knew the answer and almost cringed asking, but he felt it would've been rude not to be invested in the answer.

"Nothing," the skipper answered. "I'm coming to terms with it, Darren. My family probably perished. I grieve in my cabin every night so that I can still do my job. But thanks for asking."

"If you ever need someone to vent at, Skipper, just let me know."

"I appreciate it, COB, but now that Squadron Five has been stood-up here in Pearl, I have a few other COs in the pool of 'equals' that I can talk with about stresses." The Hunny's CO changed the subject. "How's the crew fitting in at the Training Center?"

"About as expected, sir. I think the one thing that keeps them from going U.A. is the fact that the world's on fire right now. They know all the branches are preparing for the possibility of war. Had we merely been dealing with the homeport disaster, I think a lot of these kids would've disappeared already.

"Interesting perspective, COB. Have they picked up on the record time that the shipyard is repairing our boat?"

"A few have, sir. Why?"

"Several projects around the various shipyards and bases have been put on hold, specifically to give our boat the manpower and parts she needs. And though you don't know this yet, we're getting a briefing about our next mission tomorrow morning."

"Already?" Darren asked with intense skepticism. "No sea trials?"

"War time waivers, COB." Brody stood up, preparing to leave Darren in the quiet corner of the building's 'Chief's lounge' he'd found him in. He turned back. "Make sure they take the training seriously, COB. There's likely to be a lot more action where we're headed. We'll have to save our own skins next time."

TUCSON MEDICAL CENTER, TUCSON, ARIZONA

GRANGER MADISON HEARD YET ANOTHER HOSPITAL EMPLOYEE walking into the room. "I said I don't want—" He shut his mouth in shame and surprise.

Donna Wolf walked in looking ten years older than the last time he'd seen her. Granger looked down at his toes, still trapped in bed by a sling holding his arm at elevation. Though the plates and screws in his right forearm were installed and doing well, both gunshot wounds had resulted in an infection that was still stubbornly sticking its tongue out at the antibiotics. Donna wore a gaze that Granger couldn't bear to look at.

She stood in silence for ten seconds. "Say something!" she demanded.

Granger looked back up at her. "I... I can't. There are no words to—"

"You don't get off that easily, Granger!" she scolded, slowly marching over to his bed. "Two men are dead because they believed in you! In that—" she got stuck on the words "—whatever it is you all went out and did in the desert all the time! Mick and my Davey believed in you!" She barely got the words out before her emotion erupted once again from her eyes. Her face red, she moved right next to him on his left side. "Tell me why my husband died!" she screamed as she grabbed his left hand with both of hers and began to squeeze.

Granger's eyes filled with tears, running down his flush face, some of them spilling onto his burn scars. He kept his gaze on her. "They died for America, Donna," he said softly. "No. For Americans. For all people who can't fight for themselves." Granger felt her hands relax just a small bit, a slight release of tension.

"They're going to keep doing the smuggling," she said, a little more calmly. He felt her grip lighten up a bit more, though she kept clutching his undamaged hand.

"And someone will need to shut that one down, too," he said passively, still giving her the respect of eye-contact. "But it'll have to be someone else. I'm done."

"What!" This nearly boiled her blood pressure. "The hell you are! Dave wouldn't have wanted that, and you know it!"

Granger was confused. "But—but..."

She moved her right hand up to his left cheek. "Granger. I don't know when I'll forgive you. But I won't let anger control me. And Dave looked up to you like a long-lost brother. They all do. If you truly want to honor my husband... honor Mick... you won't quit."

She started to walk away from his bed but stopped and looked one more time. "Just be smart about it. Get more guys. Get better stuff. I'll help with that. But I know one thing for certain—if you quit, if my husband's death was for nothing, you'll be angry at yourself for the rest of your life."

MANHATTAN, KANSAS

THE POUNDING ON THE DOOR WOULD'VE GONE UNANSWERED had Morris Dooghan not recognized his father's commanding voice. His head spun as he got out of bed to move to the door. He'd barely gotten up for water or the bathroom in the two days since tragedy struck.

"I don't know why you've been ignoring your mother," his father said before the door was two feet opened, "but I had to drive up here and check on you—and now I'm pissed!" His father stepped into the small second floor apartment with the claimed authority that fathers can sometimes have over their adult son's lives. He scanned the room, looking for William or signs of a Thanksgiving meal...something. The room was dark and stale, messy... "What's going on, son?" he asked, voice turning to inquisitive worry. "Why did I have to drive up here on Thanksgiving night? I should be watching football."

The grave look on Morris' face betrayed him, the corners of his eyes crusty from the salt of shame. "I—I don't even know where to begin, Dad!" was all he could get out in a voice that began to crack.

"Where's William?" Mark Dooghan asked his son with grave concern.

"He's dead. Something... I can't really talk about it, Dad..."

Mark pulled his taller son in for a hug. "Grab your stuff, son. I won't let you sit here and suffer. You're coming home."

CAMP DAVID, FREDERICK COUNTY, MARYLAND

PRESIDENT JEREMIAH ALLEN WALKED INTO HIS RESIDENTIAL quarters and found First Lady Frances Allen sitting on the large sofa, MacBook Pro on her lap as she worked on one of several charity initiatives she was involved in. The retired teacher was a sucker for anything involving helping children. The propane fire warmed the ceramic decorative logs, which in turn warmed the room set to a rustic décor. As soon as she saw her husband, she picked up the landline phone on the oak and granite end table next to her. "Could we get a hot plate of dinner sent in for Jeremiah, please?" Even to the staff, she called him by his first name. She hung up the phone.

"What doom and gloom have the networks been saying today?"

Jeremiah asked as he went to the 'kitchen' and got himself a big glass of water.

"That you're the first president to not pardon a turkey since 1962," she said, smirking.

Jeremiah downed the water and immediately headed for the liquor cabinet in search of a scotch. "There's much greater travesties happening today," he grumbled as he poured.

"Anything you want to talk about?" she offered.

"Nothing I should," he said, knowing he should skip the drink and get a nap before the next crisis. "Russia is taking actions that lead me to believe this naval battle they've been playing with is about to hit the ground. China is taking actions that lead me to believe they're about to attempt to shut down the internet and our power grid. And I fear that my attacks on the cartel strongholds are probably the catalyst for a much more nefarious movement disguised as a 'protest.' In other words," he said as he plopped next to his wife and grabbed her hand lovingly, "where are we going? And why are we in this handbasket?"

There was a knock on the door. Jeremiah started to rise, but Francis stopped him. She answered the door and allowed the Navy Culinary Specialist in to deliver the food. After the young woman left, Francis took the metal cover off the large plate of turkey and traditional fixings. She carried it back around the end table and set it on the coffee table. Francis Allen took the drink from his hand, startling him.

"Wh-What?" he said as his eyelids shot open. The red had already started to creep in on the whites of his eyes.

"Shhhh," she shooshed.

Francis took a quilt from a cedar chest that contained the household goods they had shipped to stay at the presidential retreat for as long as he was president. She selected a smaller quilt made by Jeremiah's grandmother in 1945. It was soft and pliable, and it had a faint mothball smell to it. She placed it on his lap and torso and sat down next to him once more with her minicomputer, wondering how many children had already perished since that horrible earthquake and volcano had erupted.

William Beaumont Army Medical Center, El Paso, Texas

Lou set the phone down when he heard a woman's raspy voice. The sound of various machines played over the muted television in the hospital room. It had been showing several episodes of 'Ridiculousness' over and over, though Lou had not been paying much attention. So much had happened. It seemed the only thing to take his mind off thinking about the three soldiers that had died in Rosie's rescue operation was the realization that he needed to go back to Maryland and face his life. He'd spent nearly an hour on the phone with his brother, who just had a hard time understanding how a colonel on a light-duty boondoggle could have been shot in the side and foot.

"Come in," he mumbled as he looked over. He instantly tried to straighten himself, a useless task in the elevated hospital bed. "Ohhhhh... Hi!"

"Hi..." Rosie said sheepishly. "I...uh..."

"It's okay, Rosie," Lou said. "You don't have to say anything."

She was still decked out in patient gown and robe, walking steadily behind a walker that was barely bearing weight. She moved over to Lou's bed. "I guess it's cool that the hospital let me stay... me being a civilian and all..." She looked around at Lou's instruments and started to get a bit emotional.

"They kind of toss the rules aside for terror events," he said. "How are you?" He wore the concerned look of a father or older brother.

"They're letting me go tomorrow. The Rangers are taking me directly to Dallas for a debrief," she explained. "I think the military might be there, too."

"You look like you're moving well," Lou said, not sure how much small talk he was up for. "At least you're done wearing diapers. Right?"

Rosie chuckled, though not as much as Lou had hoped. She grabbed his hand with both of hers. "I…" She got stuck and tears began to well up. Lou remained quiet this time. "I—I wish I knew how to repay you!" Her chin began to quiver. She let go of Lou's hands and started wiping both eyes.

"I think you might be the bravest person I've ever met, Rosie," Lou said calmly. "I've been the one doing the saving… Now I got to be the one getting saved…" He paused, searching for words. "I… I don't know if people like us ever get to repay the things we need to. But I guess… I guess I'd like to think that the world is a better place because of people like us… I'm not sure if that makes sense…"

Rosie nodded. "It does. I get it." She took a chance to change the subject. "How long do they say you need to be in here?"

"Several more days, at least. The kidney was toast—the round just shredded it. But I got lucky apparently—it went right through and missed everything else. And…" he laughed, "God gave me a second kidney!" This got Rosie laughing a bit. "The heel hurts like the dickens, though," Lou admitted. "I'm going to need one of those pirate-leg casts for a while, apparently."

"That'll make it hard to drive, won't it?" she asked.

"It will, which means I'm stuck with that squared-away Marine for a few more months." Another laugh.

After an awkward silence, Rosie asked, "What do you think will happen next?"

"That's a good question…" Lou pondered. He grabbed the corded-remote attached to the bed's guardrail and turned off the muted television. "I think our world is going through a drastic hitting of the 'reset' button. Something that some folks have been bragging about for years… while others were warning about it." He pointed to the empty visitor's chair, hoping the tough but vulnerable woman would have a seat. "But I'd love for you to stay awhile and tell me what a seasoned cop thinks about it."

EPILOGUE

SOUTHWEST BERING SEA

THE TWO YUAN-CLASS TYPE 039A SUBMARINES MAINTAINED three steady and extremely quiet knots, six hundred feet below the Russian flotilla floating metaphorically overhead. The closest ship, one of two Udaloy class destroyers, was six miles to the south. The last true combatant ship this far north was a medium Slava class cruiser. The ships were escorting nine Russian landing ships capable of a variety of tasks related to amphibious invasion. With them came an assortment of helicopters and landing craft. Most of the ships had left the North Fleet under the initial lead-out of nuclear-powered icebreakers. Three Alligator class amphibious ships had been en route all the way from the Baltic Fleet. Since the early days of the conflict, Russia had been positioning itself to be prepared for all possibilities against its two Pacific foes.

The Yuan submarines were two of China's growing fleet of a newer class of submarine, nicknamed AIPs—their source of power was diesel combined with compressed hydrogen—it was a chemical process that was considered 'air independent propulsion.' This new propulsion threat had worried the U.S. Navy for two decades, ever since a Swedish AIP sub repeatedly launched mock torpedo threats on a U.S. aircraft carrier during wargames. The subs were much quieter than their nuclear-powered counterparts, not needing nearly as much noise-generating equipment as a reactor. And though not as quiet as the traditional diesel-electric submarine, they did not need to regularly surface and run a generator to recharge batteries. This allowed them both the ability to stay submerged for far longer than diesel boats and evade at higher speeds without fear of killing the batteries quickly.

0130, Ma Nan thought as he checked the clock mounted to the sub's bulkhead. He felt the ship begin to increase its rise angle. *We're coming up to periscope depth. It should be starting.*

"Everyone, conduct another triple check of each other's equipment," he said, his voice boldly concealing his nerves.

Like himself, every man in this special forces unit was an officer, though twenty-six and with four-and-a-half years' experience, he was the oldest for his squad. They were part of the Naval Special Commandos, a sub-unit of the Type One Wu Jing. Unlike the 6th, 8th, and 12th Special Warfare Groups, the NSC specialized in maritime operations. And though training had been slow for the last two years, Ma knew something was amiss. *It's like some sort of switch flipped when America had that earthquake,* he had told the three teammates he was closest with. Chinese soldiers, elite or not, did not cast large nets in which to toss their opinions. The risk of superiors finding out their deepest thoughts was too great.

"They should be starting already, huh?" Zhu Yong said excitedly. He began to look over every inch of Ma's dry-suit, oxygen rebreather, weapons, and all gear that had been attached with lanyards. He finished by double checking that the swim fins duct taped to Ma's calves were secure.

Ma began to perform the same check on his buddy. Before he could speak, the compartment's red lights turned on and the white lights dissolved. "Prepare for dive operations!" they heard a nameless submarine sailor blare into the compartment's overhead speakers. A flurry of sailors began to check pressure gauges and the condition of valves with checklists.

"First four!" Ma heard a submarine officer bark. He nodded at Zhu and two others from his eight-man squad. In all, it would take each submarine four evolutions with the 'lockout chambers' to get the thirty-two commandos out and into the black, cold Bering Sea.

Under the yellow and green glow of chemical lights, the commandos retrieved inflatable boats from topside compartments and lashed them down onto the submarines' topside as trained. They partially inflated the rafts, which made them start to strain against their lashings, their air cells searching for the surface as if starving to breathe. Though they couldn't see the sister sub a mere seventy meters away, there was a small comfort in knowing they were there.

At 0215 on the surface, within ten seconds of each other, three two-hundred-kilogram solid tungsten hypersonic projectiles screamed from a low space orbit of thirty miles in altitude, piercing the hulls of the three Russian combatant ships with such inertial energy that the act of hitting fuel or ammunition spaces was merely an unnecessary bonus. The force of the six-foot-long skinny heavy bullets ripped through the steel and titanium with enough force to peel the ships open like cans of cat food. Before a sailor could even sound an alarm, the high-speed devices were already several hundred feet down, well on their way to their final resting places on the sea floor. The ensuing explosions finished the job, the ships sinking in under three minutes, the fastest being eighty-four seconds. Emergency rafts popped off automatically when the vessel's hulls reached twenty-five feet of submergence.

The escort ships had been leading the pack, spread out over a width of twelve miles and length of nearly forty. The initial ships to witness the brazen attack spent a few seconds reviewing their own data. *What the hell just happened?* Those closest then kicked up their pace and went to battle stations, rousting sailors from their racks in the middle of the night. They would need to begin searching for survivors immediately.

The Naval Commando Unit's target was not any of these ships, but rather the last ship in the procession, the *Ivan Gren.* It was the lead boat in its class of transport ships and capturing it intact was critical. And as Ma and the other thirty-one commandos braved the cold and dark hostile ocean, the two submarines had quietly placed themselves directly to the port and starboard of its heading. When the ship was two hundred meters away, the submarines turned on the red light on top of each boat's rudder for two seconds.

It's time, Ma said to himself excitedly. He gave the hand signal and the commandos of the two squads on this sub began to unleash their inflatable boats. Free from their bindings, the craft began to rise, with the commandos positioning themselves over them. The more the crafts ascended, the faster the air inside the cells expanded under less oceanic pressure. It was a chain reaction of speed, as the cells were fully pressurized when the little boats broke through the six-foot waves, all of them positioned near a corner of the ship that was just passing through. *As we practiced!* Ma commanded in his head, not believing in telepathy, but hoping in that moment that his men felt his encouragement.

Two men enabled the small electric motors within seconds, allowing the black rubber boats to begin keeping pace. Two others launched a compressed gas tube that sent powerful magnets to the ship's hull with a thud. Though loud, the reality was that those spots on the ships were carefully selected based on the far side of the hull being some form of water or fuel tank or unmanned machinery space. Within twenty seconds, all four craft were lashed and matching speed with the mother ship, which helped a bit, but didn't completely dispel the rough tossing the men were receiving.

After ensuring all seven other men in his boat had removed diving helmets and rebreathers, he looked at the two on the bow. They had reloaded the compressed launcher to throw heavy lines and hooks up to the bow of the tall ship. The final task for this dangerous boarding evolution was to get the big climbing net hanging from their prey's structure near the deck above.

"Now!" Ma Nan yelled with a wave. "For China!"

The End.

OTHER WORKS BY AUSTIN CHAMBERS

The Cascadia Fallen Trilogy:
Tahoma's Hammer
Order Divested
Spiritus Americae

The Splintered Moon (novelette)

And… A small request for assistance…

If you enjoyed this book, it would be tremendous if you were able to leave a review. Reviews help me gain visibility, and they can bring my books to the attention of other readers who may enjoy them.

Please consider leaving an honest review of this book. You can look under the book's name on Amazon, Goodreads, or Bookbub. Thank you!

JOIN SECTION 8!

Want to stay updated? Join Section 8 and get some cool FREE writings!

The Splintered Moon tells the tale of a young, expecting couple as they try to bugout unprepared when a piece of the moon heads toward the Earth! The Prospects is a "Chapter 0" to *Tahoma's Hammer*, which tells the pre-story of the Scumbags in the Prologue. You'll also get a map from the trilogy and a true short story! And at time of publication of this book, I'm also giving away the first book in the Cascadia Fallen trilogy, Tahoma's Hammer!

It's completely free to sign up, you can opt out anytime, *and I never give away or sell my list.* You can enroll at the bottom of my website's home page. **Works that are given away for enrollment are subject to change.**

ABOUT THE AUTHOR

Navy veteran Austin Chambers took an "early retirement" from a naval shipyard to pursue working from home. In addition to writing fiction via blending the post-apocalyptic and military thriller genres, he also dabbles in preparedness and has a YouTube channel for that passion, called Crossed Cannons Readiness. He lives on a small homestead in Washington with his beautiful wife, their youngest son, and an awesome mouser named Combat Kitty.

Made in the USA
Monee, IL
12 February 2022

90355552R00239